A QUEEN'S SHADOW

MELISSA
KIERAN

ALSO BY MELISSA KIERAN

THE WOLVES OF MORAI SERIES

A Warrior's Fate

A Queen's Shadow

CATAEA
THE LAND OF WITCHES
GREAT OCEAN
TO THE FAE RUINS
N
W
E
S

To you, the reader.
Thank you for making my dreams a reality.

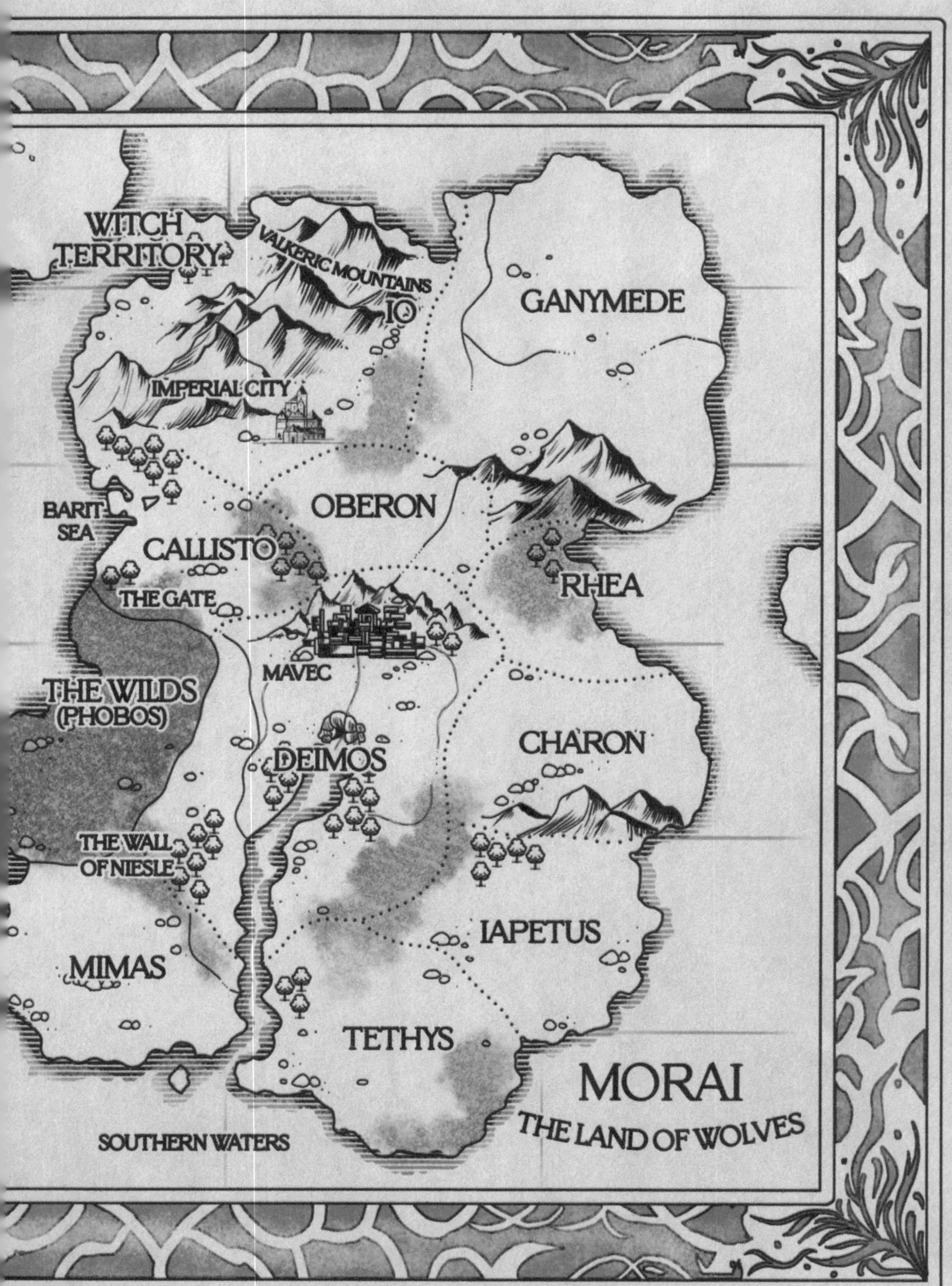

WITCH TERRITORY
VALKERIC MOUNTAINS
IO
GANYMEDE
IMPERIAL CITY
OBERON
BARIT SEA
CALLISTO
THE GATE
RHEA
THE WILDS
(PHOBOS)
MAVEC
CHARON
DEIMOS
THE WALL OF NIESLE
IAPETUS
MIMAS
TETHYS
MORAI
THE LAND OF WOLVES
SOUTHERN WATERS

AUTHOR'S NOTE

A Queen's Shadow is a direct continuation after **A Warrior's Fate**. This novel must be read before AQS in order to understand book 2.

Need a refresher for book 1?
Check out: www.melissakieranauthor.com/wolves-of-morai-summary!

~

This book explores some potentially triggering themes. Visit: www.melissakieranauthor.com/wolves-of-morai-content-warnings for the full list, and please read with care.

A
QUEEN'S
SHADOW

PART I
A QUEEN'S DESCENT

CHAPTER 1

ISLA

One could claim this tavern was no place for a queen, but Isla wasn't a queen quite yet.

She watched the gathered merry crowd from her spot in a shadowed corner booth of The Obsidian Isle, her tawny-gold hair left in loose, wild waves doing well to shield her features.

Though her rule over Deimos was imminent, not many in the pack truly knew what she looked like. Not yet, anyway. All they had to glean from were blurry grayscale images in newspapers and the lips of gossips whose opinions of her appearance ranged from favorable to brutally harsh.

She took hold of her mug of ale, the wood smooth in her calloused hands, and brought it to her lips. She cast her eyes on the man sitting at the oakwood bar across the room as she sipped. He was drinking heavily, chatting up a female patron who seemed very interested in what he had to say, to Isla's surprise. The chestnut-haired woman's pale fingers danced over his palm as she leaned into him, batting her eyelashes.

His movements had become a bit more exaggerated as the night went on, the bourbon he'd been calling for one after another having a steep effect, so much so that the bartender had been watering down his latest rounds.

At one time, the man, Warrior General Eli of Iapetus, had been her commander.

As the woman threw her head back with a howling laugh, Isla narrowed her eyes. Eli had never struck her as particularly funny, not enough to warrant a guffaw like that—unless she counted his poor attempts to court her these past months.

She was too far away to parse what they were saying over the drumming of dancing feet on wooden boards and the croon of the performer goading them on. So, with a steadying breath, Isla burrowed deep into herself, into a familiar beating of power. Her wolf was weak, though—still injured—but it reacted to the brush, nudging back at her inner reach as if accepting the care.

Isla sighed.

She was disappointed, yes. But mostly, relieved and grateful. At least her wolf was there.

"Have we met before?"

The slurred question came from Isla's side.

She glanced up to find a dark-haired man looking her over, his bushy brows raised above glistening, drunken green eyes. He was decently attractive—perfect for any *other* woman in this bar to snatch up for the night.

He couldn't have known who she was. And if he had, then maybe he had a death wish.

Isla forced a polite smile and calmed the thundering of her heart. "Can't say we have."

"You're right. I would've remembered." He took an uninvited seat on the other side of the booth. "Finley."

A soft laugh spilled from Isla's mouth as she folded her hands on the table. If Finley were observant, he'd notice the paler patch of her sun-kissed skin where her mating ring sat—and then he would've run. "I'll save you the trouble of having to repeat these lines later tonight." Isla flipped her hair to the side.

The spot where Kai had sunk his canines into her neck, claiming her as his and his alone, couldn't be missed. In fact, it had darkened again after he'd marked her a few days ago, a result of Isla's own sensuous taunts as he took her against the wall of his office.

"You—you're mated?" Finley's eyes had widened, his entire body

rigid. Isla could practically taste his fear as he glanced around, the small beads of sweat on his brow catching the low tavern lights. "Is he, uh... is he here?"

"Lucky for you, he's outside." Isla adjusted her hair again, masking the spot.

It wasn't a lie. Kai *was* currently hiding amidst the shadows of Abalys. She couldn't even call him an overprotective bastard about it. If the roles had been reversed, if he'd wanted to go out tonight to scale the seedy river town, she would've done the same. They were a team now, the two of them.

"Outside..." Finley let out a breath before rising to his feet. "Outside. Uh, have a good night, then."

Isla lifted her hand in a gentle wave. "Have a good night."

For a moment, Finley lingered, perplexity coloring his features. Like he recognized her from *somewhere* but couldn't quite place where. For his own sake, Isla hoped he couldn't figure it out, only to spare him the mortification of knowing the woman he'd flirted with, who'd turned him down, was not only his future queen but the mate of his alpha.

Given how his nostrils flared, how he stepped back, how the fear became a tangible coat on her tongue, he'd become the wiser. He left her without another word, just the slightest bow of his head.

"Well, then." Isla went for her ale again, wishing she could tug at the bond and share her amusement with her other half. But like her wolf, her soul connection to Kai had been wounded. She couldn't feel him anymore. Not in the way she once could.

Back to Eli, she supposed.

Turning her head, Isla sought the general out—but he was gone.

No. Not gone. *Leaving.*

The general moved towards the exit with his hand pressed to the woman's lower back as they weaved through bodies to the door. Isla stood too fast to be subtle, catching the eyes of several surrounding patrons as she reached into her cloak, brushing the hilt of the dagger strapped to her hip when she went for the money in her pocket. The coins clanging on the wooden table were her farewell as she followed them.

Humidity and a rolling, briny mist greeted her when she stepped onto Abalys's plank-lined streets. It was one of the warmest summer nights she'd faced since she'd come to Deimos. Though still nothing like the heat she'd grown up amidst in the north of Morai, in Io.

Eli was several yards away now, moving quicker than expected along the winding canal's edge, heading towards one of the many bridges that crossed the spidery, golden-aura-speckled waterways. Isla hung back, pressing into the shadows, cloak clasp loosened, hood pulled up, counting her heartbeats. And then, tapping into a warrior's grace, the predator's instinct she'd honed to use even if she was as good as merely human, she followed them.

Unlike Deimos's royal city of Mavec, where nightlife trickled out of the clubs and gambling dens into the crystal-laden cobblestone squares brimming with life, many of Abalys's frequenters remained inside, their liveliness nothing but a muffled rumble across the air.

When Eli and the woman slowed to a stop in front of a three-story apartment building, Isla fell back into a darkened alleyway. She pressed her fingers into the cool brick of the building beside her, peering around its corner.

As the woman reached into her bag, Eli shoved his hands in his pockets and glanced around. And for a moment, Isla swore she glimpsed the poise of a warrior general—ready and at attention—not the bumbling drunkard she'd seen at the bar.

He *had* become inebriated unsettlingly fast...

There was a sudden warmth at her back.

Isla tensed, her fingers twitching to draw claws that would not emerge before they went for the hilt of her knife.

But a steady touch kneaded into her muscles, feeling that tension, her nerves, her fear. Then she felt Kai brush back her hood to press a kiss to her neck in a silent apology for sneaking up on her.

Isla relaxed against him, breathing and relishing the feel of his body, relishing in the subtle things. His scent. The softness of his curls, his lips, and his beard as he dipped his head. How gentle he was with her when everything about him was so... hard, steady, stable.

Not a rogue. Not a witch. Not a monster. And yet, she was... disappointed.

She'd known he was following her. Could've figured it out, even without the vague sense of him at all times. But he'd gotten a jump on her, just enough. And she didn't care that he was an alpha blooded with power and prowess, that he'd made history a few months ago in one of their people's greatest trials. She should've been more aware of his approach.

Isla didn't turn or speak until the woman and Eli had gone inside—but not before Eli gave the area around one last look over.

She sighed through her nose, her nails scratching at the building's brick. "I don't trust him."

The words had been hard to get out because of *why* she didn't trust him, what he represented. Her past, her home, her family. She recalled what she'd learned from Ameera this morning about Eli's movements for the past few days. It was why she'd felt so driven to witness his doings for herself tonight. The last member of the warriors they'd caught sneaking around the territory, as Eli had been for the past few days, was Callan... and he'd been doing so to spy for Imperial Alpha Cassius.

"If it helps," Kai began, his voice low as he continued kneading at the muscles of her back, sore from her training with Rhydian that morning and likely from hunching over books at Jonah's these past nights. "I don't think Lysa is suspicious."

Lysa?

Isla turned, meeting eyes the color of storm clouds and chaos. Eyes she adored. "You know her?"

"I know a lot of people," Kai said, his lips twitching upwards. "The Isle used to be one of our 'spots.' She's worked the floor for years, reading palms, telling futures, guiding wolves towards their mates. Couldn't vouch for how good she is, though. She told me my future was in the bed of a small brunette with hazel eyes. Can't say I ever made it there."

"Of course."

That description sounded *a lot* like Lysa herself—but Isla couldn't fault the woman at all. If she'd been faced with Kai, even back then, while he was only the second-born prince, she may have tried the same tactic.

She looked over him now, the "gift" the goddesses had given her. After years and years of agonizing over finding her mate, after giving up and *finding herself* instead... she'd made it to him, made it here. To a pack, to a destiny that had always been hers.

That thought, the reminder of what was coming faster than she was prepared for, made Isla's stomach turn.

She turned back to face the apartment building. "So, should we just... wait here?"

"You don't think he'll be very long?" Amusement gilded Kai's tone.

"If he's anything like you."

Kai let out a heavy breath, feigning being wounded. And then Isla was twisted, her back pressed against the brick wall. She did her best to maintain her snarky, challenging facade as Kai's body enveloped hers. But, Goddess, the shadows and moonlight adored him as much as she did. The contrast caressed his face perfectly, in the way she wished she could mimic with her fingertips, with her lips.

Kai's fingers dipped below her chin, tipping her head back for a better view of her face. Her mouth. "So, your claws came back, huh?"

"Lucky for you." She found herself inching closer, arching into him with a desperation she should've been too proud to convey and dragging her nails over the skin of his forearm as she'd done many times down his back.

A brush of his mouth against hers and his tongue teasingly sweeping over her bottom lip had her toes curling. But then Kai stepped back, leaving her cold and her body wound tightly.

"Bastard."

Her curse earned a chuckle in return.

Tonight had been one of those rare times without obligations when they could've spent the entire night in their bedroom, tangled up with each other until dawn broke. Or even just catching up on ever-elusive sleep. But instead, she'd wanted to go out.

To follow Eli, yes, but something else weighed like a boulder on her chest. Something, or *someone*, she was hoping to find or even simply glimpse while traveling along the winding river tonight.

A swallow caught in her throat as Isla glanced back at the streets, her heart constricting at their barrenness. She waited for a shadow that didn't appear. One that had been following her, both of them, and protecting them from another threat they couldn't see.

Again, she felt a hand beneath her chin, and Isla let Kai turn her face to look at him.

His eyes searched her fallen features, and before he could ask her what was wrong, she lifted onto her toes and kissed *him* this time. Sweetly. Gratefully. He knew; he had to have known her ulterior motives, and he was here all the same.

Even if her mother had a heavy hand in the greatest tragedy of his life.

When she dropped away, as if he could taste the unspoken words on her tongue, Kai laced his fingers through hers and stepped forward out of the shadows. "Come on. I'm going to hope for his dignity that they'll be a while, and this place up here makes some decent food. We can eat while we wait."

~

The scent of earthy spices flooded Isla's nose as she and Kai settled onto the stone of a nearby rooftop, a musky wind lifting the warm steam from the bowl cradled in her hands and brushing it across her face. Gnawing on a piece of bread she'd dipped in the savory broth, she watched her mate closely as he craned his head against the breeze, his posture shifting, his eyes narrowing with an animal focus.

She followed his gaze upward to the starless sky looming above them, the silver winks of the constellations blotted out by thick, roiling gray clouds. Even with her dulled senses, she could scent the shift in the weather in the air, the heady metallic tang before a downpour.

"Another storm," she observed aloud, her voice light with a hint of excitement.

Kai's features tightened for a heartbeat, then softened. "I've never seen anything like it."

The bread in her mouth felt leaden as she swallowed. "Should we be... worried?"

"No, no." Kai shook his head, though a bit too quickly for her liking, even with his slight, reassuring smile.

Isla angled her body toward him, eyes narrowed. "Are you feeling okay?" It was, perhaps, a question she'd lobbed at him a few times too many as of late.

Kai breathed through his nose. "Would you believe me if I said I was fine?"

"Probably not."

"Would you accept it if I said, 'Don't worry?'"

"Even less likely." Isla placed her bowl down by her side, her gaze still fixed on him. "How do you feel?"

Kai shrugged, giving her his full attention with that look in his eyes. The easy, disarming one that was meant to distract her from her concern. "No headache this morning."

Isla hummed, not falling for the charm. "An improvement."

He'd had them for weeks since his challenge against Brax. Weeks of hiding the wincing. Weeks of pretending he wasn't trembling in sleep from nightmares he didn't want to talk about, only to jolt awake and hold Isla tighter, making sure she was there.

"I've been thinking." Isla's voice dipped quieter, barely audible above another lazy stretch of wind. "What about Raana? You said it yourself; you felt like her magic called to you. Maybe I could call Adrien and see if we could talk to her. If she felt something from you, then maybe she could tell us what it is."

Kai's features pinched again. "I wouldn't trust any communication over the phone, especially with Io. I didn't lose the challenge. If Cassius didn't have it out for me before, he does now. He looked like a fool putting us all through that."

Isla couldn't disagree. The reminder of the Imperial Alpha made her scowl, heat pricking beneath her skin.

She stiffened when Kai gave her a long once-over, his gaze sweeping from her boots to her eyes with slow, deliberate intent. "You're still feeling okay, right?"

"Other than the fact I can't shift, I feel fine." Isla noted the tension in his expression. "Why are you worried?"

"Because it's you, and I can't stop myself," he said simply. His voice held that quiet ferocity that had always tugged at their bond. "Raana said her magic was... different, and it felt strange when she was healing you. Like you were still pulling away."

Isla exhaled sharply through her nose. Just what she wanted to be reminded of. She'd done her best every day not to worry about what it meant to be healed by magic she didn't understand. She had enough on her mental plate without imagining herself sprouting a second head.

"Adrien was fine," she reasoned, as she routinely did in her own mind.

"Adrien was healed by Raana's mother, a witch," Kai said. "Not a witch with fae blood—however the hell that's possible."

Isla let out a long breath. "You said she mentioned her father was fae. But he couldn't actually *be fae*. The veil between worlds became like stone after the War of Realms. We've been entirely divided for a millennium. It must be somewhere distant in her bloodline."

Frankly, she didn't even know if it was possible for mortals and immortals to bear children.

"If that's the diluted blood of fae," Kai murmured, stealing another bite from his bowl, "I don't know how this realm survived the war against them, let alone defeated and banished them."

Isla couldn't fathom the scale of the chaos and destruction of that war. Sometimes, she could barely wrap her mind around the other worlds out there—the realms of fae, demons, and deities. Their existence made her own feel small and fragile.

"So, whatever it is you can do," Isla began, sorting the words carefully, "the power you feel—it responds to her magic... but you don't think you have magic?"

"At this point, I don't know. I don't even know what I want to be. If it gets out regardless, I don't think there's getting around it being a disaster—with the other alphas, our own people. The entire continent will look at me as an anomaly, as a threat to the balance of things. It'll put the people I love at risk. But..."

"But?"

Kai met her stare, his eyes shadowed. "If I hadn't been so afraid of this, if I'd embraced it, I could've ended the fight and gotten to you sooner. I could've found you. I could've gotten to the witch. Maybe I could've killed her."

"What happened to me isn't your fault." Isla sighed, uncurling her legs beneath her and shifting to kneel beside him. "I went down into those tunnels. I killed the bak before they got into the city. I did my job—what I've been trained to do."

"Warrior Princess or not," Kai's voice guttered as the raging guilt swept in, "my job, my duty, above my throne, above my people, is to protect you. To love you."

Isla offered him a smile. "Loving me is a job?"

Kai snorted, the corner of his mouth twitching up, exactly as she'd hoped. "Alright, smartass."

He leaned down and kissed her, and Isla deepened it, wrapping her arms around his neck, shifting until she was flush against him. His hands spread warmly across her back, anchoring her. As she broke the kiss, she whispered against his lips, as though sharing a secret meant only for him, "It works two ways, you know... that duty."

"I know."

"Good... and you remember my promise."

Kai's breath tickled her lips as he moved closer still, their noses brushing. "To and through eternity."

He'd recited the words just as Isla made her way onto his lap, her legs bracketing his hips, the moon and city behind her as she settled. "Do you think things will ever become simple? Where we can just be happy, old, and in love." She spoke amidst the phantom caress of his mouth against hers.

"I can probably only guarantee those three." Kai laughed softly, his hands slipping beneath her shirt, palms warm against her skin. "I will do everything in my power to make you happy, I will love you forever, and we are going to have a long life together. Whether it will be simple, I'm not sure, but my gut says it won't be."

Isla shivered as his touch swept over her stomach, spreading warmth in its wake. "I suppose that's fine as long as in the end, it's you and me."

Kai hummed in agreement before meeting her mouth with his. A kiss, slow and sure, sealing the promise between them. "I'm not going anywhere."

CHAPTER 2

KAI

It seemed the world was as off-balance as Kai had felt these past few days, weeks... months, really... with Deimos experiencing an endless chaotic cycle of torrential storms amidst periods of blaring sunshine.

With a barrage of rain imminent, he and Isla headed east off the boardwalk, away from the winding canals and river towards the stretches of lawless land that bracketed their borders.

Rogue territory.

Apparently, Kai had to give Eli more credit. Nearly three hours had passed while he and Isla sat on the rooftop, and the general had not yet emerged from Lysa's apartment. Kai put his money on a half hour, and Isla gloated for the ninety-plus minutes that followed. Sometime in the next few days, he owed her a back massage. Though with the way those ended, he hadn't necessarily lost the wager at all.

As their investigation fell more fruitless with every passing, uneventful minute, Isla's smile faded, and Kai couldn't have that. So, he proposed a switch in objectives. They'd been out anyway and close to the borders, too. Any hour now, if they hadn't already, his scouts would be returning from the rogue lands, hopefully, with some intel about what was occurring within them or the dominions beyond.

After all that had occurred with Callan and the intelligence Kai had been gathering since becoming alpha, he suspected Cassius had planted eyes throughout the packs, and Kai, despite the laws against it, wanted his own. Though he had no plans to launch an attack and incite a war, he needed to be more proactive in protecting his people. He had to pinpoint exactly where the threat was and build their defenses against it.

It didn't help that there was danger in every direction. Cassius in Io. Rogues slipping into the southeastern territory. A murderous, vendetta-driven witch who was somehow able to control the minds of the rogues and deadly monsters, goddesses knew where. A witch who didn't want them *dead*, according to what she'd told Isla, but still had nearly killed them both.

The fact that they didn't fully understand her motivations, other than the fact she wanted to kill Cassius—who fucking *didn't?*—probably made her more dangerous than anything.

"You son of a bitch!"

The ringing curse wrenched his attention forward.

Kai immediately recognized the voice. The expletive had been directed at *him* quite a few times in that tone.

They scaled a final gentle hill before the landscape opened to the sprawling borders protecting Deimos from the rogue territory. And there, before the network of stone and vines, two forces collided on a patch of drying grass.

Goddess, spare them.

Kai could barely hold in his laugh as Rhydian and Magnus, clad in their guard uniforms, hands locked on each other's shoulders and biceps, knees bent with snarls on their faces and eyes and lumerosi glowing, tried to knock the other down.

"Don't drop your shoulder!"

At Isla's call, Rhydian buckled.

Kai watched her hand descend from where it half-curved around her mouth, a smirk painted on her perfect lips and a mischievous glint in her eye.

His bona fide brother seized and straightened, turning to glimpse them on the hill's precipice, distracted just enough for the predator before him to pounce. Magnus rocketed forward with a triumphant battle cry, tackling Rhydian into the dirt outlay of their grass patch.

Isla laughed, and Kai heeded the sound, the image of her and her smile, then tucked it away somewhere safe for those moments when she wasn't there to abate the darkness, not necessarily from his power but from the shadows that had haunted him for far longer than he cared to admit.

"Is this what we pay you for?" Kai asked as he and Isla approached. "Novice mistakes and shit-poor fighting stances?"

Magnus, who'd been howling at his victory and only now noticed them, went rigid. Kai gave him a small tip of his head. "That wasn't directed at you. Nice work."

"Thank you, Alpha," he said, only breaking his harsh posture to sweep some of his light hair from his eyes—eyes that eventually slid to Isla.

Tension rippled between them, and Kai worked to hide his amusement.

So, he'd learned, back when Isla was training with Deimos's guard along with her warrior unit, she and Magnus grated endlessly on each other's nerves. The guard, a key member of Rhydian's team, had a particular disdain for Io, the Imperial Alpha, and the Warrior Rite that he'd always desired to enter but had always been denied access to. So, meeting the Imperial Beta's newly anointed warrior daughter went as well as one would expect. Kai wished he'd been there the moment that Isla blurted that she was his mate during one of their many squabbles just to get him to shut up.

"Warrior," Magnus said, conceding a bow. Kai knew Isla got a small satisfaction from it.

"Guard," she replied curtly.

"Shit-poor, my ass."

They all turned to Rhydian as he rose from the ground, swiping his hands over his uniform and brushing away Magnus's reach to aid him. He speared his eyes over Kai and Isla. No bow or formality; it wasn't necessary. "The distraction got me, yes. But why the hell aren't you two at home? It's the middle of the night."

"We were out and thought we'd come visit," Isla said.

"Out?" Rhydian's gaze flicked to Kai, questioning. He'd known of his intentions not to leave the House tonight, and yet, here Kai was. In answer to the silent question, Kai gave a subtle shrug, and Rhydian shook his head. "Stubborn, workaholic bastards, the both of you."

They had no answer, no defense. Kai only asked, "Have they returned yet?"

Rhydian's features shadowed. "No."

Shit.

Kai ground his teeth, casting his eyes over the border. A heaviness settled over his heart as he recalled every scenario if they'd been caught or killed. How it would be handled. And as if beckoned by his emotions, his power breathed. A deep inhale and exhale as if it wanted Kai to acknowledge that it still lived. That it could be used.

Isla squeezed his hand, but he didn't look at her.

"There's still time," Rhydian said, pulling Kai's gaze back to him. "We told them the night of the quarter moon. The night hasn't ended yet, but a few hours ago, a... family came through claiming that they're pack members of Charon. A man, a woman, their child. The kid couldn't be more than three or four years old. They were pretty shaken up, and the father had blood on him. Thyra took them to the inn down by the bend of the eastern canal. I sent Belle to check the other breakpoint further north."

Both Kai and Isla remained unmoving.

"A family?" Isla let out on a breath, turning her head in the direction Rhydian had pointed. "That makes it ten people fleeing from Charon in the past week."

Kai steadied himself with a breath, his mind becoming a mess of scenarios, plans, and logistics. The situation they found themselves in was precarious. Pack loyalty wasn't only a part of the continent's law but the code a wolf lived by. One could not defect without their alpha's approval, and yet, increasing numbers of Charon's members had been appearing at their borders, seeking refuge from the state of affairs in their pack. From the anecdotes Kai had gathered, the ever-prideful, bull-headed Alpha Locke's rule had slipped into a tyranny.

He hated to ask, "And everything checks out?"

"From what I can gather," Rhydian said. "They're definitely not rogues, but I didn't have them go too far. In case."

"How far is the inn from here?" Isla asked, wriggling her shoulders as a subtle hint for Kai to release her from his hold.

"About a ten-minute walk," Rhydian said.

Isla sighed, looking down and then over again. When she met Kai's eyes, her own were filled with hints of that steel will and determination he'd fallen in love with months ago. "They must be terrified. I'll check on them and bring them some food. See if they're still awake and want to talk."

It wasn't a bad idea, but—

"I don't want you going alone." Kai brushed a hand over her lower back.

She pursed her lips. "I'll be fine."

She probably would. She was a warrior, after all, and far from fragile and delicate. He knew he couldn't keep her caged, knew he couldn't protect her from everything, but...

He remembered the cold of her skin as she was dying in his arms.

"We're too close to rogue territory. I'm not risking anything."

"Kai," she breathed his name before stepping closer to place a hand on his chest. She lifted onto her toes to place a kiss on his mouth. "I'll be fine." Soft, sweet words. A caress over his lips in this small space just for them. "Overprotective bastard."

He couldn't deny appreciating this obvious tactic of manipulation, especially with how her body pressed into his. Both Magnus and Rhydian had respectfully dropped their gazes.

Kai hummed and said nothing, only brandishing a slight uptick of his lips as she turned to walk away. He let her get a few steps ahead before he called out, "Magnus, I'll take your post. Go with Isla to the inn."

"*What?*"

Isla whipped around, teeth bared, while a slightly alarmed Magnus bowed at the waist. "Yes, Alpha."

"Kai," Isla hissed, hurling all that fire and determination at him through her stare.

He slid his hands into his pockets. "Give me shit for it later."

The glower didn't leave her face.

He flashed her a smile and let the slightest bit of mocking and playfulness slip in as he crooned, "I love you."

The growl she gave shouldn't have been as arousing as it was. "Asshole." She turned her back but wouldn't walk away completely without grumbling just loud enough for him to hear, "*I love you, too.*"

He knew if he laughed, she'd launch herself at him, so he stamped his lips together as she and Magnus strode away, the guard keeping a wise few paces behind his future queen.

"She's going to kill you," Rhydian said, also, it seemed, afraid to show any amusement until the two of them were out of sight. He lifted his head to examine the cloudy sky.

"I'm looking forward to it," Kai answered truthfully, thinking of that passion being thrown at him. He turned his attention back to the border wall.

Rhydian said, "I thought you told everyone to be scarce around the House tonight."

Yes, he'd had plans. Plans that began with dinner and ended with her struggling to keep those wonderful sounds of hers contained. But then she'd wanted to trail Eli—not entirely strange, given her need to be involved in everything—and then he'd noticed something else. The black cloak, torn and covered in dark blood, that hadn't made it entirely under the bed to its typical hiding place.

Her mother's cloak.

At the thought, his power writhed.

Murderer.

Kai battled away the thought, tried to stifle the void that tried to push and push. He wondered if Rhydian could sense it the way Isla could.

In a breath, Kai allowed it to cast out and gave it an outlet. He shrugged. "Plans change."

A small bite must've slipped into his tone because Rhydian jeered, "You seem pleased by that."

"Who wouldn't want to spend the night trailing the general who brought their mate across the continent just to get in her pants, instead of being at home in bed with her?"

Rhydian's smile was too wide for Kai's liking. "Still on that mating edge, brother?" He must've understood, even if he and Davina had mated over a year ago.

Kai ran his tongue over his bottom lip, as if he could still taste Isla there, still feel the press of her body and her touch on his chest. On edge wasn't the half of it. Their bond was still new in a way, still fresh. Broken and healing, but still had him in that newly mated male frenzy, wanting to be on her, *in her*, to the point where it was near maddening.

He said, "As long as it's the two of us, I don't care where we are."

"Very diplomatic answer." Rhydian twisted his head in the opposite direction to where Isla and Kai had come from. "So, you took Meera's tip then. Do you think Eli's up to the same shit Callan was?"

Kai opened his mouth to answer, but then closed it. As if he'd caught an animal on a snare, his senses snagged on something beyond the borders.

Go see.

Either his natural inclination or that power beckoned. He took a few careful steps forward, avoiding the crunch of the drying grass. Rhydian didn't even bother questioning; he only followed.

"I don't know what information Cassius would have him gather that he didn't have Callan get already." Kai lowered his voice as he approached the wall's weathered stone. "He has to know about the tunnels. He knows what my father was planning, to an extent at least. He knows we're dealing with a witch, and the witch came from his prison." He moved along the wall until he reached a small fissure, enough for one to slip through—where his scouts were meant to slip through.

Another breath. He closed his eyes, focusing.

Thunder rumbled—but not loud enough for Kai to miss the sound of a branch cracking beneath a foot. Someone was out there waiting... watching.

His nostrils flared as his eyes snapped open.

Then the Alpha of Deimos entered the rogue lands.

～

Behind the border wall, the forest was still, silent but for the sound of water pattering off bare branches of trees onto the leaf-littered floor. A vapor swirled around Kai's legs, a fog in the distance by whatever uncharted body of water lay beyond.

Rogue territory, undesirable and nearly uninhabitable, was unclaimed by any of the kingdoms. The wolves who ended up here could've easily tried building their own societies, unchecked by the Imperial Alpha, but it wasn't in their nature. Rogues had become so mostly due to their heinous actions against fellow wolves or their desire to be free from a pack's constraints.

Kai paused just before the fog's edge, clocking Rhydian close behind him. He could sense so much of his brother's feelings—the doubt, confusion, and apprehensiveness at being in here—but he still guarded Kai's back. Always had.

"Something's out here," Kai finally enlightened him, and as if the Goddess had made it a point to spear her dwindling light through the clouds for him to notice, he caught a glittering within the leaf litter. Too perfectly piled.

Kai advanced, mindful of the still-muted forest and guided by instinct, he carefully brushed the perimeter of the spot until he revealed a chain. He tugged it and then beheld a brutal spike meant to tear through flesh and bone. Several spikes. A hunter's trap, not unusual, used mainly by those who couldn't shift to score game.

But here...

He crouched to examine it more closely and then twisted, noticing the trajectory the trap had hoped for its prey. It had been perfectly placed so that anyone approaching the fissure in the border would be snared; anyone going out or trying to get in.

There was a whisper of a blade unsheathing, followed by heavy breathing and footsteps. A rattled battle cry was cut short as Kai's hand, extracted claws digging into flesh, clamped around the charging man's scrawny neck. Not enough to kill, but enough that the warmth of blood coated his skin. He brought him to the ground rough enough to knock the wind from his lungs and wrench the dagger from his hand.

His wolf howled within him, that power singing a war song as Kai breathed raggedly through clenched teeth. This man, whoever he was, couldn't shift. The doorway of his mind, unused, was more difficult to find, but somehow, Kai had traced it, and the void rose, spearing for unfortified walls before Kai could leash it.

Thoughts that weren't his own assaulted him along with shrieking, overwhelming emotions of fear and aggravation. The sensation of pain that wasn't his felt like pinpricks on his own consciousness. It should've hurt. There should've been some consequence to something as vile and intrusive as this. As he glimpsed people he did not know, heard words that were never meant for his ears, and felt joy, horror, pleasure, and suffering that wasn't his.

Pull. Fucking. Back.

He couldn't let this consume him entirely. Never again. No matter who this was.

A weak tug of something inside him, a glimmer of a dimmed light. A better part of him.

Kai breathed, then released.

The man ripped a panicked, frustrated scream so violently from his lungs that Kai wondered if he'd taken away that ability, too. His body squirmed amongst blood-matted leaves, his feet kicking and his nose leaking crimson from Kai's unintended assault.

Kai released his grip on his neck, leaving his claws out and dripping gore onto the man's chest as he pressed his foot to his throat instead. He could feel Rhydian behind him, sense the rise of his power and Rhydian's apprehension that he hoped wasn't towards him.

"You have two seconds to explain why you're laying traps by my borders before I crush your windpipe," Kai growled, bringing his wolf forward and allowing his eyes and lumerosi to glow their signature blood-red.

The man, a rogue, Kai could only assume, gurgled a curse through the blood in his mouth.

Not a mindlessly brash rogue, then. He knew to be afraid.

The man braced his hands on either side of Kai's booted foot, pushing up to lessen some pressure, but Kai only pressed harder. "This isn't your territory," he wheezed, "you have no jurisdiction here, Alpha."

Alpha?

"And yet, you address me properly." Maybe he'd just been cast out. Rogues didn't respect hierarchies. Apparently, he hadn't unlearned that yet. Unless...

Kai sifted through the memories and feelings again, recalled the voices he'd heard, the shouts of agony, the words.

He narrowed his eyes, his canines feeling sharper than usual as he drew a horrendous conclusion. "You're not a rogue at all, are you?" The man's stiffening seemed enough of an answer. And if he wasn't a rogue, then these traps... "Did someone send you out here?"

There.

A fluttering of the man's heartbeat. A sinking sense of doom so potent that Kai could taste the bitterness.

Fuck.

Those shouts became a clear image of terrified people bounding for freedom, only to be snared in these jaws, hoping they'd bleed out before they could be dragged away. A bounty hunter meant to capture Kai's spies or wrangle Locke's fleeing pack members. That family... His own men...

How many had been taken?

Kai swore he could feel the man's rasping breath against his sole as his face turned a faint shade of purple.

Kill him.

It was a thought that came too easily. A little more force, and he could. His power fed off his own malice. It wanted to dig and pry and tear and shred and rip apart. It wanted retribution—but Kai pulled back. Back, back.

"Are you alone?" Kai's voice was lethally calm, cold.

As if he could sense his fate was at a crossroads, the man nodded. If he lied, Kai would know anyway. It felt like he had a hold on the man's bones, his breath, his soul. Whatever wolf lay dormant beneath his skin, he found that too and had it cowering. The lumerosi on his arms and his back burned. "How many other traps are there?"

"F... four. A... at each of the... these t... *trees.*" Gasping now, the man pointed out several of them with a shaky hand.

Kai wouldn't turn his attention away, but there was Rhydian still at his back, guarding him. "Some of the trees are marked, likely so he wouldn't accidentally trip them," he said with no waver in his voice, a mountain of force, another threat in his own right.

"How do you disable them?" Kai asked.

Several attempted labored breaths fell before he could say, "A... a pin by the back mechanism."

"Rhydian."

"Yes, Alpha."

Rhydian fell back to make work of disarming the snares while the man's eyes fluttered, turning glassy. If Kai didn't let up soon, this was over.

End it.

But if he could learn who he was working with, overhear his conversations with Locke, see plans through his eyes...

To protect his family, his people, to protect Isla—

"Rhyd, leave that one alone!" Kai called to his brother, who'd been crouched beside the last of the snares.

He ignored the temptation of his power, having the same sinking feeling as before. If he gave in to it, he'd lose another fragment of himself when he already struggled to keep himself pieced together.

Kai lifted his foot and stepped back from the man, who let out a cry of relief as he scrambled for his throat. "Th... thank you."

Maybe he'd lost too much air. That was why he was so delusional.

Kai nodded sideways to the trap. "Walk."

The man blinked. "What?"

"*Walk,*" Kai repeated, and echoing throughout the skies was the boom of thunder. The rain hadn't fallen, but he could feel it. "I'm giving you the option of someone hearing you before you bleed out." He took another step back. "Make me say it again, and I'll leave you gutted here."

The man barely deliberated.

He rose, keeping his hands where Kai could observe, and began his walk towards where Rhydian stood, his head low. He knew if he ran, they'd catch him. But what Kai should've expected, maybe had in the back of his mind, is that the man would use his distance between them to reach into his pocket and pull out what looked like a small capsule. Before either of them could react, he shoved it in his mouth. One bite, one bob of his throat, and he fell into a writhing heap on the dirt, foam forming at the corners of his chapped lips.

Kai didn't move; he just watched as Rhydian ran up to him, checking for a pulse at the side of his neck. "He's dead." Shock laced each word. "He's dead. What do we do?"

Wordlessly, with veins filled with both fire and ice, Kai wrenched the man's dagger from the dirt, then took hold of the man's collar, dragging his limp body to the base of one of his marked trees. Above him, in the bark, Kai carved his family's sigil as an acknowledgment, a warning.

He tossed the blade in the leaves beside the corpse and turned for home.

Then the rain began.

CHAPTER 3

ISLA

Isla parted the shade of the inn's room with two fingers, watching the fat drops of rain pour over Abalys's streets. Lightning struck across the darkened sky in an amethyst whip, followed by a heavy crash of thunder that rattled the brick building's foundations. After speaking with Nefel, the father of the family who'd fled from Charon, she needed something to pacify the rage and guilt warring in her heart.

He hadn't initially been open to talking, but Isla had come offering food and comfort, a listening ear, and a sturdy shoulder. While their daughter was being soothed by his wife—the poor thing, afraid of the storm, even with all she'd just endured—Isla learned of what they'd gone through for the week it took them to trek the rogue lands to make it to Deimos. The rogues they'd run from, who Nefel had needed to kill, the decline and instability of Charon, and the hell they'd endured in what was once their home.

Grimacing, Isla turned to where Kai lay in the small bed, blankets slouched low on his hips, his muscled body bare but for that fabric as he studied the ceiling. His hair draped in loose waves over his forehead, drying from having been in the storm. With his brow pinched and his jaw tensed, he was clearly deep in thought.

In his hand, he twirled her dagger with expert ease that shouldn't have been as attractive as it was. The absent action served as a small reminder that even if he didn't bear the mark as she did or the official title, he was a warrior by rite all the same.

As if he'd felt her stare, Kai's focus shifted, the hard edges of his face smoothing as he took her in. His eyes drew up and down her body, clad in only her tunic skimming the tops of her thighs, the rest of her clothes left on the vanity.

He threw an arm across the covers, an invitation and request.

Isla gave him a soft smile.

The bed creaked as she joined him on the hard mattress, and when she leaned over to kiss him once, he threaded his fingers through her hair and kept her there for a few moments, lips gliding smoothly over hers. Not a fiery embrace but a grateful one.

I'm happy I have you. I'm happy you're here—words he didn't need to say for her to understand.

When he'd arrived at the inn alone and entirely drenched, she had known something had happened back at the borders. She'd even felt it before she saw him, nearly leaving Nefel because of it. But even without that otherworldly sense, she would've known from the way he'd embraced her when she met him in the lobby, the way he'd kissed her like he needed her to breathe. Magnus, Thyra, and the concierge at the desk had been forgotten. All that existed was her, his grounding force.

He hadn't been ready to talk then. Not while they made their decision to spend the night here rather than trek for hours through the downpour to get back to the House. And not while he started up a fire in the small wood stove in the room's corner or stripped and left his clothes near its steady heat to dry.

So, Isla waited, accepting every gentle graze of his hands and soft wordless kiss he stole until he tucked into their bed, her knife in his hands, spinning and spinning like his mind must've been.

Shadows had clouded his eyes, but now, as she settled cross-legged beside him, she could see that the storm had cleared just enough.

So, with her voice so low it nearly got lost in the crackle and pop of the flames, she asked, "What happens now that they haven't made it back?"

Not *what happened*, not *what did you do*. That would be too accusatory.

Kai let out a heavy breath, his hand drifting over her bare leg, mapping patterns over her skin. "There are only so many options. We continue to wait, hoping they'll make it back tomorrow, the next day... maybe. Or we send out more scouts to track *them,* but given the circumstances, it could just be a suicide mission. With Eli sneaking around here, and Locke with his own spies in rogue territory."

Isla jerked back. "Locke's what?"

"Spies, bounty hunters. They're setting up traps by our borders to either get their people back or find proof of ours drifting out. Locke must know we're taking members in, figures we'd send out people to monitor, and if he can prove it..." Kai swallowed hard, darkness creeping over his face. "Goddess, I have a headache."

"We don't have to talk about it now," Isla said, not wanting to push him. "Everything's clearer when the sun's up. I'm convinced our wolves take too much control at night." She combed her fingers through his hair. "Tonight definitely didn't go as planned."

Kai scoffed. "I don't think anything will ever *'go as planned'* for us."

Likely not.

"But I got to spend it with you. That's all that matters."

Isla laughed. "Such a damn charmer."

With a sigh, she tucked herself beneath the covers, lying so she could face him. They needed something to banish this dark cloud hovering over them. And the answer always seemed to be each other.

She traced a line over his neck, his collarbone. "What *did* you have planned for after dinner?"

Kai's breath caught, hearing the suggestion in her tone, the desire to play.

Leaving the knife on the side of the bed, he rolled to face her.

His hand found her thigh, skimming the skin not covered by her shirt. "Well... while we were *cooking* dinner, all I wanted to do was bend you over the counter, but I knew once I got my hands on you, I wouldn't be able to stop there." He continued his trail up, grazing the smooth skin of her stomach, reaching until his knuckle skimmed the underside of her breast. "I probably would've given you the option. To either clear the table and take you right there, bring you to the couch in the living room, or carry you upstairs."

Isla shivered and arched up towards his touch as he palmed her breast, pinching her nipple between his fingers. "I think I would've picked the table."

A grin spread across his face that silently said, "*of course,*" because he would have done the same.

Despite the loose fit, her shirt felt like too much. She rose to pull the garment over her head, and when she settled back onto her pillow, she tucked both her hands beneath her flushing cheek, purposely shielding her body from him. "What else?"

"Such a tease," Kai lamented lowly.

Rolling her eyes, Isla moved her arm. Kai's eyes took their time surveying every bend and curve of her body with an intensity and adoration that made her heart pound. He opened his mouth to speak, but before he could say anything, she leaned in and pressed her lips to his. Kai's hand went up to cup her face, his fingers curling around her neck.

"You can do more than look," she murmured over his mouth, taking his hand and dragging it down her body, over her breasts, down her stomach, to the waistband of her panties, lower...

"*Fuck.*"

She wasn't sure which one of them had said it.

Her breathing sharpened as Kai ran his fingers over the damp material of her underwear. "I was this wet for you when we were eating, too."

"Were you now?" Pushing the fabric to the side, Kai dragged two fingers over her slickness, teasing her and making her grab his shoulders, digging her nails into them.

He easily slipped one inside her, making her arch and moan. She kissed him again, long and slow, her tongue slipping into his mouth to tangle with his as Kai added a second finger. He pumped them in and out of her once, twice as she ground her hips for more pressure, more friction.

"More," she breathed the word.

Kai dragged his teeth over her bottom lip. "Lie back for me."

Isla obeyed.

As she moved to her back, nearly falling off the too-small bed, Kai brought his fingers to his mouth, and she watched as he savored the taste of her, removing her underwear.

Kai chuckled. "So eager."

"I could say the same."

Kai moved atop her, kneeling between her parted legs, the blankets shifting and falling away completely and leaving them both bare to the room. Isla greedily took him in, the way the shadows and firelight caressed his skin. The muscles of his arms, his abs flexing with each heavy breath, his length jutting out between them, thick and powerful and so *hers*.

Goddess, she needed him.

"Kai." A desperate, demanding plea. She stretched out a hand to touch him, the tips of her fingers grazing the smooth shaft and making him twitch, moisture already beading at the tip. She caught it on her finger, not breaking eye contact as she brought it to her mouth, sucking it away.

Kai's eyes blazed, and he dropped to envelop her again.

They became nothing but carnal need and insatiable hunger. A clash of mouths and teeth, grabbing hands and heavy breaths. Her ache to have him inside her was unbearable.

"Kai." A command this time.

"This bed's too small for me to fuck you the way I want to," he told her, his voice guttural in her ear.

"Then don't fuck me on the bed," Isla growled and pushed him.

They went crashing to the floor.

Their coughs and laughs filled the room as Isla fell atop him and braced her hands on either side of his head.

"Maybe a warning next time," Kai suggested, his touch ghosting over her waist.

"Sorry," Isla said, leaning down until she was pressed against him again. "Now, how did you want to take me?"

Kai smirked, and his hands held her hips as he leaned up to kiss her. He wrapped his arm around her as he lifted her, and she'd been so distracted by his lips, by his touch, that she hadn't realized how much he twisted them until craning her neck was the only way to maintain their contact.

When they broke their kiss, Isla, now on her knees, faced forward, finding nothing but the hearth before her. She felt Kai running his touch over her back and lumerosi, mapping her etching of the moon. She gasped as his hardness pressed against her, and he flattened his hand, guiding her forward.

But before she bent too far, his breath was hot against her skin as he whispered, "On your hands and knees, beautiful."

Isla ran a tongue over her bottom lip and obeyed, placing her hands on the warmed hardwood. Her breaths sharpened as Kai nudged at her entrance, the tip of his cock running along her wetness. He didn't tease her long, bless the Goddess, before he pushed himself inside her. Slowly. Letting her luxuriate in every inch of him as he filled her, stars bursting behind her vision.

Fuck, she loved him. Loved this.

"Goddess, I'll never get enough of you," Kai breathed, holding her hips as he waited for her to adjust to him. Or perhaps, to gather himself.

"Move." Isla wriggled her hips, moaning at the subtle movement and its explosion of sensations.

Now, Kai listened, drawing back nearly to the tip before pressing back in.

Once. Twice.

Slow at first.

But then he gripped her tighter, his hands finding her hair. His name became a whimper on her lips as he drove in harder. Over and over.

Pleasure branched through every corner of Isla's body, her muscles going limp as the night's darkness and all their worries were dashed away in this stolen moment. In him.

Kai leaned forward until his chest was pressed to her back, his arms curling around her body until his fingers found her clit. "You take me so fucking well." His teeth were a teasing graze against the skin of her neck as he circled the bud. "Come with me, beautiful."

Isla's body shuddered as she nodded, a wordless, *yes, yes,* on her lips.

She didn't last much longer after that. Neither did he.

Her inner muscles clamped down on him as both found their release, Kai holding her steady as he spilled and spilled himself inside her.

The room became silent but for the crackling hearth and their spent breathing.

Then, beyond the inn's window, thunder and lightning crashed.

CHAPTER 4

RAANA

Raana awoke in a cocoon of darkness, heavy and suffocating, laid thick over her body like tar. In the confined space, her hands went to her throat, finding her skin clammy yet freezing beneath her fingertips.

She'd been dreaming again. Of the dying queen, the king kneeling at her side. Of pushing her own magic too far as she tried to heal her.

Raana hacked, trying to gasp down air, but the shadows pressed in further, lapping at her skin, as cold as ice, *colder*. Not trying to hurt her, but not understanding—

Her voice was a rasp as she commanded in the common tongue, "Let me out."

Raana's skin prickled and pulled in response to the shifting black. Soft streams of moonlight greeted her from the outside world, but barely.

They will kill you if you don't keep them under control.

She winced at Helene's voice flooding her head, the words not said out of concern but as a demand. Leash this power that no one understood, least of all herself, or be damned to die by it. Be damned to curse them all.

Heart thundering, lungs constricting, Raana lifted a hand to the unrelenting dark and braced the other below, tangled in her sheets. An anchor, a reminder in case things got... complicated. She commanded again, "*Go.*"

Like old paint, the shadows peeled away, a patchwork of light fully gracing her skin. The tendrils slithered along the edge of her threadbare mattress, over the hardwood floors. They bled and blended into the corners of the room, where they'd wait, she knew, like little beasts for her next order. The shadows as extensions of herself weren't anything new. But them being so responsive, as volatile as her emotions, even while she slept, was *entirely* new.

Tears stung Raana's eyes as she panted, the night air bloating her chest. Sweat coated her blankets and every inch of her body as she tallied the cracks in the ceiling, timing each count with her heartbeats, focusing on the strength of each pulse. Alive... *beat*... awake... *beat*... real.

She was no longer in those tunnels.

The rusted lantern on her bedside table had been snuffed out, leaving only the faint glow of cinders to accompany the aura spilling through her bedroom window. As she lifted her head to sweep over the tiny space, she realized the few sparse pieces of furniture within it had moved, as if a wild gust of wind had swept in and blown them over.

Her grip constricted on her sheets as she forced herself to rise, slowly pulling her bare legs up until her knees touched her chest. She pictured it, the shadows rushing towards the bed in a wave of ebony from every crevice of the room, devouring her, *protecting* her. A threat was a threat, even if it was her own mind. Even if it was these nightmares... or rather, memories.

That night, within the hidden underground tunnels of wolf territory, she'd saved the life of Isla of Deimos.

She'd been dying—the luna, the queen—teetering just on the edge of oblivion while the king, the alpha, her *mate*, watched on, unable to do anything to help her. Raana still heard his broken plea when she was quiet enough, still felt that overwhelming anguish of his when she fell into her own despair.

Bile rose in her throat as she looked at her hand. Her knuckles strained, and her brown skin paled from her tight grip on her bed's damp fabric. Her iron ring, enchanted and carved with delicate but powerful runes to suppress parts of her magic, seemed to absorb the embers' faint glow and the moonlight's softness as she stared into it.

You're fae.

The alpha's voice echoed in her mind. Kai figured the truth out much faster than she'd expected—before her glamor could even fall away. It had taken everything in her, then, not to vomit on the stones.

After a decade of hiding what she was from the world—after sacrificing a life full of friendship and family—in that moment, it became for nothing. She'd risked everything.

With a shaky breath, Raana released her hold on the sheets and swung her legs over the edge of the mattress. She needed a bath. A hot one. Needed to wash the night away. A drink wouldn't hurt either... maybe a good book, too.

Relit lantern in hand, Raana padded barefoot to the threshold of the room. She opened the door and looked upon the darkness of her living room, dining area, and entry hall...

The cottage wasn't a grand space, but since her thirteenth birthday, this had been her home. Though hideout and prison may also have been suitable descriptors.

While most young girls worried about their first bleed, the swelling of their breasts, and maturing into a woman, she'd had to worry about her ears becoming arched, the sharpening of her teeth, and the shifting of her eyes to something brighter than their usual earthy brown hue. Becoming ethereal, otherworldly... becoming a monster.

She had no knowledge of who her father was, and her mother, before her death, hadn't left any trace of his identity behind either. Raana hadn't even known she was part fae until she began changing, and then Helene had finally told her the truth.

Raana was a child born of mortal and immortal blood, something unheard of, beyond the fact that the fae "no longer walked the world." It just *wasn't* possible.

And yet, her mother, a mortal witch, had carried her in her womb for a year, a babe of eternal shadow and broken promises with the stars. She'd held her in her arms for one fleeting moment before...

No wonder Helene couldn't keep the resentment from her voice when she'd laid out her confession. She was forced into solitude, to care for Raana all these years out of loyalty to a ghost.

A quick match to the hearth in the sitting room brought the cottage to life with light. Raana crouched beside it for a moment, letting its heat seep into her skin and banish the shadows' chill. They were a taunt along the wood-stained walls, but she ignored their draw, their murmuring, as she rose and took the few strides to the kitchen.

She hung her lantern on a hook beside two cabinets—one containing a sparse supply of food and the other holding a myriad of special herbs, roots, bones, ash, and the blood of varying animals. The fundamentals of potions. She'd never been particularly great with brews. She could read a recipe, but feeling the preternatural draw to the perfect mix of ingredients for her desired result—a poison, a salve, any remedy —was beyond her. Not beyond those of her past, though.

Her eyes slid to the tome on the scratched-up countertop, the worn leather-bound book opened to pages cornered by a raven and serpent before the sun with passages about cloaking spells and suppressing brews. All things she'd tried and all that had failed in hiding her immortal features as the power of her iron ring began to wane.

Aside from potions, her ancestors, Scornn witches, were skilled in divination. If only they, or her mother, could've foreseen what would befall her and helped her out. Left some extra notes behind in the yellowed pages of the family grimoire.

With a sigh, Raana closed the book, tracing its cover, etched with the same raven and serpent with a finger, before going into the cabinet. She pulled out a bottle of wine, some crisp bread, and cheese. The sheen of a spider's intricate web caught her eye as she closed the door, the little black beast perched in its center, watching her, waiting. A soft smile passed her mouth, though she felt something in her chest ease in a pathetic way. "I won't hurt you."

As if it had understood and acknowledged the kindness, the creature began its leisurely climb across its terrain.

Raana's smile fell.

Spiders, creatures of the surrounding forest, and the shadows—those were all she had for companions in these weeks Helene had been gone. Not that her being home meant for joyous company, but it was... a body. Another living, breathing person. All she'd known her entire life.

When Raana had returned from her time within the wolves' territory, all Helene had left behind was a note saying she'd gone to the mainland to look for some better work, more clients in need of her healing gifts. It wasn't unusual as their land on the edge of Morai fell to ruin, and more took the leap of moving to Cataea, even if a life of poverty was their likely fate. She wasn't sure when Helene planned on returning since she'd taken many of her things.

Raana popped a piece of bread and cheese into her mouth before taking her bottle and glass to the bathing room. They teetered on the edge of the sink while she gathered other supplies: another lantern, some lavender salts, her opalescent crystal conduit on its silver chain, and one of the books she'd gotten from the local bookseller. *A Dalliance with Defiance*, a less-than-chaste tale about a princess swept up by a castle guard for several nights of "forbidden passion." Perfect for a night of escapism.

When her bath was filled, Raana took hold of her conduit again, the feeling of her magic simmering in her blood, migrating, focusing into the stone in her grasp. She held it beneath the surface, muttering the incantation she'd memorized in the mother tongue of the First Witches, invoking the magic of the Spirits to take what she'd offer and give her something in return. Power crackled at her fingertips before steam began to rise.

She pulled her hand—and the crystal—from the water, looking upon her reflection as she had when she was a child and had first harvested the stone herself. So much had changed since then, and Raana would do anything to protect that hopeful little witchling from the harsh truths she'd come to learn about herself.

After peeling off her gown and releasing her dark curls from their tie, Raana let out a relieved sigh as she sank into the water's heat. It burrowed deep beneath her bare skin, loosening her muscles in tandem with a swig of alcohol. She slipped down until she was entirely submerged. It was so quiet down here, but also so... loud. Her thoughts roared, the rush of her blood in a constant battle for dominance.

Witch. Fae.

Mortal. Immortal.

Ever since she'd taken her ring off that night to heal Isla, ever since she'd pushed her magic too far, it was as if she'd awakened, revitalizing the immortal blood in her veins. And she had no idea how to dampen it again. Mortal spells were useless. Fae lore—*true* lore, beyond the eerie stories and tall tales—was scarce.

They will kill you if you don't keep them under control.

Gripping the slick edges of the tub, Raana yanked herself up, sending water flying over the washroom. She was lightheaded as she gasped for air, harshly wiping the water from her face and eyes. Her fingers gently glided over the edges of her ears. Smooth, not pointed.

Mortal. Immortal.

Witch. Fae.

She shook her head, having half a mind to go back under the water and scream, but she wouldn't let the feelings consume her. There would be no more darkness tonight.

No. Tonight was for these words of scandal and seduction.

With a heaved sigh, she dried her hands on her scratchy towel and took hold of her book, settling back against the edge of the tub and thumbing through the pages until she snagged on a sentence about the dashing knight removing his tunic.

Raana had only gotten through a few stolen kisses and lecherous touches when the sound came.

Thud.

A knock on her front door.

She nearly dropped the book into the tub as the pounding fist rang out again. Again. Again.

Her body locked up, and darkness gathered at the corners of the room. Raana acknowledged the shadows with a glance, as they crept in closer. Ready to protect, ready to attack at her whim.

What the hell was happening? Who had gotten up here? No one was supposed to know about this cottage, let alone make their way up to its door. She had wards for miles through these peaks to at least *alert* of any intruders.

Raana slowly lifted from the bath, took hold of her conduit, then quietly returned to her bedroom to grab a new nightgown. The knocking had stopped, but she knew the person or thing on the other side hadn't left.

She sought the best weapon she could on her path, the steel fire poker from beside the hearth, and clutched it in one hand between paling knuckles while the other held her crystal. Her damp curls dripped a path behind her as she crept towards the door, muttering an incantation beneath her breath. Offensive spells, as with potions, weren't her strong suit, but hopefully she'd muster enough to stun them and knock them on their ass for her to use her weapon. The shadows were her last resort. The crystal seared and glowed within her grasp as she continued her chant.

After a few breaths, Raana took hold of the door's knob and wrenched it open. Then she was left dumbstruck, jaw hanging open, as she stared at the man on her doorstep.

The Prince of Wolves.

RAANA

The prince had come with no interest in pleasantries, it seemed. He brandished a sack of coins, likely light and inconspicuous enough for her to barter with at market, and demanded she be ready to leave within the next twenty minutes.

Raana had remained there for a moment, still stunned. Her eyes wild. The thrum of magic spluttering. Her curse dead on her lips.

"Adrien—are you... Are you *kidding me*?" She scowled at the annoyingly good-looking, rugged man, worn from traveling through the mountains against the howling night winds and taking up most of the entryway. She inclined her head, attempting to see over the shifter before opting to glance around his side.

What the hell was he doing here? Better yet, how was he even...

"Foolish of me to expect a warmer greeting," Adrien remarked, amusement gilding his deep tone as he likely clocked her makeshift weapon. But Raana barely heard the words. She tore her eyes over his frame. Searching until—

There.

A bunch of ebony, white-speckled flowers stuck out of his jacket pocket. Nightsweet, deceptively simple and beautiful, was eradicated from the mainland because of its effects when woven with twine and soaked in salt water. A secret Helene had taught the wolf prince that *any* mortal—witch, wolf, or simple human—could wield against magic like Raana's *weaker* protective spells.

Raana abandoned the poker and drove her hand straight into the folds of Adrien's coat, running into the solid muscles of his stomach. She didn't care at all that he was a prince... or an apex predator.

The flowers burned at her touch, and the tell-tale nausea hit her hard and fast, poison exterior, made more potent after the salt treatment, leeching into her skin. With an agitated growl, she carried the bushel to the hearth and chucked it in. The fire fell to embers before erupting into cold, black hissing flames, the wretched blooms incinerating and leaving nothing but a disarmingly pleasant scent wafting through the air.

Raana lifted her arm to block her nose, but her eyes remained open, watching as the darkness ebbed and bowed before becoming its rightful smoldering sun once again.

Click.

She twisted at the sound of the closing door and found Adrien had invited himself inside. His keen eyes swept over the small expanse of the cottage as his boots creaked along the floorboards. He followed the trail of water she'd left from the bathing room to her bedroom, but instead of falling back to the puddle gleaming behind him at the entryway, his gaze settled on her.

Raana noted the slightest uptick of his brow, intrigue passing over his face. His gaze meandered up her bare legs, over the thin black nightgown she'd pulled on that barely covered her body. And though nothing beneath it was a mystery to him anymore, Raana folded her arms over her chest.

She blamed her shiver on the... chill he'd let in from the summer night. Not on his close attention. Not the fact that one look at him always brought up memories of an evening not too many months ago.

When she wasn't busy having horrible nightmares, sometimes she dreamt of him, remembered him. His mouth drawing over her skin, the strength, power, and presence of his body as he moved against her. In her.

One night of bliss and freedom in that ramshackle inn because she'd been too distracted to worry. By alcohol. By *him*. Her natural-born enemy, reluctant acquaintance, and one-time lover.

The last time she'd seen him, he'd stood by the cottage entryway, and they'd agreed they wouldn't see each other ever again. She'd already gone through a few days of pathetically lamenting that decision before she got a hold of herself and accepted it.

So, what the hell was this about?

Before Raana could ask, Adrien said, "It looks different." He pulled out what was typically her seat at the small, off-kilter dining table. As he sat, making the chair look frail beneath his long-limbed, muscle-bound frame, he dropped the sack of coins to the wood with a heavy, glorious clank.

Raana met his eyes, more golden than green in the reflection of the firelight. Somehow more... animal. Maybe she should've been more afraid of him. Wolves and witches had a bloody history, mainly over the territory within and surrounding these mountains.

"You know, bringing nightsweet into a witch's home warrants a wicked dealing of fate by the Mother," she said lowly, lifting her head. She wasn't entirely sure if it was true, but she remembered the tales.

"Good thing you're only half-witch, then. I guess I'm only half-fucked." He followed the words with a challenging grin that tied her stomach in knots.

Spirits, why couldn't Helene have struck a deal to aid in the healing of an *ugly* prince?

Raana bit the inside of her cheek and nodded towards the burlap. "What's in there?"

He toyed with the bag's strings. "A bit of silver. A bit of gold. One to spend, the other to hoard, lest others become suspicious of your sudden haul."

Raana hummed, toeing the ground and doing her best to hide her excitement. Gold. She'd be good for months.

Adrien trained his eyes over the cottage again, inclining his head, and she knew it was because he was listening with that animal hearing of his. That, or trying to catch a scent. "Where's Helene?"

She hated that the question felt like a jab in the gut. "Ehime... Auren... Elsun. I don't know. Wherever and whoever will pay her more."

Adrien's brows furrowed. "I thought she never wanted to return to the mainland?"

Exactly how much had her "mother"—what Adrien had known Helene as until he'd learned the truth of Raana's parentage a few months ago—disclosed to him during his healing sessions with her?

"It's becoming more difficult to have a choice, I'm afraid. A lot has changed since you were last here. And to my knowledge, you're entirely healed, so she wasn't waiting around for your call or expecting you to fill her pockets."

A wave of concern crossed his features. "Have you been alone since I brought you back?"

Raana forced herself not to stiffen. "Yes."

"It's been weeks."

"And? Nothing wrong with having your own company." At his questioning stare, Raana sighed. "You're a wolf—a pack animal. You wouldn't understand."

"I'm human first."

She waved him off and looked down into the fire again.

He already knew it all, why she kept to herself. Knew bringing people in close risked exposing her secret, and exposing her secret put not only her life in danger but also the lives of anyone who heard it. He was *one* of those very people. His friends were now those people, too, even though he didn't know it. Isla and Kai had sworn her to secrecy within those crystal-laden caverns. The three of them were the only ones who would know Isla was healed by not just a witch, but fae-kissed magic.

Her eyes slid to her middle finger, to her iron ring, her portable prison, and then she turned for the kitchen. Being around him while drinking alcohol may have gotten her in trouble in the past, but tea... tea wouldn't be a bad idea right now.

As Raana worked to get the kettle and track down her lavender and mint leaves, she heard the scraping of a chair against the hardwood flooring, followed by the heaviness of Adrien's footsteps. She refused to turn as he neared, opting to take another bite of the cheese she'd left out instead.

A sudden warmth spread across her back as Adrien reached over her shoulder to take some for himself. She was so bare in this scrap of fabric that his hand, his skin, brushed against hers.

"Help yourself," she said, cursing internally for sounding so breathless.

A low chuckle from him—that she felt in the subtle places they connected—had her body thrumming. "Such a gracious host."

Raana was so aware of him that she even clocked the way his breath ruffled her hair. It was aggravating how easily he could get under her skin. It had to be that she'd been deprived of human contact for so long. But even that realization didn't change that she wanted him to press harder into her. To be firm in the fact that he was there, that someone was, to warm the chill that hadn't left since she'd woken from her nightmare, despite the fire and the bath.

When Adrien reached again, Raana turned, momentarily stunned by the rush as she took in his features for the brief second he wasn't looking. Long lashes, a straight nose, stunning eyes, a pillow-soft mouth, and a cut jaw graced with a shadow of stubble. A Spirits-damn prince, yet she'd kissed along that jaw, traced that mouth with her tongue, and made him groan *her name* as she took him deep into—

Adrien met her gaze, and Raana shook herself back to reality, praying that he didn't notice. A moment of pause said he may have, as did the way his eyes darkened, but he only told her, "You should get ready to go."

Somehow, blissfully, that broke any delusion his closeness had brought about, dispelling the heat she *didn't* need. "You think you can just show up at my house and demand I leave, and I'll go with you? No questions asked? You never even said where we're going."

Adrien reached over again, but rather than food, he grabbed the kettle. Raana was left damn-near freezing as he moved away, circling her to go to the sink and fill it. "I'll tell you on the way. Get packed. You're wasting your ten minutes."

Ten?

"You said twenty."

"And we've wasted half of it." He perched the kettle on the stovetop and glanced around the counter for whatever he could use to ignite the flame.

Raana rolled her eyes and turned to grab the spark rocks from where she'd left them by the altar dotted with candles, sage, and crystals. A small tribute to the Mother and Spirits. "If you don't tell me, I don't see any reason to go."

"What's this?"

Raana spun from the altar and felt like her stomach had plummeted into her shoes. Adrien's eyes ran over her grimoire, his hand perched next to it on the counter as if questioning if he should touch it. For most of her life, she'd kept the item hidden. Even Helene had asked where she'd whisked the book away to. A grimoire wasn't necessarily something kept private, or not as private as she kept it, but to her, it was like a wound she couldn't quite close. One she didn't want to expose or explain to anyone.

She carried the rocks to him, keeping watch of his hand, ready to sweep the book into her own. "Nothing of your concern."

Adrien raised his brows, likely noting her nervousness and the rise of her stupid heartbeat. Then, with a speed she couldn't match, he blocked her path.

She leveled him with a deadpan stare. "Really?"

Adrien flashed her that stupid grin. "Go get ready."

"Are you a child?" she sneered, pressing forward and futilely attempting to outmaneuver him, only to end up crushed against his broad chest. She reached around again, bracing on his arm as she lost her footing. But she was too distracted by her annoyance to care about the feel of his muscles beneath her fingers, how perfectly their bodies fit together, or that her nightgown was riding up on her back with each failed stretch. "Adrien, may the Spirits fucking save you, move or I'll castrate you."

Adrien's laughter flooded the room, blooming that sickening warmth in her chest. "Well, that's a new threat." Raana met his eyes then, the challenge within them. They sparked something in her that she hadn't been expecting but should've. They always seemed to. "Make me move, princess."

He delighted in getting this rise out of her, too much. Too. Damn. Much.

Raana felt a cold lick at her fingertips and knew shadows ebbed along her skin. She became aware of what lurked in every corner of the room, everything the darkness caressed. Everything that could be used against him, including the fire poker she'd abandoned.

She calculated her next move. Should she circle his arms in dark tendrils to pull him back? Form them between them like a wall and drive him away?

She could walk through the shadows and appear behind him, one of her favorite skills she'd developed years ago. Slipping from darkness to darkness, a secret stalking through the world. If there was one thing she enjoyed about her immortal power, it was that.

But... her magic had been so unpredictable lately.

Raana willed herself to calm and stepped back, pushing the darkness away. She went to spark the stovetop. "It's my mother's grimoire."

In her periphery, she noticed Adrien had sidestepped, glancing back at the relic. "Your mother's grimoire..." He seemed to test the word *mother*. "Your..."

"Birth mother, yes," she finished for him, just as flames erupted. She placed the metal canister over the blaze and turned to him fully, allowing a woefulness to color her tone. "The one who died giving birth to me. The one who left me nothing but those spells and the words of our ancestors to remember her by. To figure out who she was, who *I am*. Who has left me to wonder how different things would be, how much I'm missing by not having her in my life."

Adrien blinked at her, his lips twitching downwards. "You're guilting me?"

Raana had been moving as she spoke and reached around, ripping the book from the countertop and holding it close to her secretly cracking chest. "Pity is its own kind of magic, Your Highness." She nestled the book onto the middle shelf of the potion cabinet as she bit into her thumb, the tang of blood coating her tongue. She pressed her injured, leaking skin to the closed wood and muttered the locking spell, feeling a shock tremor up her arm and a wave of dizziness as it pulled at her magic. Blood was much stronger than a conduit in directing power, but more costly. "Try to touch it, and you'll get warts."

"You know that magic doesn't work on me."

"It'll still keep you out, though." She staunched the bleeding with the skirt of her nightgown and leaned back against the door. Another form of defense. "Now, where do you think you're taking me? I thought we decided this"—she gestured between them with a finger—"was over. We're even. I risked your hide; you risked mine. We're both alive, and now we move on."

"Well, you were so perfectly inconspicuous on my father's guard the last time that he wants you back. Not to guard, but to look at the Wall protecting us from being consumed by the monsters your people created." Adrien mirrored her position, leaning back against the countertop, casting an assessing eye over her body as if sizing up whether she could keep him from the cabinet.

"*My people?*"

"Witches. Dark magic. The darkest kind, I hope. I don't want to imagine it gets much worse than the bak."

Raana had heard of the bak. The beasts had been down in the tunnels beneath Deimos. Isla had killed them and was coated in their reeking, dark blood. Raana hadn't ever actually seen the creatures, but they sounded—and smelled—horrid.

Adrien continued, "We'll be in Io first for a day at my family's estate in the countryside to keep you hidden while I meet with my father, and then we'll go to Callisto for a couple of nights."

Callisto? The name sounded familiar, but—"I don't have your map memorized."

"It's on our western border. It's not too far. Closer than Deimos."

"Good, because that journey was awful."

"It will be nice not to have you vomit on me."

"I didn't vomit *on you.*"

"Over me."

"Sorry, I'm not used to riding around in those metal contraptions you wolves call cars."

"The witches are getting there, so I've heard."

"Maybe on the mainland," she murmured.

Adrien hummed as if agreeing to disagree. He rose from his lounge. "If we're going to make it back before sunrise, we need to go now. Grab the bare minimum you'll need. I'll be giving you clothes anyway, so you blend in." He cocked his head. "Or I can just tell my father to forget it and take back the gold."

Raana narrowed her eyes. "I dare you."

Adrien answered her challenge with a grin, and the kettle finally whistled as he headed for the door. Raana, poised at the countertop, felt that piece of her rise, beckoned too many times now not to play.

The room darkened, a hollowness filling her ears.

Her shadows, the little beasts, crawled from the corners of the room, creeping towards his retreating form. Adrien surveyed them, had the audacity to meet her eyes, look back at them, and scoff. He snatched up the bag and kept moving.

Raana's blood chilled, then, and her eyes darted from him to the shadows, to the fire poker she'd abandoned on the floor. She stepped sideways, running on an ancient, ingrained instinct as she called upon the darkness to gather, to swallow her up.

It happened in a blink: her body, beneath what felt like freezing water, became part of the black space she whipped through.

Adrien's hand had been on the doorknob, twisting and pulling.

The exit slammed shut as Raana appeared between him and the wood, the metal poker now in her hand and pointed at his chest, having been claimed by her through the darkness.

"Drop it," she commanded, and delight flashed in Adrien's eyes. Flashed in hers, too. She couldn't deny the high that came with using her immortal power, the natural way it responded to her.

They remained like that, nothing between them but deep breaths, before Adrien spoke.

"If you want a chance at killing one of us," he began, his hand lifting to shift the steel bar over an inch, over what Raana assumed was dead into his heart. "You aim here." He pushed it up higher, to the base of his throat, and her breath caught at the ease with which it pressed into his flesh. "Or here. The strongest of us don't break easily anywhere else. Don't give us a chance to think. Don't let us draw our claws."

As if to emphasize the point, sharp protrusions erupted at the tips of Adrien's fingers, and Raana dipped her eyes towards them, the claws that could carve her to bits right here. Shifting looked horrendously painful, but it was done with such lethal ease. Wolves were predators crafted by a deity.

These lessons, he always fit them in when he could. Always had. To keep her safe while she was with him. To keep her safe in general. Witches weren't naturally endowed with brute power. Those who became such forces were molded that way, undergoing intense, soul-shredding training within the Bend between the Great Cities. They were never the same again, or so she'd heard.

There was a pause, and Raana felt like her heart was about to beat out of her chest. Before she could blink, he swiped her weapon to the side, entirely disarming her and pinning her beneath his heavy body. The wood of the door dug into her back.

"Don't take your eyes off us," he said. "And you *need* to be quicker."

Raana glowered, her blood heating then chilling as she called upon the darkness again, as she ebbed through that pool and appeared behind—

No. In... front?

Adrien was facing her, grabbing and whirling her to pin her to the wall again.

This time, he'd been bowed over, low laughter falling from his lips so close to her ear, her neck. One of his forearms rested beside her head while his other hand pressed to the wood of the door by her hip, his thumb barely skirting her skin. But just enough.

Spirits, save her.

"Also, work on being less predictable." The deepness and nearness of the words made her shiver. With a heaved breath, her pebbling breasts brushed against him. She caught his fist clenching and felt him adjust his stance, but he didn't rise until he whispered, "At one time, the fae were the most feared beings to walk this world, and for good reason. Don't squander the power you have with novice mistakes."

There was a hidden seduction in his words. She could be feared and powerful if she'd embrace who and what she was. But that meant risks she couldn't imagine taking. Even just the thought of it had anxiety tightening her chest.

Raana beat it down, distracting herself with the man before her and what hummed between them. Both she and the prince walked a fine line of discipline, one she could shatter right now if she wanted.

Actually...

Raana angled her face towards his, speaking low and smooth, "Who said the shadows were my only power, Prince?" She got closer, closer until she knew her breath fanned across his lips. Adrien's eyes dropped to her mouth, clearly distracted. Raana hid her smile as she reached up to touch his face, darkness slowly filling the space between them. Too late, Adrien realized it, and she pushed. As he stumbled back, the shadows keeping him off balance, she laughed and reached for the bag of coins he'd dropped. "Try not to think with that little thing between your legs."

Adrien scoffed but was still grinning as he righted himself. "You and I both know it's not *little*."

Raana waved him off, refusing to agree. "I'll be ready in twenty minutes."

CHAPTER 6

RAANA

The late-summer sun was a brutal kiss to Raana's skin, even within the confines of the vehicle rumbling over the sandstone streets of Io's Imperial City. She bit down on her tongue to keep her nausea at bay. Not only was the ride uneasy—not only was the unrelenting heat made worse by the two massive bodies at her sides—but the prospect of what awaited her at the end of this journey made keeping down her breakfast feel impossible.

Because before she was to inspect the wall in Callisto, Imperial Alpha Cassius wanted an audience with her.

A surprise to both her and Adrien as they gathered themselves after her cottage at one of the royal family's estates within the mountains. Winslow, the Imperial Alpha's liaison, had intercepted them just as they were about to leave with the order and "suitable attire for their guest." And despite Adrien's vehement protests, Raana found herself here, swathed in a simple dress fit for a citizen of this kingdom, heading for her potential doom.

She wrinkled her nose as she met the prince's gaze in the mirror for the umpteenth time in the thirty minutes they'd been traveling. Amusement and concern shone in his eyes before she dragged her gaze away from him, sitting in the car's passenger seat, to Winslow, driving them at his side.

The fact that the liaison had been the one behind the steering wheel appeared to be a shock to both the prince and the guards. Their questioning comments to him regarding his driving received an excuse Raana took as bullshit, given the amusement on Adrien's face. One glance of his back told her she may have been the reason for the unusual setup. Something that was confirmed when Winslow met her stare in the mirror and stiffened, his sun-tanned skin blanching.

Afraid. He was afraid of *her*. She didn't know if he could shift, but regardless, he had much over her in size.

A sweeping breeze carried the scent of fresh bread and salt, and the sounds of cawing gulls. Raana watched the people carrying their wares in wicker baskets as they hustled by shops draped and painted in vibrant colors, beyond the motif of burgundy and gold she'd seen almost everywhere. The guards at her side had tensed as if they knew what would follow.

It had been an initial proposal that she and Adrien travel in separate cars to dispel any swirling rumors if the Crowned Prince were spotted with a *mystery woman*. But the suggestion was met by protest from them both, most fervently by Adrien. She wouldn't be leaving his side, and anyone who had a problem with that could fuck right off—not his *exact* words, but it was something to that effect. Now, she was trapped in this vehicle bearing a crest of a wolf, a crown, the sun, and the moon... a clear symbol of the royal entourage.

And *everyone* took notice.

The ruckus built steadily, in time with her nausea. One person noticed their car, saw the prince, then another, and another. Whispers became shouts, hands shot in the air, heads were bowed, baskets dropped, and then the preening began, daughters tugged by mothers and fathers into the car's vantage. Into *Adrien's* vantage.

With a twist of her gut—as Adrien lifted his hand to his citizens, that heart-fluttering grin across his face—Raana remembered the prince's love life was a spectacle. He needed to find his mate, his one true match, and that someone *did exist* out there. A woman who'd literally been *made for him*.

He'd had a lover before, she remembered. More a wife than a soul-bound partner, but he still regarded her as his mate. He wouldn't talk much about her to Raana, but she'd known losing her had been the reason for him needing to be healed by Helene. Severing the bond between wolves tore them apart at their foundations.

Raana didn't want to watch much more of the fawning, and her chest had begun to feel tight as the crowd multiplied. People converged on them in a way she wasn't quite used to, as they had in Deimos, and even then, she'd needed to bear down and fight through it. So, she directed her gaze elsewhere, to the palm trees swaying in the balmy breeze, to the distant gates that stretched high, their golden tops nearly blinding in the blaring sunshine, and the gargantuan building behind them. That had to be the Pack Hall.

Raana blinked wide as she took it in. It was a palace, really. A monstrous feat of marble and stone, columns and archways, gold and burgundy in billowing flags and drapes. More citizens had been camped out beside those gates, waiting for them, for any one of the royal line, maybe. Some held cameras, already snapping the bulky contraptions, replacing flashbulbs as they approached, with notepads in their hands.

Raana jerked, feeling warmth against the bare skin of her leg, just below her knee, enough to make her breath hitch and become shallow. Her body had chilled, and darkness crept into the corners of her vision. She'd been creating indents in her palms, too, from how hard she was clenching her fists.

She lowered her gaze, then followed the fingers caressing her skin to their source. But Adrien hadn't turned to look at her; he wouldn't even meet her eyes in the mirror. He was still focused outside on his people, waving and pretending he wasn't doing anything at all. He must've sensed her panic, the writhing of her magic.

She couldn't settle or return the touch in thanks, though, sensing another set of eyes on her, from within the car. She didn't need to turn to the female guard on her right to know she'd noticed the prince reach back while everyone else was preoccupied scanning their surroundings. And she didn't need to turn to know her gaze was filled with both curiosity and disapproval.

Raana gave her leg a subtle shake, hinting at Adrien to remove his hand.

She didn't meet his eyes in the mirror.

❧

Inside, the Pack Hall was everything Raana had expected. High ceilings that echoed their footsteps and their very breath, the alabaster interiors splashed with deep reds and golden yellows, gilded at every opportunity. Only Winslow's assistant, a young woman named Ravona, Adrien, and the female guard, whom she now knew was named Sandrine, had escorted her to the second floor.

Any ease of nausea she'd been granted upon exiting the car was long gone. She began picking mercilessly at her nails, not caring at all about the skin she peeled away. Her heart hammered, and despite Adrien now walking at her side, his arm a reassuring brush against hers, it couldn't be alleviated.

She didn't understand.

She'd been in much scarier places than this opulent establishment—within the depths of mountains, in the bowels of cursed woodlands, on hallowed ground known for its vengeful ghosts—but she'd never felt on edge like this before. And it wasn't, she knew deep in her bones, the prospect of speaking to Adrien's father that had her feeling like this, even if the thought of the highest King of Wolves was intimidating as all hell.

Raana had noticed when she'd been within wolf territory weeks ago, had sensed it while walking the mountains, and she'd sensed it with every step now. The shadows were different here, in the way they moved, the way they felt, and how they seemed cautious of her. And yet, there was something here in this hall, in this path they walked, something that stirred the darkness and had it whispering to her in vague tongues. Not wanting to protect her, not wanting her to wield them as a weapon, but wanting her to... see.

"What's wrong?"

Raana jumped as the words warmed the shell of her ear, and she felt Adrien's hand wrap around hers. Damn it all to hell, she supposed. Whatever way she was behaving must've been bad if their ruse of not giving a shit about each other had completely collapsed. Adrien slowed their steps, and neither Ravona nor Sandrine questioned them as they fell behind. She missed his heat when he dropped her hand.

"I don't know." She could've easily said *nothing*, but it felt like lying would land her in deeper shit.

"I can stall him and give you a minute," Adrien said. "It shouldn't kill him to talk to his son for a while."

Raana's mouth lifted a bit at the quip. After the quickness of the morning, settling for even a moment didn't sound so bad, but... "No, I'm fine. I just needed to catch my breath."

"Are you sure?"

She forced a wider smile, her *yes*. "Stop worrying so much. People might start to think you like me."

Adrien laughed through his nose. "Goddess forbid."

By the time they moved, Ravona and Sandrine already stood before their destination—one of the many rooms in this hall—and remained there as Raana and Adrien stepped inside.

Raana had looked a crawler dead in the eye and killed it. She had held a woman's life in her hands, healing her while the man who loved her more, it seemed, than the world itself watched. She, herself, was a monster unlike any in this world, crafted by shadows and the darkest of things, with little knowledge of the true extent of her power.

But the Imperial Alpha scared her shitless. Because unlike everything else that she *knew* would kill her, knew *how* they would kill her, he was entirely unpredictable.

Even with Adrien at her side, Raana felt herself shudder beneath the Alpha's attention.

Cassius's eyes were dark, such a deep brown that they seemed black, nothing like the golden green hue of Adrien's. His features were harsher, too. Finer lines etched by his brow, his mouth, likely due to too much scowling. He was still handsome, in a terrifying way. She figured Adrien would look the same in thirty years, though, hopefully... kinder.

Across from Cassius stood a stockier, familiar man. With friendly pine-colored eyes, so opposed to the wolf opposite him, and a warmer smile to match, though it didn't make him less intimidating.

Imperial Beta Malakai—Isla's father. A man who had no idea his mate was alive.

Another secret Raana had been sworn to keep in the depths of that arena. A witch may have been responsible for orchestrating Kai's father and older brother's deaths, but the one who'd dealt the killing blows had been Isla's mother, assumed dead for years.

Raana could barely wrap her mind around how twisted that was, and she had to check herself from wondering at the magical capability the witch must possess. Skilled with poisons and able to use coercion and mind-control. It was the darkest of their gifts, forbidden in practice; a law disregarded by some radical coven leaders who cared not for the High Witch's wrath. Even the prospect of that scope of power lingering in one's future should've been picked up by one of Her Highest's dutiful seers—though they'd somehow missed Raana's fae heritage during their census for magical potential. Divination itself was an unreliable ability.

"Hello again," Beta Malakai greeted from where he stood by a map of their continent on the wood-paneled wall. Cassius, on the opposite side of the work, said nothing, only leveling her with that assessing predator's stare.

Raana bowed low to them both at once, then shifted her feet so they pointed towards the Imperial Alpha. "Your Majesty."

When she rose, Cassius's lips lifted into an unnervingly pleased grin. "You've trained her well."

Raana felt Adrien tense, and she fought to keep a scowl off her face while Adrien answered, with a bite in his voice, "No training was necessary."

Silence fell, and Raana felt one with Malakai as they took in the two Alpha-blooded wolves. She wished Adrien would drag her away or that she could call upon the shadows to get her the hell out of there. But all her effort was focused on keeping them *away*.

When the room had become insufferable and suffocating, the oak-colored walls closing in, wall lamps burning hot, Cassius finally said, "Leave us be."

Us.

Oh, Spirits, save her. Mother, bless her. Whomever the hell the fae worshipped... help.

She'd been prepared for it, but hearing his words made her heart drop into her stomach.

Malakai bowed his head to his leader, and Raana felt Adrien's hand wrap around her arm. "I'll be right down the hall. Not far."

He'd brought his face close to hers to speak quietly, but closer than he should've in front of his father, of all people. But she just focused on him, on his eyes, steeling herself, her breath, and nodded.

As he and Malakai left the room, she heard Adrien mutter to the Beta, *"Before you eventually leave for Deimos, I have a coronation gift I want you to bring Isla, and a mating gift for them both."*

So, Isla was going to become queen soon if she hadn't already.

"Sit."

Raana snapped to attention as the door closed, sealing her fate, as Cassius gestured to the seat before him, a grimace on his face that made her wonder if he'd heard Adrien's parting words. The demand in his voice couldn't be missed. Raana slowly approached the leather chair at the center of the room, smoothing out her dress.

Cassius began pacing behind the chair across from hers, hands in his pockets. "I have to say, it's shocking."

Raana took a deep, steadying inhale, pretending his movements weren't those of a predator stalking prey through a forest. "What is, Your Majesty?"

Spirits, she sounded so weak, and her heart was going to explode. There was no way he couldn't hear it. Her thumb began playing with her ring, spinning it over her skin. If she didn't relax, if the shadows reacted, the Alpha would kill her without hesitation.

"How I didn't realize it sooner." Cassius ceased his movements. "How no one has. You're what? Twenty?"

Why did her age matter?

Raana cleared her throat. "Twenty-two, Your Majesty."

"Twenty-two years," he said humorlessly, pressing his hands to the back of the couch, looking down at her with narrowed, hungry eyes. "Fae have walked the world for twenty-two years—more, most likely—after centuries, a millennium, and not one of the witches, no one at all, has figured it out."

Raana's blood chilled, her entire body locking like she'd been encased in ice.

Fae.

Fae.

This had to be a nightmare. She hadn't just heard out of his mouth what she thought.

"I—I'm sorry, Your Majesty?"

This couldn't be real. It couldn't be real, couldn't be...

"My son was wrong. Training *is* needed, then you'd know better than to lie to me." Cassius's tone was threatening, but still, he wore that voracious smile, a fascination glinting in those near-black irises. "I know that's you, making the room colder. It's the shadows you control, correct? Darkness."

Raana couldn't breathe. Her hands shook, and her fingers pressed so hard into her ring that the iron and subtle runes burned her skin. "I don't know."

His eyebrow quirked, head lifting in that detecting, animal way. "Not entirely a lie." Then he was moving again, away from her. "You truly don't know what you can do. No one to teach you. Your parents—"

"Are dead."

So quick to retort. All formality gone. As if a part of her didn't want him even thinking about her parents, let alone speaking of them. People she'd never even met. Ghosts standing at her side in that room.

Raana flinched when she'd pinched herself to the point she drew blood, the pain a sign this was not a nightmare. There was no escaping this. A drag of her tongue over her teeth had her tensing. Were they becoming sharper? Were her ears...

The corners of Raana's eyes stung as the tips of her fingers became cold, ebony cresting her crossed legs to gather by the tips. No, *no.*

She flicked her hand, shooing them away, not wanting to lift it to check her appearance, a prayer on her quiet mouth that the Alpha hadn't noticed.

There was no need for her to lift her head to catch the plethora of weapons on display in this room, aside from the fact that the Imperial Alpha was a weapon himself. He'd put her down like an animal right here in this chair if she posed any threat.

As if to remind her of that, Cassius rested against the display case holding a brutal-looking sword with an ornate handle. An antique, but just as lethal in the right hands. "Your mother, maybe, but I can't imagine an immortal meeting such a... mundane fate. Perhaps that's my own blind optimism. Foolish, considering the horrible ramifications it could mean for the fabric of our world if your father were alive, roaming Morai..."

He paused, stepping closer with his weighing stare. Raana had no response and would not move, focusing only on resisting her own magic. She wouldn't even let her mind wander to that thought she'd had herself on many occasions, if her father still lived.

Cassius seemed to delight in her show of restraint. "Forgive me. I'm not usually a man who struggles for words. I hope you realize what a wonder you are."

Wonder... that was one way to put it. But it only went so far when her existence, like her absent father's, meant horrible ramifications for the world. So, when she couldn't come up with a response, she knew she'd soon start to annoy more than please him.

Her fear and panic threatened to consume her, but she couldn't let it show so clearly. "How did you... What did I do wrong? Where... When did you figure it out? Did Adrien—"

She cut herself off because of her inevitable fumbling and not wanting to bring the prince into it.

But Cassius finished, "Tell me? No, though, this has helped me better understand my son's infatuation with you. A rare find, indeed."

Infatuation—despite everything, the word rang hollow.

"Then how?" Her voice strained, pressed, broke.

Cassius only gave her a smile, a pitying one that dug its claws deep into her, that... that sent her mind reeling back. To a letter, to missing clothes. To lonely, hollow weeks...

"No." The word had been nothing but a breath from Raana's mouth.

Now, Cassius sat on the couch before her, as if he'd succeeded in his goal to break her down to something helpless. Someone who wouldn't fight back at all.

"I'm surprised how simple the choice seemed for Helene. Release you to me, or be turned in. I expected a counteroffer of some sort, but she didn't even ask for gold."

Raana's ears were ringing. Helene's face flashed in her mind. Her crinkled, cold chestnut eyes, her dark hair streaked with gray. The woman who had raised her. Who she'd even called *mother* until... until that mask the older witch had worn broke to pieces the night she told Raana the truth of her heritage. When fragments of hatred and resentment began to flicker in every word spoken by her.

The only person in her life she'd ever felt she could remotely rely on.

Other than...

Other than...

She looked up into Cassius's face, seeing a fleeting vision of a person she'd given so much to. Her darkest secret, her body, her...

"What do you want?" Raana choked out, his words registering. *Release her to him.* "Why make a deal for me? What do you need me for?"

Anger glazed her tone. At Helene, yes. She wanted to scream and rip Helene to pieces. But this man, this conniving bastard—he'd started this. He'd sent her world crumbling.

Cassius didn't seem phased at all, and his apathy straightened her spine. "I want you to work for me."

Raana blinked blurry, rage-filled eyes. "What?"

"You have a skillset I covet," he said, rising to his feet again, a reminder of who held power here. He moved like he wore a crown, heavy and gleaming and everything he was entitled to. That the world was. "The readings on fae are scarce, archaic, in languages barely studied and only by the oldest scholars. To my understanding, of the two immortal fae courts, only one sect within them can wield shadow as you do. I've seen sketches, some translated anecdotes. Nightmarish things, they are. Darkness made flesh, possessing the ability to be everywhere and nowhere, to see the unseen, to hear the unheard. Incarnates of death, at their worst."

A lump had formed in Raana's throat. Where had he read all of that? She couldn't find anything of the sort, but then again, the resources he has access to as a King of Kings...

Darkness made flesh. Incarnates of death.

"How much does that ring hinder you?" Cassius asked, disrupting her thoughts. "It's iron, I know. Helene taught you to enchant it. It keeps you appearing mortal, but how much does it restrict your power?"

She wanted him to stop speaking *her* name. Each mention was a punch to her gut.

"I don't know," Raana answered quickly—too quickly—still pressing back against the shadows that wanted to crawl over her skin, to lash out and protect her. Not so much to fight but to prevent him from seeing what she could do. "What are you expecting of me by working for you?"

A feral grin crossed his mouth. "All in due time. Though I appreciate the initiative. You'll learn once you've accepted my offer and sworn your fealty by blood before your deities and our own. I'm gracious. I'll give you time to consider until after you and Adrien have come back from Callisto."

Adrien...

Had he known of his father's plans?

Cassius seemed to pick up on the way her features had shifted, and his tone had become... gentler but still firm. His movement slowed; his words chosen carefully. "My son has duties he will need to fulfill as my Heir, which include finding a mate, a future queen of the realm. And though I am gracious, I am not blind. You're an interest of his, and I'm not sure how much you were involved in his healing, but as a show of gratitude, I'll allow it to continue as long as it remains hidden and as long as you both know when it must end, it ends. Our bonds are absolute. Our loyalty is to one, and only one above all. When it's time for him to assume his duty, entertaining you will no longer be an option. Don't make me have to remove it, remove you. Because I will."

The threat in his words couldn't be missed. Raana's mouth was agape, trying to process. He'd *allow* her to be Adrien's mistress until his mate came along? One of the prince's conquests. A rare find, indeed. A dangerous one to remain a secret forever.

A cocktail of rage, disgust, and hurt coiled within her. Mostly because she realized she was a fool.

"Yes," she agreed quietly.

Cassius nodded, marking an end to their conversation. When he turned from her, Raana took the hint and rose to her feet, shaking darkness from her hands. Her entire body was loose and trembling. "Your Majesty." She was impressed by how firm her voice sounded.

It made Cassius turn, his features betraying his slight surprise at the tone.

Before he officially dismissed her, he said, "You can also be assured I won't imprison you. Not like the others. You're too valuable right now. Though there will still be precautionary measures taken, I'm sure you understand."

She opened her mouth to ask what measures, what *others*, but then closed it. He'd turned away again.

For a moment, Raana didn't know what to do with her body, with her urge to call upon the darkness to sweep and swallow and whisk her off to any oblivion but here.

CHAPTER 7

ADRIEN

"Isn't it a bit early, Your Highness?"

Adrien didn't even glance at Sandrine as he splashed bourbon into a glass. He'd been in the room for all of ten seconds before the dry bar in the corner called to him like a beacon on a stormy night.

"No." The prince knocked the drink back, savoring the burn in his throat as he refilled the glass.

Sandrine made a disbelieving sound, flipping her coppery hair over a crimson-clad shoulder. "So, who is she that has you so wound up?"

Another drain to the dregs. "I'm not wound up."

"Yeah, okay. And I didn't see that little caress back in the car or find it strange that the two of you are hiding out in your vacation home or that your scent when you're near her becomes just *a bit* too detectable."

Adrien contemplated pouring another, but instead, set the glass back on the bar's crystal surface. "I don't recall you being so nosy."

"Some say nosy, others perceptive. It's a good trait as a guard."

"An annoying one," Adrien muttered, turning to find her standing with proper form, shoulders and legs square, hands behind her back. "Do you ever stop being a guard?"

Sandrine gave him a flat look and relaxed, though she didn't move from her spot. "I won't deny she's pretty, but she isn't of Io. At least, I don't recall ever meeting her. I can't get a scent off her either, other than how

59

she clearly also feels about you—like every other mateless woman on this continent. I believe I caught an accent, too. Did you pick her up in the southern territories or something?"

The southern territories? Wrong direction, but good enough, he supposed.

"Yeah," he said gruffly, running his hands over his face as he took a seat on one of the leather couches.

"I hope you get better at lying before you become the Alpha, for your own sake," Sandrine said. "Were you always so bad at it?"

Adrien narrowed his eyes at her, though she wasn't wrong.

He didn't answer. Instead, he rested his head back and let his eyes trace the ceiling. This sitting room, like others on this floor, was littered with old books and maps. He glanced over at the piece draped on the wall, similar to the one in the lounge he'd left Raana in with his father.

It had taken every scrap of willpower to leave her with him and not to go back in there right now.

His shoulders were practically up to his ears. *Wound up.* Yeah, he was. *The last thing you, of all people, need is to be screwing around with a witch.*

At Isla's voice in his head, Adrien grimaced. What he'd give to have her here, slapping sense into him right now.

As if she'd sensed, tangentially, where his mind had gone, Sandrine asked, her voice light with mocking, "What is it? Are you lost without your other half? I don't think you and Sebastian have ever been apart for this long."

Adrien didn't bother lifting his head. "He'll be back; don't worry." If he remembered correctly, Sandrine had fawned over his lifelong best friend when they'd been teenagers. But then again, Sebastian charmed everyone—even those Adrien thought the Imperial Beta's son had no shot with. He wondered how things were going with him and Kai's friend, Ameera, while he was in Deimos for Isla's coronation. Intimidatingly beautiful, a warrior, and unattainable. One of his many types.

"Not Isla, though," Sandrine said.

Adrien furrowed his brows at the mention, the barely perceptible bite to her voice. "No, not Isla." The words stung more than he'd braced for.

"You know, a part of me always thought you two would've ended up together, especially after she ended things with my cousin. And you—" Sandrine cut herself off.

Adrien tried to ignore where her words had been heading, banishing any thoughts of his own past, and forced a laugh. "I love her, but not a chance in hell. There never was."

Even when she'd been with Sandrine's cousin.

Callan, Isla's shitty ex, was a warrior as she'd become. The two of them had been put on assignment in Deimos a couple of months ago to deal with rogue attacks on the pack's borders.

Sandrine snorted, and at a look from Adrien that said *stop having a stick up your ass for two seconds and relax*, she sat on the chair across from him. "Her coronation's in a few days, isn't it?"

"On the Equinox," Adrien said before testing out slowly, "Luna Isla of Deimos. Long may she reign."

Sandrine snickered. "Of all the packs on the continent."

"Deimos isn't so bad."

"I heard from other guards that your father received death threats while he was there."

"As he does in Mimas, Tethys, Rhea, and Iapetus. My father is the Alpha. If his life wasn't in danger from some radicals or rogues, then he should fear that he's lost track of where the threat is."

Sandrine hummed. "I also heard you ran off, too. That you weren't supposed to be there for the challenge."

Adrien shrugged. "I had to be there for a friend. Alpha Kai is Isla's mate, her *fated* mate. I couldn't leave her to deal with watching that alone."

His statement had something sparking in Sandrine's eyes, her brows raising. "So, what I don't get," she began carefully, "If he's her fated mate... they were in the Hunt together. Surely, they knew they were fated, then. But they obviously didn't *reject* the bond. Yet, Isla came back here for a month before going back to Deimos and taking the throne."

Her words sounded so rehearsed that they made Adrien clench his teeth. It had been distrust and suspicion in her eyes. It didn't take much to figure out what she was alluding to. Isla, a luna by destiny, living secretly amongst Io's citizens. A spy.

He obviously knew the whole tale and had confronted her about her logic and their reasoning for choosing to do *nothing* about what lay between them, but was it his to disclose? Before he could muster an answer, the door mercifully burst open.

Or maybe not so mercifully.

Raana was a whirlwind, and Adrien shot to his feet. Magic seared in her blood—he wasn't sure how he could sense it. She was on the precipice of something dangerous. It was apparent on her face, too, her soft features drawn in lethal lines. "What happened?"

"I need to talk to you." Her voice was hoarse, broken. Cold. "Now. Alone."

Sandrine had also risen, her feet spread and shoulders squared, lumerosi and eyes glowing that common pale blue. Her fingers splayed, ready to draw claws, prepared to uphold her duty to protect him.

Adrien's heart was a war drum, and his wolf crested, a burn beneath his skin as his own markings flared. "Stand down." A command that made Sandrine stiffen. "Leave us."

The guard gave a subtle shake of her head as if she also had the preternatural sense of the threat rising in the room. "Your Highness—"

"*Go.*"

Reluctantly, she obeyed—but not without a glower at Raana. When the door had closed behind her, a wave of black cascaded over the wood. Shadows forming a barrier, hardening.

Keeping others out. Or... him in?

Adrien should've been more afraid of the woman before him. A phantom wind billowed her hair, her dress, the crystal glittering near her throat. Her entire body, from her toes to the crown of her head, seemed to hum with anger—with power. Adrien swore that on an exhale, he could see his own breath.

Only once had he seen a glimpse of this. Of her. The *true* her.

In the face of it, Adrien pulled back his wolf. Not much, but enough to take the burn from his eyes, his markings.

If she had something to throw at him, he'd be ready to weather it, but more than anything, he needed to keep her mortal. His voice was a tender caress as he chanced a step. "Raana."

Shadows greeted him, curling around his feet like feral cats. Her magic, her *fae* magic, probed him, his intentions, if he was a threat. His wolf wanted to rise to it, to fight it off. But when it came to faerie magic, Adrien, all of them, were almost powerless. He'd need to weaken her beyond reason to land a blow, as they had in the past against her ancestors.

Raana's mouth opened and closed, her chest heaving, eyes glossing over. "*Helene.*"

The name had barely been a whisper.

Adrien continued to advance. "What about her?"

Raana wouldn't meet his eyes, but he could see the way hers flickered. And that wasn't shadows crawling up her arms; the darkness spider-webbing there was skin-deep. Her features, her face, her ears, all of it... had shifted. His eyes darted to her hand, still donning that ring.

"Raana," he pressed as the light seemed to flee from the room, from her. A shiver raced up his spine, ice filling his veins. Those cats at his feet scraped at him with claws and teeth, teasing, testing. He bared down when they bit, the magic nearly tearing his clothes when they tried to lock him in place away from her. They failed.

When his hand touched her cheek, it was freezing, unbearably so, but he didn't move, even when her shadows tried to pull again. "What happened to Helene?"

Her eyes met his—primal, ethereal. Fae. A universe born and destroyed within them with each blink. "She's—she's never coming back."

It was a numb, distant sentence. Disbelieving.

"What happened?" Adrien kept his body from tightening, from letting his reaction feed into hers. What the fuck did his father do?

Raana's jaw tensed beneath his fingers, and her hand wearing that ring reached up to touch his, squeezing for reassurance that he was actually there. "She told him. She told your father. She told him what I am, and she left. Forever." The final word was breathless. "It wasn't worth the risk anymore—I wasn't—so she left, left me to *him*. She's gone."

Raana dropped her hand from his and stepped back, wrapping her arms around herself. Shadows swept over her, seeming to drape her like a cloak. The room brightened, warmed.

For a moment, Adrien couldn't form words, wanting to process everything she'd just said and not have her rehash it again. His father had paid Helene to leave her?

"Why?"

"He wants me to work for him."

"He wants you to what? *Why?*"

"He wouldn't say." When she turned to him, her eyes were that familiar, rich brown again. "Not until I swear *fealty* to him." She seemed to spit on the word. "I have until we return from Callisto to decide."

Adrien wasn't sure where his emotions wanted to settle, not sure where his mind even could. Helene had betrayed her like this? His father *knew* what she was?

That frightened him more than anything, and he was overcome with such a visceral need to hide her away. "What if you say no?"

"He'll either hunt me down or tell the entire world, I'm sure," she said and practically fell into a chair. In time, the darkness dripped from the barricaded exit. "He said I wouldn't be treated like *the others*. Do you know what that means?"

Adrien stiffened.

Lie.

It was his father's voice in his head. His tutors, instructors.

It's not for her ears.

It was his duty to uphold their pack's secrets, the wolves' secrets, and what had been going on with the witches in the prison had been a decade-long one, even if he'd only learned the truth months ago.

But... he couldn't bring himself to lie to her. Not now, not when she was like this. Inevitability seemed to linger here, Fate a taunt in his ear. She would find out. He should've been grateful that his father didn't tell her himself before Adrien could.

"Do you remember when I told you, or you asked, about witches who were caught trespassing in our territory within the mountains?" Raana straightened and nodded. "They weren't—they weren't executed as I'd said."

She tilted her head, shadows rolling off her shoulders with the movement. "Then where are they?"

He swallowed. "They're in our prison within the peaks. We call it the High Ground."

Raana blinked. Once. Twice. "Why would you lie to me about that?"

An honest question.

Adrien scrubbed at his jaw. "I wasn't allowed to tell you the truth. To tell anyone the truth." Though he'd told Isla, even Sebastian was in the dark.

Raana shook her head as if trying to dislodge something from it. "Why does it need to be secret, though? People only hide things when they feel guilty, when being caught comes with consequences. Our treaty—you can imprison them if you wish. Why must that be a secret? I would think you'd all rejoice at their capture. Or was not killing them too merciful?" They were biting, curious words.

Killing them might've been, Adrien thought with a sickening twist of his gut.

He hadn't truly known what went on in Valkeric—prison to the wolves' greatest felons, those who'd committed crimes so heinous that living as a rogue was too little of a punishment—but he'd heard the horror stories.

It was why he still thought of Lukas, a competitor from the Hunt a few months ago who'd been sent there after trying to kill his fellow wolf during the sacred trial. He'd tried to kill Isla, too, afterwards. Somehow, the Wilds had driven him to sheer insanity.

"My father doesn't want anyone to know that they're there because of their purpose—or what he hopes their purpose will become." A flicker of her eyes urged him to get to the point. "He wants to use them for our protection, on our inner and outer borders. Something he's not so sure other packs would be keen on."

Raana's fists flexed and clenched in her lap, shadows curling her wrists like manacles. "Protection against what? Our magic doesn't even work on wolves."

"I don't know." Her eyes scanned his face for deception. "Truly, I don't."

"You're his *Heir*."

Adrien fought to keep his voice from matching the malice of hers. "I know."

As the words settled, as the truth did, Raana's shoulders shook. She was looking down at her clasped hands as she muttered, "Entitled prick." Her stare was scalding when it met his again. "We were always told that you wolves, with your prosperous empire on your lonely continent, would destroy yourselves. That there was no need to fight you to bring it down. Don't drag our people into this. We're not weapons at your disposal for your petty wars."

"There is no war," Adrien snapped, harsher than he meant, feeling the words with a touch of fear. "*Your people* should've never been in those mountains in the first place. You don't even know what they were doing. What they were planning."

Raana didn't respond; she only glared at him.

Adrien dragged his eyes over her one last time before heading for the exit. "Don't leave this room."

"Where are you going?" she called, worry tinging her voice.

"To find out why my father wants you."

∼

Adrien sat silently in front of his father in the Imperial Alpha's office. He'd caught the Alpha in the hallway as he'd been ascending the stairs to the third floor along with a horde of guards, more than Adrien had ever seen him travel with within their own walls. He didn't need to contemplate their purpose.

No one was permitted into the atrium of the Imperial Pack Hall, comprised of frosted glass walls with gilded panes; the only one with a clear view of the Imperial City and open sky beyond it. An observatory of sorts, made more so by his father's brass telescope, perched by a latched opening in the glass. From where Adrien sat now, he could see the entirety of this place he'd called home—the Valkeric Mountains, a sliver of the Barit Sea. In a couple of hours, the sun would fall, and the moon would call up the city's famed lights, much like stars. He'd seen the same in Deimos, but their stars had been crystals embedded into the earth and their streets. Crystals that glowed at night as if they'd absorbed the Goddess's energy and reflected it into the world.

He remembered coming up here as a child, wondering at this floor, at this office, what would all come to be his. All this space... yet, it felt like a cage.

There was another map beneath the plating of his father's desk, and atop it were small figurines. Carved wooden flags on stands with the insignias of the other packs. Adrien traced his eyes over a long river cleaving the south of the continent down its center. Along it, in a line across their territories, were Tethys, Deimos, and Mimas. Io, along with Iapetus and Charon, was positioned west of Iapetus and Charon's borders.

Adrien asked as Cassius swept a hand over the glass, washing it all away, "What's this for?"

"Contemplation," his father said, sitting in his high-backed chair. Adrien had always wondered why he kept his back to the city. "Let's not waste each other's time, Adrien. I'll have to work on drilling the importance of confidentiality into her before we start."

Adrien fought to stop his body reacting, keeping his face impassive at his father's grating tone.

Start what would've been a logical follow-up question, but something else had gnawed at him. "Did you threaten Helene?"

His father laughed humorlessly. "No."

"So, why did she—"

"She chose her life over the girl's. People are simple. Greed is simple. Cowardice is simple." Cassius waved a hand, dismissing, "I thought you'd be happy you get to keep your little pet."

Adrien snarled, feeling his wolf snap to the surface. "Don't talk about her like that."

In response, his father's eyes flared crimson, the blood-red glow bearing down on him, pushing at him. An alpha requiring submission from his subordinate. "*Careful*," he seethed, though something like pride swept over his face. As Adrien's wolf retreated, Cassius's did as well. "You've hidden her from me for how long?"

Adrien's nostrils flared. He could lie—but he hadn't been much for that today, had he? "I found out a few months ago."

An indifferent nod. Adrien would've thought his father would be angrier about the deception. "Does anyone else know?"

"No. It's just me. I promised her that."

"Good. I'm sure you know what would happen to her if it got out." A silent threat rippled beneath that sentence. "I will tell you the same as I told her. Have your fun, get whatever you need out of your system, and don't get caught. No doubt your prospects will remain if the secret slips, but I'd rather not deal with the headache."

Raana hadn't mentioned this.

Adrien's blood heated, feeling like he'd just exposed a vulnerable edge to a predator. He wouldn't let it reflect on his face. He may have remembered too late that laying bare emotions was as good as lying down for a blade. "My prospects?"

"Alpha Baldor of Rhea—his daughter's a year past age with no mate in sight. I've had Winslow arrange for her to come here for the Winter Solstice. The chances of her being your fated are slim, but it should be a suitable blood match."

Adrien's gut twisted. "I don't want to think about finding a mate right now." *Especially not choosing one.* Before his father could elaborate further on whatever he was attempting to arrange, Adrien asked, "What are you planning to do with the witches? Are they truly for protection? When you release them, where will they go? How will you explain it to our people, to the realm?"

Cassius tapped his fingers against the glass. "So many questions."

Many that also hadn't been the one he intended.

"I'm just trying to understand you. I'm your Heir. If I'm meant to follow in your footsteps, I should be able to defend your decisions."

"Have I made a decision you cannot defend?"

Several.

But maybe one weighed the heaviest of them all.

"You approved a challenge of an alpha against a rogue wolf," Adrien began, low but firm. "Even with the rogue's claim—*months* after the atrocity—they have no right to rule over anything. If we can't prevent that from happening, what is the purpose of our keeping order between the packs? Deimos had already seen us in a poor light, as had the southern territories. This has only created more discontent."

"I know."

Adrien's brows lifted. He knew? "So, why approve it?"

His father fell silent, contemplative. Without breaking eye contact, his hand reached out, picking up one of the discarded figurines. He squeezed Deimos between his fingertips as he brought it up between both of their faces. "When Alpha Kyran and his heir passed, I thought the Goddess had done us a service."

"They didn't just pass," Adrien argued, not allowing his voice to rise. "They were *murdered*. Murdered in cold blood by a witch who should've never been able to breach our lands."

"An unfortunate tragedy."

"Our failed purpose."

Cassius's grip on the wooden figure tightened, ruby-red threatening his eyes as creases cut his face. "Alpha Kyran was building an army," he laid out in a plain, frank tone. "Planning an attack of some sort; I still don't entirely know what his plans were. But he was rallying pack members from Charon to join his ludicrous cause to rise against us." At Adrien's stunned silence, he continued, "For months, all those audiences with me were for the purpose of tracing our territory, our defenses. It's why I denied his last request. Why I started bargaining with the witches."

Adrien opened and closed his mouth, shaking his head. He knew their packs had their disagreements, but... "Attacking us would mean civil war. He couldn't have been that reckless."

"One would think," Cassius said, propping the piece back on the map, right over Mavec's eight-pointed star. "Our packs have a long history of strife that I don't have time to explain to you today. But as greed and cowardice are simple, so is pride and how it destroys and distracts. It has been my own shortcoming in the past, even regarding this. I thought I could handle it myself, but I must call upon something, *someone* greater."

"What are you talking about?"

His father leveled him with a glare. "Alpha Kai is a problem that needs to be addressed quickly, and *that's* why I need her."

CHAPTER 8

KAI

The moon lingered above the trees, low and sharp, a hooked blade refusing to dull even as morning approached. Sharp enough, Kai lamented, to carve him open if the power under his skin didn't do it first.

Dawn crept across the sky in strokes of oranges, reds, purples, and blues, the air kissed with a dewy mist that filled his lungs as he sprinted through the forest. He'd awoken just before daybreak, that twistedly intoxicating essence digging at his insides—a shout caught in his throat, his heart hammering, and the phantom warmth of blood on his hands.

But unlike most nights, it wasn't the gore of Brax coating him like a second skin, but that of the bounty hunter from the rogue lands. Kai may not have killed him by his own hand, but if the hunter hadn't ingested the poison...

The power pulsed through his veins in time with his heartbeat—too strong, too awake, as if the nightmare had torn something loose. It was a living thing pacing along his bones as it had that night.

If the hunter hadn't ended his life, Kai would have done it for him.

As horrible as it was, he was thankful for his and Isla's weakened bond, so she wouldn't be roused by the chaos he felt inside. She was still sleeping when he'd slipped from their bed. Still sleeping when the palace had stirred with the morning minutiae and he'd taken off running.

The forest had accepted him without ceremony, swallowing him as sunlight struggled through the branches. Pines rose on either side, their needles dark and wet, their trunks gleaming where early light struck them. The ground was slick beneath his bare feet, earth chilled, snapping twigs and needles sharp beneath each step.

He ran harder.

He needed this burn. The strain. Needed, then, to release the leash on his sense, just enough, to find some type of relief.

Everything he'd already observed erupted in stunning new clarity. The scent of the tacky sap over the bark, the morning calls of the birds rousing the branches, the pinpricking heat of the sun. His vision wavered at the edges, shadows stretching where they shouldn't. For a heartbeat, the fog along his ankles seemed to breathe.

The world pushed in.

This void within him embraced it.

Kai felt like nothing but a pawn in its game.

Stop.

He sucked in a sharp breath as something inside him went taut, the sensation hooking beneath his sternum and twisting through his spine. His power, his sense snagged on something... wrong.

Kai slowed to a stop, his bare chest heaving. The morning sounds, scents, and smells thinned.

Kai turned, the forest seeming to open around him, branches bowing aside as though wary. Of what, he wasn't sure, but something innate told him it had to do with the way darkness seemed to gather between the distant trunks, where the ground sloped downward into a deeper part of the woods.

Where he felt as if something... watched.

It pulled at him, at his wolf, at the void. Kai knew he should've resisted it.

Go see, Alpha of Deimos.

And yet, he followed.

CHAPTER 9

RAANA

They hadn't gone back to the estate before being loaded into the car meant to drive to Callisto, but Raana didn't care. She had nothing there. She had nothing anywhere. Whatever illusion she'd had of her life, of *a* life, had shattered the instant Cassius opened his mouth.

Or perhaps it had *been* shattered for years, but she'd been too foolish to notice.

She and Adrien hadn't spoken once since they'd left Io's borders. Whether he'd found out his father's intentions for her, she didn't know. And again, she couldn't bring herself to care.

The prince was either angry with her or keen on giving her space. Either way, she didn't protest. Silence, not having to speak, was welcomed. Every time she opened her mouth, even to take a breath, she felt like screaming or sobbing—and every time she berated herself to get her shit together, it only made her more volatile. It was a wonder she hadn't encased the entire vehicle in shadows as they drove, damning them all. Just as Helene had always predicted.

By the time they'd arrived at Callisto's Pack Hall, with watercolors of dusk falling to inky darkness, Raana couldn't even muster the energy to marvel at the building nestled into the lush, verdant landscape. The garden pathways and creeping vines over brick foundations.

She was an empty shell as they were greeted by staff clad in deep green uniforms and brought up and up and over to where they'd be lodging—

"We're in the same room?" Raana rasped, standing before the threshold of a guest suite as the Imperial Guards who'd come along made a sweep of the space. An assurance that there were no traps laid for the Highest Prince.

Adrien finished thanking and dismissing the staff member who'd directed them to this wing of the hall. "We are," was all he answered, his eyes doing their own pass of the terrain from where he stood in the alcove.

Raana pursed her lips. "You neglected to mention that."

"It didn't seem important."

"Really?" She'd said it with such disbelieving force, the most emotion she'd allowed herself to show in hours, that it made Adrien turn her way. She folded her arms, adding softly, "How will this look to others? You and I staying together?"

"I don't care."

Another flippant response. One that felt purposeful, to get underneath her skin.

The guards, one of them Sandrine—who couldn't seem to look at Raana without a distrustful sneer—concluded their search, deeming the room safe. They bowed to Adrien as they stepped out, and Raana—now in a more modest version of their custom uniform—received a shallow, frigid movement in farewell. Adrien's keenness towards her was undeniable now. After what had happened at the hall. She was sure that they had opinions. And she was equally sure they were not favorable.

The prince's new plaything.

With a low grumble at their forms, retreating to their bedrooms down the hall, Raana turned to her own—hers and *Adrien's.*

She was too tired to fight, so, without meeting Adrien's eyes, she stepped along the path he'd cleared for her into the suite.

It wasn't long until a bitter laugh tumbled from her mouth. "Oh, *of course.*"

Only one bed.

A grand one, thankfully, unlike the small mattress at the inn during that chilled, rainy night. Four mahogany posters were set in the middle of the rustic enclosure. It looked divine. Soft. Silk pillows and a gorgeously embroidered duvet that she was sure cost more than half the wares in the cottage. The estate had been just as luxurious, Io's hall boasting as much, if not more splendor. The *wealth* of these people. These places. These kingdoms.

Would she need to become used to it? Not embracing the abundance but observing it?

While she stood in her spot, Adrien closed the door. He walked to the modest living space in the corner of the room. Two oak-colored chairs and a couch set before a tall, arched window overlooking the distant forest. To its side lay a bookshelf, ridden more so with knick-knacks than actual reading material.

They'd be together all night... did she want their only conversation to be the one they'd had at the door?

"This story didn't end well for us before," she said, gesturing to the bed.

Adrien turned, following her movement. "*Too well,* you mean." He let the taunt linger before he sat, getting comfortable on the couch. Arms behind his head, ankle balancing on a knee. "I can sleep here."

"No." The answer was too quick, and an agitating smirk played on his lips. His brows raised at her apparent invitation. "I mean, *no*. You're the royalty here. I'm a 'guard.' If anything, *I* should be on the couch."

"You're a lady," he said. "You should be comfortable."

Raana snorted. "A *lady*?"

"You had me on the floor last time this happened," Adrien said.

"That was different," Raana argued. "We were in some small, obscure town. You weren't *the Imperial Heir*."

"I'm always *the Imperial Heir*." His tone was almost mocking. Tired.

Raana sighed. "It was different. Though it didn't stop much."

"It did not," Adrien conceded jovially. "Because you were *cold*, and I was too courteous. But it's summer now, so I won't believe you when you start pretending to shiver so I'll come warm the bed."

Raana scoffed. "As if I needed trickery to seduce you. You were at your wits' end, panting after me like a Spirits-damn dog by the time night fell."

Adrien's flattened brows showed he didn't much appreciate the comparison. He uncrossed his legs. "It was the height of the season."

"The *season*," Raana drawled. "Which translates to all you wolves becoming lecherous bastards because of *nature* and *instinct*."

"More or less," Adrien grumbled. "Though, don't play the innocent card. I remember well you begging me to fuck you."

Such a crude, easy sentence.

Raana's cheeks heated, her blood, too. The distance between them suddenly felt too great. Too much. Her grip on her forearms tightened. "I wasn't *begging*."

"Demanding," Adrien said, waving his hand. "Either way, it was insanely attractive."

"I was caught up in the moment."

"We've been caught up in many moments, lady."

Many moments—and they had led nowhere because they were wiser now. Because they knew better.

Raana sighed through her nose, then realized he'd successfully distracted her. For a fleeting moment, everything didn't seem so horrible. She'd almost forgotten. She wasn't sure why that made her feel stupid and... guilty.

"I'm going to get washed for bed. We have an early morning, right?"

The corner of Adrien's lips tilted downwards, and he only nodded as she turned to walk away.

~

The mattress was far too big. Far too chilly. The ceiling was so far away, its surface smooth. No cracks for Raana to count as she stared, only a chandelier with jewels like emerald raindrops, which she didn't bother lingering on.

She twisted her head, her loosely tied curls a whisper against the silken pillow, and glanced across the patchwork of darkness to where Adrien slept, *actually* slept. His chest rose and fell steadily, the faintest snores escaping his parted lips. He was directly beneath a stream of moonlight, the Goddess's fingers seeming to trace every contour of his body, every honed, lethal, deity-blessed muscle lovingly.

He'd taken the couch. Wouldn't hear any more argument for it. He'd offered for her to join him on the sofa if she was adamant about *sleeping with him,* but mentioned it would be a waste of such a beautiful bed. Smartass.

Raana had learned, while he readied for sleep, that this hadn't been the original plan. According to the guards she'd heard chattering outside while they waited for a final order from Adrien, Raana was supposed to be staying in her own suite across the hall. And they did, in fact, now believe her to be his harlot. Why else would he change the plan? Why else keep her so close?

Why else—but to keep an eye on her. She, who'd been on a spiral for what felt like endless hours. Her, whose life would never be the same again. She, who had taken these four walls and him and pretended, tonight, that they were a fortress. That this room, their banter, and this too-big, too-cold bed were all that existed.

She wouldn't ask him whether he'd learned the truth of his father's intentions for her. Wouldn't let herself think about the witches in their prison that he hadn't been entirely truthful about. Even if she had "no right" to know in the mess of politics and nonsense.

She'd worry about them once they returned to Io. Would see if there was something she could do to help them—somehow.

Somehow...

Cassius had said he wouldn't "imprison her like the others," but "precautions" would be taken. *Precautions.* She may as well have been his prisoner at that point.

Raana rolled onto her side; her tongue clamped so hard between her teeth that she drew blood. Her splintered heart fractured further, that hollow wound festering.

She was alone. She had no one.

But she couldn't cry anymore. Couldn't let this break her. Couldn't give Cassius, Helene, or any of them the satisfaction.

Her fingers wrapped around her conduit, still around her neck but resting on the soft, white sheets. It burned within her touch as she muttered not an incantation but a prayer. Not to the Mother or Spirits, but to whoever the hell would listen. Asking for answers, begging for a way out before the darkness of sleep claimed her.

~

Raana's eyes flew open, her body rigid, and her bed sheets soaked with sweat.

No, not sweat.

Not sheets, either.

Raana's fingers drew over the frigid, wet stones beneath her touch. Wildly familiar but wrong—so wrong. The air felt hollow as she slowly rose, her eyes drawing over dank cavern walls embedded with translucent crystals. Familiar. And wrong.

"Isla."

Raana was on her feet, faster than consciously possible, and she turned towards the voice. Kai's voice. "Isla."

Her steps were rapid and hollow to her ears, her pulse hammering against her skull as she scaled the rock. Running, running, running until—

She was already there. Kneeling before a woman's limp, broken body, her sallow skin covered in blood.

"Isla."

She looked up for Kai—but he wasn't there. Only a shadow, a figment of darkness amongst the swirling, ebony backdrop of this void. And Isla—

Light. That was all she'd become. Warm and rich and... fading. Those auras Raana had detected, how she'd help reunite the king and the lost queen, she'd traced through the world with her magic. Those pieces were there now. Light in dark, dark in light. Where they belonged to each other.

Something grabbed her. Something foreign from beyond the darkness. An icy grip that bit into her shoulder, that her shadows tried to fight away.

It had been there that night, too, something she hadn't confessed. She wondered if either one of them could sense the threat, the danger that loomed. The thing that watched like a cat from the depths of the cavern.

"Raana."

Binds tore through the void, wrapping around her, strangling her. Strangling Kai, Isla, who'd been reunited again, just as she'd seen them when Isla had awoken. But then they were ripped right from each other's arms. All of them torn and pulled into oblivion.

"Raana!"

Light flared, and the world swirled to nothing but ash and blood, rot and rubble.

"Raana!"

She screamed.

With her chest heaving, body leaden yet trembling, Raana's eyes cracked open. The room spun, tilted, and whorled before her.

And—Adrien.

Adrien was there, right before her face. His hands were warm on her shoulders, then brushing over her cheeks as he tore his gaze over her. "What happened?"

Panic flared in his eyes, dimming gold flames, and was equally present in his voice. And she could... sense him. An aura of power rippled through the world around them.

"What?" Her mind was swimming, and Spirits, her mouth was dry. An attempt to sit up had only been a thought before she gave up on it.

"Your nose is bleeding." Adrien brushed his thumb over her upper lip, collecting the warmth that Raana now realized lingered there. He narrowly avoided her tongue as she darted to it, the taste of iron flooding her mouth.

What the hell?

She was still lying in bed and, with the slightest turn of her head, noticed some of it had dripped down onto the powder sheets, which were also soaked with sweat.

"A nightmare," she breathed, the words grating her parched throat. She wasn't sure if relief was the proper emotion. All of it had felt so real. She still sensed the darkness at her throat and wondered, despite herself, if Isla and Kai, in their distant palace, were okay.

She scanned the room, seeking any shifts of the furniture, searching for that unending cold. The chandelier above swayed, its little jewels tinkling and twinkling in the moonlight.

"Why can I scent you?" At Adrien's gentle but warning question, she snapped her eyes back to him. Concern knitted his brows. "The enchantment's gone."

Raana's eyes blinked impossibly wide.

Gone?

That concealment spell should've kept her hidden as long as she hadn't performed any magic. Wielding shadows, her immortal power, was a fortunate exception. So, when had she—

Raana jolted, bringing a hand to her mouth. She suddenly found the strength to sit up. "I'm going to vomit."

It was with a shifter's quickness that Adrien retrieved a bucket from the washroom. Quickness Raana had to be grateful for as she retched the moment the little pail was placed in her lap. The bile stung, and the hollowness of her stomach made it fairly apparent that she'd barely eaten yesterday.

A soft tug at her head signaled Adrien gathering her fallen curls in a hand. He wrapped them again in her tie before his touch pressed against her back. He ran his hand soothingly up and down her spine. Not too firm but enough to let her know he was there. In a lull, he asked, "Does this always happen after nightmares?"

Raana spat and groaned, resting her forehead against the bucket's edge. "Not this part."

She couldn't think of any time the nightmares had made her ill like this.

It felt like her body had been run over by a carriage, several carriages pulled by several mammoth-sized, ornery horses.

There was a brutal beat at the back of her skull in time with the heavy drum of her heart. Weak. She felt so *weak*.

Perhaps that was why the spell had worn away. Such a vehement reaction to the horror in her mind had drained her. It couldn't do. *No one* could scent her. Hopefully, she had enough energy in her to execute one last spell.

"I need blood," she choked out before blindly reaching out a hand to Adrien. "My blood. Freshly drawn."

Out of the corner of her eye, she saw him hesitate. He clearly understood but still asked, "Your nose?"

"Doesn't count," she exhaled, opening and closing her fist. "It's okay. I'll forgive you."

Adrien sighed, and Raana could hear and feel more than see when he shifted, drawing one of his claws. A shudder ran down her spine as the cool black tip pressed to the fragile skin of her palm. One slight caress, and blood pooled. Adrien dragged only an inch, soft as a lover but still lethal, before pulling away.

It was enough to work with.

Raana grunted her thanks as she used the crimson to draw the rune over her skin, murmuring words in the First language. Magic seared as she closed her fingers over her palm, and upon opening her fist, she watched the rune seep back into her skin. Her small wound healed. A witch hidden once more, and hopefully—

Raana checked for her ring, still perched on her finger, and then lifted her hand to her ears. Still round. Thankfully, the exhaustion hadn't tampered too much with *that* enchantment.

"Shit," she cursed as the use of that final dreg of power caught up to her.

She heaved again, and this time, Adrien didn't linger after she'd finished.

Head still hung over the basin, Raana heard the sounds of running water and the shuffling of fabric. The prince had left the room for Spirits knew how long. At least, by the time he'd returned, she'd stopped puking, and the room had, mercifully, stopped dancing.

"Here."

Raana lifted her head to find Adrien had extended a glass of water. A wet washcloth, some wafers, and a new shirt and pants were also cradled in his muscled arms. Her own nursemaid.

An unbelievably attractive, half-nude nursemaid.

Raana allowed herself the gratuitous once-over of his body. The cut of it. The way his pants slung low on his hips, revealing the devious lines that cut down his stomach and disappeared beneath the waistband.

The corner of her lips rose, and she battled away the heat rising to her face.

She reached for the water, offering a *thank you,* along with, "Fussy."

Adrien only hummed, a smirk playing on his mouth as he settled back down beside her. Had he caught her staring?

A few moments passed, and the only sounds were her swishing and spitting, before Adrien lifted the cloth. He didn't ask or offer; he just began cleaning the dried blood from beneath her nose himself. She'd forgotten it had even been there.

"I won't lie—you look pretty badass." He chuckled.

Raana snorted, trying to ignore the way her heart fluttered at the care, the attention. "Bloodied from battles with my own dreams."

Adrien pursed his lips, bringing the reddened towel down from her face. "Do you want to talk about it?"

Raana swallowed the next mouthful of water, then reached for one of the wafers, too, if only to give herself more time to think of an answer. But that contemplation only went so far. "No."

Not her truth to share, and she didn't have the energy for the full explanation.

She cleared her throat. "What happened with me?"

Adrien knew what she meant. He shrugged. "It was all pretty fast. I felt the cold first, then something like wind, and when I woke up and looked over, I couldn't see you."

"The shadows," Raana breathed, lowering her head. "They've been doing that a lot lately when I'm sleeping, especially if I have a nightmare. They try to protect me, but—they can become too much."

"Well, they let me through to you."

She lifted her head. "They did?"

With a nod, Adrien reached a hand over her shoulder, past it to the darkness that had loomed there, a specter over her body. Raana watched with surprise as it unfurled and caressed his skin, dancing along it. Adrien smiled, almost smugly. "I think they like me."

"I don't think they can *like* anything," she argued, though she wasn't truly sure, given how they acted.

"Well, they obey you," he met her eyes, "so, *you* must like me."

Now, warmth flooded Raana's cheeks. For what, she wasn't sure. It was an innocent statement, a simple flirt and tease from someone who'd already been beyond, who'd seen the most intimate pieces of her. At least, physically.

She lowered her lashes and bit into another wafer, the food helping to rebuild her strength. With an extension of her fingers, the tendril of shadow coiled and tightened around Adrien's wrist. "For now."

A wider grin and devilish glint took to the prince's eyes as he examined where the darkness held him, bound him. He tried to pull, flexing and clenching his fist as it kept him firmly where he was. "Interesting."

A dark, dangerous word said with a glance her way. A glance that held reminders of times past and had the heat Raana felt drifting elsewhere...

In the throes of that night months ago, the shadows were present as they always were—but she'd never thought of... involving them.

The image she'd conjured then brought a proper deep flush of red to her cheeks. It wasn't helped by the fact that Adrien, in all his half-bare glory, only sat a foot away from her on this too-big, too-cold bed.

He wouldn't speak the words, but the look in his eyes conveyed his thoughts, his... potential offer.

"You know," he began teasingly, still tugging at that bind. "If you wanted me in bed with you, you could've just asked—no need for the magical tantrum."

Raana scowled, and with another flick of her fingers, the shadow around his wrist became a force pressing against him. A weak attempt to push him off the bed that barely had him faltering as he grinned. "Fuck off."

Raana wasn't sure how many hours had passed between when she'd shot awake from her nightmare, gathered herself to wash up for bed and change again, and emerged back into the room, not feeling entirely of death, but thankfully, darkness still prevailed outside.

Maybe she could catch at least a few hours of sleep.

Upon entering the bedroom, she found Adrien had returned to his couch, paging through one of the volumes from the bookshelf. He looked up and surveyed her oversized nightclothes, borrowed from him. "I'm a bit disappointed you didn't bring your nightgown."

She flashed him a deadpan look. "This arrangement is hard enough without me in anything scandalous."

She settled back on the bed as Adrien set the book aside. "I'm not really tired anymore."

Rather than lying down, Raana scooted closer to the edge of the mattress, tucked her legs beneath her, and faced him. "I'm tired, but I don't know if I'll be able to sleep."

The beige rug on the floor may as well have been the ocean that had separated them for the years before Helene had forced Raana to leave Cataea. All for her safety, all to keep her hidden, but—Raana missed her old life. Her coven.

Helene could have that life again now, couldn't she? Now that she was rid of her burden.

"Raana."

Her name said gently carried from the other side of the room. Raana lifted her head, and Adrien asked, "Where'd you go?"

She narrowed her eyes. "You're very nosy."

Adrien shrugged and leaned back in his seat. He spread his arms over the back of the couch as he lounged, and Raana had to push back the thoughts of how inviting he looked, that spot in his lap perfectly open for her.

"We're both just sitting here. I mean, I have no problem looking at you all night, but talking could be nice, too."

"Everything we *should* be talking about, I don't want to talk about," she said. "Otherwise, I'll remember that I should be mad at you for lying to me... even if you couldn't tell me the truth."

A frown passed Adrien's face, albeit briefly. He tilted his head to the side, considering. "We don't have to *talk,* then."

"Really?"

"Your mind's pretty deep in the gutter, Scornn."

"Your words aren't very subtle, Your Highness." Leaning back on her hands, she cast her eyes to the side. "Sleeping with you shouldn't be the way I avoid my problems. My feelings."

"Sleeping with you shouldn't be how I want to avoid mine."

Raana snapped her eyes back to him, her blood heating despite herself as she hung on to that one word. *Want.*

She ignored the intensity of his predator's gaze surveying her. It invigorated her, though. Dug deep, stripped her down in a way she didn't quite mind.

"So difficult being a prince," she teased. "Your biggest issue is what now? Finding your soulmate?"

For a moment, she regretted the words that had come out, fearing she'd opened a fresh wound of his—or a new wound of her own.

Ridiculous.

She knew this. He was not hers and could never be hers.

Before Adrien could comment or counter, as if to make herself feel better, to appear that she didn't care, Raana said, "You know, I probably could—find her, I mean. Or figure out what she's like."

Several emotions passed over Adrien's face then, each one pelting her harder. Shock, once he realized she wasn't joking, then doubt, fear, and then, what made her stomach sink most—the smallest glimmer of hope.

He'd banished that fast, though. He'd banished it all for aloofness. "And how is that?"

Part of her wished she hadn't answered. Wished she hadn't spoken at all.

"I'm adept when it comes to reading auras. Of power, of people. The way your bonds work—with mates being a part of each other—I might be able to find her in you."

His brows furrowed. "Like Isla and Kai?"

"Exactly." Raana adjusted herself. "It may have been easier to detect because they'd bonded, but I could separate them. Isla as warmth and light, and Kai as... cold. But not a bad cold. A refreshing cold. The soothing kind."

"So different," Adrien noted.

Raana's shoulders rose and fell. "And yet, perfect for each other, it seems."

She hadn't missed the smallest downturn of his mouth before he righted it. "So it seems."

Choosing not to dawdle on it, she continued, a bitterness settling in her chest. "Technically, you're holding a piece of the woman you're fated for, even if it hasn't been 'awakened' yet. If I could find it, feel it, within you, within your aura, I could tell you what she's like."

Silence fell between them, and Adrien glanced out the window behind him. To the moon, the stars, and the forest beyond. A part of Raana hoped, desperately, he'd decline the offer.

He turned back to her. "Is this magic?"

"At a point, it would become so. It's a natural gift I have. I don't need my conduit or any incantation unless I'm trying to track someone across space. As long as you yield to me and drop all your defenses, I shouldn't have to dig into my magic... or we could keep staring at each other?"

"Tempting." Adrien grinned before sliding over on the couch. "I'm at your mercy."

Raana did her best to hide her disappointment and didn't bother commenting on what dangerous words those were. She could've sworn wariness colored Adrien's face as she rose from the mattress and crossed the great breadth of ocean to him.

Did he not trust her—or did he truly not want to know?

Raana placed herself on the plush surface beside him, right where her knee bumped up against his. One of the hands Adrien had placed on the back of the couch fell to her side atop the cushions, his fingertips brushing over her thigh, electrifying her skin. Raana didn't flinch away, didn't ask why. Just accepted what felt like a current between them.

She surveyed him for the umpteenth time that night. His handsome face, those tattoos, his body. His hair was disheveled as if he'd been running his own stressed fingers through it, and she remembered when it had been her hands tugging at those raven-black tresses. When she couldn't get or feel enough of him. A man that was everything she shouldn't want, shouldn't have, *couldn't* have.

And now, she was about to find out exactly *why* all of that was true.

Outstretching a hand, willing her heart to settle, Raana laid it upon his bare chest.

"Yield," she reminded him as a force of *her*, not her power, collided with what felt like a stone wall.

Then, as easily as an inhale and exhale of breath, his barriers tumbled.

The rush of it was overwhelming, almost euphoric, and Raana's eyes slid closed.

It was like observing a spider's web, a finely woven blanket. She envisioned and felt and tasted. Color, light, life. Different cords, different experiences, all bearing the same essence. *His* essence. A crackling fire. A summer storm. She needed to find what varied.

Adrien couldn't have been more different from Kai. Where Raana had found some unknown, deeper common ground in Kai's aura, his power, Adrien's essence seemed to clash. It pushed where Kai had found a way to pull. And where Raana had felt the Alpha of Deimos whole, despite what had been occurring with his mate, Adrien had been fragmented. The most obscure pieces of him were torn away, lost forever.

Taken by the first woman he'd ever loved. The woman he'd offered his soul to.

She felt Adrien's fingers brush against her leg again. Her heart stopped entirely when she opened her eyes to meet his, the gold beneath simmering.

This was... intimate, more than anything else that had occurred between them. Sleeping together the first time had been a feverish rush to rip off clothes and satisfy a deep ache for something primal. They'd given themselves to each other, but not entirely. Not the way he opened to her now.

And for a moment, she may have understood, may have felt why the mate bond of wolves was as wondrous as claimed. To have a connection like this, to be a part of someone in this way, to have them with you, woven through you *always*.

She wanted to stay.

She wanted to push herself forward, to twine herself, her power, her magic with him and his.

But—

Not hers.

And then, as if in answer, she felt it.

A chasm unlocked. Something new, something fresh and bright.

"Spring."

The word tumbled from her mouth.

Adrien blinked, his eyes beginning to dim. "What?"

Raana backed away. Her cheeks were searingly hot as she stared at him. "Your destined mate. She feels like spring. She's soft like meadows. Like fresh blooms and gentle rains."

Adrien swallowed thickly, scanning her face as he took in that fact and seemed to tuck it away. Raana didn't know how long they remained like that, gazing at each other, before she pulled her hand away.

Silence held for beats and beats of Raana's heart, and she looked down at her hands as if she could still feel him there.

"You remind me of winter."

Raana snapped her head up, meeting Adrien's stare. *Winter?* "Biting and frigid?"

"Stunning." The word rolled off his tongue easily and bounded through her. "Until the ice beneath you melts away, and then you're drowning." His hand had been traveling up her side, over her waist. She didn't flinch at all as he brought his touch up to her cheek, brushing a curl away and tucking it behind her ear. His fingers were gentle over the edge of it. "You're dangerous. Forbidden—and inevitable."

Raana hung onto the last word. "You're the one who keeps calling upon me."

"I know." Adrien's eyes scanned her face. Dropped to her lips. Back to her eyes. "I can't seem to stop, no matter how many people tell me to."

Raana's breath caught, and she suddenly didn't know what to do with herself. Her hands, her body. She said, "You should listen to them."

Adrien gave a slight shrug. "Probably."

She cleared her throat. "Are you going to?"

"Probably not."

A sharp breath slipped from her mouth, and she found her fingers moving lazily over the skin of his arm. She was quiet while she thought, refusing to meet his eyes while she tried to remind herself of the reality. But reality didn't exist. Not in this room. Not now.

"You know, you're just something else I'm going to lose," she told him. "You're not meant for me; you never have been. So, no matter what I feel. No matter if it's lust, no matter if I *like* you. It means nothing. It goes nowhere because this story doesn't end with us. It can't."

"Raana." Raana looked up and felt like she'd melt under his gaze. "Right now, there's only you. It's only been you since we met, even before I *liked* you. Even when we're a mountain apart. You never leave my mind. And I'm a selfish, stupid prick to make you go through what I've already endured. Wanting someone who wasn't mine, not truly—but I can't stop wanting you. I can't stop wanting us to figure this out."

Raana gnawed on her lip. "Our paths are set."

"We could die tomorrow, for all we know. Our paths could *end*," Adrien said. "And instead of the two of us in that bed right now, we're here, on this couch, pretending we're not thinking the same thing."

So much for being wise.

A barely there grin passed her lips. "You know *exactly* what I'm thinking?"

Adrien smirked and gripped her hips to pull her into his lap. Raana felt like her heart would beat straight out of her chest as he looked up at her. "Am I close?"

"It was more so about you on top of me, but this will do," she said, wrapping her arms around his neck. "Kiss me."

A fire seemed to light in his eyes before he leaned a bit closer. His whisper tickled her skin. "I won't be able to stop."

"Then don't."

CHAPTER 10

RAANA

The world became Adrien's mouth, hands, and body against hers. Nothing else mattered from today, this week, this month, or from any other part of her life. Not as his lips moved against hers.

At first, the kiss was gentle. A soft brush that set her body alight. It deepened from one breath to the next—yet remained unhurried.

"Fuck, I missed you."

Adrien's words were guttural against her lips, and they unchained something in her. Something primal, something buried. A hunger, a want, a need.

Months—it had been months since anyone had touched her like this. The last had been him. All she wanted was him. In her thoughts, in those dreams.

Raana clawed herself closer, her touch running over Adrien's shoulders, his chest, feeling the ridges of that intricate tattoo etched into his skin.

One of his hands swept into her hair, wedging into her curls, loosening them from their tie, and angling her head to take more of her. His other hand had slid beneath the hem of her shirt, his fingers tracing over the smooth skin of her stomach, trailing a blazing line up, up, up—so close to skimming the underside of her breast. Raana bowed into his touch, into him, her breath becoming heavier.

More.

A demand of her blood.

Raana nipped at his lip, traced her tongue along its softness, and moaned at the taste of him when he opened for her, his tongue meeting hers.

The kiss became ravenous as if they needed each other to breathe. To survive. Adrien echoed her small sound with his own groan as he flexed his hips and dragged her closer, grinding her against him in time with his hand cupping her breast, teasing her hardened nipple.

Spirits, save her.

Or don't save her; leave her here. With this. With him.

His hardness pressed into her, rocking exquisitely against where she wanted him most.

Her body went taut. Her clothes and her skin became too much. The last time they'd been together flashed through her mind in delirious waves—his first thrust into her body, the ecstasy, the euphoria as he stretched her, filled her. The sounds of his pleasure mixed with her own until she could barely remember her own name, wiped away with each pounding stroke.

She ached for that now. For there to be no space. No world but the one in this room. To watch, to feel him come undone, again and again.

More.

For one beat of her warring, thundering heart, Raana leaned back from him, roughly breaking their kiss to grab the hem of her shirt and pull it over her head. She tossed it back into oblivion before her hands came to rest on the waistband of his pants, dropping further to palm along the hard, considerable length of him. Her mouth dried out. Adrien cursed, bucking into her touch. And though the night air was a cool caress against her skin, as were the shadows that she realized now ebbed around them, with the way Adrien stared at her then, taking in her half-bare body with darkened eyes...

Her blood became a scorching river.

"Gorgeous," he murmured as he dragged his stare up to her face, the corner of his lips lifting. Everywhere he touched her held a current. Her hips, her waist, her breasts. "But I thought I told you, when I finally had you again, I'd take my time."

Raana bit down on her tongue, whimpering as he pinched her nipple before soothing the hurt with a caress of his thumb. "And I thought I told you I'm not very patient." She wrapped her arms around his neck and tugged herself closer until there was no space left but between their mouths. Her lips barely brushed his as she whispered, "Fuck me now. Take your time later."

Adrien chuckled, his hands sliding down her body to grab her backside. "Here you are, demanding again." He guided her forward and back, and Raana moaned, tipping her head as pleasure struck through her like lightning. Her nails dug into his back as he did it again. Again. Slow and controlled, her body shuddered as she pressed into the movement, embracing the delicious friction as Adrien met her, building a rhythm that had her dizzy. A tight knot coiled in her lower belly.

His voice was gritty with restraint as he teased, "I don't remember it being this easy to get you off. How long has it been?"

"Too long," Raana breathed, the ache to have him inside her becoming unbearable. She lifted her head again, meeting his eyes. "I need you."

Adrien's nostrils flared as if he could scent her arousal, how wet she was for him.

Then he growled, a guttural, animalistic sound that burrowed deep before he met her mouth in a hard kiss.

Raana's legs tightened around him as he tucked his hands beneath her thighs and lifted her from the couch. The shadows trailed them on their walk to the bed, bowing over her skin to his, as greedy for him as she was. As if they, too, craved his strength. His stability, his power.

Adrien dropped her onto the mattress, and seconds felt like an eternity before he covered her body with his again. His fingers twined with hers, pinning her arms to the bed as his fervent kisses traveled from her lips to her jaw, to her neck.

"Adrien," she moaned his name, squeezing him between her thighs and lifting her hips, trying to find that friction again as he began to lick and nip at her skin. He ground against her just as he dragged his tongue over a spot near her collarbone... and scraped his teeth along it.

"*Adrien*," Raana gasped again, arching into him. The sensation traveled straight down to her core. So... sensitive. He may as well have had his head buried between her legs, then, as he nipped, licked, and sucked along that space, sending her straight to the edge of ecstasy. Maddening and perfect. She couldn't remember her body ever responding like this.

Adrien tensed, his lips, his bite hovering over that spot. His breathing was ragged, his grip on her hands constricting. For a moment, she swore he shook his head.

"*Raana*." Her name had been spoken softly, desperately.

And then Adrien moved up to kiss her again, and there was something about it that was tentative. Afraid.

And the way he looked at her when he pulled back as if he was seeing something—her, something in her—for the first time...

His eyes shuttered. "I—I have to tell you something."

Raana blinked, the seriousness of his tone stunning her, taking the edge off her want. Still, she asked, "Can it... wait?"

"No." Adrien swallowed, adjusting himself to rest on his elbow, taking some of his weight off her. "It can't. I can't do this without telling you the truth."

Raana loosened her legs' hold on him, a pit forming in her stomach. "About?"

Adrien stared blankly at her body, avoiding her eyes as he went deep in thought, seeming to pick over his words. His stare had hardened when it finally met hers again. "I know why my father wants you. He told me today."

Raana stiffened, her heart ratcheting up and breath hampering for a whole new reason. "And are you—are you *allowed* to tell me?"

Another bob of his throat. "He didn't tell me no."

Somehow, having him on her, having him this close, felt like too much. "So, what is it, then?"

More hesitation. A slow, deep inhale.

"He needs you to kill the Alpha of Deimos."

CHAPTER 11

ADRIEN

Looking down at Raana, flushed and half-nude beside him, for a moment, Adrien felt like an idiot—and an asshole.

His own body was still wound up tight, the scent of her arousal still staining his senses. He wanted her. Goddess, he wanted her. So damn much he'd nearly marked her moments ago. It had been a tremendous effort of discipline not to give in to her demands on the couch. To not tear off what remained for them both, plunge his cock inside her, and let her ride him until they were both screaming. Forget who could hear them.

But he couldn't do that; he couldn't allow her to give herself to him without telling her the truth. She'd dealt with enough today, and he knew her well enough to know if he'd taken her body *and then* disclosed this—something that felt so world-tilting—it would feel like another betrayal.

For a long while, she didn't speak. Only lay there. Only stared at him as though she was in some trance. Her body was so still, he thought she'd bleed into the pooling shadows around her and disappear forever. The darkness gently rolled over her skin as if soothing her, shielding her again.

Adrien took the moment her quiet shock offered to roll off the bed and locate the shirt she'd thrown.

He only made it a step.

"He…" Raana began, just above a whisper. "He wants me to *what*?"

Adrien breathed slowly, taking the few more movements to retrieve her clothes as time to gather himself. He needed to keep his emotions in check, if only not to feed into hers. "Kill—" Goddess, he could hardly say it. "Kill Kai."

If Isla were here, she would've already been on him with her claws at his throat. She would be storming Io's Pack Hall, trying to rip apart his father. And Adrien, frankly, wouldn't fault her.

Raana blinked. Once. Twice. Her hands had barely moved from where he'd once pinned them. "I can't tell if you're serious right now."

Adrien gritted his teeth and handed her the shirt. "Why would I joke about something like this?"

"Because it sounds *insane*." She'd blissfully softened her voice just as it began to rise, and though she'd taken the garment from him, she didn't put it on. Slowly, she sat up, her eyes fixed on the window and its distant forest view. She folded her knees to her chest, seeming to test out the words, "He wants me to kill Kai."

Adrien didn't move. "Yes."

Her look of fear and panic broke something in him. "Adrien."

A desperate plea for him to be lying, for it all to be a joke.

Adrien lowered to the bed to sit beside her. "I know."

"*Adrien*."

"*I know*." Firm, reassuring words. This was something they both had to weather.

Raana looked away from him, back to the forest, bathed in the moonlight. "I don't know where to start—*why* or how he thinks that would even be possible?"

He'd had the same two questions when he was up in his father's office.

He'd *also* thought his father was playing a twisted joke.

Adrien dragged a hand through his hair. He hoped there were enough walls and barriers to evade eavesdropping ears, keen even if they spoke quietly. "Which do you want first?"

Raana wouldn't look at him. "The why."

"He said he's a problem. A—threat."

"A threat?" Her brows raised, her gaze going distant as if picturing Kai standing before them. "To whom?"

Adrien's shoulders rose and fell. "To everyone."

Her forehead pinched. "How?"

"He doesn't know."

"I'm sorry." She whipped her head around to look at him. "He doesn't *know*. But he needs me to—to *kill him*," the words seemed to grate her throat, "because of it?"

Every beat—precisely as it had been between him and his father.

And it still made as little sense.

Adrien just felt... wrong. Dirty. Unfamiliar in his own skin. Simply entertaining the words felt like a betrayal. To Isla, to the camaraderie he'd experienced with Kai, and the mutual respect and understanding between them. A slight to his own honor as a wolf.

"Being Alpha is a thankless job," his father had told him as Adrien sat there, stunned and furious. *"It requires sacrifice and choices that not everyone will come to understand or appreciate. That's why we are the ones chosen to shoulder the burden. Separate your personal feelings from the job that must be done."*

The ease with which his father had spoken still chilled him—held a weight, like he'd made those decisions, those sacrifices many times before. Some, Adrien suspected, he would never become privy to.

But *this*?

The walls of the suite closed in, his wolf feeling caged in this prison he couldn't escape.

He slid a hand over the mattress, stretching to caress Raana's thigh, but something sharp and cold coiled around his wrist, halting him. The shadows weren't permitting him through to her this time. A glance at her grimacing face told him she'd been responsible for it.

"What else?" she said through gritted teeth, her body trembling. "There has to be more than that."

There was—a lot more. And though Raana would struggle to understand all he meant, Adrien would rehash it with a small hope that maybe he, himself, could fathom his father's reasoning.

He drew back his hand, but not far. He let it linger close enough that she could reach for it if need be.

"My father said that on the day of the Hunt, our warrior rite, when we were all standing at the Gate, he felt our ancestors calling to him, telling him to pay attention." *Absurd* had been Adrien's initial thought at that until he remembered his own training. An alpha's otherworldly sense, gifted by the Goddess. "Kai was there to compete, and when the call came for him and the other Hunters to shift, my father said he felt... something."

"Something?"

"Power," Adrien said. "Unchecked, raw power. Like an ember of a flame." Raana's lips twitched downwards, her spine locking straight. "What?"

She glanced at him, then looked away, her throat bobbing. "Nothing. I thought you all were powerful. Especially alphas. I mean, your eyes remind me of flames."

There was a kick of her heartbeat, a distance to her voice. Both made Adrien narrow his eyes. She hadn't shared the entirety of what was on her mind, and she had a point, but—

"I guess it must've been different. I hadn't sensed anything when I watched them, but my father's an alpha, the *Alpha*, so his senses are sharper than anyone else's. He said he felt it again when we were in Deimos. When Kai killed that rogue during the challenge."

"But the rogue killed himself," Raana said softly. "He clawed himself to death. I watched it."

At those words, the gruesome display reeled through Adrien's mind again. The blood and gore splattered over the arena stones, the screams of horror from those who could and couldn't bring themselves to look away. And Kai...

A wolf who'd fought for his life. Who'd fought to defend his home, his family, and most of all, his mate.

Adrien would be lying if he said the image of Kai's wolf standing there, covered in carnage, with a stare promising instant death to the next person he crossed paths with hadn't caused his own to bristle—not in fear, but in preparation to fight back.

Adrien dragged his hands over his face with a soft groan. "That's what I told him, but he thinks Kai *made* him do it."

Another contortion of Raana's features. "How? Wolves aren't able to coerce."

"An alpha can demand, but even that's just a *strong* suggestion you'd be foolish to disobey." Which sure said a lot about him. "I believe there would be a line when an alpha commands you to claw yourself to death, but my father can't think of any other explanation. He's certain in what he felt and saw. So, that's why he wants you."

Adrien could sense her heart pounding and could hear it, too. Raana wedged her hands into her curls, resting her elbows on her knees and shaking her head. "I don't get it. What can I do? I'm not some trained assassin. I barely have offensive magic."

"I know."

"Then how, in the Mother's name, does he expect me to kill a wolf, let alone an alpha?"

Adrien steeled himself.

It was time for the most absurd part of it all. He pulled his hand away completely, resting it in his lap as he followed her gaze to the moon and forest beyond the window. "Have you ever heard of the dark moon?"

"No."

"Neither had I," he said. "But it's happening sometime soon, and you may be the only person in this entire realm not affected by it." He paused, allowing the information to settle. Though Raana looked at him, he didn't look back. "It's once every five centuries. Apparently, the world shifts, and the moon just... disappears, which is how it gets its name. It seems like an eclipse, but what happens is... not good. And no one realizes until it's too late."

He went quiet again, but Raana pushed, "*What* happens?"

Adrien sighed. "The entire mortal realm tips into chaos. We'll lose our ability to shift. Sirens lose control of the tides. Your mortal magic turns against you. Crawlers become ridden with bloodlust, even turn against each other, and even humans are left to equal madness."

Now, Raana was quiet, staring at him blankly. As if in response to the looming threat, darkness curled over her shoulders. "And how long does that last?"

Adrien shrugged. "An hour, two, as long as it takes for it to pass. My father only knows of it from scrolls he dug up from the catacombs beneath the hall. All anecdotes from five hundred years ago."

"Why have I never heard of it?"

He'd asked the same.

"Trying to get a person to remember the issues of last week is hard enough; forget a centuries-old phenomenon. Frankly, I don't even know if it's real. It could just be some stories from bored ancestors."

"Pretty brutal stories for boredom."

"It was a different time then," Adrien said, not bothering to add that it was around when they'd had an entire pack destroyed by dark magic, too.

In his periphery, Adrien caught Raana dipping her head. "So, where do I fit into this?"

"You're immortal. Or at least half-immortal, so in theory, your power with the shadows shouldn't be affected."

Her features twisted, and she lifted a hand. Darkness gathered in her palm, delicately dancing over her flesh before curling up her wrist. "So, how am I supposed to kill him?"

Adrien watched the movement in slight awe. "He didn't get that far."

Raana hummed, then dropped her arm, the shadow becoming smoke and dissipating into the air. "I could never do that. Even if I *could*, I wouldn't."

"I know."

"Is that all you can say?" she snapped, whipping her head to him before her face dawned with clarity. Still, desperation shone in her eyes. "I'm sorry." She turned away again. "I just—that can't be why he wants me. It can't be because I can't do it. I won't. And knowing he set my life on fire for this..." A ragged sound escaped her lips.

"Hey." Adrien chanced closing the distance between them, and this time, the shadows allowed him through, even curling around him. He took that as an invitation and wrapped his arms around her, pulling her to his chest—skin to skin.

Raana let everything go, then.

Her body shook as she sobbed, and Adrien could only hold her tighter. Rage roiled in his gut. His father had done this; Helene had done this. Yet another woman in his life whose existence had been fucked up by knowing him.

Adrien did his best to keep his mind from Cora, from what he'd had to do. Otherwise, he'd be right there beside Isla, ripping his father apart.

Despite him holding her, Raana's skin chilled, and the darkness pressed in. He needed to keep her mortal, especially here. He gently stroked her hair. "I told him you wouldn't do it. I told him *no one* would do it."

And his father's answer to that had been more comments speared at him in that flat, condescending tone about how he was nowhere near ready to ascend to his destined role. He'd needed to bite his tongue to keep from barbing; he just hadn't been broken down enough to embrace the role in the way *Cassius* had wanted him to. Callous and cruel. Maybe the way he needed to, but he wasn't ready to lose himself yet.

"It doesn't mean anything," Raana murmured, tears dripping onto his chest. "If I can't serve his purpose, I'm as good as dead. He'll kill me or tell everyone what I am, and then *they'll* kill me—or keep me alive, which might be worse."

The wavering of her voice had his wolf rising. That innate urge to protect, protect, *protect* at all costs, pounding through his veins. He slid his hand down to her cheeks, brushing away the wetness. "I won't let that happen."

Her eyes locked on his before tracing his features. "You can't guarantee that."

He couldn't, but he'd try. Damnit, he'd try.

But it was going to hurt.

Adrien swallowed, and this time, he let his mind drift to a little over a year ago. "What if—what if I could get you out of here? Out of Morai without my father knowing."

Raana stiffened against him. "How could you do that?"

"A boat off the coast, in a blind spot provided by the mountains." He didn't want to explain all the details just yet. "I've done it before for... someone."

"Who?" Raana asked, then appeared to want to grab the words out of the air.

"Corinne." Adrien pursed his lips. "She was—"

"Your mate," Raana finished softly, brows raised in surprise.

Adrien nodded and scowled as what he'd never spoken to anyone— not even Isla, not even Sebastian—rose to the surface. "He was going to kill her."

The words were like acid on his tongue.

For a moment, he let them hang there, allowing reality to set in. Raana remained quiet, though she waited for him to continue. "He didn't want us breaking the bond because of how it looked to the other packs and the effect it would have on me. It was a joint decision, but she had to deal with some of the greater consequences. Banishing her and her mate to rogue lands wasn't enough of a punishment for—for what she... couldn't control."

He needed to believe that last part—that she couldn't control what she felt for a man she barely knew because Fate had willed it so. But either way, the woman he'd loved for nearly a decade of his life was gone. And after all that, how could he ever think of anyone but his destined mate?

Adrien cleared his throat, guilt gnawing at his stomach as he loosened his hold on Raana. "A few weeks after she was banished, I suspected he was planning something, so I went into rogue territory and got them out of Morai. I never knew for certain, but a part of me believes she'd be dead right now if I didn't get her out. Whenever I think about it, I—"

Hate him. Adrien couldn't finish the treasonous sentence aloud.

Silence fell between them.

"I'm sorry," Raana eventually said, her icy touch going to his face. Her gaze hardened, and she spoke lowly, "Your father is a horrible man."

Adrien despised the defensive piece of him that rose. "He's my father."

"And for lack of better terms, Helene was my mother." Her voice broke, and she lowered her hand to his chest, over his heart. Adrien opened his mouth to protest that this was different, but closed it. "It's all an act. They can say they love us, pretend to care, but in the end, we're just pawns to them. Obligations or ways to maintain power."

The words and the truth he found in them cut him like knives. "It doesn't matter. He doesn't need to love me or care about me. I just need him to approve of me enough that he passes down the title when it's time."

Raana furrowed her brows. "I thought you were guaranteed to become Alpha when he dies."

"He'd find a way to fuck me over. He told me as much after the bond was broken."

Raana sneered, her eyes blazing, yet her voice remained soft. "If it's yours, then take it."

Adrien's pause of contemplation at that may as well have been another act of treason. "I could never do that to my mother. And despite all the shit he's put me through, put the people I love through, it's all personal. *Our people* love him, and so does most of the continent, despite his detractors. Challenging him sounds simple, but the ramifications..." He winced, feeling a headache coming on. He didn't want to talk about this anymore. "If you want to leave, I can get you out of here."

Raana's jaw clenched. "Won't you get in trouble? I don't think that will help with getting his approval."

"It's worth it," Adrien said before quipping, "It will be my final and greatest act of defiance."

Raana's mouth quirked to the side in some semblance of a smile. "Then yes."

Her words were a punch to the gut.

Adrien nodded. "Tomorrow night, then. After we do what we have to at the Wall, we'll leave once night falls, but we'll have to be quick." He placed his hand over hers on his chest, feeling the metal of her iron ring. "Which means you'll probably have to take this off."

Fear washed over her face, but it was slowly replaced by determination. "If it means I have a chance at getting away, then it's worth it. I'll just have to figure out a way to get my grimoire from the cottage—and the gold, too."

"We'll figure it out."

Raana's eyes gleamed as she hummed in agreement. And then in a flash of movement, she leaned up and pressed her mouth to his. Though it was gentle, Adrien felt a rush of heat take over his body along with the sinking desire for them to have had a chance.

Raana pulled back enough to murmur, "Thank you."

Adrien didn't know how to answer, at a loss for words as he traced each line of her face while he could.

Raana kissed him once more before leaving his grasp. Still not bothering with her shirt, she crawled up the bed to the pillows and pulled back the blankets. Settling beneath them, she gestured beside her. "Do you think you can handle sleeping next to me?"

Adrien grinned, trying to keep his mind from buzzing as he surveyed her half-naked body. "Can you?"

Raana didn't respond, only shot him an innocent look, biting her lip and shrugging.

Adrien held her darkening stare as he made his way to her, but before he could take his place at her side beneath the covers, she grabbed his face and brought it to hers again. And this kiss was not soft, gentle, or innocent. She murmured over his lips, "If I only have one night left in Morai…"

Adrien got the hint. With a low chuckle, he pressed his body down onto hers. As she wrapped her legs around him, he said, lips skimming her jaw, her cheek, her ear, "Try to keep quiet this time."

Raana moaned and arched into him as he moved down to her breast, taking her nipple in his mouth. "I make no promises."

Adrien laughed again and took his time dropping down, down, kissing his way across her stomach until he reached the waistband of her pants. He removed them in one fluid movement, his mouth going dry at the sight of her, bare and gleaming before him.

"Fuck," he cursed, feeling his cock twitch. He wanted nothing more than to bury himself inside her, but despite the fact that daybreak was fast approaching, he'd take all the time he could. He bent down, gripping her thighs and spreading them wide, kissing up her skin until he reached what he'd been dreaming of for months. Breathing in her heady scent, he flicked his gaze up to hers.

Raana's breathing was hard, the rise and fall of her chest a taunt. "Please," she whispered, her fingers twisting in his hair while the cold of shadows cascaded over his back.

Adrien smiled. "Keep quiet," he reminded her before lowering his mouth.

At the first swipe of his tongue, she screamed.

～

It wasn't the first light of morning that woke Adrien. It was a pull. An unnerving, cold, stomach-dropping pull that roused him from a sated sleep.

There was emptiness beside him, the lack of a weight on his chest from where Raana had rested after they'd finally given in to sleep last night.

Adrien peeled open his eyes, glancing around the room that was slowly coloring with the dawn. The silence of the space made his chest tighten.

"Raana?" he called out, shooting upright.

Another tug, cool against his skin. Adrien glanced at his ankle, where darkness pooled and pulled at him. Darkness that seemed to have no master. He surveyed the room again, looking for a note or any indication of where she could've gone. But there was nothing.

Something wasn't right.

CHAPTER 12

RAANA

Everything felt wrong. Breathing felt wrong. *Existing* felt wrong.

A hacking cough fell from Raana's mouth as she rose from where she'd been splayed, drying mud covering her from head to toe, weighing down her oversized nightclothes. She blinked against a mist rolling through the withering trunks of decrepit trees, the sulfuric taste of it coating her tongue with every inhale.

Was this another nightmare?

Her watering eyes adjusted to the world around her. Devoid of color, of flourishing life, as if everything good and vibrant had been sucked right out.

Moving her hands beneath her, then her knees and bare feet, she tried to get up—but fell again. She cursed at the pain that shot through her body, so weak and exhausted and covered in... blood. It was all over the front of her shirt and crusted beneath her nose.

Raana inhaled. Exhaled. Every breath made her feel more light-headed. With a soft whine, she forced herself to lift her head and take in her surroundings again.

Where the hell was she?

Deep in her bones, she knew it wasn't safe—wherever this was.

Last she remembered was being in Adrien's arms. Last she remembered was his soft snoring as she'd muttered another prayer to whoever would listen for more time with him. Then darkness—sleep. She'd fallen asleep, hadn't she?

Her head fell, and more coughs rasped through her throat. As she became lightheaded, she focused on her conduit, still dangling from her neck, and then her eyes drifted to her hand, where the iron ring was caked with mud.

Still there. Good.

Too late, she heard something shuffling through dried leaves, and then, the feeling of warmth against her back. Raana jumped, gasping, and weakly tried to spin away from whatever it was. The world tilted and turned as she scrambled, ending up on her back anyway. She waited to die in this horrible place, but instead, she was staring up at a woman.

Raana blinked, her vision spotty, her current state of mind questionable. The woman—stunning with long, inky dark hair spilling from the hood of her cloak and eyes such a bright blue Raana could see them through the shadows—reached out a hand. Raana's eyes slid over what sat perched on each of her fingers. Rings of crystal. Crystal, she recognized.

Her eyes widened, and her gaze flew back to the woman's face. Her nose and mouth had been covered, perhaps to make for better breathing.

"Witch," Raana rasped with the most certainty she'd ever had in her life.

From the crinkle of her eyes, Raana could tell the witch smiled slightly. "As are you—partly, at least."

Raana couldn't focus on what the woman had alluded to, instead honing in on the brutal scar spanning her face, straight down from her hairline and disappearing beneath her covering. It looked painful, though healed enough that it was a puffy pink. It looked as though she'd been clawed by an animal.

Maybe one out here?

Ignoring the witch's outstretched hand, Raana tried and failed to get to her feet herself. "Where am I?" Another hacking cough sent her body shuddering.

Rather than wait for Raana to accept her gesture, the woman crouched to her level and lowered her scarf to reveal her thin mouth and exactly how far that scar spanned. Straight across to her chin, right through her lip. "I believe they call it the Wilds."

The Wilds. *The Wilds*? Raana had heard that once before.

With her breath shuddering, Raana inclined her head and turned, seeking a wall of stone, seeking some sort of gate, but all she saw before her was forest. And behind her—ruins. What was once a village was obliterated.

Now she knew what was so unsettling about this place. It was as if she could sense the dark, corrupting magic infecting her everywhere she came in contact with the earth, and with every breath she took. Even the shadows felt worse here, more biting and foreign.

"How the hell did I get here?" she asked, turning to face her. "What are *you* doing here?"

"I was about to ask you the same, child," she said with a matronly softness before reaching for Raana's hand. Her skin was warm as she held it and observed the iron ring. "You know, if you cease to dampen your true power, all of this will likely be easier to tolerate."

Raana recoiled, now fully coming to terms with the fact that this witch knew what she was. "I don't know what you're talking about."

The woman grinned. "You evaded the High Witch's seers, but you can't evade me. Especially not here."

Raana nursed her hand and ring as if she'd been burned. "Why not here?"

"Because here, all we witness is the truth." As if to make a point, the witch glanced at the destruction, though Raana hadn't known what she meant.

Spots began to crowd her vision, but not the familiar empowering darkness she was used to. Fear struck a deep part of Raana with the knowledge that the woman was right. If she didn't take off her ring, she'd die.

"Who are you?" Raana asked, her fingers running over the metal.

The witch turned back, and now, her smile was bitter and sad. "Nerissa," she said. "Of the Althary witches in Ehime. "

"You're from the mainland?"

Nerissa laughed through her nose. "We are all from the mainland."

Raana was about to ask how Nerissa had gotten *here*, but bile had risen in her throat, and she turned to vomit. It was only Nerissa's grip that kept her from falling into it.

"You need to take the ring off," she spoke gently as if cooing a lullaby.

"Clearly, you've used magic you need to recover from, likely what got you here, and the atmosphere isn't helping much either."

Raana didn't need to hear anything else. She took hold of the ring and removed it.

Silence.

For a moment, everything was silent and hollow as Raana stared at the raw, paling skin where her ring had once been. She'd dropped the metal in the dirt, not wanting to see or think about it.

It felt like hours passed. Maybe all of eternity.

The glamor had gone first. In one blink to the next, her flesh had healed, and her skin took on the slightest glow. Ethereal. Otherworldly. She hissed at a tinge of pain when her ears arched, and she felt the points of her teeth press against her tongue. The stunning clarity that came with her heightened senses, she could've done without, but she knew she'd get used to the reek of the world. That had been the easy part.

Because then came the power.

When Raana gasped now, fortunately, the air did not sting, but it burned. In the way an icy wind burned. She reeled, bowing over her knees as her magic erupted, a torrent of shadows rushing towards her body and drowning her beneath them.

She hadn't known she was screaming until she stopped. Her throat was raw, and the only iron she tasted was her own blood.

Looking down at her hands, the night in the tunnels of Deimos came back in flashes. When she'd pushed her magic too far and tapped into this piece of her she'd never fully understood. As they had then, her fingertips shone with an iridescent light that felt alive, dimming and brightening, traveling and retracting with every breath she took. It bled into a night-dark black that inched up her arms like elbow-length gloves.

Darkness made flesh—it was the Imperial Alpha's voice in her mind, and she felt a pulse as her power responded to her rage. The darkness crept higher, her body becoming impossibly cold. If she allowed it to consume her, she would become shadow itself. It had only happened once, and she'd vowed to herself she'd never let it happen again.

"Remarkable."

Raana lifted her head, having forgotten Nerissa's presence entirely.

She walked back towards her, dropping her hood to give Raana a full view of her face. Somehow young and aged at once. She had to be about twenty years older. And that scar—

"What happened to you?" Raana realized too late how inconsiderate the question sounded.

But before she could apologize, Nerissa said, "I'll tell you the whole story once we—"

"We?" Raana jerked back, shadows dancing around her, ready to protect and strike. Though she felt no safer. "I—I'm not going with you. I need to get back to..."

Adrien.

In her haze, she'd forgotten, and now, he was all that mattered.

She looked down at the blood-stained shirt she wore. One of his that she'd thrown on after she'd been wrapped up in him last night. But she wouldn't let her mind get lost in those moments. Not now.

Nerissa's features darkened, and her tone dripped with malice. "Don't be foolish, girl."

Raana's sharpened teeth pierced her tongue as she felt a gnawing in her gut. It was as if a veil had just been lifted, and she could finally sense Nerissa's aura. How bleak it was, but also how powerful. Something about it felt forged, not entirely what it had once been. She'd never sensed anyone like it.

At that moment, a wave of shadows slid over her back, reaching her ears with their whispers. And as they spoke, Raana felt it.

They weren't alone.

Her blood chilled, and she got to her feet with immortal agility and strength.

Pairs of red eyes watched them from the darkness. When she spun to Nerissa, the smallest trickle of blood leaked from the older witch's nose that she dabbed away with her sleeve. Somehow, she was exerting power.

Raana nearly buckled as the bak emerged from the trees—three of them. Her stomach bottomed out. They appeared worse than she'd ever imagined, their bodies nearly five times her size, crafted of solid muscle and seeming to leak a putrid, dark aura from their pores. It was peculiar, that aura. The fact that they had one, and even more peculiar, that they did not attack. No, they stood as dutiful soldiers. Waiting. Waiting for...

Everything made sense, then. *Everything.*

Raana stumbled back, away from Nerissa, the shadows keeping her from falling over. She attempted to angle her body to maintain a view of all that surrounded her, but who knew what hid amongst the trees? Where had these beasts even come from?

See the unseen, hear the unheard—that alleged dark fae skill would be helpful right now.

Raana breathed, "You're the witch who tried to kill Isla... The one who took her mother and killed Kai's family."

Nerissa pursed her lips, and Raana chanced one more step, but heard a growl and stopped. She didn't know where to look and lifted her arms slightly at her sides as if to raise the shadows if need be. She tried to recall Adrien's lessons. She needed to be quick. She needed *not to be* predictable. She needed a weapon. But he hadn't taught her how to kill bak—only wolves.

"And you're the fae who saved her. May the realm rejoice," Nerissa said, uninterested. The scar across her face, bestowed by Isla, seemed more pronounced now. "It was never my intention to kill her. It was merely an error in judgment. I thought she was stronger." She inclined her head. "What else have they told you about me? What have they left out? Did they mention the prison I escaped? Did they mention the king ripping us from the mountains?"

Raana blinked her eyes wide. "You were in the prison?" At Nerissa's nod, and with eagerness coloring her tone, she asked, "How did you escape?" If she'd gotten out, maybe the others could, too.

Nerissa glanced up, looked over, and somehow, in this place that seemed devoid of wind, a breeze swept by, rustling her hair. "More stories for another time."

"There will be no other time," Raana pressed. "I'm leaving."

"To go where?"

A taunt lingered in those words as if she knew they would hit Raana like a blow. Knew she had no one. But—

Again, her mind went to Adrien, to last night.

She realized she had no idea what time it was. Everything in here was gray, and barely any sunlight streamed through the trees. He had to be worried.

"He's in *here*, you know."

Raana snapped her head up, seeing Nerissa's cruel smile. "I don't know how he found you, but the Prince of Wolves is behind the Wall. Reckless. Foolish."

Raana's entire body seized up. He couldn't be here. Not alone. Not with these beasts lurking around.

As if she could read her thoughts, Nerissa said, "All it will take is one command from me."

"No." The word ripped from Raana's throat. Nerissa had control of these beasts—they were her eyes and ears. Her weapons. The darkness on Raana's arms crept higher, more of it rising from the trees. She felt sweat bead on her brow as she struggled to get a hold of it. "If you touch him, Spirits help you."

She took one step towards Nerissa—then barely had time to react.

A blade cut straight through her.

No, not a blade.

Raana screamed as she collapsed to the mud, her hands cradling her torn and bleeding middle as one of the beasts who'd snuck up on her roared in triumph.

Blinding pain seared through her as it lunged again, and Raana called upon the darkness to sweep her up just as its claws went for her head. By the time she realized she'd moved, another beast was waiting. It swiped as shadow rushed for her, nearly too late.

Then, there was another.

Raana's blood, soaking the earth, marked the path she traveled. Darkness to darkness. Over and over. Each distance shorter as she became weaker, evading death again and again while her fae magic struggled to heal her and move her simultaneously.

She wasn't sure how many times she'd managed before she could hardly remain upright. Her knees crashed to the ground, and all she could do was brace herself as a bak charged, all snarls from its hungry, drooling maw, its claws raised high to strike—

It froze.

Raana's breathing sawed and shuddered through her body as she curled into herself, shaking her head. She didn't even feel like a person. So much of her magic, mortal and immortal, had drained away.

"What do you want?" Raana sobbed through clenched teeth. "*What do you want?*"

The beast backed away, barely, but enough that Raana managed to breathe one lungful of air. She could feel her wound knitting beneath her fingertips through her tattered shirt.

"Stay."

Raana struggled to lift her head, only glancing at Nerissa once before resting it again. "Why?" Such a weak, pathetic word.

She flinched as delicate fingers combed over her curls. "Because it would be an affront to allow you to waste your potential. I may not be fae. I may not possess as strong a gift of divination, but I can teach you so much." Again, with that soft, motherly tone. A manipulation, Raana knew. "I will keep you safe, and when it's time, we'll both have the retribution we've earned."

Though Raana despised it, Nerissa's words struck deep and true. In some twisted way, she felt comfort. She felt understood.

"Then let me get him out." With the small plea, Raana fought upright, her arm still cradling her stomach. "Let me get him out of here safely, and I'll stay."

Nerissa's eyes glinted, seemingly pleased. "Only him."

What? Why did that matter? Had Adrien brought others with him?

At Raana's questioning stare, Nerissa hardened her gaze, signaling she *meant* what she said, and Raana would come to understand.

With her lip quivering, Raana said, "I—I don't care. Just let me get him out."

Nerissa stepped back, gesturing sideways in invitation, allowing her to go.

But Raana did not rise; she let down her defenses and closed her eyes, hoping this hadn't been a trick as she left herself vulnerable to an attack. She drove down, deep, deep, deep into whatever dregs of power she had left. She focused. For several heartbeats, she sorted through death and destruction, rot and rubble for that summer storm, for that flame.

And then let the darkness carry her away.

CHAPTER 13

ADRIEN

Adrien had been twenty when he entered the Hunt, and he had hoped he'd never have to see the Wilds again. Hoped he'd never have to face another bak. But here he was. Standing before the Gate welded with archaic patterns and protections, meant to be the last barrier between the wolves and the horrors beyond.

But he didn't care anymore. Raana was on the other side of the Wall, and he needed to find her *now*.

"Your Highness, I apologize. I don't understand."

Adrien gritted his teeth, feeling his wolf rise to the surface as he glanced at one of the three Callisto guards at this post. "Open the Gate and let us through."

At the demand, the small sliver of shadow, easily missed, where it circled his wrist beneath the sleeve of his shirt, seemed to pulse.

He wasn't sure why or how it had become attached to him, but it had guided him here, to where Raana had gone. It still baffled him how she'd managed to slip away at all. She'd been in his arms when they'd fallen asleep. But the shadows, all that was *unknown* about Raana and her origins, seemed to hold answers. So, if somehow that was how she'd gotten here undetected, his biggest question was why? If it was about escape, he could think of no worse place to run to.

The guard's eyes shifted from Adrien to his fellow squad mates to the two Imperial Guard members at Adrien's back. Sandrine and Dante had caught him just as he was leaving the Pack Hall and had refused to leave him on his own in another territory. He'd needed to put on quite a show to lie about where he was heading, about why Raana wasn't with him until he fully understood where the shadow was guiding him. And then he'd needed to conjure a new, grander tale as to why he needed to go behind the Wall immediately.

He didn't want to drag them in there, but they refused to leave his side.

When the guard hesitated far too long, Adrien added, "It's my father's order." Not that Adrien's word should've held any less weight here, given the Imperial Alpha's absence. And he let that fact linger in his voice, let it shine in the fire of his wolf's eyes. What he was, what he represented.

The guard stiffened, bowed, and then fell back. As he gathered at the Gate's heavy lock with the two others, Adrien braced himself. The keen and scrape of the metal was like a shot in his mind, bringing back the memories of trying to wrench it open to save two hunters, Kai at his side, when the exit would not budge. So much had happened that night. *Why* had that happened?

Adrien stripped off his clothes, Sandrine and Dante following suit, before the three of them shifted. Adrien's paws had barely hit the ground before he snarled and began running, kicking up dirt and grass in his wake.

The Gate screeched and slammed behind them.

He wasn't sure what hit him first—the sights, smells, or heaviness of the earth and air, weighed down by the darkest of magic. It was incredible how vividly he remembered walking through here the first time. Maybe because he'd done so many times over in the nightmares that followed.

After a good distance from the Gate, Adrien slowed at a clearing, his heart hammering as he attempted to catch a scent, but the desolate land's pungent odor assaulted his senses.

"This place is horrible," Sandrine observed, mind-to-mind as wolves, the only time they could ever do so as they weren't fated mates. She came to stand at his side, her wolf's eyes that off-white iridescence, her lumerosi snaking over her legs and back pulsing the same hue. Judging

by the fact that Dante hadn't even flinched, the statement had only been projected to him. *"Why are we here? What are we looking for?"*

Adrien turned his head, scouring in another direction. He wasn't sure where that small sliver of shadow had gone. Perhaps it feared his wolf— or feared this place.

"Anything that will help us figure out why the runes are failing."

Lie. Lie, lie.

Sandrine seemed to detect it. *"Why would we need to come in here for that?"* Adrien could hear a tremor in her voice, which he entirely understood. It had surprised him that she came in here at all. She'd never shown any interest in the Hunt or being a warrior like her cousin, which meant all of this was a matter of loyalty to protect him and his family.

"Imperial Heir!"

Dante's shout came from behind them, and Adrien whipped around, lowered on his haunches, prepared to fight the monsters of his people's greatest nightmares.

But it hadn't been quite the monster he expected.

His wolf nearly let out a whine in relief—relief that was short-lived. It morphed into rage and fear. Raana panted against a tree, using the bark for support as she clutched her side. Blood covered her entire body, her body that was...

Goddess above.

Adrien took in her arched ears, her skin. Though it was the same light brown shade, it now possessed a glow. But then there were her hands, true iridescence at her fingers that bled into an ebony that crawled up her arms.

Adrien sprinted towards her, ignoring the astonishment of Dante and Sandrine behind him, standing incredulous and afraid.

Raana collapsed as he reached her, and he dipped his head so she could wrap her arm around his neck. As wolves, they were much larger than their human forms, and she seemed impossibly small like this. She gripped his fur to keep herself upright, and for a moment, she buried her face into him, trembling violently.

Though it went against his better judgment, Adrien shifted back. As he fell to his knees, he caught her in his arms and held her tight. His entire body went cold, and he could feel her being thrumming with pure power, unfamiliar and vast. It was as if he were clutching a fallen star, and he never wanted to let her go.

Tears pooled in the crook of his neck where she lay her head and sobbed. Amidst her chilled skin, he became aware of the warm, dried blood on her shirt—*his* shirt—the iron scent cutting through the sulfuric smell of the Wilds.

"What are you doing out here?" he asked, his voice shaking slightly. As he brushed the back of her hair, he accidentally bumped into the arch of her ear. She winced, the spot sensitive.

Raana only breathed, "You need to leave."

Adrien straightened, then leaned back to look at her face—her eyes slightly different, and bloodshot, crimson smeared over her cheeks. He gritted his teeth. "What the hell happened to you?" He'd kill whoever touched her. Whatever touched her. He moved back further, observing the brutal wound across her stomach. His fury worsened. If the cut had been any deeper, her insides would've spilled onto the mud. "We need to get you back."

"No." She placed a hand on his chest, and Adrien flinched at the shock of power. "Please. You need to go and leave me here."

Adrien's eyes went wide. "Are you fucking crazy?"

Raana reached up to his face. "Do you trust me?" There was an urgency in her voice.

A growl sounded behind him, and Adrien spun to find both Sandrine and Dante crouched in position, eyeing Raana with predatory intent.

Adrien's wolf rose to the surface, violent and fast. "Fall back."

Though he hesitated, Dante obeyed, but Sandrine didn't move.

"Fall. Back," Adrien repeated.

Sandrine still refused, but her eyes had fallen behind him. They went wide, and then she barked, the sound ringing through the woods. The roar that echoed it from only a few feet away rocked Adrien to his foundations.

He'd never forget the piercing red of a bak's eyes, especially emerging from the dark, tangled thickets of trees. The beast gradually revealed its monstrous body, long, heavy limbs dragging over the forest floor.

Adrien didn't think; he didn't even feel. He pushed Raana behind him and shifted.

Years of training slammed into him all at once. What he'd learned, and all he'd taught others.

But even with that deeply ingrained knowledge as he lunged for the bak's lower half, knocking it off balance, and clamped his jaws around its thick neck... he couldn't help but feel it was too easy.

Like the beast had wanted him to kill it, let him.

A sacrifice.

A distraction.

Adrien spat at the acrid taste of the bak's blood and looked up to find them surrounded. Several more crept through the trees, like a small army.

What the fuck?

So, their behavior during the Hunt hadn't been a one-off. They truly did work together as a pack now.

Adrien counted seven of them. Two wolves—he and Dante—had competed in the Hunt, but Sandrine had not, and Raana was—

Adrien glanced behind him, where she was finding her feet. He took one step back to allow her to use him while he calculated his options. Split up, spread them out, and pray there weren't more. Stick together, end up in a mess of claws, teeth, and limbs, end up cornered...

"I'm sorry." Adrien felt the pull as Raana's small voice came from his side, and he turned just as she wrapped her arms around him.

Then darkness swept up over them both, taking away his sight, sending him underwater, sending him through space.

Adrien crashed through the world.

He let out a groan as his body, feeling like it had been tugged and twisted in so many wrong ways, crashed down onto the earth. He'd fallen onto his back, fallen out of his shift with Raana's body splayed beside his, one arm still draped over him. The sunlight of late morning was near-blinding, and it took a moment to adjust to inhaling clear air. Raana coughed violently, blood spraying from her mouth.

Adrien shot up, wrapping his arms around her and letting her lean against him. Jaw slack, he took in the world around them. They were no longer behind the Wall; they were in front of it, and the Gate was nowhere to be seen. He stared at the stone, wide-eyed, realizing what had just happened. Realizing Sandrine and Dante had been abandoned to face an army of bak.

"What did you do?" Adrien asked desperately.

Raana took slow, deep breaths. "I needed to get you out."

"But we left them in there," Adrien gritted, still disbelieving. Those were *his* people. His guard. He'd abandoned them. They were going to fucking die, and he'd brought them in there.

Silver lined Raana's eyes as she became pale. "She said I could only save you. And I couldn't—I couldn't—"

"She? Who's she?"

Raana fought to her knees and leveled his stare. "I'm sorry," she repeated and then lightly grabbed his face. "Even," she struggled for a breath, and then she leaned forward, brushing her mouth against his. "Even with a wall between us."

She leaned back, tears cutting through the dirt and blood on her cheeks.

Adrien barely had time to process before darkness swirled, and Raana vanished.

CHAPTER 14

RAANA

Raana was certain that if she traveled one more inch, she would die. She wasn't sure where she'd ended up on the other side of the Wall, only that she was so far deep into the forest she could no longer see the barrier that separated the Wilds from the outside world. Shaking violently from where she'd collapsed amidst the mud and leaves, she brought her hands to her face, unaware of where the cuts on them had come from, the wounds not healing as her body struggled to keep up with her injuries.

By now, she was all out of tears. And for now, she was all out of fight, too. She wanted to sleep. Needed to sleep and escape whatever this new reality was. What she'd just done...

Those two wolves had to be carrion now. There was no way they'd survive, and she wasn't sure Adrien would ever forgive her for it. It terrified her that she'd do it again. Anything to ensure he was safe. But now, he was at the mercy of the one person she trusted the least.

Adrien would need to explain all of this to his father—her escape, the dead guards. It had to have been a test, him telling his son of his plans for her. A test to see where his loyalty lay, if he'd confess secrets—and he'd failed.

The Alpha never made mistakes; Raana had learned that much. No action was taken without intention. No word spoken that he did not

117

expect to reach the wrong ears. Whether she was under his control or not, he wanted her to know his suspicions about Kai. Wanted her to know about the dark moon, about how Raana, on that day of chaos, would be capable of killing him. As if he'd known she, too, had figured out that Kai was different and powerful in ways a wolf should not be.

Raana didn't even react to the soft touch on her back. Hadn't even heard the incoming footsteps.

"You did well, child," Nerissa cooed, and the praise made Raana sick. "You will forget him in time, as he will forget you."

Raana bit down on her tongue so hard she tasted blood. Adrien forgetting her would be a mercy.

Nerissa began speaking, though it wasn't to her. Raana couldn't even get herself to turn to look; her muscles were liquid, yet her bones were lead. An order to *pick her up* was followed by a grunt that sounded like a human, a *man*.

Strong arms hooked beneath Raana's knees and back, and her teeth rattled as she roughly fell into a broad chest. She cracked open her eyes briefly to catch a flash of coppery hair and amber bloodshot eyes. Eyes that didn't glance at her once. Eyes that appeared vacant—dead. She didn't recognize him at all. Dante and Sandrine were nowhere to be found. Neither were any bak.

Raana winced as Nerissa came into view, running a pointed nail over the skin of the man's neck, across his throat, a mockery of a lover's caress that ended where Raana swore she saw faint scarring by his collarbone. Though the man's eyes were distant, his face twitched, and he squeezed Raana gently. She could've sworn he did it twice more, as if trying to get her attention. But still, his features were blank.

She remembered exactly what Nerissa's greatest gifts were—*potions and mind control*. Had this man been one of her victims?

Raana's throat was so dry she couldn't swallow. She'd once wondered at Nerissa's power, and now she feared it could be used on her.

"What now?" she asked, the words raw.

Nerissa stepped forward and brushed back a curl that had matted to Raana's face. "Now, you rest. We have much to do, but we can start tomorrow. It won't be long until the moon is dark, and we will be ready for when the story begins again for a final time."

Raana felt her eyelids becoming heavy as Nerissa gently moved her thumb over her forehead. The conduits on her fingers were warm against her skin, and Raana had been far too weak to throw out any resistance or build any mental walls. Her breathing slowed. "How—how... do you know... about the moon?"

Before exhaustion claimed her, Raana caught Nerissa's smile. "There's someone you need to meet."

PART II
A QUEEN'S DAWN

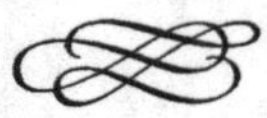

CHAPTER 15

ISLA

"**Y**ou're going to make yourself dizzy."

Isla halted her pacing of the antechamber of the Western Ballroom. She twisted to where Kai, handsome as ever in his traditional dark suit, sat in a plush armchair, a glass of whiskey swaying between his fingers as he observed her with amused-yet-wary eyes.

Isla folded her hands, twisting her mating ring on her finger, setting the glimmer of the gemstones over the surfaces of the room. "If I don't move, I'll lose my mind."

It wouldn't be long before Marin came to usher them to the double doors leading to the ballroom. And though this wasn't the first time Isla had stood at Kai's side and addressed a crowd, the stakes now felt substantially higher.

Maybe it was because of the rigorous preparation that Marin had put Isla through. A review of the party's guest list to ensure she knew the names and personal histories, and ensure she knew how to navigate every conversation and each dangerous detour that could arise. One wrong word, one accidental insult, and she could make an enemy of a gamma's wife, a wealthy merchant pivotal to their economy, or an influential reporter who helped with pack morale and their support of her and Kai's rule.

She'd handled court before, putting on the facade of a proper lady with precision as deft as a blade, but never to this scale. Never as the *center* of attention.

Everyone at this gala wanted to speak with *her,* to impress *her.* Wanted to judge *her* and get to know who was about to represent them to the rest of the world.

A foolish girl with a brash attitude in way over her head, given all this power by an entity almost beyond their understanding, beyond their control? Or the queen they deserved. She'd claw tooth and nail to prove the latter.

Kai leaned back, stretching out his long legs and patting his thigh in an invitation always hard to refuse.

With a sigh, Isla crossed the room, her low heels clicking over the marble floors that reflected the warm light of the sconces on the art-splattered walls. Settling on his lap, her eyes dragged down to the alcohol in his hand. Kai lifted it, an offer that may have been more of a *joke*, but Isla took the brown liquor and threw her head back to drain it. Features curling, she shook her head, feeling like her throat was ablaze.

"Goddess, I hate whiskey."

Kai laughed, taking the empty glass from her hand and placing it on the silver-plated table at his side. He lifted his hand from where it wrapped around her waist to the skin of her arm left exposed by her gown, his touch its own flame. "You might need it. You're freezing." He rubbed along her skin as if to warm her up. "Are you feeling okay? Do you want my jacket?"

Isla had become so accustomed to the chill in her bones that she barely dallied with the discomfort most of the time. And though this was another bout of him being a *fussy bastard*, she didn't mind it at all as she leaned into him. "I'm fine. It'll go away. I think it has something to do with losing my wolf, missing that energy."

She needed to keep her voice quiet. Other than Marin and their close friends, no one knew she could no longer shift, and if anyone became privy to that, they'd use it against her, against them. Physically. *Politically.* Even if she were coming to terms with the fact that she didn't need her wolf to be powerful, it wouldn't change others from seeing her as weak.

Kai hummed, pressing his lips to her shoulder. "Maybe I can help."

Next came a kiss on her collarbone, then another at the crook of her neck. Then his teeth nipped at her skin. Up and up, higher and higher...

Isla's blood heated, and a fluttering began in her lower belly as he licked and bit just soft enough that it wouldn't mark but enough to make her heart thunder. Enough to make her recall the last time he marked her so vividly, making her nipples pebble and her back arch. Her eyes slid closed, and she wrapped her arms around him, tugging herself closer.

"Just get through a few hours of this," Kai whispered into her ear, kissing below it, his voice like liquid gold. "And then I will sneak you away and worship you properly."

The breath she let out may as well have been a moan.

Kai's hand ventured to the slit in her ivory gown that had left her leg on display. His fingers curled to the inside of her thigh, the touch to her skin making her shiver despite the heat as he drifted up into dangerous territory.

Isla knew what he was about to find. Her eyes fluttered open as he reached the junction of her hip, where a fact became very evident.

"Fuck." Kai sucked in a breath, his eyes drifting to where his hand was hidden beneath the fabric. His gaze met hers, dark and dangerous.

Isla gave an innocent shrug, her fingers tugging at his hair near the nape of his neck, making a sound rise in the back of his throat. "Underwear didn't work well with the dress."

Kai's fingers dropped so close to her arousal that it made her core clench. "How unfortunate."

He kissed her mouth now, and her breathing stilled at the gentleness that juxtaposed whatever wicked act he was about to commit, merely an inch from what pooled between her legs.

A knock rapped at the door.

"You're fucking kidding," Kai muttered in a ragged breath before he called out, "Yes?"

"Is now a bad time, Alpha?"

Isla furrowed her brows. She'd been expecting Marin to come and sweep them away, but that deep voice belonged to Sol. She and Kai met each other's eyes, the same question of the delta's presence bearing on them. After the other night, Kai instructed him to brief another set of scouts to send out into rogue territory. They'd decide whether to send them out in a couple of days.

Still, Kai asked, "Is it important?"

"I'm here with Imperial Beta Malakai."

"Hey."

"And the future luna's brother."

Kai released his grip on her hair, and Isla's body went cold and hot with mortification all at once.

Intrusion aside, her father wasn't supposed to arrive until tomorrow afternoon, having a conflicting duty in Io. But no, he was here, and she was sitting on her mate's lap, moments away from...

"You're cute when you're flustered."

Isla whipped around to face Kai, who brandished a slightly smug smile. She whispered sharply, her eyes dropping to his crotch, "You might want to hide that while you're talking to them."

"Believe it or not, they're a bit of a mood killer."

"Big, scary alpha afraid of my dad and older brother?"

"I can take Sebastian, but your dad is your *dad*, and I'm nowhere near good enough for you. Fated or not."

Such a good answer.

Isla smiled and rolled her eyes, pecking once more at his lips before turning for the door. With a hurried glance in a large, gilded mirror, she smoothed out her clothes, then her hair, and ran a finger along the outline of her rouge-painted lips.

She carefully twisted the lock and pulled back the door, feeling like her chest would burst when she beheld her father. The Imperial Beta of Io was a hulking presence, the tallest of the men who stood in the doorway, making her, and sometimes even Sebastian—who could've been his twin if he hadn't gotten some of their mother's prettier features—look small. He wore a dark suit stitched with patterns of burgundy and gold.

"Are we interrupting?" Sebastian asked tauntingly, and Isla cut him a glare. He even earned a narrowed look from the woman beside him.

Isla shouldn't have been surprised to see Ameera, gorgeous in a cream dress that hugged her body perfectly, not there accompanying her brother, but there with Sol as somewhat of an apprentice.

Ever since Ezekiel was imprisoned, the position of Kai's second had been vacant... and he wanted Ameera to take it. Not because it had been her father's but because it suited her—her, the warrior general who'd known him and been by his side since they were children. After an initial outright refusal, telling him no one would want a *traitor's daughter* as the pack's beta, she told him that she'd consider. Shadowing Sol allowed her to get into more of the inner workings of the court and Kai's stripped-down, now-replenished council. Anyone he'd felt had ill intent towards him or Isla was gone.

So much had been changing within the pack's hierarchy that Isla feared they teetered on a fine line, and others would see that as instability and an opportunity to strike.

"My little warrior," Imperial Beta Malakai boasted, his arms splayed.

Such an old endearment. Isla didn't hesitate to enter her father's embrace, which had once made her feel like the world couldn't touch her, but now, an uneasy feeling slithered inside her as she remembered whom he served. Who he'd probably just left.

He had no idea what a monster he had for a ruler, for a friend—or did he? Was it ignorant for her to assume her father knew nothing of what Cassius was doing? Would it be improper to ask if he'd confronted Cassius upon learning his friend had known he was sending *Isla's mate* into a battle to the death?

And he couldn't have known the most damning thing of all. That Cassius had knowingly sent her mother into peril to cover up his mistakes, and likely figured she'd been captured by the witch and left her for dead.

As rage built up inside her, Isla's mouth opened to say it right then. He needed to know. Sebastian needed to know. They deserved to.

But... not now. If they learned the truth, they might go after Cassius right now, and she wasn't prepared for that fallout if it went horribly wrong.

Selfish.

Guilt gnawed at her stomach.

Isla pulled back, schooling her features. "You're here early. I didn't think you'd be able to make it until the coronation. I haven't even made sure the guest wing of the House is ready. I would've arranged for dinner, or—"

"You've never arranged anything for me," Sebastian said, adjusting the cuffs of his navy suit jacket.

Isla looked him over, thankful he cleaned up remarkably well. He could annoy her to no end, but he played the part of dashing—and sneaky—court member perfectly. She just needed to give him a speech to keep it in his pants for *one night.*

"You show up unannounced *and* make yourself perfectly at home without my assistance."

Malakai looked between his two children that he hadn't seen in weeks, a smile tugging at his lips. "Don't pester your sister," he told his son before directing his gaze back to Isla. "You've been busy, I'm sure."

Isla waved him off. "Only a little."

Her father's eyes drifted behind her, to where she knew and felt Kai standing, allowing them their moment. Malakai bowed. "Alpha."

"Imperial Beta." Kai stepped forward, taking his spot at Isla's side. He reached forward to grab the beta's hand... the same hand he'd been gripping her hair with only minutes earlier. She shook off the thought so violently that Kai must've felt something through the fractured bond, glancing her way.

"I'm happy you could make it," he said to her father, dropping his hand. "I hope you had an easy trip."

"The rain made for some muddy trekking, and we ended up getting stuck," Malakai conceded. "But we made it."

A moment's hesitation and a locking of his muscles. Isla hated that she noticed her father's small ticks, his tells. *Lie*, the word flashed across his face, to her, like a beacon.

Kai blew out a breath. "Rainy season coming down from the north as well? It's been pretty bad here."

"Unfortunately."

Kai had caught him off guard, somehow. What wasn't he saying?

"Well, thank the Goddess," Sebastian mused. "With all the droughts we've had the past few summers, it's nice it's finally turning around. Maybe it will have cooled off by the time I go back."

Her father swallowed, and his smile was too tight. "Indeed."

There.

A pit formed in Isla's stomach. If he hadn't truly been in the north, where had he been?

"I'm sorry to interrupt."

Isla's attention was drawn to Ameera, who stepped forward. Sol watched from behind her, a touch of pride in his eyes as she took charge, and the mischievous intrigue in Sebastian's stare, the hum he'd let out, made Isla want to knock him upside the head—if Ameera wasn't already planning to. But...

Had Ameera just fought a smile? At *him*?

Hands behind her back, the warrior general bowed to both of them but directed it at Kai, "May we have a word, Alpha?"

Isla scanned the seriousness that crossed her face as Kai, seeming to fight his own look of pride, nodded. "Of course. If you'll excuse me." He brushed his lips against Isla's cheek, and there was a faint tugging sensation inside her. An urgent attempt to communicate through their bond, but nothing came through. So, he could only whisper, "I'll be right back," before an easy, "I hope it's not raining."

Isla battled to keep her shoulders from falling. So, he'd picked up on her father's lie, too.

When the wolves of Deimos had gone, leaving only the Imperial Beta and his children, Malakai asked, "Do they leave you out of a lot?" His features were a mix of perplexed and concerned.

"I don't think he's leaving me out," Isla said. "They just don't want to rip me away from you. Kai will brief me later."

Malakai hummed. "And he's treating you well? You're happy here?"

Isla laughed. He was truly in overprotective father mode. The war of emotions continued to rage inside her. "Yes, Dad. I'm very happy."

"It surprises me every day," Sebastian drawled, sauntering further into the room and mindlessly scanning the art pieces as she had been. "He genuinely loves her. I have no idea how."

Isla folded her arms. "You're in true form today."

Sebastian stepped closer and threw an arm around her shoulders. "Someone has to humble you before they put that big, fancy crown on your head, Pudge."

"Humbling and annoying are two different things."

Before Sebastian could retort, a deep chuckle fell from their father's mouth, and Isla found his eyes solemn, his shoulders sunken, likely weighed down by a burden she couldn't see. "I've missed you two."

It broke Isla's heart.

With her and her brother standing opposite him, it felt like they were speaking over a wall. One being built brick by brick from Cassius's lies and mortared by her own destiny. And though she knew the words to say to send it crumbling, she wasn't sure if they'd all be able to crawl out of the rubble.

～

It was nice to hear that she and Kai were *a beautiful couple,* but it felt like more than half of their guests had been given a script on how to address them, and they followed it verbatim.

Since the moment they'd entered the gala, arm in arm—in the way she'd once, heavy-heartedly, watched Kai do alone within this very ballroom—conversation followed the same template. A deep bow and a lingering look over her dress—because what she wore was somehow pertinent. A compliment as individuals, then as a pair. Questions about how they met, how they'd felt *when* they met—a story they kept chaste. And eventually, some talk of an heir.

It hadn't occurred to her how little people held back, how unafraid they were to pry about when they planned for children. But she would bear their future alpha, she supposed, so maybe that made them think they had some say, some stake in the matter. She wouldn't be surprised if there were bets about when a royal baby would be born, and wouldn't be surprised if Sebastian was running the books.

Isla wished she'd been better prepared for certain conversations, but from the moment her feet hit the ballroom floor, she had her sights on her father. She kept tabs on everyone he spoke to and how they reacted to his presence. Once, months ago, Kai had used her in such a manner. Given the natural animosity between their two packs, anyone who seemed a bit *too friendly* with her—or even too vehemently opposed—would find themselves under Kai's suspicions.

But using her father like this... felt gross. It felt wrong. She didn't *want* to know if there was corruption or collusion, but she knew she would. It would inevitably be unveiled now with her position, but she had to prepare for how deep it went, how twisted it was, and how she'd react. She could only imagine how Ameera had felt as everything with Ezekiel came to light.

About an hour before the dance company they'd hired for the night was to begin, Isla and Kai split, all part of Marin's calculated itinerary. Even who they each would speak to was pre-chosen. Isla remembered both dreading this moment and feeling the part of her that thrived on challenge fiending to rise to it—intrigued to see some *truer* colors now that she didn't have the Deimos-born alpha at her side.

Partway through her rounds, Zahra appeared, beautiful and regal in her marigold gown, the color standing out against her brown skin.

"They'll try to catch you off-guard," Kai's mother, the former Luna of Deimos, muttered to Isla as she smiled away the official who'd bustled up to Isla once she'd been alone. "They want you to make promises that you can't keep, but you can bet they will hold you to them. Everyone in this room will remember each word you say and every move you've made."

Isla swallowed, trying not to let her features fall as Zahra schooled her. It was counseling she needed, truly. Who better to teach her the ins and outs of being queen than the one who'd served for nearly twenty years?

She'd once thought to ask for guidance, but wasn't sure whether Zahra would even be up to it. Isla had taken her position because her mate and eldest son had been killed, and truthfully, she didn't know how to look Zahra in the eye in the few conversations they'd had, knowing that her own mother had been the one to deliver the deadly blows that stole her family away. Zahra had been with Alpha Kyran in their bed when Apolla had poisoned him.

"Marin made sure I was aware of that," Isla told her, lowering her voice. Some of their guests were eyeing them, eyeing each other, as they hovered nearby, unsure who would make the next move. Would Isla approach them, or would they dare interrupt her and Zahra? "I received a list of potential requests and how to respond."

Zahra smiled, effortless and stunning. "I expected nothing less. And I notice you're making them a bit more personable, which is perfect. Better not to sound like you're a wooden board, or the gossips will talk about the stick up your ass." Isla snorted as Zahra sipped from her glass of sparkling wine. "You're doing great so far. Poised, well-spoken, handling high pressure—Isla?"

Isla wrenched her head back to Zahra, her blood pounding, but she couldn't stop herself from taking one more glance at her father within the mess of the chatting crowd and weaving servers. *Who* he was speaking to.

General Eli.

"Who the hell invited him?" she muttered under her breath, narrowing her eyes. Words and smiles were being exchanged, nothing secretive it appeared, but Eli's hands were clenched behind his back. Her father's posture was strong, authoritative. What were they saying?

Isla was just about to excuse herself from Zahra when she felt a hand on her back.

She turned to find Kai, who also noticed the exchange, but drew his focus back to Zahra. "Sorry to interrupt, Mother, but I need to steal my wife for a moment."

Isla's stomach fluttered. *His wife.* She'd never get sick of hearing that. Though she wasn't technically "his wife" until they had their mating ceremony, he'd taken to calling her it.

A twinkle of mischief, of mother's understanding, flashed in Zahra's eyes as she looked between them, and a gloss seemed to take over her stormy irises. She'd once told Isla that the only thing that had kept her from being swallowed alive by her grief after the bond and the fabric of her wolf had been ripped to shreds when Kyran had died, when she'd lost her son, was the fact that she would never leave Kai to bear the weight of the world alone. But now he had Isla.

"Of course." Zahra waved her hand. "I'm not unfamiliar with your escapes."

"This isn't an escape," Kai said, not the least bit convincing. "I've outgrown that."

Isla furrowed her brows and glanced up at him. "You have?"

Morning after morning lately, she'd woken up without him in their bed. Apparently, he'd taken to morning "runs" to rid himself of suffocating, pent-up energy. Power.

With a smirk sliding across his lips, Kai shushed her.

Zahra hummed. "Do what you must. Just be back to thank the performers for attending before they begin."

Isla and Kai watched as she spun and walked off, pausing a few feet away to pluck an hors d'oeuvre and a new glass of wine from a platter that swept by.

Isla furrowed her brows. "Did your mother just encourage us to sneak away to have sex?"

Kai's expression was an equal mix of perplexed and perturbed. "She's hinted to me on more than a few occasions that she wants grand-children."

Isla pursed her lips. She'd mentioned it to her, as well.

"Well, until it doesn't feel like our families are two seconds from clawing each other to death, everyone needs to be patient. We could never bring a child into this." Isla met his eyes, seeing some solemn agreement in them. She knew he wanted a family—and the thought of it melted her—and they'd agreed to wait a year, at least. Hopefully, things didn't get worse. "But that's not why you need me, though, is it?"

Kai frowned. "Meet me in the Warrior Galley in five minutes."

"What is it?"

Kai looked up and away, scanning the crowd with a soft smile on his lips, like she'd told him something endearing. They still needed to put on a show. "If I tell you, you'll leave now, and I need you to wait so it's not obvious."

Isla resisted the deadpan on her face. "You act like I have no self-control."

Kai leaned down to kiss her cheek. "Five minutes. Schmooze one more guest."

Then he walked away—and Isla schmoozed no one.

She waited a minute, sure, but then she was gone. Snuck out, easy and inconspicuously, with the help of a strategically maneuvered waiter, a friendly guard, and some heavy night-dark curtains blocking one of the many secret doorways within these walls.

Every Pack Hall had a Warrior Galley, meant to honor the wolves who'd gone through the perilous Hunt and survived, as well as those who hadn't. Here, the galley lay within the North Hall, the original hall that had stood on these grounds since Deimos was founded a millen-nium ago. The history chiseled into these walls would take Isla a lifetime to learn.

The double doors that hid the galley displayed Deimos's insignia—a representation of Kai's bloodline—two wolves, *twin* wolves, lunging for the moon. Thinking about it now, after what she'd learned about Deimos and Phobos, their connections, and how they'd been one pack of Ares, she wondered if there had been a reason for it.

She pressed a hand to the warrior's crescent below the symbol and pushed the heavy doors open. Moonlight barely edged through the windows, trickling beyond the latticework of stone slabs and columns, etched with countless names—a long legacy of strength, ferocity, and triumph. Ebony silks were folded in underlit glass cases, those of warriors past, taken and embroidered with their names and when they'd succeeded. Beside them were the sharp claws of bak, their razor-sharp teeth: trophies and proof of their victories.

And at the pinnacle of the cases, displayed grandly on the back stone wall, Isla caught a flash of red amidst all the obsidian. There, hanging beside a silk of black that belonged to the Alpha of Deimos, was that of the first warrior luna in the pack's history. Hers.

Isla rested her hand on the glass box just below their silks. Six sets of claws and teeth, two slain by her and four by Kai, lay on velvet sapphire pillows in such an elegant display for a brutal act.

A shadow appeared in the corner of the glass, a figure slipping from the darkness of the room so carefully that she knew it *wasn't* Kai.

Heart ratcheting, Isla's hand went to her side for a blade she didn't carry. Fingers splayed for claws she could not summon.

Then they became a fist, solid and ready to strike.

Isla whirled, but the intruder knew her well. Too well.

Adrien caught her hurtling fist in his hand and smiled.

CHAPTER 16

ISLA

For a moment, Isla could only stand there, jaw unhinged and fist in hand as she took in the Wolf Prince's features. His raven-black hair and golden-green eyes gleamed in the streams of moonlight. With the way the darkness cut him, he looked so much like his father that it sent a tremor of rage down her spine—one that made her fear what she'd do if she ever saw Cassius again.

Adrien dropped his hand and, in turn, hers. "You and your mate truly are made for each other."

Isla still didn't speak, taking in his face carefully to banish the image of Cassius away—and to make sure she wasn't dreaming. He looked... rough. Not his clothes, those looked fine, if not wrinkled and covered in smears of dirt it appeared he'd tried to wipe from his face and body. But his eyes... something broken lay within them.

Adrien began, "Are you—"

Isla lunged forward, wrapping her arms around him and effectively cutting him off. There was no need for questions yet, even if she had too many. The first being, what the hell was he doing here?

The tension in his muscles melted away with each passing second as he circled his arms around her waist and rested his head atop hers. She was sure a smartass quip sat on his tongue about *her* needing *him* after this time apart, but it was too obviously a lie. From how he hugged her right now, he needed her, too. Needed a friend. With her and Sebastian here in Deimos, she couldn't think of who else he truly had.

Heartbeats passed where they didn't move or speak. Isla sniffed, the earthy, rain-kissed scent of his body unmissable even without her animal senses, even if she hadn't plucked a leaf from his hair. Had he been out in the storm last night? Had he *run* here? There was no evidence of any Imperial Guard. Hell, no one seemed to know he was here except Kai.

She leaned back, taking stock of his pursed lips, those eyes that held words he hadn't spoken.

Letting out a deep sigh, she gripped his face between her hands. "You're a dumbass for sneaking up on me like that, *and* you look like shit."

The smile that burst across his features sent a course of relief through her. "I wasn't aware there was a party."

"There's *always* a party—I don't even remember what this one is for." Isla stepped back from him, not even thinking to worry if any of the dirt had gotten on her dress. "What are you doing here? Or better yet, *how* did you get here without anyone seeing you?"

"When we left last time, I noticed some weak spots in your outer defenses by Rhea's borders. I'm guessing because you've collapsed a lot of your guard south towards the rogues. You don't have many watches through the mountains between Ifera and Mavec, so I cut through those passes."

Isla blinked and probably shouldn't have been surprised or impressed. "And the hall? There are people everywhere."

"Tunnels," Adrien said, as if it were obvious, and he was disappointed she didn't figure it out. "Every Pack Hall on this continent has an underground tunnel system. These check another off my list. Only Mimas and Charon left. Maybe you should consider a few more sentries around here."

Isla flattened her brows. "Any other faults in our pack's protections?"

"I can try sneaking in again and let you know."

"Not necessary. How did Kai find you?"

"I don't know, but I didn't make it three feet out of the room the tunnel spat me out in before he nearly gutted me."

"Maybe next time, you'll give us some warning before showing up, then." Isla and Adrien turned towards the entryway, where Kai strode into the room, hands tucked into his pockets. He said to Isla, "And next time, I'll suggest you leave right away—but then, you probably won't even show up."

Isla narrowed her eyes and subtly flipped him off from her folded arms.

Kai barely fought off a laugh before asking, "I'm assuming the Imperial Alpha or his Beta outside don't know you're here." He took a spot by one of the many columns, leaning against it. There, he had a vantage point of them and the door. *Always alert, always protective.*

Adrien shook his head. "Not yet, but I'm sure they will by morning. I cut my time in Callisto short, and since I'm here, I wanted to stick around for your coronation, if that's okay."

Excitement bubbled in her at the last sentence. She'd wanted him to be here, but because of the Equinox holiday and the fact that he couldn't appear to "play favorites" with Deimos, with her, she thought he wasn't going to attend.

Her joy was short-lived, however, as her mind snagged on the few words before that. "Why were you in Callisto?"

Adrien swallowed, backing up an inch. "Do you have time for a long story?"

Kai and Isla glanced at each other, not needing a silent conversation. Even if they didn't have time, they'd make time for this. If Adrien was so freely offering up information, it was valuable. They'd be fools not to take it—though with a grain of salt. Keeping an eye on her father and Eli would have to wait.

"My father sent me to Callisto to look at the Wall and its enchantments. Alpha Kane reported that the Gate's lock is breaking down and eroding. And other than that, there's still the smell of corrupted magic, and the bak are venturing closer than usual; close enough that guards spot their eyes through the iron occasionally, and... and on my way here, I noticed some rot seeping through from below, along the edges of the stone. Dark magic. Still in Callisto, but closer to Deimos than the Gate. My father doesn't know that part yet."

Fear spider-walked over Isla's bones, and for a moment, she swore she could hear the Wilds beckoning her, wanting her back—wanting her blood. A collapsing Wall answered why the bak had been coming through the tunnels, no longer repelled from anywhere near the barrier by magic.

"We've already dealt with rot." Kai barely seemed phased, but he was always exceptional at masking his emotions. "Almost a decade ago, it wiped out an entire village in one of our regions. I wouldn't be surprised if you never learned about it. Io never seemed to give a shit."

And there it was: some emotion buried deep within that jab, despite the ease with which it was delivered. And despite everything, she felt the hit.

Adrien glowered. "I wouldn't put it past your father to have kept it from us."

Something in the air shifted, then power rose from them both. They weren't about to break into a brawl, but it was a show of dominance Isla had to resist rolling her eyes at. Frankly, neither of them was wrong, so there was no use arguing about it.

Isla lifted her hands between them. "Play nice. Both of you." She narrowed her gaze at Kai—a silent *you better behave*—before she asked, "How did they stop it from spreading? You never told me."

"I don't remember, but I think it just... stopped."

Isla dropped her hands and sighed. What happened ten years ago that could've triggered it? In the same way the spread of rot had been triggered now. "Didn't the witch escape your father ten years ago?" she questioned Adrien softly, trying to hide the bite from her voice.

Before Adrien could answer, Kai said, "If she's strong enough to mess with the behemoth that is the Wall, which we needed multiple witches to enchant, she wouldn't need anyone to help with her vendettas. She would've destroyed us all years ago."

His logic was sound.

"Who did you bring with you?" Kai asked Adrien. "I know you're familiar with... *magic*," the innuendo in his tone earned a sidelong glare from his mate, "but I can't imagine the Imperial Alpha has you as a high-level advisor of such things."

Pain lashed across Adrien's face so violently that he didn't have time to throw on his mask before Isla noticed. "I didn't go alone." An answer so quiet. "I brought Raana with me."

Isla stiffened, and even Kai tensed. She asked, "You brought Raana back into wolf territory? Did you leave her in Callisto? Is she here?"

Again, that look of anguish struck over his features. "I don't know where she is." With his eyes shadowing, Adrien had to turn away. Moments of silence passed as he paced, wringing his hands and looking over the warriors' names. His power ebbed and bowed, as if he were fighting to restrain it and contain his emotions.

Isla jumped when she felt something wrap around her, not an arm, but something like a wind or force pressing on her—protecting her. Like a literal rope, a tether of power. She turned to Kai, still against his column but watching her, Adrien, and the door. This feeling, this force, was separate from their bond. Something physical, something *him*, and something within her reacted to it. Her wolf, probably. She didn't balk at it, though. She never would balk at him—though she may have called whatever shield this was unnecessary.

She raised a brow. *New trick?*

Kai simply shrugged. *You could say that.*

"Do you remember Sandrine? Callan's cousin?"

She spun back to Adrien, who'd ceased his moving. What did she have to do with anything?

"Of course," Isla said. "I liked her much more than Callan. She may have been one of the few people who supported me going into the warrior program."

"She's dead."

Isla jerked back, feeling the words like a punch in the gut. Her knees weakened beneath her, and she swore Kai's power kept her upright. He pushed up off the column, ready to be a true steady force if need be. She and Sandrine weren't particularly close, but death...

Goddess, she was sick of death.

"Dante, too." Isla shook her head. Another guard she had a vague memory of. "How?" Kai was at her side now, a hand pressed to her back.

"It's my fault. I..." Adrien clenched and unclenched his fists. "I brought them into the Wilds."

"You *what*?" She didn't expect such icy rage to rise in her, darkening the corners of her vision. "You better be joking." He clearly wasn't. "What were you thinking? Why would you ever go in there?" If they had died, he could've just as easily, and she wasn't sure if she'd ever recover from that. "Did your father make you?"

"No," Adrien answered with some bite, his lip curling as he rubbed at his wrist. Isla could've sworn there had been darkness there—tangible darkness—but it disappeared from one blink to the next. "I needed to find Raana. I don't know how she ended up in there." Adrien let out a ragged breath, shaking his head as if he were weathering a barrage of memories all over again. "We hadn't made it far into the Wilds when we were surrounded by bak, and then Raana showed up covered in blood. She told me to leave, to leave her. And then when I refused, she—she got me out. Left Sandrine and Dante to die, but took me. Said that *she* told her Raana could only save me."

Isla could feel Kai's fingers tightening on her back, but he remained silent. "She? Who's *she*?"

"That's what I asked, but she didn't answer me before she shadowed away. I'm assuming back into the Wilds."

An incredulous laugh came from behind her. "Well, that's just fucking great."

Isla turned just as Kai stepped back, pinching between his brows. "It's the witch. That has to be where she disappeared to. As if one who murdered my family and nearly killed my mate wasn't bad enough. Now, there's another one running around that's half-fucking-fae." He snarled, "You Imperials just love screwing up your jobs and dragging them into our territory, don't you?"

"*Kai*," Isla seethed, trying to get him to back down. Though she understood his point, Adrien was already beaten up enough about this by the look of him.

She hadn't seen him look at anyone like he did Raana, except Corinne, and he'd chosen her as his mate. There must've been much more to his and the witch's relationship than having slept together the one time he'd told her it had happened. And though he'd promised nothing would come of it, because it would never and could never work out between them, it seemed easier said than done.

"Watch it." The prince bared his teeth, but then something seemed to dawn on him. "You know what she is?"

"She told me, but even if she didn't, traveling through shadows like that isn't something a witch is capable of."

Adrien glanced at the ground. "She never told me you knew."

"She evidently hid a lot from you."

For Goddess's sake, he was relentless. Isla was a few moments away from shoving Kai out of the room. The warning look she gave him now was the last he'd get before that happened.

As if he could sense that he was pushing too far, too hard, Kai softened his voice but only slightly. "Raana helped us, and I am forever in her debt for that, but that witch said she doesn't want us dead. Maybe Raana has been working with her this entire time."

"She hasn't," Adrien said firmly, though the slightest doubt may have slipped through. "I *know* she hasn't."

Kai looked as if you were ready to say something, something that would cut deep, but refrained. "How can you be so sure?"

"Because she wanted nothing to do with this continent. Nothing to do with the world. She was trying to get away from here, from my father." In a hush, he added, maybe not for their ears, "Unless *nothing* was real, I don't think going with the witch was always her intention."

Isla caught the undercurrent, though. It could be her intention now.

"Why was she trying to get away from your father?"

"He knows what she is—*all* that she is—and he propositioned her mother to give her to him so she could work for him."

Isla blinked. "Like his other witches?"

"He had a special job for her skill set, but she didn't want to do it." Adrien's eyes slid to Kai. "He wanted her to kill *you*."

"What?" Isla snapped, not realizing she'd stepped in front of Kai in reflex as if to protect him, until he rested a hand on her shoulder.

Kai let out another loud laugh. "I was wondering how he'd try again. I thought he'd at least have the dignity to do it himself."

Adrien's jaw tightened, and for a moment, he paused. Like he stood at the edge of a cliff or had just gone to hurtle himself off it, but now dangled by one last finger. Finally, he said, "He's afraid of you."

Isla tried to keep her temper in check. "He *admitted* that to you?"

"More or less."

Kai inclined his head. "Why are you telling us? You're his heir. You should be protecting his plans."

"Because I'm done," Adrien said. "He has taken and twisted so much of my life, hoping to mold me into a mindless monster he can control, but I won't break. I'm sure there are parts of this plan I'm missing. He wouldn't have let Raana go to Callisto after telling her all he did with the risk that she'd flee or come to tell you. And he would've never told me because he hasn't fully trusted me in years. The moment he learns I'm here, I'll lie, but he'll know I told you. Even if I truly didn't, he wouldn't believe me." His tone was thick as he steeled against his emotions. "I love my pack, and I want my crown, but I only have a few people left. If getting those things means hurting them," he focused on Isla, "then I'll fight instead."

Isla's heart clenched, and all she wanted to do was grab him and pull him into a hug, but her shock must have held her back. "You'd *challenge* your father?"

"If it becomes the only way, it would be better if I were the one to challenge him than anyone else to keep the continent from teetering into mayhem." Tension settled in the room like a thick, dark cloud, the traitorous words winding around them all. If this had, in some alternate, messed-up reality, been a setup, she and Kai would be screwed for not refuting him. Adrien's eyes slid over Kai. "Did you genuinely kill Brax without touching him? He didn't lose his mind; it was you."

"A little bit of both."

Fear flashed in Adrien's eyes. "How?"

"I'm still figuring it out."

Adrien rubbed at his wrist again. "I think my dad knows a lot more about what *it* is than he's letting on. I don't think he's just blowing smoke up my ass when he says you're a threat. He genuinely believes it."

"Good." Kai's voice was a lethal calm. His arm slid around Isla's waist, holding her close. "Because the next time he threatens my mate, family, or home, you won't get a chance to challenge him. When I see him, I'll end it. I'm not the Imperial Alpha; I don't need to be concerned about the rest of the continent."

Isla slid her hand over his, feeling that power rising. She stroked her thumb over his skin, reassuring him, *I'm here. I'm safe.*

Adrien said nothing, seeming to understand, but his eyes betrayed other unspoken words. Isla had pried information from him far too many times to miss it. "What aren't you saying?" she asked. "What else is there?"

Adrien took a long breath of resignation. "Have you ever heard of the dark moon?"

CHAPTER 17

RAANA

When Raana closed her eyes, she dreamt of him.

When she settled deep enough into the threadbare pillow, she could pretend any warmth it offered was from Adrien's arms. She could pretend the press of her suffocating shadows was his body against hers, feeling his kisses pepper over her shoulders, her neck, his hands roaming and exploring her skin. Unrestrained. *Unafraid.*

Once she awoke, she sat in her own darkness.

She didn't bother chastising the icy shroud draped over her body as the shadows protected her. It would've been easy to say she needed protection from Nerissa. Easy to say it was from the horrific monsters that stalked the forests beyond with their skin-tearing talons and teeth. But what Raana truly needed safety from was her own shredded heart. Because if she remained in the shadows, if she steeped within her own darkness long enough, the rest of the world didn't exist, and she could feel nothing. She could remember nothing.

Not that the closest person she'd ever had to a mother had betrayed her. Not that a target the size of the mortal realm itself had been placed on her back by the King of Wolves, and... not that she'd betrayed the one person who may have cared about her.

Within a week, she'd lost everything.

But there was a voice, a tug, from somewhere she couldn't see, telling her to *get up*. And for some reason, she always listened.

Even now, begrudgingly.

The halls of this ruined palace smelled of rot and horrid things, but Raana no longer scrunched her nose as her keener senses took it all in. She moved like a wraith through the narrow, dilapidated corridors, the sound of her footsteps dulled by the shadows that rippled by her feet and behind her like the train of a gown.

It had been three days since Nerissa had brought her here. Of them, she'd been conscious for two—thanks to the unfamiliarity and overuse of her magic that horrible day—and she'd spent them doing this: exploring their new refuge in all its destroyed glory. And it was going... well, terrible, quite frankly.

Every door she passed on this floor was locked or warded—or both —and she'd almost killed herself trying to overtake the spells to get inside.

But maybe this time...

"Shit!"

Lightning shot up Raana's arm when she wrapped her fingers around the rust-splotched door handle. She pulled it back, shaking away the pain and redness as she glowered at the entrance. She should've known—

Iron.

Every damn door here was locked and made of *iron*. And even if they appeared to be crafted of wood, somehow the cursed metal laced them.

For a little while, she thought Nerissa had been responsible for every obstacle she encountered, but the elder witch hadn't been hiding out here long enough to install solid iron doors. At least, Raana didn't think so. Which meant they'd been installed long before her time, back when this place was still brimming with life rather than decay.

Five hundred years ago.

The ghosts of the past would be happy to know their enchantments and protections, clearly meant to deter magic, still held after all these centuries.

Her shadows hadn't seemed to learn from her mistakes. She watched, brows drawn as they struck the barrier like asps, recoiling the moment they touched the surface in a trembling smoke.

"That was foolish," she scolded. She wasn't sure whether they were only protecting her or if they were equally curious about what lay on the other side.

At that thought, the ground shifted, and a low, steady groan reverberated through the walls.

Raana stumbled back as the stone beneath her feet shook so hard she wondered if it would give way, and a gust of wind rushed down the corridor. She threw up a hand, the shadows curling around her as rock and debris hurtled by.

That was the other thing. This palace, this former Pack Hall of Phobos, as wolves had once called the kingdom, was haunted. Or rather, it was cursed—imbued with the dark magic that had destroyed all else around it.

It was another reason Raana found exploring so difficult. Doors and hallways were constantly changing. Just yesterday, a trip to locate the decrepit kitchen area had her walking in circles before she gave up and *circled more* before returning to her dusty bedroom. Good thing she hadn't really wanted to eat, anyway.

Despite the inconvenience, she couldn't deny her fascination. Whatever this magic was, it was unlike any other she'd ever sensed. Different from any witch, *too powerful* for any witch, and different from her, too. Nerissa hadn't done this either.

It tickled at the back of her brain, how nothing seemed to add up with the tales she'd heard. What kind of magic had truly destroyed this place?

A rasping squeak drew Raana's attention to the door she'd once stood before. Only now, it was different. It was no longer dark wood, but a lighter hue, and the knob had become a handle. She wouldn't need to touch it, thankfully, as it was open a hair.

She stepped forward just as the source of the squeak came scurrying out of the room.

A twisted, sad little thing that Raana imagined was once a rat before the corrupted nature of this place took hold. It swept through the mist of darkness at her feet, running for its life, and her shadows, either wanting to play or just be assholes, clung on.

The rat writhed, screeching in pain and terror as a tendril coiled around it and squeezed.

"*Enough*," Raana snapped, and the shadow released its grip, spooling back into the others around her feet. They all seemed to collapse into it, reprimanding the rebellious shadow for falling out of line. For a moment, she nearly smiled.

Raana lifted her head to the ajar door. *Now, what was that rat running from?*

She angled her head, tuning into her enhanced fae senses. Even the air felt different along her skin.

Oh.

Raana grimaced.

She was here.

She walked forward and carefully pushed the entrance open the rest of the way. There were no wards or lightning this time.

The scent of rotting flesh hit her like a slap to the face, and the room pulsed with a noxious smoke whose source seemed to be the cauldron Nerissa hunched over. She wasn't wearing the scarf she used to cover the scarring of her face.

This room had once been a ballroom. A grand, sweeping, spacious place now with crumbled high ceilings and a floor of shattered glass, partially from the fallen chandeliers that had once dripped like starlight. But also...

Raana turned to the only other source of light besides the lantern Nerissa had at her side and the fire blazing beneath the obsidian pot at her knees.

Even destroyed, the stained-glass window was beautiful.

Fragments littered the floor in shattered pools of silver and midnight blue. A gaping wound to match the one left in her chest. She was sure that if she peered into herself, the way she peered out into the rot of the Wilds, she'd see as much destruction.

She'd sacrificed the lives of two wolves to save Adrien. Maybe that's how she'd ended up here. A monster who belonged with other monsters.

"You found your way to me," Nerissa said, her voice soothing yet haunting in its ease.

"More like I was brought to you. The halls shifted."

Nerissa hummed, seeming unfazed except for her slightly lifted brows. She plucked one rat of many scurrying creatures from the small cage, squeezing it tightly in a fist.

Raana watched in awe, disgust, and fascination as the elder witch honed her focus. She muttered words in the witch's First Language under her breath. The rat stilled, and its jaw opened on a hinge. Barely reacting, Nerissa reached over to the vial on a rack at her side. It was then that Raana noticed her other wares—vats of dark blood, monstrous organs, claws, and teeth.

From those beasts. Ingredients for whatever potion she brewed.

Nerissa dropped a rivulet of liquid onto the rat's tongue, then released it. The creature ran... then collapsed in a convulsing heap before it stilled.

Potions... or poisons.

"Mother above," Nerissa seethed. "Too much heartstring that time." She scribbled some notes down in the leather-bound journal at her side. It was filled with recipes and clippings, as well as drawings of plants and animal anatomy.

"Could I ever do that?" Raana asked, curiosity getting the best of her. "Potion work like this, I mean. You're creating brews from nothing but your mind, and they work—most of the time."

Nerissa's features curled slightly at the jab. "Likely not. It's a rare gift of my bloodline, like the persuasion. As divination is yours."

"I haven't really tried divination."

"I think you have without even realizing." She flipped to a new page. "I once killed a man with a cocktail, not realizing what I'd mixed. All subconsciously. My magic drew me to different ingredients." Raana's eyes widened, and Nerissa waved it off. "Don't mourn him. No one did. He was a bastard." She pursed her lips, going back to an older page with what looked to be a siren's tail, before flipping back. "Magic like this comes on gradually, divination likely even more so. If it didn't, it would overwhelm you and drive you mad. It's why I'm convinced the High Witch never learned about you. Seers cannot be seen, not truly. Which is why when she finds a powerful witch, one who may be greater than her, she binds them to her by blood before they reach their potential to keep them grounded and close."

An undercurrent of malice laced each of Nerissa's words. Raana didn't remember much about the High Witch or the mainland, where her image was splashed around on every corner of the three great witch cities.

Nerissa plucked up a vial from a bag behind her, the contents of it shimmering despite the low light. "Are those... siren scales?"

"Yes." Using a small set of forceps, Nerissa pulled one of them out.

Raana gaped. She'd never seen a siren. Their isles—for when they dwelled on land—were located in the far west of the world, their ocean kingdom likely just below it, though she wasn't sure if it ever had truly been charted. "How did you get them?"

"I plucked one out of the ocean myself." It was said with such conviction that Raana had nearly been convinced, but then she amended, "A merchant was peddling them, and you know they're authentic because..." She tapped the scale on the lip of the cauldron, a metallic clang reverberating in the room. "They're like plated armor." She dropped the scale into the vat. The liquid shone, then bubbled and steamed. "Sirens are the closest relative to the fae that we have in this realm. It's said the fae who didn't want to leave the mortal lands jumped into the ocean, became it, to evade our persecution after the War, and now they call mortals to the sea with song and promises of power to devour us in retribution. I'm sure the walls of their kingdom are lined with the bones of the gullible." Nerissa took hold of the large wooden ladle and stirred the brew, the air filling with a scent of sweetness. "You've never been curious to learn about your father? About where that shadowed blood comes from?"

Raana took a few steps away and turned, glancing into the endless forest and the beasts stalking around them. "According to Helene, he got my mother pregnant and left her. He wanted nothing to do with me, so why would I want to know anything about him?"

"Because you're smarter than that," Nerissa said. "He gave you power unlike anything else. If you could learn exactly where that ends, you would be an unstoppable force."

"And if I don't want to be?"

Nerissa sighed. "I understand your fear; I understand that you have been broken, but if you do not reforge yourself, it will be a tragedy like no other." The words were almost soft, matronly. They rattled in her skull.

I understand... I understand.

It was likely the words were Nerissa's persuasion, but Raana still tucked them close, packing them into her wounded heart.

"You and I are similar, child. Too powerful for our own good."

"If you're so powerful, how were you captured by the King?"

It was an honest question. Maybe one that didn't need to be delivered as snippily as it was. This woman was a murderer, so she should tread more carefully.

"Because greater forces than I conspire."

Spirits, did she ever stop speaking in riddles?

Raana folded her arms and spun to face her. "You know, you told me that there was someone I needed to meet and that there was work we needed to do before the *dark moon* that's supposed to screw the mortal realm to hell. But I've done nothing but wander these halls and play with my shadows for days."

Nerissa wafted her brew. "Because you're not ready. We can't trust you yet. I know what you'll do when you learn the truth, and we can't risk things not falling the way they're meant to."

We, we, we.

Raana felt her shadows rise. "So, what do I have to do to prove myself, then?"

Nerissa smiled as if that was exactly what she'd wanted Raana to ask. As if she were a rat just dropped into her cage. She tipped what appeared to be ground bone into her brew. "The coronation of the Luna of Deimos is coming soon, and during the ceremony, both she and the alpha will cut their palms and mix their blood with ashes and oil in a call to their Goddess to complete their union and their sharing of her power— wolves can have animosities towards us, but they have their own magic in their rituals. I'll need at least a vial full before the combined blood is brought to the temple and locked away where you'll never be able to get it."

"No."

The answer was immediate, assured. Blood magic of any kind, whether the blood of the caster or the blood of others, was dangerous and absolute. Whatever spell, all its force, would be for Kai and Isla and them alone. A wolf's immunity may not even matter. Raana wanted no part of that.

"Very well."

Raana blinked. That was too easy. "What do you need it for?"

"You aren't ready to know."

She growled under her breath. "Are you going to hurt them?"

A foolish question because... *murderer*.

An exasperated breath left her lips. "Never intentionally."

Raana's shadows coiled around her arms, snaked up her legs, and draped over her head like a cloak, settling like a crown. She could kill her and stop all of this.

"You could *try* to kill me, but you won't. Even if you're fae, it's not in your nature. Not yet. Sacrificing those wolves doesn't count." Nerissa met her widened eyes. "I don't need the ability to read minds to see you, girl. You wear your emotions clear as day, and I know how desperately you want to redeem yourself to him."

Him.

She spat the word.

Him... the Prince of Wolves. Spirits, Adrien probably hated her. She'd left him with hell to deal with and was responsible for the death of his friends.

"You're *better* than that, Raana." It felt strange to hear her name out of Nerissa's mouth. "Smarter. Surely, you know where your story ends. He would sooner drive a blade through your traitorous heart than take you as his queen. You wouldn't even be his mistress."

Raana could barely swallow. She remembered that aura of spring within him—his fated mate.

But then she remembered how he kissed her, the way he touched her.

He'd seen every dark, broken, and monstrous part of her, and he'd been the only one who had never walked away. He ran *towards* her, and that mattered far too much.

So, she'd left him before he could break her heart.

"There is no fairytale for *any* of us," Nerissa finished, taking another rat from the cage. "The sooner you realize that, the better off you'll be."

She watched as Nerissa went through her routine again. The dropper, the control.

"If I don't go, will you send one of your..." Raana trailed off, unsure what to call the wolves Nerissa kept hidden away within these walls. All under her manipulation and control—as Isla's mother had been. "Soldiers?"

She didn't know exactly how many she had. All she remembered was the man who'd carried her here in her magic-driven stupor—half awake, half *alive*. She'd searched for him, for some type of dungeon, but with the moving hallways, there wasn't much hope.

"Yes." Nerissa dropped the rat, allowing it to scurry away. Then it froze and cried out. Its skin seemed to bubble, expand. The creature grew and grew, its eyes flaring red, and then it died. More notes. Raana was going to be sick. "If you don't go, I will need to use other means, and with those, harm is much more likely. You're quicker, quieter, and can inflict minimal damage."

Raana was out of options. If she didn't help, Kai and Isla could be hurt, but if she did...

"Whatever you're doing with their blood won't hurt them or anyone they care about." Raana pointed to a small blade on the ground by Nerissa's folded legs. "Swear it to me right now by your own blood, and I'll go."

A small smile slid across Nerissa's lips as she reached for the knife. "It's not wise to make a bargain with the fae. They never truly give what they promise."

"Then you're lucky I'm half-witch."

CHAPTER 18

ISLA

Isla woke to an empty bed, though she didn't remember falling asleep in it.

Her shaking fingers raked over silken sheets, heady with Kai's scent but absent his warmth as the fog of her recurring nightmare cleared. She wrenched up, a gasp caught in her throat, and her body covered in a cold sweat as her hand dove under her pillow for the knife she kept there. The iron tang of blood stung her nose, but—

Not real.

With her heart thundering, she blinked, and steadily the raucousness of a battlefield, of that woman's voice, faded to the faint chirping of songbirds, and the metallic tinge of blood turned... floral? The vision of strewn corpses was replaced by their empty bedroom.

Empty.

Kai.

His side of the bed was bare, and even their duvet had somehow ended up on the floor. Adrien's voice, his warning of Cassius's plans, crowed in her head along with her nightmare's taunting.

He'd gone out on morning runs before, but today was her coronation.

Where the hell was he?

The bond felt wrong. Lately, it always felt wrong. But right now...
right now...

Isla moved, ice flooding her veins as she gripped her dagger so tight
the hilt indented her palms. She had to find him, even if he was just
downstairs. She needed to see that he was okay. Needed to get death out
of her head. She had to—

Flowers.

There were flowers on her bedside table next to a framed photo
crowned by an amethyst ribbon. Grayscale and grainy, the image of her
mate grinned, those dimples on display as he wrapped an arm around
her as she cupped his face in her hands, her lips smooshed against his
cheek in a loving, playful kiss.

The ice melted, and Isla's shoulders dropped.

The photo was from their date night a couple of weeks ago—their
first ever, unless their time spent researching, spying, or fighting counted
—taken by a local photographer who'd snapped them while they were
on a walk. Rather than asking him to trash the film as Marin likely
would've advised them, so they wouldn't be seen as so "commonly," they
had asked if he'd take another. Kai must've gotten a copy after it was
developed.

Isla lifted the silver, woven branch frame, a smile tugging her lips as
her gaze shifted to the stunning bouquet of autumn blooms, in hues of
burgundy and orange, browns and golds. She grabbed the folded note
near the book she recalled reading last night when she'd been in the
library. After talking with Adrien, she'd wanted to begin learning all she
could about this *dark moon*, not wasting a moment to pick up a tome about
charting the stars to gauge celestial events. Kai must've carried her back.

> *FOR THE MOST BEAUTIFUL*
> *QUEEN IN THE FOUR REALMS.*
> *BE BACK SOON.*
> *I LOVE YOU.*

Isla ran her hands over the ink and brought it closer to her nose to
catch his scent. *Real. Alive.* She let out a heavy breath, unsure whether
she was about to cry in relief or over how much she loved him.

He had to be safe, then. Wherever he'd gone. But the bond, something inside her, still felt... wrong.

But she couldn't linger on it for long, not with the blush pink that crept over the floor as dawn peeked over the mountaintops.

The countdown had begun. At dusk, as the sun faded and the goddesses rose with the moon to witness, the coronation ceremony would begin.

And she would be crowned the Luna of Deimos.

Late afternoon hit, and Kai was still missing.

Marin hadn't known that he'd left at all, let alone where he'd gone, and neither had Sol or any of the staff or guards. Isla couldn't make a huge fuss about it when she'd asked them, having to frame her question as something easy in passing, but she should've known that someone would see right through it.

Isla had dealt with Ameera's scrutinizing stare for ten minutes too long before she dismissed Marin's arsenal of doting handmaidens so the two of them could talk. The general carefully sat on the lip of the bath within the ornate bathing room, specifically situated in the Northern Hall to prepare the luna for events. "How long's he been gone?"

Isla's heavy sigh rippled the lukewarm water. She ran a sponge over her arm, dousing herself in the smells of spearmint and jasmine. Not as calming as she would've hoped. "Since this morning. He left me a note saying he'd be back soon, but didn't say where he was going."

Ameera pursed her lips. "All meetings today were canceled for the coronation."

"I'm aware."

Her voice softened even further, wary of any listening ears. "You can't feel him?"

Isla kept hers equally so. "Barely."

It had been with sheer grit and determination that she took the fragments of the bond, of herself, and hurtled each across the bridge between them, trying to re-forge the tether with whatever fire she possessed. But he was only a whisper of a tug, if anything. Perhaps, sometimes, she felt her heartbeat in phantom rhythm with his, but that could've just been in her mind as a comfort. Telling herself that he was alive.

"Could he be getting you a gift?"

Isla sank lower into the water, letting its warmth envelop her, just above her shoulders. "He already did." There was a steady pressing on her skull, right between her brows. A tap, tap, tap on her mind, but not from the bond. Not from Kai. Stress, anxiety, she didn't know what it was from, but with each ticking second since she'd woken up this morning, it was relentless. "What I do feel... is something's wrong."

"With him?" Ameera's body had become rigid, muscles in her arms flexing as if the word had triggered something deep within her, and for a moment, Isla saw a flash of wild emotions on the general's usual flawless, fierce exterior.

"No, not him," Isla answered quickly, but then reeled back. "I think he's fine. It's just... something."

It wasn't nearly as placating as she'd hoped, for Ameera or herself. The general was already rising. "I'll gather my band of fools, and we'll look for him." Rhydian and Jonah, Isla assumed. "It's not the first time he's disappeared on us."

Isla offered a soft smile in thanks. "Where was he the last time?"

Ameera's jaw tensed, and a bitter rage lingered under her words. "In Callisto, because he'd entered the Hunt and never thought to mention it to us."

Isla opened her mouth to defend him, to say he hadn't been thinking straight in the early months that followed his family's deaths, but it seemed Ameera had already figured that for herself.

The mention of the Hunt snagged in her mind. She recalled all they'd learned from Adrien the previous day, including about the spreading rot. If Kai had gone to investigate without her...

"Check along the Wall, the wasteland," she told Ameera, who didn't question why. Only nodded and left the room.

Two hours and forty-two minutes passed.

Two hours and forty-two fucking minutes, Isla was left with the silence of her paranoid thoughts as a team of stylists and artists scrubbed and plucked and preened her, rubbed her skin raw, and then soothed it to smoothness before lathering her in lotions and subtle perfumes. Two hours and forty-two minutes that she endured the pounding in her head.

And still no Kai.

In the small moments of reprieve from being prepared like a fine holiday meal, she tried to distract herself by reading, returning to her book on charting the stars and celestial events. Frankly, that only led to more frustrations because there was nothing about this supposed "dark moon" that Cassius had told Adrien about. Nothing about losing their ability to shift, the loss of magic, or bloodlust-ridden creatures.

The only interesting thing she found was how, on the equinoxes, the stars could be used to map the other realms. With the veil at its thinnest, constellations took the form of the eternally sealed doorways between their worlds, and the darkness of their sky—the reason it could be so unique and beautiful on nights like tonight—was because it was bleeding with the darkness of others. The realm of the fae, demons, deities, or all of them at once.

Isla shook away the chilling feeling of being watched.

Only hours remained until moonrise.

"Hey, careful, careful!"

From where Isla had been reaching for her glass of sparkling wine, she snapped her gaze up at Davina, who'd been with her for most of the afternoon. She looked beautiful in a rust-colored dress that, coupled with her dark makeup and coppery hair, made her appear as autumn incarnate.

Every one of their friends had a role to play today. While Rhydian, Jonah, and Ameera went looking for Kai, Davina kept her sane, and Sebastian and Adrien, little did they know, were Isla's eyes on her father's movements.

"I've got it." Isla drained the bubbling contents in an impressively graceful swig, careful not to disturb the pale blush that painted her lips.

"Marin will kill me if I let you ruin your makeup or dress," Maeve said from the small raised platform behind her. Isla's handmaiden had become more like a friend over these past weeks. "Or your dress."

Her coronation dress was layers of silk and velvet, of sparkling jewels and embroidery, that had been worked on over the past weeks by Deimos's most skilled seamstresses. Artisans she'd already showered in gifts and thanked a million times over. Heavy yet movable, so dark that it gobbled up the light in the room, the gown's embellishments glimmered like a sea of stars. The silver twining and diamond whorls over the bodice, tapering her waist and lining the trim that skimmed the marble floor of the dressing room, told a tale of the heavens. Even tiny gems trailed up her arms along her fitted sleeves and were carefully placed over the cape she'd don this evening.

She looked like she truly had been Goddess-blessed. If only she hadn't felt like a wreck.

"Kai would never do this to me on purpose. Something must be wrong." Isla gathered her skirts. She'd sat around and played the part long enough. "I'm going to find him."

"But Isla, your dress!" Davina rose from her seat, her hesitant movements betraying that she was all for Isla's searching and likely wanted to join her.

"I'll keep it clean." Before any arguments could come that there were already people out looking for Kai, Isla added, "*I* am his mate, and there is no point in any of this if he isn't standing next to me."

Isla wrenched open the door and stormed into the hallway, her dress billowing around her like a whirlwind of night.

Watery sunlight spilled through the airy windows of the suspended hallway connecting the North and Western Halls. Through the stone archways, Isla could see down the rolling hills in the expanse of Mavec. Not as well as she would've from the overlook before the stained-glass window, but enough to notice the bustling closer to the hall. Guards were being briefed on their posts, and ropes were set up to organize spectators and keep them off her processional path. Streamers billowed from poles, and decorations of harvest were being set across the grounds.

Marin had said the crowd that gathered would be something to behold. Though her actual anointing would take place in the throne room, where the audience would be limited, they would hold no citizen back from witnessing when she and Kai emerged to greet them as alpha and luna. A statement. She was their queen, and she would stand by Kai, stand by them, through anything.

A knot coiled in her stomach. "Where the hell are you?" Her whisper was caught in the breeze.

"Your Majesty."

Isla whipped around, beholding a bowing man dressed in a navy staff uniform. He was young, maybe around Kai's age, and his brown eyes shone with uncertainty as he rose. She wouldn't bother correcting him about her not being royal quite yet. "Yes?"

The staff member kept his head lowered as he closed the distance between them. Lowly, he said, "The alpha sent me to get you."

Isla jerked back, blinking. "The alpha? My mate, the alpha?"

Noticing that she'd drawn some attention from below, she shifted out of the window's eyeshot. "Where is he?" she whispered so aggressively that the staff member started.

"In one of the old staff quarters. I'll take you to him if you're finished... um, dressing."

Isla let out a heavy breath. "I'm very finished. Let's go."

The opening of the stone-carved path may as well have been the widened maw of a beast. Isla stood frozen at the cusp, her heart in her throat as she stared down into its dimness. The staff member—Jace, she'd learned—continued for a few steps before he realized she wasn't following.

He turned, his eyes questioning. "Your Majesty?"

Isla swallowed.

She was a warrior. She'd faced death countless times and survived. Had beaten beasts bigger than these immovable tunnel walls. But tight spaces, darkness, and the unknown... maybe she still hadn't quite recovered from what had happened beneath the arena. It felt like a boulder pressed down onto her chest, and for a few breaths, she struggled to take in air.

She should've taken a knife. Jace could easily have been lying. He could've been working for the witch—she'd never met him before, and how easy would it have been to snag a staff uniform and play the part to lure her into a trap?

"*Are you down here?*" She threw the words out, battling through that pounding in her skull. And perhaps it had been hope, but she swore she felt a tug—a pull—down the stairs.

Isla breathed, closing her eyes for a moment and digging deep. She acknowledged her fear, embraced it, and stepped into the darkness.

Isla wouldn't let Jace follow her back as they descended the stairs. The underground network must've also connected to the kitchens because it smelled divine, of autumn spices and the roast of a harvest.

When they came upon an old door that seemed to be crafted of worn iron, Isla paused and stepped to the side, inviting Jace to open it, while the risk of him pushing her in and trapping her here lingered in the back of her mind. The heavy entrance groaned open, and Isla leaned forward to peek inside, her nose twitching at the pungent stench of antiseptic. It wasn't a grand space, reminding her more of a safe room than living quarters, but she barely took in what lay inside. All she could focus on was a bare, muscular back and its familiar tattoos. Kai was hunched, head hung, until he met her gaze in the smeared mirror in front of him and turned sharply to face her.

Isla hadn't realized she was moving until she stumbled, eyes blinking wide at the blood-soaked bandages over his chest.

Though his features were tight with pain, a smile slid across his mouth as his eyes drew over her body. "Wow."

Isla's incredulous gaze snapped between his eyes and his wound. Once. Twice.

"What the hell happened?" She reached him as Kai gripped the vanity to support himself and reached across his chest. Isla immediately went to work on the poorly dressed injury, delicately pulling back the bandages to find the cuts still gaping, still leaking blood, though slowly. "How long ago did you get these?"

Kai cleared his throat, his nose twitching in pain as he shifted his shoulder. "A few hours ago."

"A few *hours*?"

A barrage of questions ran through her head, but they could wait. He wasn't healing properly.

"Thank you, Jace," Kai said, dismissing him.

But Isla called, "Wait!" She kept one hand braced against Kai as she counted off on her fingers. "I need thread, a needle, a candle, some matches, boiling water, and the strongest alcohol you can find. Please be discreet."

Jace bowed dutifully. "Yes, Your Majesty."

When he left, closing the door behind him, Isla felt her muscles tighten. This room was so small and smelled of blood, just as the tunnels had when she beheld Sebastian's near-dead body.

Breathe.

She felt the brush of a hand on her hip, and she turned to meet Kai's pained eyes full of concern and comfort *for her*. Like *she* was the one with holes in her chest.

Isla willed her fingers to be steady as she peeled the bandages away. "What. The hell. Happened?"

"I—*fuck*." Kai let out a ragged breath as she exposed the wounds and apologized, pressing lightly on the unmarred skin around them. Three deep slashes from his collarbones to his mid-torso.

From claws.

"I found a tunnel," he confessed, and Isla's fingers froze. She lifted her gaze again, harsh and imploring. "And there were bak in that tunnel. I killed all three, but one landed a good blow. I'd spent too long on my shift, used too much energy. My wolf is knocked out."

Three bak. *Three.*

Isla pointed to the small cot. "Sit." Kai obeyed, and she helped lower him to the mattress. Pacing a few steps back, Isla observed the soiled bandages, her injured mate, the drops of blood on the vanity, and then her, dressed like a queen, the jewels of her gown and woven into her hair glittering in the lantern light.

"You're stunning."

Isla spun back, unsure whether she was about to cry in relief or frustration. Unsure if she wanted to berate him for being a reckless asshole or kiss him until she couldn't breathe.

"You scared the shit out of me," she said, turning to gather what was left of the clean bandages and the antiseptic. She set the supplies on the bed beside her as she sat to face Kai.

For a few heartbeats, they just stared at each other, and no other part of the day mattered. Because he was here. He was alive. He was safe.

Kai cupped her face in gentle hands, holding her glossy gaze as he said, "I'm sorry."

His kiss was just as soft, and when his mouth met hers, Isla swore something cracked within her—but it wasn't a well of emotion. No. It was a spark of energy. An ember. A stoking of a flame. Not of lust, but something different. Something greater. Her mouth fell open as the warmth spread, the energy crackled.

When they parted, barely, still brow to brow, his breath was hers, and hers was his. *Alive and okay.* Both of them. "Why were you hunting in the tunnels alone?" she whispered.

Kai's fingers ran delicately over her cheek, her neck. "I never thought I'd end up there. I just needed to get out. Get away."

Isla leaned back, placing her hand over his. Was that why she'd felt so off? "Is that power acting up?"

Kai's throat bobbed, and now Isla could see the shadows cast over his eyes. "It's been worse today than any other. I was up a few hours before dawn, and it felt like I was about to burst right through my skin. I could barely think straight, see straight. I was afraid that I'd..."

He trailed off, but Isla knew where he was going. She squeezed his hand. "You can't hurt me, Kai. You cannot, and you will never."

His brows scrunched, fear and doubt evident. "I don't understand why it's so bad today. It's like it *led me* there. To the bak, to that tunnel."

A knock on the door had them separating.

Jace returned with everything Isla had requested, plus a small cauldron of boiling water conveniently stuffed into a small wicker basket. She thanked him and asked if he'd quietly inform Ameera of Kai's return and to just *leave it* at that. They'd decide how and what to explain later.

With wares spread over the mattress, Isla got to work. Kai lit the candle while she carefully threaded her needle with the boiled thread. Her mind reeled back to the lessons in suturing wounds that had been part of her warrior training. Although healing occurred naturally most of the time, some wounds needed manual manipulation.

"Hold still."

Kai handled the first piercing of his skin, at the top of his cut near his collarbone, remarkably well, though he did take a long drink of whatever bitter alcohol Jace had found. As Isla moved down his skin with expert precision, each stitch brought a vision of her mate taking on three of those horrendous creatures and surviving.

"That's seven bak you've killed now," Isla said, gnawing her lip between her teeth.

Kai chuckled, then drank. "You were beating me by one; I couldn't have that."

Isla snorted. *Prick.* "Don't make me laugh, or I'll mess this up." She narrowed her eyes in focus as she pulled the thread tighter. Given the depth of the wounds and that it had taken them so long to heal, he'd probably end up scarring. Frankly, she didn't think he cared. There was a phantom pinch at her shoulder, where the twisting vines of her injuries lay from the Hunt.

Halfway down his chest, Isla couldn't resist asking—she needed to know more.

And so, Kai explained how he found the three bak all tucked together like they'd made the tunnels their home. Their den.

So strange.

Kai's voice softened, and his eyes drifted to the gashes in his chest. "They were so *not like bak* that I thought I was hallucinating, but I could scent the Wilds so clearly. And once they realized I was there, they didn't attack at first." His jaw tightened. "It almost seemed like they were yielding."

"To you?"

Kai nodded. "And I truly thought about walking away, but the idea of yielding or leaving didn't last long for either of us."

Isla listened as he broke down every maneuver of the fight, every duck, lunge, and weave, each landed blow, because he knew she'd want to hear it and knew she would stow the information away for future strategy. He told her how that power had pushed, how he thought it may have helped him, gave him an edge in an impossible battle, as if he could predict every move as they cornered him.

His trek home after he'd cleaned off in a lake and gotten the bleeding to subside had been hell without his wolf.

"All I wanted was you and a fucking bath." Kai tilted his head back to rest on the wall behind him. Isla had just finished her work on the largest slash marks and observed the one below it. It was shorter, cutting just to the top of his abdomen.

She met his gaze as he repeated, "I'm sorry. I'm sure today's already been a lot."

"I feel like this is the most relaxed I've been. Probably because you're home, but..." Isla sighed. "I would take on three bak, or I would stand before that witch and rip out her throat, but the crown... I put on a decent front, but I'm scared. Of the coronation, of ruling, and then being the queen every moment after. I'll do whatever I can, whatever I must, but I can't guarantee I'll do it right."

"You can't do it wrong." Kai reached out a hand and brushed her cheek. She most definitely *could,* but she appreciated the sentiment. He added, "*I'd* be lying if I said I haven't been scared, too, regardless of my bloodline."

"What made it easier?"

"I met a beautiful woman with a smartass mouth and legs for days." Isla was beaming and needed to put the thread down as Kai continued, his thumb stroking her cheek. "And everything that had scared me just became challenges. Challenges I *wanted* to face. Even without doing anything with our bond, I wanted to become a better man because you were out there. A woman who would stop at nothing to get what she wanted. Who loved her family and her home so much that I could see it in her eyes and could hear it in the way others spoke about her. Who loved as fiercely as she would fight for anyone, regardless of who they were. I wanted to feel that if we found our way back to each other, I would deserve to call myself your mate. I wanted to deserve you." He paused, and his eyes trailed over her once as if in disbelief that she was sitting there. "All of the things that make me love you so much that I can barely breathe when I look at you are exactly why you will be an unbelievable queen."

Isla wasn't sure where she'd thrown the needle as she lunged for Kai, careful of his injury, of the blood, and crashed her lips to his.

That ember within her sparked again, sending heat pounding through her blood as her fingers tangled in his hair, as his hand gripped her hip. There was such a deep, fundamental *need* for him that it was maddening.

"I love you," she murmured over his mouth, their breathing ragged. "And not that you needed to, but you have earned every bit of my heart."

Once Kai was patched up, Isla let him guide her through the tunnel system to the kitchens and the source of that divine smell. To say the cooks were surprised was an understatement, but they were more than happy to give them the first taste of the beef stew they'd been preparing, before they had the rest of the night off for the coronation and holiday.

Bowl in hand, she watched as Kai and the cook discussed cutting techniques before Isla and Kai found a corner of the kitchen to talk.

On her short stool, set before a small wooden table, Isla dunked a piece of bread into the hearty broth, while a symphony of pots and pans echoed around them. "Before we seal up the tunnel, I want to see it, map it, and look for any more markers. I don't know if you got to talk to Jonah last night, but he figured out the pattern of the symbols on the ones we have, and it looks like if the tunnel connects to us, it's etched into it. I know we have more pressing problems, and more just got thrown at us last night, but it's good to know."

Kai, now on his third bowl of stew, scraped the bottom with his own bread. "We can go tomorrow night."

Isla's brows shot up, her prepared rebuttal for his absolute refusal dying on her tongue. Just the other day, he didn't want her walking around rogue territory alone. "You'll be well enough?"

Kai rolled his shoulders. "I already feel better, thanks to you." Finished with his meal, he leaned back in his seat, a healthy flush having finally returned to his face. His eyes slid across the kitchen, the blaze of the oven gilding his irises, his brow pinched.

"What are you thinking?" Isla asked, bringing a chunk of beef to her mouth.

"Too many things." He fell forward again, resting his elbows on the table. "Did you find anything in your search of the stars?"

"No." Isla pursed her lips, setting down her spoon as nausea stirred in her gut. "A part of me is hoping this is just some elaborate lie from Cassius to scare us. This is the last thing we need."

"Or maybe it's exactly what we need and explains why everything's going to shit." At Isla's confusion, Kai elaborated, "Patterns. Five hundred years ago, a cosmic cataclysmic event sent the mortal realm spiraling. *Five hundred years ago*, a pack was destroyed like never before—all ties and traces of it *allegedly* erased by the Hierarchy. Cassius is the only one who knows. Maybe his ancestors have always been the only ones who knew and used it to their advantage. Now, the creatures created in that time are acting strange, everything is being covered up again, and the whole world just seems off, and I..."

"You?"

"I have no idea what's going on with me, but I can *feel* something wrong. It's as if *my ancestors* are trying to tell me to be cautious. To watch out." Kai's jaw tightened, and he tapped his finger on the table, thinking, debating. "Aneurin was the final Alpha of Phobos. He was my blood, and he went up against the Hierarchy—or tried to—and he was destroyed by the Imperial Alpha. Through a *witch*."

Patterns, patterns, patterns.

Isla swallowed, the stew sitting heavily in her stomach. "You think history is repeating here, with us?"

"It's a theory." Kai's mouth thinned. "Fate apparently lacks originality."

Fate also *apparently* hated her.

Isla couldn't stop her fingers from curling into fists. The disdain she'd once had for the deity reared its head. This all completely tracked with the goddess's wicked games.

The phantom scent of ash lilies tickled her nose, and her hands felt sticky with blood that wasn't there. Despite the oven's heat, an unnatural chill settled in her bones as she recalled a battlefield, a war, a dagger over her heart, and a voice.

If you fail, they all fall.

CHAPTER 19

KAI

Every time Kai walked into the throne room, his insides turned to lead. It had been over five months since his coronation, and still, it hadn't gotten easier.

There had been no celebration that day. He didn't recall much from the week—hell, the *month*—that followed his father and brother's deaths, but he did remember that.

He hadn't been sure why they hadn't waited to crown him. At that point, he'd already been hurried through the Alpha Rite, where he was brought to near-death, saw the heavens, survived the "endless forest" to reach the Goddess, who blessed him with her power and "bore him anew."

So, dealing with all the pomp of a coronation while everyone was still in mourning seemed unnecessary, even downright disrespectful, if he were being truthful.

He had been nothing but a puppet then, barely able to grasp any type of reality. Survival had been his only goal—it was all they needed him to do, frankly. Make it to the next day, then the next. Figure it all out as he went, or their kingdom would come crashing down. Just as much as his life had.

"Alpha Kai of Deimos!"

The boom of the High Elder's voice proclaiming his imminent arrival

166

brought him back to himself as he stood in the antechamber behind the throne room. Kai swallowed the lump in his throat and steeled himself as he gave his sore shoulder one last rub. Four elders clad in their signature pale blue robes, and two priestesses in their obsidian garb, with silver and moonstone circlets over their brows, stood before him. Slowly and straight-backed, they began the procession into the sacred, cavernous space.

The scent of jasmine hit Kai first, the incense burning on the altar that lay a few feet before him as he crossed the archway. He was certainly getting sick of that foreboding smell. Every time he'd been around it, in a call to the goddesses, it hadn't meant anything good.

But *today*...

When Kai focused his hearing, he couldn't miss the crowd's roar beyond the Northern Hall's stone, and Goddess, did he wish he was out there to see it. To see Isla's face as she took it all in—the waving hands, the beaming grins, and the shouts of her name. Guards lined the streets from the Pack Hall all the way down to Abalys. He wasn't going to let anything ruin this or threaten her today.

Seven steps lay between the ground and the dais, and the two thrones were perched on the inky marble platform, high above them all.

The seats themselves were simple, their darkness woven with gilded vines like veins, yes, but the true grandeur of the alpha and luna's chairs lay in what surrounded them. The stone had been carved with depictions of wolves, forests flourishing with life and their beginnings, below renderings of the Goddess, Fate, and Eternity. The moon, the stars, and the night sky. Three women, three sisters, ethereal and eternal. Creator, Weaver, End. Always watching.

With the lunar rise, the crystals wedged into the stone seemed to pulse and glow, much like the ones in tunnel walls and those that lined Mavec's streets. A phenomenon that made their kingdom unique.

A lilt of notes bounced off the walls as a steady hymn fluttered from the choir in the corner of the chamber. On cue, the procession walking the curve of the fourth step divided, and without thinking, Kai's body knew where to take him. Up and up until his booted foot hit the sleek, night-dark marble, and he rose to the pinnacle of what may as well have been a mountain for how hard it felt to breathe.

For a moment, Kai paused, his eyes sliding over the two empty, glorious thrones, with only the goddesses dwelling above them. The silver branches of his crown clawed deep into his scalp, sitting so heavy that he ducked his head. Every time he came up here, he remembered his father. He remembered Jaden. Remembered this seat was not his. Had never been *his*.

And yet still, he had to take it.

Every step to the throne felt like powering through quicksand. The crescendo of the choir faded to nothing but white noise because of the sound within him—a roaring that rivaled that of the crowd outside, a thrashing of something wild and haphazardly tamed against his ribcage.

You are no king.

Kai shook the thought, said in his father's voice, out of his head. Shook off the weight of five months of suppressed feelings. Shook off the pain. Shook off the guilt and shame. He became numb.

His knees touched the edge of the metal, and he turned and took a seat.

All eyes were fixed on him.

He wasn't sure how silence could be so Goddess-damn loud. How eyes and auras could scream at him, pounding against his skull so hard that he gritted his teeth.

His eyes drifted to where his mother stood, a soft grin on her face that did not appear as it had on the day of *his* coronation. Back when he could see the grief, the facade she fought to maintain, so clearly in her eyes that he made a vow never to break. He'd come the closest to that shattering point when Isla had nearly died.

You do not deserve this.

His chest constricted, his fingers tightening on the cool arms of the throne.

This room was too confined. There were too many people. Too many sights, smells, and sounds, too much havoc inside for this void to feast on as it fought to tear itself free, fought to tear him apart.

He sought out his friends, his family, any distraction amongst the spectators on the long wooden benches that had been brought in for observation, but each glance felt like leveling a blade at someone's chest. One strike, and he'd cut too deep.

Pull back.

The double doors of the throne room opened, a gentle breeze sweeping through in their wake.

And there stood the most beautiful woman he had ever seen.

All who had been seated, including him, rose to their feet, turning to Isla, who waited at the entrance. The two shifted wolves given the honor of escorting her—one of them Rhydian—dropped into low bows.

Isla was meant to step forward, but she froze, her eyes sweeping the crowd. She clenched and unclenched her fists before she clasped her hands. She was nervous, looking for her family.

"Isla."

He didn't think his call had made it to her, but something had. Isla lifted her eyes to his, and the distance between them vanished. They stood upon the broken road they had crafted once before, just a handsbreadth away from embracing, but enough for a phantom touch.

With a smile threatening his lips, Kai said, *"Just focus on me."*

Isla's head dipped in the slightest nod, then she straightened, knocked her shoulders back, and moved. Her cape trailed behind her like a sea of stars as she passed each observer, all of them gawking, dropping into bows, and not rising until she was well away.

Perfectly in sync with each of her movements, Kai descended the steps as she climbed. Asked and answered. Beginning and end. Until they met, finally, at the altar's edge, where he took her soft hand in his.

As the two of them united, the choir ceased, and the room—the *world*—waited on bated breath.

The High Elder descended from where he had lingered just below Kai on the sixth step and threw out his arms. "Let us begin."

CHAPTER 20

ISLA

Isla had never been to a coronation. She'd never been great at visiting the temples to worship the goddesses either, and during her lumerosi ceremonies, any stories from the Elders were of strength, power, and promise. But she'd never heard so much of the *beginning*.

She listened from beside Kai behind the altar as the High Elder, a portly and astute-looking man, told the tale of Selene, the Goddess—a woman who once walked upon the mortal realm as flesh and blood in defiance of the higher deities to live amidst those they'd created. He told of her sisters, Destinare and Aeterna, who soon joined her. But before they were united, amidst the treacherous, uncharted land that was the world of those who would come to pass, Selene had been attacked by a demon from the realm of the damned when all paths between the worlds were open, only to be saved by a wolf in what became known as the Forest of Selene. A location that Rhea was able to tout as belonging to them.

As the story was recounted, and the High Elder explained her creation of the wolf shifters as protectors of the mortal world from those of the others, Isla's eyes trailed over the spectators. They were mostly high-ranking officials and other elders, and then there was her family. Her father sat with Sebastian and Adrien, her brother and best friend failing to keep grins off their faces, while her father...

He wasn't watching her. His eyes were fixated on her mate, his brows pinched.

Isla felt her wolf rise in a way she hadn't in a while, in a way that would've thrilled her if she wasn't so uneasy. Her father was acting strange—too strange.

She felt the brush of a hand against hers, the interaction hidden behind the solid marble. Both she and Kai did well not to make it obvious, not flinching or paying each other any mind. Kai's pinky twisted around hers as if to say, *what is it?*

Isla breathed, her eyes dropping from her father's roaming ones to the material on the altar as she tiptoed across the bond she'd worked even harder at reforging all morning. But even if she could find a way to communicate with him, she wasn't sure what she'd say or if she even wanted to acknowledge her fears about her father.

The Elders began shuffling, and Isla turned her head to watch as a box was brought forth. No more than a hands-breadth in height or width, but long enough to expand beyond the chest of the young woman who held it. Given the way her blinks timed with each of her steps and how her hands trembled, she was eager and anxious. The metal-worked body of the box seemed heavy, too.

Slowly, Isla pulled her hand from Kai's as they, not the story, became the center of attention.

It was almost time.

Heart in her throat, Isla watched as a heavy fabric was lifted from the altar, revealing a golden basin, its shell swiped in intricate details and patterns of dark paint. Inside were two crossed pieces of muddy-colored bark, dried enough that the small limbs must've been cut free long ago.

"Wood from the Forest of Selene sprouted from our goddesses' spilled blood." She recalled that from Marin's lessons, as well as the oil in the palm-sized carafe that the High Elder lifted, harvested from the tree's labors.

Isla counted off her fingers to banish the downward spiral of her thoughts, briefly contemplating her next moves if this went horribly wrong. Because this moment, this ritual, would change *everything*.

She hadn't gone through the Luna Rite—she wouldn't have survived it without her wolf, even with Kai as an anchor—which meant her wolf's eyes had not yet shifted from their common blue hue to a queen's signature amethyst.

If she stood before this crowd and the shift didn't happen, not only would her mating bond with Kai be called into question, but her inability to shift would be wholly exposed.

Kai took hold of her hand now, stroking his thumb over the back of it as she fought to keep her breathing even. The Elder who held the box undid its latch and slowly pried open the lid.

What the hell?

Isla started, clamping her lips shut to prevent the words from falling out of her mouth. She blinked a few times to make sure what she was seeing was real, giving Kai's hand a tight squeeze.

An eerily familiar dagger sat upon the cushioned surface lining the box. A blade that may as well have been the one Jonah had been keeping in the safe of his bookshop apartment. The one Lukas had tried to murder her with.

The dagger. But it couldn't be.

She sought Jonah in the crowd, unable to stop herself, but he seemed more confused and intrigued by her attention than some mastermind with a plan.

Snapping her gaze forward again, Isla could feel Kai's eyes on her, and she ran, *sprinted,* across the patchwork bridge of their tenuous bond, yelling into the smoky void for him to pay attention. Asking if he'd known—if somehow there were two of these.

"Nearly two millennia ago," the High Elder continued, his voice heavier. "Our goddesses crafted a blade of stone and stars and sky, of their essence, and used it to offer their blood to create the first of the alphas. Made in its image, blessed by the divine sisters, with this ceremonial dagger, our alpha will offer his blood, his goddess-blessed power to his fated."

Isla wasn't sure why, but a deep part of her screamed to stop this. To pause, to let her think. Her mind whirred, trying to scrape together a reason for the similarities.

Kai had the blade in his right hand now, his gaze never leaving hers, a darkness clouding his eyes that made her wonder if he was fighting a thunderous voice of his own. A voice that may have made him hesitate as he looked down upon the hand that he'd already cut once. A voice that was telling him to run, to fight.

Isla felt Fate shove at her back, hard, digging her claws in as her delicate whisper caressed Isla's ear, *I am not done with you yet.*

No.

Kai drew the blade across his flesh, and the scent of his blood made something in Isla's body twist. Come alive.

The crimson pooled and dripped onto the marble floor from the tip of the dagger as he turned and held it out to her. All the while, an Elder poured the oil over the wood in the basin, using a match to set it ablaze. The heat, though gentle, wrapped around Isla with grabbing fingers, leeching into her skin to pluck at those ever-present cold spots on her bones. The smoke that invaded her nose carried the scent of jasmine.

With a hand sturdier than she felt inside, Isla reached for the outstretched dagger, her fingers brushing Kai's as she took hold of the ancient hilt. His touch burned as much as the fire would've, and she couldn't fight her desire to melt with that flame.

Isla took in the dagger, making note of how it compared to the one in Jonah's keeping. This blade did not sing to her as the other did. It felt odd in her hand—too light, too tawdry.

Wait, she thought, scrambling to make connections, but Fate pushed at her again.

There were so many people watching her, watching them. Waiting. Isla breathed, fixating on the pale flesh of her right palm.

She pressed the cool metal to her skin and slid, not feeling pain but adrenaline. She couldn't draw in a breath, as if something had coiled around her insides. Her wolf even wobbled to its paws, standing at attention. Waiting, too.

"Bound by destiny, blood, and power, alpha and mate will call upon the deities for a final blessing of their union and an entrustment of their gifts to lead us all."

Kai held out his hand for her, looking and feeling more ethereal and otherworldly in his crown than Isla had ever seen of him before. And when she took his hand...

Nothing had ever been so intimate.

Not even when they slept together had she felt this stripped down and exposed. Never had she felt so certain that he was *everything.* That her soul would find his in every universe, over every lifetime. That it had. Over and over and over.

There was a shifting inside her, between them. Everything peeled away to find this final pure essence of *her*. Of him. Of why they'd been created. The pooling blood between their palms was molten ore, forging a universe between their clasped hands that they would not allow to fall and break. *Could not.*

Isla's body moved of its own accord, Kai's too, as they extended their arms over the blaze.

Together, they would do this. Together, they would get through everything.

Their grip on each other's hands tightened, a crimson rivulet seeping beyond their grasp and kissing the writhing flames.

And then, everything erupted.

CHAPTER 21

ISLA

Shouts and gasps of awe, shock, and confusion echoed throughout the room, a backdrop to the roar of fire. Isla had narrowly avoided being singed by the blaze when Kai had shielded her, stepping them back and slipping onto the steps behind them.

An electric current surged through her blood, her entire body pulsing with energy, with... power.

With her breathing ragged and her bloodied hand soaking the fabric of Kai's shirt, Isla peered up from where she had buried her face in his neck, wincing at the bright spots in her vision. Wincing at how loud the world was. In a way she hadn't experienced in nearly a month, but also in a way that was *more*. Looking at Kai right then felt like looking at a god. Striking and untouchable, the fire cast a dark reflection on the bends of his crown, the shadows dancing over his face, darkening his eyes that gleamed with the flame they looked upon.

She turned her head, unable to see beyond the fiery plume that stretched so tremendously it nearly brushed the high ceilings. It was beautiful, ferocious, and daunting. The crystals embedded in the walls around them seemed to quiver with a resonant lunar aura that could've only been divine.

"This didn't happen last time. To my parents or me," Kai muttered, and Isla met his gaze, a simmering red beneath his irises. Suddenly, his breath caught, his jaw dropping as his eyes locked on hers.

Isla gripped him tighter. "What?"

Kai cupped her cheek, his gaze glossing over as he fought a too-wide grin. The aura of his wolf overpowered her senses, dominating the room, and the mysterious power within him seemed to caress her bones with phantom hands, considering her in a way it never had before.

"Your eyes," he whispered in wonder, in disbelief.

Isla blinked. "My eyes?"

Kai tilted his head to the side, and Isla followed to where the ivory marble of the altar had been so polished that she could see a blurred version of herself, her eyes now illuminated a deep shade of violet.

"Oh, Goddess." The words fell on a breath, a near-choked sob.

She closed and opened them again. And again. Still, the color remained.

This was... real.

Tears sprouted too fast, and for a moment, she ignored everything else around her. With her eyes finally alight, her lumerosi burning, she had to see, to know. She tried to shift.

Her back arched, but not from the pain of her wolf taking hold, but from the agony of being dunked in an icy lake, her wolf trapped behind a patch of frigid darkness, like the bars of a cage of her own making.

"No," she panted, her features twisting. "No, please."

Kai placed his fingers beneath her chin, turning her head to him. "Give it time." His throat bobbed, and his jaw tightened as she still glowed and burned. "You're incredible."

The rasp in his voice, the simplest truth of all this, washed away any disappointment Isla had felt.

She leaned forward, thankful for the altar that shielded them from the crowd, and for the fire that still burned, though it began to dwindle. "You're not alone anymore." She brought her hand up to his face. "Never again."

"Never again," Kai echoed, and the kiss they shared, the small sound she'd made as his lips moved along hers, as his essence dug into her skin, was less than chaste. They weren't in that throne room anymore. They were somewhere else—somewhere more extraordinary and above the world—within themselves, crafted by darkness and cut through by burning light.

Eternal, ever-present, and powerful enough to rattle the realms if they wished.

The flames had ebbed to a steady smolder by the time they broke from their embrace, and when they rose, Kai offered Isla a hand while the room beheld them with reverence. Maybe even fear, *puzzlement*. Even the elders and priestesses looked surprised.

So, blood spawning a bonfire mustn't have been common at all.

Isla watched the elders smother the basin, leaving nothing but blood and ashes behind. Then, Kai's hand left hers as he stepped back and up to the step just below the dais. Isla remained where she was as a new priestess emerged from the antechamber. The back of her eyes stung as she beheld what lay in her hands. A crown crafted of silver and obsidian gemstones, as magnificent as the one Kai wore, sat on a velvet pillow.

Hers.

The final piece. The last adornment.

Isla bit back against another rush of tears.

The priestess ceased her steps a foot from Isla, bowed to her, and then shifted to offer the High Elder the crown as he stood at Isla's back.

"May the goddesses take witness," the High Elder proclaimed. "May the wolves of the north, south, east, and west take witness. May the beings beyond hear this call." He reached for the crown, holding it firmly between his spiderweb-veined hands, and leveled it above her head. "Isla of Deimos, do you swear to give your life, body, blood, and soul to this kingdom and its people?"

Isla swallowed, her gaze fluttering to the crowd where she found her family. The boys were still smiling, maybe even glassy-eyed, and her father...

Her spine locked up.

The only way she could describe how he looked was distressed, as though someone had him pressed against a wall with a knife to his throat. As if he hadn't truly grasped the reality of this coronation until the oath.

Isla of *Deimos*.

Their stares met and held, as they had throughout her life. With every word of wisdom, every expression of affection, every admonishment. They may have fought and disagreed, and she may have felt lost, trapped, and misunderstood, but she never questioned how much he loved her. Never questioned that he was her greatest supporter. She was his fighter, his little warrior. Especially after her mother had... gone away.

She should've been there beside him. Her next words were her first step in rectifying the hell Cassius had put her family through.

"That is my vow," Isla said, her voice echoing off the chamber's wall. Steady. Certain. She pushed her shoulders back and kept her head high. "From this breath until my very last. I promise to nurture, protect, and guide Deimos and its people, *my* people, with all that I am and could become."

"Then let it be so."

Isla's breath caught as the crown lowered onto her head, settling heavier than she'd expected it to be.

The High Elder stepped away from her, tucking his hands in the sleeves of his robe. "It is my honor to present Her Majesty, Luna Isla of Deimos. Long may she reign."

"*Long may she reign*," the words echoed back, and Isla found the rest of her family in the crowd—Davina wiping her eyes, a now-guard-uniform-clad Rhydian beside her with an arm over her shoulders, and a surprisingly smiling Ameera and Jonah. Their eyes drifted from her to the man behind her.

Isla turned to Kai, who waited on the final step before the dais. The dimples in his cheeks were visible despite his attempts to hide his grin. He subtly knocked his head to the side, possibly even tugged at the bond, urging her to *hurry up*.

Isla took hold of her dress to keep it out of her way as she ascended the steps. Her hand, the wound still fresh, slid into his, and together, they took the final step.

Isla didn't look at her throne, though. Or him. Her gaze drew up to the goddesses etched into the stone, stopping on Fate, the beautiful deity with a thread woven between her hands.

That tapping was back again. The pounding on her skull. But Isla brushed it away and allowed Kai to guide her to sit.

She turned, facing the spectators, and lowered onto the thin, cold cushion, the high back making her feel so small. With her hands braced on each metal arm, Isla watched as Kai hesitated, giving the crowd a chance to appreciate *her*, it seemed, before he took his place.

Isla's joy bubbled into a laugh as the cheering began, then a chant of her name, and more calls for a long reign. With cheeks hurting, she twisted to Kai, who seemed only to see her. Then the choir began and was joined by an orchestra somewhere beyond the walls.

As the world beheld the Alpha and Luna of Deimos.

CHAPTER 22

ISLA

Isla wasn't sure where they'd ended up, but frankly, she didn't care. All she could focus on was the feeling of Kai's lips on her neck, his hands on her hips, waist, and breasts. The brushes of his skin beneath her fingers as she worked down the buttons of his shirt. Fresh from their time parading on the veranda, waving and beaming at their people, they had crashed through a door in the Northern Hall, not even bothering to check what or who lay inside.

"Kai," she moaned his name, the backs of her thighs colliding with something solid, a table maybe, sending whatever had been on it clattering to the floor.

Isla turned, Kai's breath hot on the shell of her ear as she finally took in their surroundings. A private showroom or well-decorated study, barely illuminated by the moonlight spilling through the window, the art and sculptures that surrounded them were shadowed. On the floor by their feet, a ceramic bowl that had fallen from the raised display platform ceased its rolling. She couldn't see if it had cracked. Couldn't make out if the piece had been valuable. Hell, all of this must've been.

"Shit."

"It's fine," Kai breathed, grabbing her ass with both hands as he lifted her, wincing slightly as she hooked her legs around his middle.

Isla tried to wriggle from his grasp. "You're hurt."

"I don't care." Gripping her so tightly she thought she'd bruise, he pinned her between him and the wall.

Goddess. She savored the feeling of all his strength and power lined up against her. Her nails scratched at the bare skin of his back, his muscles flexing beneath the touch.

"Do you know how impossible it is for me to control myself around you?" he ground out in time with his hands slipping beneath the heavy fabric of her gown, baring her to the cool air and the heat of his skin. "Do you know how badly I want to destroy this fucking dress?"

"Don't rip—" Isla whimpered as he pressed his hips forward so perfectly that her core throbbed. "Goddess, just get this off me."

Kai chuckled, dragging his teeth down the column of her neck, biting at her fluttering pulse. Her body tightened when he clamped down on the sensitive space between her neck and shoulder, not enough to darken her mark again, but enough to remind her who she belonged to. "Is that a command, *Your Majesty*?"

Isla moaned as his touch slid higher, mapping every bend, curve, and hollow of her body, claiming it. She rolled her hips, needing more friction—needing him inside her. His fingers, his tongue, his cock, she didn't care. The ember that had bloomed earlier when they kissed had become an inferno that raged hotter than the sun itself. More than a lust for his body. More than lust entirely.

It was madness—all-consuming madness.

Somewhere in her haze, Isla must've said yes, because her feet were on the ground now, realizing just how pliant her body had become. From him. For him.

She turned and braced her hands on the wall in front of her, beside a myriad of fine ceramics displayed in a glass case that she could see Kai in. He worked at her back, unthreading the laces of her gown, a smug smirk as he purposefully took his time, kissing her neck and skimming his knuckles over her spine. Occasionally, he'd grab her face, twisting her head back to kiss her lips, nip at them. She rubbed her thighs together in a demand for him to hurry up, earning another deep laugh.

Once her gown was a heap on the floor, the cool darkness of the room swept over her flaming skin, her nipples pebbled and aching against the silk of her slip, her body screaming for him to touch her, just *touch her*.

As if he could hear those screaming thoughts, Kai answered, his arms snaking around her and pulling her back against his bare chest. Her gaze focused on the two of them in the glass, their crowns still glinting on their heads.

She bit down on a whine as he skimmed over her peaked nipple, his other hand dropping lower to her underwear. He shredded through it before his gentle fingers grazed up her sensitive inner thigh. Coaxing, teasing, not quite reaching where she needed him.

"Do you remember the first time I got to hold you like this?" Kai's voice was a deep rolling purr.

Isla's mind reeled back. Every touch of his had been branded into her, every embrace an imprint on her soul. The way their bodies molded. The way his thumb skimmed just beneath her breast, how his fingers traced her hips.

She whispered, "When we touched for the first time."

A maddening accident after everything they'd done to stay apart.

Maybe being pushed into him in the chaos of the rogue attack was another one of Fate's cruel games.

Kai hummed, his fingers climbing higher, his head dipping lower into the crook of her neck.

Isla reached up, wrapping her arm around him and twisting her fingers in his hair. She braced her feet further apart and stretched out to give him more access. He heeded the hint and took advantage, hands mapping a greedy path over her skin. She felt him smile against her neck, and they made eye contact in the reflection of the glass case.

"I damn near lost my mind," he said, his touch ghosting over where she ached for him most. "I still don't think I've recovered from it. Not being able to touch you, taste you, the woman who ravaged, ruined, and saved me with just one look, a few words." Isla gasped as he finally pressed his fingers to her clit, moving in lazy circles that sent pleasure zapping through her. Her toes curled, and she rolled her hips, breathing his name. "After that night in the gardens, you became every dream. Every waking thought."

With her eyes sliding closed, she lolled against his shoulder, baring her neck entirely to him as he worked between her thighs. His circles grew tighter, *faster*, with just enough pressure to have her straining and digging her nails into him. Her lower belly knotted; her muscles burned.

"You became mine," she exhaled before a whimper fell from her lips. "And I—I hated you for it." His muscular arm held her closer as her legs shook, as he crept her nearer to bliss.

Kai's chuckle rumbled down her spine, igniting every nerve. "I never hated you, you know. Just the fact that I couldn't have you. Because I knew *this...*" Tighter and tighter. Faster. Relentless. Isla was like a bowstring pulled taut, completely prepared to fall apart. "Getting to watch and feel you come undone would be something I'd never experience, and that was a tragedy—because *look at you.*"

There was enough command in Kai's voice that Isla opened her eyes. In the reflection of the glass, she took in their embrace, the way he held her, and how her body responded to him. Her slip may as well have disappeared; the silken fabric was hiked up her hips and pulled down below her chest.

"You're a goddess," he whispered into her ear, and it was an effort for her not to fold entirely. "One I plan to worship for a very, *very* long time."

It was difficult to oppose that. "But the—the party."

"Can wait." He scraped his teeth over her mark, and Isla felt the bond lock up, thrum from that deep chasm of *them* they'd unearthed during the coronation. "So, do you want to come now, or do you want to play?"

Isla bit her lip so hard it nearly bled, watching as Kai touched her, worshiped her. She was so close that thunder rumbled in the distance, a precursor to the streak of lightning that threatened to strike through her. But—

"S—stop."

Kai immediately ceased his movements but still held her tight as Isla sucked down air, trembling legs rubbing together in her tumble away from oblivion. A unique form of torture, but the ecstasy that awaited when she climbed that mountain again and finally fell would be worth it. Especially if she had him buried inside her.

Suddenly, Kai gripped her hips and whipped her around. Her back collided with the wall; her head protected by his hand that beat it there. He corralled her as he held her stare—dark, lustful, and dangerous. "Mark me."

"What?"

Kai's eyes narrowed—the eyes of an alpha, a king, but also her mate, her equal. Commanding, yet something submissive lay beneath them. Just for her. "*Mark* me."

Isla's brows furrowed. "I... I can't." If she couldn't shift, couldn't draw her claws, she certainly wouldn't be able to draw her teeth.

"*Yes*, you can," Kai said. "I can feel you in there."

Isla shook her head. "I tried during the coronation, and I couldn't."

"There was too much noise. Now, it's just you and me." He leaned in closer, enough that she had to crane her neck to look at him. "I didn't think you were someone who backed down from a challenge."

"*I'm not.*"

"Sounds like you are to me."

Isla growled low in her throat, and Kai's grin was handsomely feral. Each one of his following words, though easy and languid, hit hard and burrowed deep. "Show the world how I belong to you. My mate, my wife, my warrior, my queen. Every breath, every beat of my fucking heart is yours. It has been since the night I met you." He moved even closer, his lips barely brushing hers. "So, take me, use me, *claim* me. I'm at your mercy until the end of time. That is my vow to you."

Isla had never welcomed such carnal possessiveness so readily. Ancient, claiming, and cruel, it tore viciously through her blood. She focused on the dark red simmer behind the storms of Kai's eyes, the way his lumerosi glowed. His wolf howled out for hers, for the piece that had been missing for far too long. Isla could feel her wolf attempt to rise in response.

Her eyes drew over Kai's face one last time before she dropped her head, closed her eyes, and *breathed*.

She needed to go back to the basics, the fundamentals, from a time long ago when she was a young pup, finally learning what potential lay in this body of hers. She felt the smallest shudder of her bones, her back arching at the now-familiar wash of icy pain.

Isla cursed, her arm snapping out as she took hold of Kai's shoulder. He closed in, the warmth of his body chasing the cold away. "I've got you."

Isla nodded, panting through gritted teeth.

Focus. Breathe. Let the energy flow.

Her energy moved like sludge. And there was that wall—a shimmering, impenetrable veil.

Claim me.

Maybe she could call on her wolf another way. Isla fed off the possessive tug, allowing that deep, ingrained desire for her mate, her other half, to take over. Her breathing shallowed as she became dizzy, her limbs feeling like they were about to shatter.

"Kai." A near whimper.

"I'm right here." He pressed in, wrapping his arms around her.

Isla's eyes fluttered open, flaring with determination as they met his, still burning that blood-red.

Kai's hold on her tightened ever so slightly. "What do you feel? What do you think when you look at me? Say it."

Isla swallowed. "Mine," she answered lowly. "You're mine."

"Good. Now, *show me.*"

Isla gave one last pull, hauling up whatever she could from inside herself, and in a flash of pain, tasted the salty tang of sweat mixed with copper in her mouth. Her tongue slid over her teeth, then recoiled at the sharpness of her canines. Her lumerosi burned, and from the way Kai beamed down at her, as brightly as she smiled up at him, she guessed her eyes glowed, too.

"There you are." Kai smiled, brushing back her sweaty hair. "I hope that didn't tire you out too much because we've only just started."

Isla failed to give him a deadpan look before lifting on her toes to kiss him, using gentle hands on his partially bandaged chest to usher him back. She'd spotted a small couch earlier with her wandering eye, and she knew exactly where she wanted him next. The moment his legs hit the base of the seat, he fell back.

As a conquering queen, Isla looked down upon him, her canines still sharp and eager to pierce his skin. *Soon.*

First, they would play.

While Kai finished the work she'd started while they moved, tugging down his pants, she lifted her slip over her head. They still wore their crowns.

With his fist wrapped around his freed length, Kai's eyes greedily drank her in. "So fucking perfect."

Isla chuffed a laugh, watching as he pumped himself slowly, her fingers twitching at her sides, eager to take over.

She lowered herself onto the couch, straddling him. Kai released his hold on himself and cupped her ass again. Isla's nose twitched at the scent of the air thick with their arousal. The peaks of her nipples barely grazed his chest, her slickness nearly dripping between them.

Cocking her head to the side, she gripped his chin and asked with seductive sweetness, "Who do you belong to, Alpha?"

"You." Kai didn't hesitate and sucked down a breath when her hand drew a blazing trail down his abdomen, muscles flexing with every bid for air. "Only you."

Isla traced a single finger along the smooth underside of his shaft before gripping tightly near the tip. Her hand barely fit around him, and yet, when they fucked, it felt like he was made for her. She stroked him, making him hold her tighter and arch his hips into her touch. A Goddess-damn alpha in the palm of her hand.

She ran her thumb along the broad head, her mouth drying at the moisture she collected there. "And what do you want?"

"Anything you'll give me."

It was said with such conviction that a thrill zapped up Isla's spine. Another leisurely stroke. She leaned in, running her tongue along the column of his throat to his ear. "Would you beg for it?"

"I'd crawl for you."

Isla hummed, allowing the sound to travel the path where she'd returned to his neck, where she let her teeth graze that spot her wolf craved. The scars of her previous bite still lingered, and she scraped along the raised, pearlescent skin, the animal inside her thrashing to be set free.

"*Isla.*"

That was a plea from his lips.

She leaned back, smirking. "Later," she whispered and rose on her knees.

She positioned him at her entrance, rubbing the head through her wetness before sliding down, down. Her muscles strained as she slowly took every glorious inch of him into her body, Kai's hands guiding until he was so deep inside her that she couldn't think.

"*Fuck.*"

She needed to hear him say her name again. Needed him to keep looking at her like she was all the realms in one.

Isla lifted and slammed her hips down, moaning at the shock of pleasure that sparked every nerve, that flared hotter when she rocked her hips, brushing that spot at the apex of her thighs. Goddess, he felt incredible. The stretch and fill to the very edge of pain.

Isla crushed her mouth to his, the kiss deep, claiming, and desperate as his tongue slid into her mouth, and they built a rhythm. He met her stroke for stroke with an upward thrust of his hips, his hands exploring her skin as she chased her pleasure. *More, more, more.*

With her back arching, his name a prayer on her lips, Isla gave herself over to him and every alive thing he made her feel. To this divine bond that linked them. To their mingling breaths, the twining of life, the pounding of their hearts as they barreled through ecstasy together.

Together. Always together. They couldn't be ripped apart. Never again. She wouldn't allow it.

It didn't take long for her to reach that precipice of oblivion again, her cries and his grunts echoing off the study's walls as the knot in her belly became impossibly tight and ready to snap.

"Isla."

A low, growling beckon—one that resounded deep inside her and made her teeth ache.

Isla tore her mouth from his, bringing it down to the tender flesh between his neck and shoulder. She wrapped her arms around him, hugging her sweat-slicked body closer as their movements slowed to an intense, purposeful, and luxurious pace, as he shifted his hips in a way that made her eyes roll back, hitting her deeper than he ever had.

Pushed her right over that glittering edge.

Her orgasm ripped through her as her teeth pierced his skin.

Mine.

The word echoed in her head along with Kai's moan as her bite dug into him, staking her claim on his flesh and feeling the warmth of his blood trickle into her mouth. And then, she *was* that golden thread, their bond, humming with pleasure, brimming with pressure, about to burst with whatever magic this universe their souls crafted was made from.

Isla pulled back, licking his blood from the corner of her mouth as she met his drunken, smug, sex-dazed smile that made her want to fuck him for hours. She wasn't done with him. Not even close. And judging by the fact he was still hard, he wasn't done either.

Kai brushed away a piece of golden hair stuck to her forehead. "That's my girl."

Isla bit back a smile at the praise. She leaned in closer again, her mouth brushing over his. "You said you'd take anything I gave you." Before they retracted, she dragged her canines over his bottom lip. "Now, give me *everything*."

She knew the unspoken words were clear to him. *Don't hold back.*

And thank the Goddess that when he flipped them, pressing her back into the couch and lifting her legs over his shoulders, he didn't.

CHAPTER 23

ADRIEN

The people of Deimos really knew how to throw a party. Adrien was thankful for the sheer number of revelers flooding the lower squares of Mavec, making it easier for him, Sebastian, and Malakai to blend in.

They sat at a restaurant by the river's edge, watching from the stone bank as boats bobbed along the water. On and around them, pack members ate, drank, danced, shopped at vendor stalls, and filled the sky with lanterns brimming with their wishes and gratitudes, if he recalled the tradition correctly.

Occasionally, thunder would rumble, a distant rolling sound, but no one seemed concerned about rain ruining the night.

It wasn't unusual to experience the same ambiance in Io—hell, the Golden Avenue was spectacular, especially around the Summer Solstice —but there was something different about this place. About today. It spoke to something deep inside him, tugging at him. It had been a while since he'd seen such pure joy. Not happiness simply because of survival, not at the expense of another, just... a celebration because they were alive. Because everything was *good*. This community had been dealt a heavy hand, but today... today was like coming up for air after being underwater for too long. Something he had desperately needed.

"Have either of you seen Isla?" Malakai asked from beside him, the plate of food before him barely touched as he scanned the mingling crowd.

Sebastian, who'd already scoffed down his meal, snuck a fritter off his father's cooling pile.

"She's probably changing into a new dress." He waved the morsel in an arc before popping it in his mouth. "I swear, every day, she goes through at least three outfits."

Despite his words, Sebastian's gaze slid to Adrien, lip curling and a knowing look in his eyes. His better guess for where Isla had gone with her mate was probably the last thing Malakai wanted to hear.

The Imperial Beta sighed and dug into his food.

"Are you alright, old man?" Sebastian went to swipe another fritter but earned a slap on the hand with Malakai's fork. Recoiling, he met his father's narrowed eyes, pine-colored mirrors of his own. "You've been white as a ghost since Isla and Kai nearly burned the place down."

Adrien grimaced.

He'd tried his best to forget about *that* moment, just for tonight. He swore he could still feel the heat burrowed beneath his skin from the tunneling flames that shot to the ceiling, sending everyone in their seats faltering back. He'd never seen anything like it before, and though it had slipped his mind, the significance of the ritual and what the offering of the blood represented, especially when burned, gave him a sinking feeling that whatever Kai and Isla had ignited served as a beacon.

A target, bigger than they may have already been.

News would spread, and he had no idea how his father would feel when it reached him. Given Malakai's reaction, he may have realized it, too. Maybe it would be a good idea to pull him aside so they could plan what to say when they returned to Io.

For a few moments, Adrien watched the Beta stew in silence, pushing around the food on his plate. "It just happened so fast."

"That's how mates work, isn't it?" Sebastian said. "Find each other and run off into the sunset? Everyone was pushing her to choose someone a few years ago."

What looked like regret flew over Malakai's face before he swept his utensil beneath a fritter and skillfully flipped it onto his son's plate, a swagger to his movements that shouldn't have surprised Adrien as much as it did. From all the tales of their youth that the prince had heard,

Malakai had always been the lightness to his own father's nature, through childhood, battle, and his rise to power. "I always imagined she'd take them back to Io."

A part of Adrien had always thought the same.

Malakai dipped his head. "Isla of Deimos," he muttered.

Even Adrien hadn't completely adjusted to hearing it yet, a sinking feeling pitting his stomach.

"She's still Isla," Sebastian reassured him, gnawing on his fritter. "A know-it-all pain in my ass."

Adrien couldn't hold in his laugh. They were words laced with love, though Malakai barely flinched.

Adrien's stare collided with Sebastian's, his best friend's lips turning down as he surveyed his downtrodden father. His knitted brows betrayed the deep concern clawing through him, and Adrien recalled the same look on his friend's face once, long ago, when he couldn't do anything while he watched his father fall into a pit after losing his mate.

Sebastian made another attempt. "Hey, you still have me."

Malakai finally lifted his head, his eyes scanning his son's face. "Yes, a know-it-all pain in my ass."

Sebastian's shoulders dropped, relieved and shaking as he laughed. Adrien couldn't help but feel the reprieve, too.

"Fair." Sebastian grabbed a toothpick and leaned back in his seat. "She's worse, though."

A resounding crackle and pop drew Adrien's attention outward to where a shimmering light burst and filtered through the cloudy sky, alongside some of the bobbing lanterns. The crowd around him pointed and gawked.

His lips ticked up in a smile. Happiness. Life.

A coolness around his wrist suddenly pulsed, and he glanced down just in time to catch the nearly imperceptible sliver of shadow skittering up his sleeve. He hoped neither man alongside him at the table had noticed.

He couldn't explain how or why one of Raana's shadows had attached to him, as if she'd somehow marked him, not with her bite but with magic. It was dangerous to let it linger, but even if he'd known how to make it go away, he wasn't sure he wanted to. If the shadows were a part of her, its *existence* told him she was still alive.

A small pulse.

Another roll of distant thunder shook the sky, making everyone gasp and look up. Some threw their arms out to embrace the oncoming onslaught of droplets. But nothing fell; only a soft rain-kissed breeze blew by, making the hair on Adrien's neck stand up and sending Raana's shadow meandering over his body to his back.

That was three times now without a hint of rain or lightning. If it meant the storm was building, maybe they should start thinking about shelter.

"Are you ready to return with me tomorrow morning?"

Adrien turned his attention back to the others, watching Sebastian's face contort in confusion at the question. "Tomorrow morning?"

A line etched itself between Malakai's brows. It didn't seem to be the reaction he'd been hoping for. "Now that the coronation's over, Cassius will expect you both back."

Adrien's gut twisted at the mention of his father. Goddess, the hell he would have to deal with once he got home. But at least he'd warned Isla and Kai of the Alpha's plans. It probably made him a traitor, but whether it was to his father alone or to his entire pack, he wasn't sure.

Sebastian's features darkened, and his voice took on an uncharacteristic coldness. "Why?"

"*Why?*" Malakai leaned in, his widened eyes narrowing. "I think that goes without question. You were granted temporary leave for the coronation, but now it's time to return home."

Home.

The word trudged through him.

A muscle feathered Sebastian's cheek. He had always been so great at hiding his emotions, but his discontent flashed like a beacon. "I want to be here for Isla, at least until things have settled. She just became luna, and today may be a day of celebration, and Kai has the pack patrolled to high hell, but those defenses will loosen. I know some people don't want her here—I've gotten into brawls with them. Fate or no."

"*What?*" Malakai's fingers tightened on his fork, his mouth curling as if to say *who,* but he reeled back, remaining silent until he calmed. "I'm sure Isla and Kai have prepared for that. She doesn't need you, and staying will only do more harm than good." He lowered his voice. "Word will travel that the three of us are here today. It'll be said throughout the continent. There's already curiosity about what this union means for the relationship between Io and Deimos. What it means for Deimos's status within the empire, if it puts them above the others."

"And what if it does?" Sebastian asked, and Malakai observed him as though he'd transformed into a whole new person.

"I think you've been here too long," he answered through gritted teeth. "The hierarchy that has survived for nearly a millennium depends on balance in the continent. Ten kingdoms, one as a ruling body to centralize and represent them within the world and equal power amidst the rest, who govern how they see fit."

This hierarchy has technically only stood for five hundred years, Adrien thought. There was no need to bring up that there had once been *eleven* packs in Morai.

"Tension is already rising. Rogues, rebellion..."

The words hit Adrien like a blow to the head. "What do you mean *rebellion*?"

Malakai turned to the prince, his features rigid as he said, "Come *home*, and I'll explain." He straightened when it seemed the crowd around them began to pay attention. "But Cassius wants—*needs*—to do everything he can to prevent it."

Sebastian sniffed, opening his mouth to retort when his gaze drifted up behind them. Adrien turned, and his brows lifted in surprise.

Warrior General Eli stood with his shoulders back, his warrior's uniform nowhere to be seen, replaced by common but elegant clothes suitable for the holiday, but didn't betray his station. Despite his well-kept appearance, the dark circles under his bloodshot eyes and a throbbing vein in his temple told of a wildness beneath.

"Imperial Heir, Imperial Beta." Eli bowed his head to both Adrien and Malakai. Sebastian also got a slight dip in greeting.

Malakai's nostrils flared, and despite the cheerful lilt of his voice, a gravely undercurrent underlined it. "General, what can I do for you?"

"I'm happy I ran into you." Eli gave a tight, almost smug smile, like he'd cornered a doe in the woods. But he was staring down at another predator. One bigger and stronger. "It's like you've been avoiding me."

"It's my daughter's coronation, General," Malakai bit out. "Avoiding you would be the least of my concerns."

"I need a word." The emptiness behind Eli's stare glimmered. Malakai seemed to trace it as Eli added, "It's imperative."

Adrien and Sebastian exchanged glances at the blatant disrespect—approaching the Imperial Beta without notice and *demanding* a conference.

"Very well."

Adrien felt his features twist in surprise as the Beta rose with a light command for their accompanying guards to stay put before he left with Eli without protest.

What the hell was that about?

Adrien felt frustration roiling his blood. So many unsaid words. So many damn secrets. Not just around here—fucking everywhere. It wouldn't be long until they built up to the point that one whisper may as well have been a scream that shattered the world.

As though in answer, the skies grumbled again, this roll of thunder punctuated by a tickle of the shadow along Adrien's neck. It settled just above his pulse and beat against it... the way Raana's heart had once drummed in rhythm with his when she was spread beneath him.

He grimaced at the spear of pain through his chest and resisted the urge to swat the shadow away.

Ta-dum... ta-dum... ta-dum.

"What do you think that was about?" Sebastian asked, leaning in.

"I don't know." Adrien's gaze snagged on the Pack Hall's pearly stained-glass window, a glittering gem amidst the swirling storm clouds—a watchful eye. An involuntary shiver trailed up his spine. "It could be anything."

Sebastian had resumed picking at his teeth, letting out a low hum. "I overheard that Kai wants the warriors gone. They think they can handle the rogues on their own." His voice wobbled slightly in question, given what Malakai had disclosed. "Maybe Eli wants to stay."

"Why would he want that?"

"Who knows? He was also making a bid for my sister, and from all I'd seen and heard before, my father encouraged the pairing, even if nothing formal was done about it. Isla would've gone on a rampage."

Adrien could only imagine. Not forcing Isla into anything was probably the best thing Kai could've done to win her.

Adrien glanced down at the food he'd ignored, skewering a cold, charred bell pepper with his fork. "Well, she's clearly off the market now, but if Eli still wants to join the Imperial family..."

Sebastian laughed. "Not my type."

Adrien smirked, lifting the roasted vegetable lazily in front of him, avoiding his friend's eyes. "You know, you've been oddly quiet about Ameera."

He met them now, watching Sebastian's eyes flash and a grin he'd seen countless times since they'd come of age slide across his face. "Who?"

Adrien snorted. "You son of a bitch." He brought the pepper back down to his plate. "You got her to sleep with you. How?" It seemed like there had never been a woman Sebastian had wanted that he hadn't managed to tangle in his web.

"We didn't sleep together," Sebastian said, but that glint in his eye...

"She told you whatever it was would never happen again if you told anyone," Adrien concluded.

"I will not confirm nor deny that statement." He gave the area around them a once-over and then suddenly shoved to his feet. "Want to take a walk?"

Adrien found no reason to say no.

Sebastian clapped a hand down on the shoulder of each of the Imperial guards who had been with them. They were relatively young, newer recruits that Adrien was surprised Malakai had approved to come along. He felt like an asshole for not remembering or bothering to ask for their names. "You two can take a load off. Eat, drink, and enjoy the holiday."

One of them sat up taller. "But the Imperial Heir—"

"Made it across half the continent without drawing any attention," Adrien cut him off. "We can manage without an escort."

With his hands in his pockets, Adrien tipped his head back to the chilly night air, the scent of spices digging into his nose. He was careful to avoid the laughing children whizzing through the streets, a few being chastised by their parents as they got too close to the river's edge. Some of them wore masks they'd decorated or beaded necklaces and bracelets they'd made—the former a tradition of the Equinox, and the latter honoring their new queen. Others had their eyes aglow, claws exposed as they engaged in a game of tag. It was reckless, dangerous even. They'd probably only just gotten a hold of their wolves.

Fifteen years ago, Sebastian, Isla, and he were probably doing the same thing.

A glance to his side, where his best friend stood, made the next breath that fell from Adrien's mouth easier than it had been in far too long.

Goddess, he'd missed his friends. As selfish as it was, he hoped Sebastian would come home.

"So," he began, his eyes tracing the luminescent crystal path before them, "is *Ameera* why you want to stay so badly? Because whatever you just fed your father about being here for Isla, I get it, but... Isla is the luna. She has guards, she has Kai, and she's *Isla*. I don't think she'll need your protection."

Sebastian opened his mouth. Closed it. He went quiet for several paces toward wherever they were moving before finally muttering, "I'm going to sound fucking crazy."

"More than usual?" Adrien joked, but Sebastian yielded no other emotion. So, this was serious, then. "What happened?"

A wave of emotions cascaded over Sebastian's face as he cracked his knuckles, stretched his neck, and observed the leafy-garland-covered storefronts as if they held answers. "I think..." He cleared his throat and swallowed. "I think my mother's alive."

Adrien stumbled, stopped, and then forced himself to keep walking.

His eyes tore over his friend's face to find any type of mirth. But what kind of twisted joke would that be? That stone seriousness, now layered with doubt, still sat on Sebastian's features.

Adrien hadn't a clue what to say. "That's..."

"Goddess-damn mad, I know." Sebastian blew out a hard breath, that cocky, aloof persona vanishing entirely, replaced by something raw. "I've... been down this path before, years ago, and I eventually agreed with everyone that I was probably in some heavy denial that she was just fucking *gone*." A crack slipped into his voice. "And I know it's almost been a decade, which is why I haven't mentioned it to Isla or my father. But." He paused and met Adrien's eyes. "Do you remember when I took off running in Abalys? When you and Isla chased after me?"

At Adrien's nod, Sebastian continued, "I scented something near us. Something *familiar* to me. I couldn't figure out why or where I remembered it from. I just followed it, but then it clicked later that night while I was lying in bed. It was the same scent that lingered in my room after she tucked me into bed as a kid. When she read me stories and swore she'd protect me from monsters." His lip curled, and Adrien could almost hear his friend's heart fissuring. "It was my mother, Adrien. Goddess, Fate, Eternity, the whole divine unit as my witness. It was her." He shook his head, his jaw tensing. "They never did find her body."

A glimmer of hope in the macabre fact.

Adrien blinked, letting his friend's words turn in his head, tossing them until they made sense.

Apolla being alive would be a miracle. It was... impossible. He remembered well Sebastian's spiral when they'd been fourteen, wanting to voyage the southern territories where she'd last been seen. They'd almost done it, almost escaped.

"But your parents' bond—"

"Fated bonds can fracture; we know that now," he said. "My parents chose each other. If she ended up hurt enough to the point where she can't reach her wolf anymore, then my father could've felt it like a broken bond."

His tone was a cacophony of despair and hope.

Adrien answered tightly, carefully. "That would mean she's been in the southern territories all this time. You think she would abandon your father? Abandon you and Isla?"

"*No.*"

The ferocity behind the answer nearly faltered Adrien's steps. He shouldn't have even suggested it. Apolla loved her family, loved her children more than anything, it seemed. She hadn't even wanted to go on that mission his father had sent her on.

Cassius *again.*

Guilt gnawed at Adrien's gut.

"I just..." Sebastian clenched and unclenched his fists. "I don't know what to do, but I can't ignore this. I need to be sure, so I'm going to find her."

"How?" It was a genuine, earnest question.

Adrien would try to help in any way he could, and Sebastian seemed to sense that with the slightest lift of the corner of his lips. "To start, I've been in Abalys nearly every night for the past couple of weeks. Which is where I crossed paths with a certain warrior general, turned spymaster and potential beta."

Adrien's brows lifted. *Ameera* as Kai's new beta? Interesting, considering what he'd heard about her father.

"What do you get when two people trying to escape their baggage run into each other at a bar?" Sebastian mused vaguely.

Adrien breathed a laugh. "An attempt at distraction."

He knew the punchline all too well. Only for him, it hadn't been a bar but an inn with only one bed. Then, a Pack Hall...

His stomach pitted, and he couldn't pinpoint one of his emotions. It was just too much. Too much pain, betrayal, then a small relief she'd escaped his father. But worst of all... longing.

Adrien cleared his throat, wanting to change the subject. "You're sure you don't want to tell Isla what you're thinking?"

"She'll think I'm nuts," Sebastian said. "And it took her so long to adjust to the loss. No point in reopening a wound until I'm certain."

Ta-dum... ta-dum... ta-dum.

Like an echo in his ears, Adrien picked up a heartbeat that drummed over his, felt it in the shadow pulsing against his neck. It writhed against him. Tried to... push him. Turn him.

Ta-dum... ta-dum...ta-dum.

Adrien stopped short, whirling around, his instinct rising to the surface as he felt a pull at something inside him. His eyes furiously scanned the crowd, sorting through the ocean of pack members. Searching, *searching...*

Ta-dum... ta-dum—

"Everything okay?"

Adrien jumped at Sebastian's voice, and his shoulders relaxed slightly. He let out a hard breath, turning back and shaking his head as he rubbed that cool patch on his neck. "Yeah, I just thought I heard something."

CHAPTER 24

RAANA

Raana felt Adrien before she saw him.

The sensation came in a whoosh, a hit of something like the wind that spawned gooseflesh on her skin and wrenched the breath from her lungs. She'd spun from where she'd been working on a mask at a vendor's stall, eyes furiously scanning the crowd for the source of what may as well have been a siren's song, for the pull she felt towards it. It would've been wiser to stay put, not to leave Nerissa's soldier—the same one who had carried her through the Wilds that day—that she'd come on this mission with alone, but she couldn't stop herself from following the call. Her iron-confined shadows whispered wildly in her ear as she sifted through the masses, her face hidden beneath her hood.

The crowd had crested and crashed like waves along a rocky coast, and when the sea parted... there he was.

She didn't know what to do with herself as she took him in as if he somehow could've changed since she last saw him. Raven-black hair, golden-green eyes, and a powerfully built body that moved through the horde with effortless regality.

He was okay. Still alive. Still breathing.

The wash of relief, sorrow, and rage threatened to drown her where she stood. He wasn't supposed to be here for the coronation. At least,

199

that's what he'd told her back in Callisto, but something must've changed. Maybe he finally stood up to his father... or had been banished.

No. That would be too easy. She imagined if it came down to it, Cassius—wretched asshole that he was—would simply see Adrien as *expendable.*

With that thought, blinding hot ire poured into her veins like molten ore, and she watched as Adrien paused. She stiffened as the prince turned his head... in the wrong direction.

Thank the Mother.

She realized now that he wasn't alone. Sebastian, Isla's brother and Adrien's friend, came up behind the prince, scanning the crowd, too. Raana took advantage of Adrien's distraction and fell back, ducking her head deeper into her hood, not noticing the tears that had welled in her eyes until she felt the wetness drip down the slope of her nose, the million apologies she owed him dead on her tongue.

For once, she craved the comfort of her shadows, wishing they would wrap her up and sweep her away from here.

She never thought she'd see him again, and more painful than anything was that for one fluttering heartbeat, seeing him left room for hope to bloom. It gave her a second to remember, to feel what being with him was like—every touch, every laugh, every quiet moment of under-standing.

The only person who had never abandoned her.

When Raana reached the vendor, Nerissa's soldier had barely moved an inch, earning a stare from the man working the booth, so she did her best to keep her voice cheerful. "We need to go."

"Too much to drink?" the vendor asked her, his salt-and-pepper mustache twitching as he grinned and subtly gestured towards her companion.

Raana forced a smile and an endearing look towards her counterpart. "Maybe a little."

She looped an arm through the soldier's, the muscles of his arm tensing beneath her touch.

Always tense. Always alert. Always under this spell.

Shame chomped at her insides as she waited for a knife to the ribs that blessedly never came. The two of them would need to play this part when necessary. At least, somehow, he seemed to understand that.

"Lighten up, friend. It's the Equinox! The winds are charging, our alpha won his challenge, and we have a new queen. His fated, Goddess-chosen." The vendor lifted a hand towards Raana. "And you have a beautiful woman on your arm."

The soldier's face didn't waver, and Raana again plastered on a smile, flashing a demure look and willing away the heat to her cheeks at the flattery. "Don't mind him." She reached for the masks she'd been decorating, frowning at the jewels that had gone off-kilter on the brow bone because she'd used too little glue.

"You should let them dry," the vendor said, a roll of thunder punctuating the words.

Raana ignored him, lifting her head with raised brows as she took in the sky. The light of the stars wheeled and shifted. Constellations illuminating, dimming... forming?

She squinted, pain lashing across her forehead as her hidden shadows' whispers caressed her ears, and she could've sworn the velvet blanket above pulsed.

"Another night of rain." The vendor's lament wasn't enough to tear her gaze from the sky. "I can't remember the last time we saw so many storms. Can you?"

Undeniable, skin-bursting pressure built from her toes, up her legs, back, neck, and head, until the tips of her fingers tingled.

"Goddess, your nose is bleeding."

Raana snapped her head down, blinking at the man as she tried to clear the gleaming map of stars from her eyes. Her free hand lifted to her nose, where warmth *had* begun to pool. She pulled back to observe the crimson. Odd. She hadn't been using magic.

The vendor's once jovial attitude began to peel away, his hardening gaze shifting between Raana and her companion. His nose twitched like he'd scented something, his eyes sliding to the iron bracelet clamped around her wrist like a manacle. The jewelry that held her enchantment and glamor together certainly wouldn't last forever.

Time to go.

With nothing but a *Happy Equinox*, Raana grabbed the masks, handed one to the soldier, and dragged him into the crowd. At a safe distance, she cut her hand on the side of her blade, quickly recasting the spell to mask her scent, just in case.

Back on task.

They'd come this far, and now she needed Kai and Isla's blood before they locked it away.

She couldn't fail. People would be hurt if she failed, and she wouldn't allow any more blood or death where she could prevent it.

The stained-glass window of the Pack Hall—so jarring to see after she'd been behind Phobos's shattered counterpart—served as their compass as Raana moved towards the hall, powering forward until she felt the occasional jerk from her companion to change directions for safer, better-hidden travel, evading the many guards that Kai and Isla had out for the night.

Raana couldn't see much of his face beyond the dark red surface of his mask, his eyes so deeply set that she could barely make out their vacant amber. Her gaze drifted to the faint scars on his neck, just exposed beneath his tunic as he moved. Two nubbed points of pearlescent skin gleamed under the streetlamps. Could they have been...

She felt the phantom caress of Adrien's teeth along her neck, the thrill of it, how her body sang at it. A wolf's bite, *where* they'd been bitten —it meant something.

Whoever this man was... he had a mate somewhere out there.

Mother above.

Raana's stomach hollowed out, disgust crawling up her throat. This was a man with an entire life, and she was stringing him along like a puppet.

Monster, monster, monster.

How did this make her any better than Nerissa?

Once they'd reached a shrouded pine forest, Raana's steps slowed, and the man whipped his head to her in demand to pick up the pace.

Before she could doubt herself, she asked, "Do you have a name?"

She couldn't see any movement on his face below the mask. Though he did swallow, and she watched the mark shift with the action.

She repeated, slower, "Do you have a name?"

"I..."

She waited for his answer, but then he ripped free from her hold so violently he nearly tore off her arm. He reached for his head, breathing hard through gritted teeth, as if riffling through his memories was too painful.

Raana gasped. Was this some failsafe for the enchantment?

"No. No, no, no. I'm sorry." Raana reached out to comfort him, but he reared back again, tears slipping down his chin from the small space at the bottom of his mask.

Something weighed heavily in the folds of her cloak. Another failsafe. A needle filled with poison strong enough to weaken his wolf and make him more complacent. It was to be her last resort since she'd need to carry him through her shadows once he was unconscious because of it. Or—

"If he becomes too much to handle, you may dispose of him. There are others." Nerissa's detachment as she handed her the blade and poison made her feel sick.

Raana struggled to swallow her disgust.

There had to be an alternative. Raana had no gift of persuasion, but she had *magic.* Even a thin veil to smooth those painful cracks in his consciousness might be enough to soothe him.

Taking her conduit in hand, feeling the stone burn beneath her touch, Raana began the chant in the First Language, stepping closer as she cooed the words. The soldier's erratic movements eased, and he allowed her to place a hand on his arm as she finished speaking. Raana was certain she was about to vomit. Not from the exertion, but she may as well have been holding a blade to his heart as she eliminated his sense of self.

"Are you okay?" she asked, feeling breathless and broken, mindlessly wiping blood from her nose and catching the tears that had fallen down her cheeks.

The man didn't answer, only straightened and turned to face the hill.

Then he kept moving.

~

Using her shadows, she'd moved them into a darkened room she'd observed from outside the Pack Hall. A gamble, considering she hadn't been sure who or what would be inside. Thankfully, it had been empty. Just an ornately decorated drawing room. It was nice to see an interior that wasn't cursed or crumbling to pieces.

Raana stretched out a hand to her companion, her heart shattering as she observed him. He may as well have been a ghost.

Once they got through this, she would help him. She would get him *out*. Away from Nerissa and away from her.

"Don't move," she commanded softly. "It's better if only one of us is in the halls, and I can blend into the shadows. I'll meet you back here. If you hear anyone, hide."

Raana stared at her open palm, her hands shaking beyond her control, making her wonder when exactly her magic's reserves would run out. Darkness slid along her fingers, welling in her hand, the shadow a swirling, ebbing mist.

"Keep an eye on him," she whispered to it. When she dropped her arm, the darkness remained bobbing where it had been.

Thankfully, the room's door opened on silent hinges, and Raana stealthily slipped into the hallway. She paused, turning her head left and right, embracing the quiet, cool darkness as the shadows danced on the walls from the lit sconces. For a moment, she swore she saw shapes, movement, and heard the faintest of hollow murmurs.

See the unseen. Hear the unheard. That's what Cassius had once told her of her power. Shadows held secrets, chronicled the past, and harbored knowledge they seemed eager to share with her. If only it wasn't in tongues that she didn't understand—the most she could do was sense feeling.

Save for some modern updates and alterations, this palace, with its arches and cavernous corridors, could've been the twin to the one behind the Wall. Luckily, this hall couldn't change its structure on a whim. At least, she hoped it couldn't.

Spirits, if only these places came with maps. Though maybe there was an option here that she didn't have back in the Wilds.

The dark magic of Phobos's cursed Pack Hall made the shadows too difficult to sift through, too difficult to trust not to rip her apart as she moved through them. But *here*?

Raana tucked closer to the stone wall behind her and caressed the darkness with her fingertips. "Take me to the throne room," she spoke softly to them. "Or show me the way. Please."

A coolness snaked up her legs, arms, and shoulders. It kissed along her cheeks, threading over her ears—a lover's embrace, pecked by whispers in unknown tongues.

They were easy, almost relaxing, until they grew louder. Until they were screams that nearly shattered her consciousness, wrapping around her neck and strangling her, shaking her, violently begging her to *know*.

Raana thrashed and coughed, but the moment she opened her mouth, the darkness swept in, pouring into her and icing her insides.

Stop!

Her shout went nowhere. The shadows heard nothing, only spoke, trying to get her to understand. Finally able to be understood. And from one blink to the next, they swallowed her whole.

This... was not a throne room.

Sprawled on a rug on the floor, a weary Raana craned her neck to observe dusty, partially tarp-covered furniture—a large mahogany desk, bookshelves, some chairs, easels with scribbled-on maps, and a dry bar.

The shadows had carried her where they wanted her. Her vision was fuzzy, her ears ringing and hollow from their shouting that had blissfully stopped once she'd been spat onto the floor.

Shaking her head, she rose onto her hands, sputtering out a shadow-laced cough. They tasted like smoke and the tang of dread and terror. On her inhale, the hair on the back of her neck stood, and she lifted her head higher, a gasp spilling from her lips.

In wonder, she fell to sit on folded legs, her neck straining as she looked up at the ceiling spanning the vastness of a stained-glass window. *The* window that could be seen for miles.

She was behind it.

Why would the shadows bring her here?

Without much moonlight, the colors of the window reflecting onto the floor were muted. Still, a wondrous sea of blues, purples, and near-blacks. Raana ran her hand through the ripples, swearing the moonbeams felt heated. So, this is how glorious the window in Phobos would have been.

Raana's eyes fell on an outline in the glass, some kind of door. Drawn to it, she rose and trekked across the expanse of beauty, the rays tickling her skin until her hand was pressed to its cool surface, feeling a slight jolt to her arm.

Iron.

She pursed her lips. Though iron, it wasn't warded. So, she weathered the pain and pushed.

"Spirits," she murmured into a rush of wind as she became one with the skies, staring down at the full glory of the city: its lights, distant crystals, hills, and the river, the way mountains cradled it like offering hands. She'd never seen something so wondrous, spellbinding, and beautiful. Ethereal.

There was a sudden pull at her wrist, and Raana glanced down to find a shadow slithering around her skin, coiling near her iron bracelet. Not touching; it couldn't. But it wanted something. Unconsciously, Raana reached for it, hissing against the flare of the always-present pain when she found the latch. When it fell away, she gritted her teeth. Her power and the shadows rushed at her in full force.

She gripped the rail in front of her tightly. This wasn't as intense as it had been in the Wilds. Her power hadn't been confined very long. But it still nearly brought her to her knees.

Breathing hard, she glanced down at the starlight glow of her fingertips as it crept up her arms like long-sleeved gloves. Her tongue ran over the points of her teeth, and she didn't have to touch her ears to know. No glamor at all.

The world had become so loud, so *vivid*, that even the air tasted different. The lingering taste of dread and terror was so potent she nearly retched.

Straightening, Raana drew her eyes up to look back at the sky and nearly fell over again. Those wheeling stars, all that pressure she'd felt earlier staring up at them, had ceased. Now, beyond the clouds, within the silky, gem-crusted velvet, she found an entire new world. A swirling, ebbing cacophony of existence that she could just barely see, barely touch. A world that felt like power, felt like fear, felt like... home.

A whisper of a wind slid over her skin, a shadow from the ones that had once more become her cloak sliding over her ear.

Turn, child.

Raana did.

Spinning, she peered into the colors of the window and her reflection amongst them. Peered at the stretch of darkness that stood at her side. Her breath caught as she turned her head, but nothing was beside her. Not a shadow, not a person.

But she didn't panic as she felt another pull forward.

Fixed on the writhing ebony, Raana didn't stop walking until her nose was nearly pressed to the glass, squinting up in that darkness that seemed to change form, beginning to clear.

Lifting a hand, she pressed her finger to the glass.

And beneath her touch, it cracked.

CHAPTER 25

KAI

Kai peered over Isla's shoulder from where she stood at one of several elongated, high banquet-style tables strewn across this quarter of the lower city. His arms bracketed her as she scribbled on a piece of parchment.

One of their many Equinox traditions was to write down three things you were grateful for, three things you hoped to change about yourself in the upcoming year, and three things you hoped for the future, personally or in general, that would be sent up to the goddesses in a lantern that would eventually burn up and rain down in glittering ash.

Isla hadn't worked on building her lantern yet, but a few feet away, he could see Davina had been busy crafting hers, her hands a mess of glitter, glue, and gemstones. Beside her, Ameera lazily drew her hand over her parchment, a vacant look on her face that, every so often, was edged with rage and pain.

He hadn't asked her if she'd spoken to her mother or father today; the former was granted permission to visit the latter, where he was under house arrest in a secure location in Ifera's countryside.

Though a different kind of hurt, this holiday had as much a bitter undercurrent for her as it did for him.

Last Equinox, he and Ameera had needed to sneak away from the soiree his parents had thrown for the pack's upper echelons to meet

Jonah and Rhydian at this festival in the city. In hindsight, maybe they should've stayed those few more minutes his mother had requested. Maybe he should've smiled wider for that final family portrait, which had now been taken down and brought to his mother's new estate.

There were so many things he could never change. So many regrets.

Isla's touch drew him from his dark thoughts, featherlight over the skin of his hand where it rested beside her. She must've felt his impending spiral.

"You're so nosy, you know that?" she teased, leaning into him.

Her body molded perfectly to his, the curve of her ass pressing dangerously against him in a way that made the fresh mark on his neck throb. He honestly wasn't sure how he could be this close to her without the deep, nagging desire to tear her clothes off again. It wasn't like they hadn't just fucked until they were sweaty, exhausted heaps on the study floor, their pillow talk slipping into meandering conversations about the dark moon, the coronation, the ceremonial dagger, Isla's nightmares, the open tunnel, and his own whirlwind of feelings.

Eventually, they'd tracked down some presentable-yet-simple clothes, leaving behind their adornments so they could easily blend into the crowd. Then they'd tracked their friends down to one of Rhydian's favorite eateries.

He twisted his hand around, capturing hers and interlocking their fingers. "Can't I know what you're grateful for?" He leaned down to rest his chin on her shoulder, nudging her head with his, earning that laugh he scrambled for and tucked away.

Isla's voice was seductive as she answered, still not revealing the parchment, "*Davina.*"

"Davina?" Kai lifted his lips to her ear, whispering, "Was it her name you were crying out a couple of hours ago?"

Isla bit her lip, her hips kicking back, involuntarily or not, making him curse softly. Another sultry laugh. "I don't remember *anything* I was crying out a couple of hours ago."

He certainly hadn't forgotten. The keenness of her moans, the look on her face, and the feel of her body against his. All of it.

He lifted a hand to draw a trail over her stomach, wrapping his arm around her waist. Isla let out a deep sigh. "You're relentless."

Kai only hummed in answer, giving her the softest kiss on the skin of her neck. She shivered, and... maybe this wasn't the best idea... his pants started to feel a bit tight. Goddess, he needed to have better self-control than this.

Isla finally pulled her hands back, and Kai stood taller, trying to distract himself with the ink across the canvas. Three lines sectioned off for each part of the custom, her handwriting neat and precise.

- *I'm grateful for my family.*
- *I'm grateful for my home, old and new.*
- *I'm grateful I get to spend the rest of my life with my best friend... even if he likes our house freezing.*

A warmth bloomed in his chest, and he couldn't hold back his laugh or resist the urge to kiss her again. "I love you," he murmured, though those words didn't feel nearly enough to express how he felt.

He continued reading.

- *I want to accept that I may never be as I was.*
- *I want to think more before I act.*
- *I want to become a better cook.*

"A better cook? What do you mean? You're perfect." Sarcasm dripped from his voice.

She lightly pinched his hand. "Oh, shut it."

The last time she'd attempted to prepare a complex meal, she'd nearly burned the House down.

Finally, Kai's eyes dropped to the last lines—hopes.

Each one felt like a punch to the gut.

- *I hope we'll get to grow our family.*
- *I hope we don't go to war.*
- *I hope I can bring my mother home again.*

Kai stiffened, and Isla had to have felt it because she did, too, her hand settling atop his around her waist.

That power within him opened an eye and beat against his chest like a war drum.

Murderer.

It had been lulled before, quieted by her, by their time together, but with the shot of emotion, all chains had been stripped away. Now, it was a thrashing against his ribcage, a pounding on his skull. He shoved it down—down, down, fucking *down*—and cleared his throat. "Are you hungry?"

Isla turned, eyes trailing over his face. "I could eat." At his lofted brows in question, she added, "Surprise me?"

Kai nodded. "I'll meet you back over there."

He kissed her temple, but before he could go far, Isla spun, inclining her head with an ask he'd never refuse.

His lips met hers in a simple kiss that shouldn't have stunned him the way it did. From one shared breath to the next, he felt himself unraveling beneath her, the threads that created the fabric of who he was hers to control as she pleased.

He'd meant it when he said it earlier: he would happily be at her mercy until the end of time, but as her essence seemed to spill into him, something inside him reacted—*violently.*

Kai broke the kiss, stepping back.

Isla mustn't have felt the vicious retreat as she stared with furrowed brows. "Are you okay?"

He wasn't sure. Whatever had resisted seemed to slink back into a darkened corner of his soul, crouching in wait.

Kai sighed. "The usual," was all he replied. "I'll be at our table with Rhyd and Jonah when you guys are done." Her stare was doubtful. To avoid it, Kai lifted his head to Ameera and Davina in the distance. "Do either of you want anything?"

"Alcohol!" Ameera answered immediately, and Kai did his best not to frown.

"I'm okay," Davina said. "Tell Rhydian to come over here in ten minutes so we can release this together."

Kai nodded and gave a wary Isla a peck on the forehead before disappearing into the crowd.

～

Breathe.

Kai took his time getting to Rhydian and Jonah, his hood pulled over his head as he maneuvered through the crowd, monitoring.

He counted each of his paces, timing them with his heartbeats, as he checked to ensure all guards were at their assigned posts. Some of them had slipped away, it seemed, in the merriness of the night, and a few he sent towards where Isla remained, ordering them to keep a distant eye on her.

He didn't catch any off scents. His rolling net of *sense* didn't snag on any volatile emotions. No rogues. No spies. No bak. No witches.

Still, paranoia gnawed at his insides, stoking his own erratic emotions.

I hope we don't go to war.

Where was Malakai? Where was Sebastian? General Eli? The Imperial Heir? Their guards? He hadn't seen them since the ceremony...

Goddess, he couldn't think like this. Couldn't doubt them and imagine the worst. They were Isla's *family*, but—

Coming to terms with the fact that Io was his greatest adversary had been a conclusion in the making for months, *years*—if he counted his father's dealings. Their love, no matter how world-shattering it felt for the two of them, wouldn't change that. Maybe the battlefield was inevitable.

"There he is!"

Kai came to attention at Rhydian's voice. Somehow, he'd made it to the table he and Jonah had commandeered without even realizing. A half-eaten feast was spread between the twins, where they sat facing each other. Street foods, entrees, and a slew of desserts, on account of Rhydian's sweet tooth, covered the table.

Jonah looked bemused. "Look who finally got off Isla's ass," he jibed as Kai fell into the seat beside him.

He shot his brother a narrowed look and, for good measure, plucked a lamb skewer off his plate. "Mention my wife's ass again." A mild, jeering threat.

Jonah's amber-flecked eyes narrowed, and Kai took a bite.

Back was the irritating desire to jump out of his skin, like he'd burst at the seams, starting at his healing stitches from the bak's brutal claw. He'd get Jonah a skewer replacement, but right now, maybe some good food would ground him.

The meat settled in his stomach like lead.

Rhydian chugged his ale, barely masking his chuckle with the wooden mug, nearly as tall as his head. "You were gone a while."

"We had a very important meeting." Despite his nausea, Kai took another bite, flavors of home bursting across his tongue. "Alpha and luna now. Needed to talk strategy."

"Oh, I'm sure."

Jonah leaned back in his seat. "You know, last Autumn Equinox, neither of you was mated, which meant I could enjoy my meal in peace without you reeking so badly of lust that even *I* can scent you."

Kai didn't bother turning his head; he only gave his friend a sidelong glance. Considering Jonah couldn't shift and had weaker senses, that said a lot.

Another bite.

No, this definitely wasn't helping.

He dug for that little glimmering piece of Isla once more, hesitant in case that hidden *thing* pushed her away again. He asked Rhydian, hoping to encourage the thought, "Does it ever stop? Wanting her so badly you can't think straight."

The oldest twin laughed, his eyes drifting into the crowd. "Wanting her all the time—not at all. But you learn to think around it."

"Madness," Jonah muttered, shaking his head.

"Just wait until it's your turn, Jo," Rhydian said. "Me last year, Kai now—we're building momentum. You or Meera are next."

"Given how rare fated mates are," Jonah answered, picking up his ale, "the fact that you two found yours brings the chances of us finding ours close to zero. I never cared for it much anyway."

"Neither did we," Rhydian said. "Now, they have us by the balls."

"Entirely," Kai echoed, rubbing his hand over his face.

In the distance, thunder crashed, and he felt it reverberate down his bones, that power chomping at his ribs again. What was *wrong* with him today, and when the hell was it going to rain?

"Alright, I have to ask," Rhydian began, leaning back in his seat. He folded his arms, the fabric of his linen shirt straining against the muscles of his arms. "I know it's the holiday, and we're trying to avoid talking about freaky shit," he lowered his voice, "but was that... normal... what happened in the throne room? You two nearly burned the place down."

Kai took the final bite of his skewer. "The fire, yes, but it didn't burn like that for my coronation or when my parents were crowned."

Beside him, Jonah seemed to tuck the information away. "The point of the ritual is to show the strength of your bond, the Goddess-given power that you have, that you're linked as the alpha and luna. You're fated, but your parents were chosen. That could be it."

Kai hadn't thought about that. "Maybe."

Jonah ran a hand over the pillow of his cropped hair, shrugging. "So, I guess the goddesses are just *really* happy you two are together."

"Seems that way."

Kai didn't even want to think about what that meant in the grander scheme of things. He leaned his elbows on the table and fell forward to rest his forehead in his palms, groaning.

Rhydian slapped a heavy hand on his back, a roughness that would've spawned a playful brawl between them if Kai had been up to shoving him back. "You've both killed the Wilds' population of bak between you. Is being Goddess-blessed truly a shock?" An exaggeration.

"No," Kai breathed. "It just means there's a wider target on our backs."

Rhydian dropped his hand. "From the Imperial Alpha?"

"From anyone." Kai sat up. "Everyone."

Do you think things will ever become simple? Where we can just be happy and old and in love, Isla's voice rang in his head.

Never simple—and now, he'd further delve into the complications.

"Since we're already violating our *'no freaky shit'* rule," Kai began, snagging Jonah's attention. "The ceremonial knife we used to cut our palms for the ritual looks just like the one Isla took from Lukas. From the witch. I hadn't realized it before, but it's the one I used—the one that's been used for generations of Alphas and Lunas of Deimos. Maybe even across all the packs, if it's meant to mimic the one crafted by the goddesses for the first alphas."

A light came to Jonah's eyes, clearly thriving off all the curiosity. The man loved puzzles and mysteries, always had. "Did Isla feel drawn to it?"

"Not in any unnatural way. Not like the one we have."

Jonah hummed, his gaze drifting out, up, and over the crowd as he thought. "I've decoded the book to the extent where I know it's chronicling Aneurin's reign and includes the war between the packs during that time. I've mapped the markers to figure out where the tunnels connect to us, but there are three things I *can't* figure out." He stuck out a hand, counting off, "*One* is why Isla feels the way she does with the dagger and diadem. *Two* relates to that because of the woman from the artwork who looks to be holding them."

Kai held in, for now, that Isla told him that the *woman* had been in her nightmare last night.

Jonah continued, "We know she's your ancestor. Isla mentioned dreaming of her. I thought I'd been piecing her together, but at most, I can assume she's tied to Ares. The wording on the back of the art is directionless—just some poem about wilting flowers, lightning strikes, and stars. There's not even a proper flow to it. It's like they pulled fragments of a longer piece and scribbled them there. I can't even fathom how or why I found it where I did. It's like someone put it there for me—which brings me to the last thing."

With the exasperated way he'd said it, Kai almost didn't want to know.

It was Rhydian who threw his arms out, like he'd heard this tirade before and presented grandly, "Why?"

Kai looked from one twin to the other, and Jonah nodded. "I hate the idea that everything happens for a reason. I fucking *hate it*." Kai knew exactly why, since they all bonded over ghosts. "But all this coming together can't be a coincidence. Deimos, Phobos, Ares, Io. Fragments of war. How everything is going to shit now. The patterns are there. And either we're mortal and just trying to craft something extraordinary from our mundane existence, the goddesses are bored and like seeing us play detective, or there's one last piece that we're missing that brings all this together and makes the picture clear."

One last piece.

The moon, Kai thought, but never had the chance to say.

He wasn't sure what came first: the pain, then the thunder, the thunder, then the pain. Regardless, he felt the reverberating slam of it through his soul, his splitting head only saved by his fingers pressed to his temples.

In one gargantuan wave, the world pushed in. Unrelenting. Brash. *Too much*. Everyone and everything. The sounds of the crowd, the scents, the auras. He couldn't breathe.

Something hit his shoulder—a hand—and it may as well have been a bolt of lightning.

Kai winced as a well of pressure built in him, making him feel like he'd burst. Rhydian recoiled slowly, grimacing, though concern shone in his eyes.

"Are you good?" he asked, but his words echoed in Kai's pounding head.

Darkness began to spot his vision as he tried to focus on him. "I'm fine."

Kai felt it then, almost saw it, smelled it, and tasted it. A link. A tether. A doorway into his brother's head.

Rhydian blinked heavily once. Twice. His features twisted as his hand went to his nose... where crimson trickled down onto his upper lip. "What the hell?"

Kai nearly fell out of his chair as he yanked the power back, jumping to his feet and putting a healthy distance between them. "I—" he panted. He needed to stay calm. Emotions drove this. *Think of Isla.* "I forgot I had to speak to Sol about something."

"On the Equinox?" Jonah asked, watching him far too closely. The doorway in Jonah's mind was shut, but Kai felt like he didn't need it. He could break down any wall.

"Busy times," he said, glancing up and away. The clouds swirled, and... were the stars moving? *Goddess, his fucking head.* "Rhydian, Davina wanted you, and when Isla shows up," he gritted out, "tell her I'll be right back."

Kai didn't linger to hear his response. And though he moved, everything went dark.

CHAPTER 26

ISLA

"This is *infuriating*."

Isla glanced over at the growling Ameera, glowering at the dazzling mess her hands had become. Her partially decorated lantern sat on the table before her. "And I'm covered in *glitter*."

"There's nothing wrong with a little sparkle, Meera," Davina chimed, tiny flecks of luster joining the freckles on her cheeks.

"You've never made one of these before?" Isla asked the general.

"No," Ameera said, wiping her hands on the cloth meant to dry her paintbrushes. Her features soured. "My mother usually does."

"Oh." Isla's stomach twisted, and she wanted nothing more than to take those words and rip them out of existence.

She knew things between Ameera and her mother had been tense since Ezekiel was locked away. From the small bits the general had disclosed and what Kai had figured, Ameera's mother saw *Kai's* actions as a betrayal of their family, and Ameera was complicit in that—a traitor to a traitor. There was no reasoning with her mother that Ezekiel had put the entire pack in danger with his secrets and lies, and that he continued to do so if he was still withholding more.

Isla drew her eyes over her lantern again, along the swirls and symbols she'd drawn reminiscent of lumerosi. Reminiscent of the ancient language of the marker and the book. It was the product of a meandering mind that would not rest. Perhaps the glittering ash that would rain down as she sent the lantern up to burn away would bring some clarity, some answers. Some peace.

Thunder crashed like a hammer upon the world, and the crowd around her sputtered and groaned.

"For the love of the Goddess," Ameera grumbled amongst them, throwing out her arms and lifting her head to the sky. "Haven't we had enough? The goddesses need to give it a rest!"

Isla held back her smile, training her eyes across the night sky. It might be best not to mention that she didn't mind it at all.

Something glimmered in the corner of her vision, and she turned to catch a glimpse of the Pack Hall's window, which seemed to shine despite the minimal moonlight.

A violent tug in her gut, at her wolf, suddenly lashed through her side, buckling her, and then there was that tap, tap, *tapping* at her skull again. A thought, a presence, just at the edge of her mind.

Kai?

"Your Majesty... *Your Majesty.*"

For a moment, Isla had forgotten the address was hers, and she lowered her head to find Ameera and Davina had closed in, their eyes fixed on whoever spoke behind her. The former became a picture of lethality and grace, her eyes narrowed and arms crossed.

Isla spun, jerking back slightly when she came face-to-face with General Eli.

"General," Isla snapped, her eyes questioning. Any anger and suspicion she'd felt towards him bubbled violently to the surface and likely rippled across her face.

"General," Ameera echoed, nearly growling. Isla could feel her take up the spot at her back. Months ago, she'd effectively gathered that the two warrior generals hated each other—Ameera deeming Eli "General Social Climber" while he'd attempted to court Isla. Passive-aggressive conversation had become an art form for the two of them.

Davina remained quiet, likely wary of whether she could trust the general, given his loyalty to Cassius.

As Eli surveyed each of them, Isla did him the honor of returning his pointed inspection. He looked haggard, unkempt. His hair was mussed in a way she knew was from his own exasperated hands, and the fear and wildness shining in his slightly bloodshot, dark-circled eyes set her warrior's heart beating.

What the hell had happened to him?

He eventually bowed low. "Apologies, Luna."

Goddess, that sounded strange coming out of his mouth.

Isla did her best not to let her unease show. "Can I help you with something, General?"

Eli rose and placed his hands behind his back. "May I have a word with you?"

"A word?"

"*Please.*"

Desperation dripped from his tone. If it was a strategy to catch her interest, it worked. She really did need to address her bleeding heart.

He added, "It's urgent, and I've heard my days here may be numbered."

They hadn't made any formal announcements about the warriors yet, but it seemed the rumor had spread.

Isla straightened, inclining her head in a way she imagined a queen would, and hoped she didn't look ridiculous. "I'm listening."

"Alone, preferably." Eli glanced at Ameera. "It's a sensitive matter."

Ameera's nostrils flared. "If you need a private audience—or any audience—with the *luna*, you can make an appointment like everyone else, General."

Harsh, though she did have a point. If Isla had felt like being an asshole, she would've told Eli to take a hike and speak to Marin about her availability. But she'd been trying to catch the general since she and Kai had trailed him through Abalys a couple of nights ago, and here he was, delivered right to her. Seconds away, it seemed, from getting on his knees.

"Just a few minutes of your time," Eli proposed again before she could end his suffering, his voice straining. For the briefest moment, his gaze flitted around them, searching and fearful. Odd. "It's all I ask."

"Very well," Isla said flippantly. Ameera let out a small grumble behind her. "Should I get Kai?"

"If you must, but I'd rather speak quickly."

Again, that shifty look, but his answer was enough to tell her that he'd be open to Kai hearing what he had to say.

"I'll let him know later." Hopefully, Kai wouldn't be too upset about her leaving him out. She took stock of her own body. No more tapping, no more tugs, and he was still... there. Whatever had been vying for her attention had ceased.

Her gaze locked on a closed shop a few yards away that had been left unlocked for festival-goers to use the facilities. "We can go in there."

Ameera said, "I'm staying close," and the undisclosed warning hung heavily between them. *If you do anything to her, I'll wring your neck before Kai even has the chance to.*

Eli swallowed. "Good."

It almost frightened her how genuinely he meant it.

On their short walk to the store, Isla clocked two guards she hadn't noticed earlier, watching her closely. Her mate's doing, most likely. But perhaps it worked out well in her favor. With the two of them on standby, she and Eli disappeared into what appeared to be an antique hub. Unlike Jonah's bookshop that boasted the continent's recent feats in innovation, from cars to small planes, telephones and radios, here commemorated the more distant past. She resisted the urge to flick at a gas lamp as she leaned against the artfully cluttered cashier's counter.

Eli stood opposite her, his body rigid and his hands clasping and releasing at his sides. Once, she'd needed to tread so carefully around him, her commander who held her dreams and life's ambition in his hands. But now, here, *she* held all the power.

"So, does this have anything to do with why you've been sneaking around my pack?" Eli's eyes flashed in surprise. "Always expect to have eyes on you. We were likely spotted now, too, and I'll probably deal with hell for taking this meeting."

She could've been dreaming it, but she could've sworn Eli cracked a small grin. "Wise advice."

"Common sense," Isla countered. "So, does it?"

Eli's features fell. "It does."

When he reached into his jacket's inner pocket, Isla weathered the shot of fear that rocketed down her spine. That terror, though, was swiftly replaced by shock.

Eli held out a shirt caked in dried blood. By the crescent embroidered into the gray fabric, she knew it belonged to a warrior.

Isla's gaze snapped to Eli's, and before she could ask, he said, "It's Callan's."

She swore the ground shook beneath her. "Callan?"

"I found it outside the guard base last week. The blood seemed... fresh."

"Last *week*?" The words cracked from her lips.

"He's been missing for a while." Eli clutched the shirt tighter in his fist and explained softly, "About a month ago, he missed training, and when I went to his room that night, his things were still there, but there was some blood, and he was gone. The next day, he didn't show up again, so I let the High General know immediately. Either he'd deserted..." He shook his head as if that was unbelievable. "Or something happened to him."

Isla's eyes fixed on his shirt, drenched in his blood. Part of her wanted to reach out and touch it, to be sure it was real. She'd gone to Callan's room that night before Eli had. She'd seen the blood on the door and the room in shambles from Callan trying to burn all evidence of him working as the Imperial Alpha's spy. It was where her mother had given her a piece of the diadem before fleeing.

"I heard from the Imperial Alpha the next day."

Isla wrenched her eyes back to his. "Cassius?"

Eli sneered at the name, stunning her even more. "He didn't want me to draw attention to it. He just wanted it to slip under the radar, and if anyone asked, just say Callan was reassigned." His voice softened in disbelief, and what seemed like pain ripped across his face. "I don't even think the High General knows what's truly going on. I had to lie to him, too. I don't know if Callan was attacked, if he ran away, but the blood in the room, and then *this*." Eli lifted the shirt. "Someone hurt him. Cassius knows it, and now, *they're* shoving it in my face. I've been looking for him, looking for answers ever since. The other night, I went to see a woman who claimed to be some type of mystic, and all she could tell me was that Callan was *lost*. Of course, he's fucking lost—and she also said I'm in danger. And I..." A bitter laugh. "I might be because I'm not going to let this go. No matter what Cassius or your father may want."

"My... my father?" Isla's voice was tight, her fingers trembling.

Any softness and sensitivity in his tone were gone. Now, Eli had become the commander who addressed warriors. Who addressed leaders. "He won't listen to me. I tried to tell him yesterday at the gala, and he brushed me aside. I finally got to him tonight, and he didn't care. Told me that if I know what's good for me, I'll drop it."

Isla wasn't sure if she was still breathing. "He threatened you?"

"As civilly as he could. He's the calm to the Imperial Alpha's storm." The words were acrid. "But I can't let it go. I swore an oath to the Goddess, whose mark I bear on my spine. I proclaimed a creed. To protect the people of this continent and my men—and women." He looked pointedly at her. "I don't work for Imperial Alpha Cassius. I'm not an accomplice in his cover-ups. And I know you no longer serve with us," his tone eased, "but you still bear that mark, too. You swore the same oath I did. You're still a warrior."

The back of Isla's eyes stung, and her jaw set. "I am," she whispered into the room that suddenly felt so silent. Her ragged, recovering breaths rattled in her skull.

Eli seemed to buckle in relief. "Then help me find him. Dead or alive, wherever he is. He has a mate, a family who are going to want answers."

Isla's lip trembled, remembering his family who'd doted on her when they'd been together, and she bit down on the flesh hard. Nausea stirred her insides as she beheld Eli, the bloodied shirt, and the dirty truths laid bare before her.

It didn't stop. It wouldn't stop. The witch. Cassius.

Her mother and Lukas had been lost in this mess. Alpha Kyran and Jaden. Sandrine and Dante. So many lives.

And her father knew... her father probably knew so much.

The calm to the Imperial Alpha's storm.

Isla braced her hand back against the wooden counter. She couldn't breathe.

And now, they had the dark moon. Now, they had to stop Deimos from being destroyed as Phobos was.

Maybe. *Maybe.*

"Isla?"

Blinking away the blur of tears, Isla met Eli's pleading gaze. He was still alive. Still here. He hadn't been fully swept away by the current of this madness.

"Help me," he repeated, so soft now it was as if he were speaking to a wounded animal. He stepped towards her. How long ago had it been that she approached him at the feast?

Isla's tongue felt like sandpaper as her vision shifted to Callan's bloodied uniform, then her mind flashed to her mother's face, bruised and beaten, teeth and nails broken, fingers twisted. Captured. Tortured. Lukas desperately clawing for his own memories, lost, scared, and confused, bleeding beneath her hands—imprisoned, in Cassius's clutches right now because he'd—he'd...

"Let it go, General." Her voice was steady and more assured than she'd ever thought possible. A queen commander.

Eli nearly stumbled in his shock. "What?"

Isla felt like she swallowed glass. "My father's right. Don't go down this road; it won't go well for you."

One would've thought she'd stabbed him in the heart. Eli took a few breaths to recover before he said with a bit of disgust, "Luna of Deimos, and you're siding with *them*."

"No." The word ripped from her so viciously she swore the room trembled. Even the lantern in the room's corner seemed to sputter, sending its shadows writhing. Isla felt something twist inside her, right where her wolf had tugged before, but this time, it wasn't an outward force but something entirely her. "I'm protecting *you*. No one else is getting hurt because of this."

His bitter laugh chilled her bones. Or maybe it was that cold that always lingered now. "I'm dead in the water anyway, Isla. I've said too much, questioned too much. And you don't test the Hierarchy. After you send the warriors back home, I doubt you'll ever hear from me again."

"Don't say that."

"It's the truth," he said with the finality of a man who'd come to terms with his own demise. "We've had our time of peace, but the continent is tearing apart. The divide between the packs is getting deeper. Mimas, Tethys, half of *Iapetus*—my own home is split about the power Io holds." His voice lowered further, but his tone remained firm. "You are a warrior. Top of your class and one of the smartest fighters I know. I always respected you for that, and I know that *you know* war is coming. And Deimos..." he gestured around them, beside her, as if Kai were there, "is led by the alpha who made history in the Hunt, who practically spat in the Imperial Alpha's face, and his destined queen followed him. His queen is a daughter of Imperial blood

*—a warrior—*Fate couldn't have made it clearer. You found each other now for a reason. It's time for change, and you two will be called upon to lead it."

Isla remained rigid, staring.

She didn't want to hear more of this but knew... knew she needed to. But first, she needed to think, breathe.

Could she even truly trust Eli? Was this some kind of setup?

"Mimas, Tethys—how do you know any of this?"

"Missions to the southern territories to break up rebel groups."

Rebel groups?

No, that shouldn't have been surprising. The Imperial Alpha had always had his opponents. It came with the territory, the power.

"I was in Tethys a few years ago," he continued. "This has been brewing for a very long time. To the point that rebels were trained from childhood for the sole purpose of entering the warrior program as a front for easier passage to the north. To infiltrate Ganymede, then Io. It's why the Imperial Alpha so rarely approves trainees from the southern territories. Cassius knows what's been happening."

Magnus. The light-haired guard had tried to enter the Hunt for years, denied again and again until he'd given up. Isla had told him there were no other motives behind it—she'd been a prick about it—but maybe he'd been right.

A vicious pull at her wolf hit with such intensity that Isla keeled over.

Her cry was lost in the thunder that boomed so fiercely that the antiques rattled, the lantern nearly sputtering out entirely.

"Isla!" Eli rushed forward to brace her as the thunder rumbled again and *again.*

Then came the wind strong enough to slam shutters and toss rocks and debris into the store's glass windows.

The onslaught of rain sounded like the breaking of a dam.

"What the hell?" Eli muttered.

But Isla paid no mind to the storm, to him, to the guards who apologized as they entered the store for refuge along with some of the festival-goers outside, drenched like they'd been dunked into a lake.

Because the bond was taut. Pulling, *straining.*

"Kai," she murmured under her breath. Something was wrong—very, very wrong.

"Isla!"

Eli called, but she was already moving, weaving through the frantic crowd until she reached the door they were struggling to close against the wind, and slipped past the guards and into the night.

~

Everyone in the city had fled for shelter. The streets were barren except for the carcasses of vendors' stalls, their wares sacrificed to the monumental storm that tore through the city. Barren but for Isla, who cut through rain so vehement it seemed like the sky was shedding its stars, her legs nearly as useless as the branches snapping from nearby trees as she battled through the downpour to find her mate.

She dug for that flickering essence of Kai within her, using that piece of their bond like a rope to pull herself to him.

Too thin. Too small. Too distant. Too fucking *distant*.

"Kai!" she shouted into the abyss of sound, battling the howls, the crashing, the rush. She lifted her hand above her eyes, hoping to protect them from the speeding droplets that serrated her arms, legs, and face like shards of ice cutting her skin.

Further and further away he drew.

This couldn't be happening.

Where the fuck are you?

Her chest hurt. Goddess, her chest *hurt*, a pit yawning open within her heart.

She found herself beyond the lower city's limits, evading the debris of the dismantling forest, dodging small rocks, leaves, and twigs until she crossed the threshold into the sodden brush, a little relief from the pounding rain. Still, here, the gale pushed and pulled her, and thunder blasted across the darkened skies, that beating hammer relentless against the fabric of the world. Isla swore as the earth shook with it, nearly bringing her to her knees.

"What the—" Her breath wrenched from her when she came across shreds of fabric. A gray shirt soaked to the point it was near-black, and equally dark pants.

Kai's.

The bond went taut and loose with every inhale, exhale, inhale, and near sob. *What the hell happened?*

He couldn't be dying. He couldn't. *He couldn't, he couldn't, he couldn't. Keep moving.*

She battled to her feet, trekking across mud.

"Kai!" she screamed again, her throat raw.

A strike of pain shot up her ankle from where it caught and twisted in the muck. She finally went down with a small cry, mud splattering over her face, hands, clothes, and neck. Darkness crept in, the cold of night seeping into her bones. Deeper, deeper. Threatening to swallow her in its hopelessness, grief, and growing emptiness.

Keep. *Moving.*

Isla fought to her knees, then got to her feet, not bothering to nurse her ankle.

Then she froze.

Red eyes stared at her from within the crypt of gnarled trees ahead, and it slammed into her as certain as death itself what a fool she was. She hadn't brought a weapon.

But... she knew those eyes. That red, though menacing, was not the bright hue of a ferocious monster but the chilling shade of blood.

She didn't know if it was rain or tears rolling down her cheeks. "Kai?" Isla's breath was a sawing, painful sound—her whisper lost in the storm's raucousness.

In response, a wolf emerged from the brush, the height of two towering men, a snarl across its maw, its dark, red-streaked fur nearly blending into the night. Its large paws tread the earth as if it were lord over all things. And in answer, all things bowed.

"K—Kai?"

Despite the fact that he stood before her, Isla could barely feel him, like he *had* drawn away and been replaced by something else entirely.

An unconscious, instinctual terror gripped her heart, flowering from somewhere deep inside. Fear... of him.

She shoved it away, locking it in a prison inside herself, because *never*. She would never be afraid of him, even as that power, his power, slithered along her body and dug beneath her skin. Asking... deciding.

A physical pinch. Only slight, but enough of a burn to make her wince.

At her recoil, Kai's wolf halted, its growl creating a puff of white before its snout. Even the rain flecking off his fur seemed to be chased away, escaping him. Whimpering, the wolf dropped onto its haunches, hackles raised as it pawed at its face.

Gradually, Isla sensed a new flood of pain, but it wasn't hers.

Just as she steadied herself to run to him, Kai was human again. On his knees, his head hung as droplets sluiced down his bare body, his muscles and markings seeming to pulse with power and energy.

Isla bound forward, dropping to her knees in the mud. "What's wrong?" She reached to take his face in her hands, but he flinched away. "Kai?"

"You have to get away from me." He panted hard through gritted teeth. "I—I can't..." His body locked up as if fighting against something she couldn't see. He shook his head, water wicking off his curls. Isla risked another reach forward, her touch ghosting over his thigh, and she was grateful when some of his tenseness eased. "Isla, please." Agony rasped his voice.

Despite the iciness of his skin, his lumerosi burned, and Isla could still feel it—something emanating from him, pushing against her.

"No," she told him, making sure her next words made it through the intensifying storm, "I'm not leaving you. I will *never* leave you."

Kai met her eyes, and the look in them broke her heart. It was grateful, terrified even. "I don't know what this is," he choked out. "I almost hurt Rhydian. I could barely stop it." His eyes drifted upwards, trailing the sky, searching for something, before the rain became too much, and he dropped his head.

The wind became impossible to bear, the storm reaching a new crescendo, so ferocious that Kai hugged her to him, shielding her head, trying to protect her body as who knew what pelted against her skin. Isla held herself closer, breathing hard, doing all she could to shelter him, too.

Lightning scored the sky, cleaving the darkness like the claw of a mighty beast, whipping so brightly she could still see behind her closed lids, even tucked into Kai like this. She could still hear it echoing long after it had finished. And deep within that echo, blended into this surging symphony, was the low cry of a violin.

The cacophonous sounds hollowed out, and Isla's breathing slowed as she held onto Kai and endured that tap, tap, tapping again. Again. *Again,* until finally, something cracked.

The violin's cry became a melody that spoke to her soul in a way nothing else had, but the man clutching her. A music that held the answers to all things, and like a serpent, an essence slithered its way into her consciousness.

"Warrior Heart."

That voice and a phantom touch to her back felt like icy, dagger-like claws trailing down her spine.

The melody exploded into an orchestra as the storm gave one last strike with all its might, and Kai gripped her tighter as the world shuddered, groaned, pushed, pulled, teetered, bent, and *broke.*

And then, everything stopped.

CHAPTER 27

ADRIEN

"What the ever-loving *fuck* was that?"

Adrien peered out into the calming night from where he and Sebastian squatted within one of many city storefronts, surrounded by others sheltering from the storm. "I don't know."

"I need to find Isla and my father," Sebastian said, voice edged with concern as the store's door flew open, and everyone began spilling outside again.

Adrien followed, marveling briefly at the cracks in the windows as he passed. It was a miracle they hadn't shattered completely. "Isla's probably with Kai, and your father is probably with—*holy shit*."

Gaping, he lifted his head. The cloud cover had nearly masked it, but the aurora was unmistakable. The ethereal ripples of reds, greens, whites, and blues were breathtaking and unlike anything he'd ever seen.

Unlike anything anyone had seen, apparently.

Slowly, everyone ventured out of their shelters, some gasping and pointing, some sobbing and cheering, seeming to view the phenomenon as a blessing—even as the landscape around them lay in tatters. Lanterns with hopes and dreams had been dashed across the land, entirely broken, and vendor stalls had been reduced to rubble, their inventory scattered over the ground and floating in the nearby river.

Adrien found his gaze now fixated on the water, unable to tear it away from the river's gentle rock, unable to ignore the steady ringing of a boat's bell. Once, twice—

The frigidness at his neck bit. Hard. And then the darkness tread his body to his wrist again. Pulling, *pulling*.

Ta-dum... ta-dum... ta-dum... ta-dum.

Adrien let it lead him and didn't bother looking where Sebastian had gone.

He wove through the wondering spectators and leapt over debris to the cadence of the shadow's rapid drumming, using it, using this sense he'd felt earlier to guide him. When he reached the fraction of the river no longer bracketed by the stone wall at the landscape's gentle decline, he slid down its muddy bank until he was at the water's edge. The shadow's pulsing eased.

It was so silent over here, far from everyone else.

Adrien turned and continued along the bank, steadying himself so he wouldn't slip into the murky drain.

He squinted at something forming in the distance, a stone in his path, maybe, the darkness not doing him any favor to discern it. But then came the smell.

Blood.

Death.

Adrien's breathing was hampered, and he ran forward as the rock became clearer—as it became a torso, limp arms, legs, then a body. He stopped short and stumbled... then stared. There was so much fucking blood, even with all that had washed into the river down with the sediment.

But that hadn't been what stalled him.

There, behind the body, with her clothes stained crimson and her beautiful eyes wide, stood Raana.

Her features remained set like stone as she fell back into the embrace of her shadows.

PART III
A QUEEN'S DUTY

CHAPTER 28

ISLA

Isla's chest heaved as she sunk further into Kai's embrace, her hard breathing hollow in her ears along with his. She wasn't sure how long she remained like that, tucked into him, inhaling his scent, assuring herself that he was in fact real—but it was enough to cement over the fissure in her mind.

Not enough to silence the echo of that music and voice. Not enough to no longer feel the ghost of nails on her back.

It was when Kai's body stirred and he sucked in an astonished breath that she finally moved.

The world was quiet around them, the wind no longer whipping through the trees and the rain nothing but a gentle, residual patter. As though lightning had indeed cut through the world, an aurora rippled across the sky like spilled paint.

"Goddess above." Isla braced a hand on Kai's chest. Beneath her fingertips, she could feel his heart beating fast. His breathing ratcheted up, a rapid rhythm that his pulse barely kept up with. Panic.

"Hey." Gently, she took his face in her hands, thankful he didn't turn away this time. He simply stared at her, lips parted as he panted. Choked. "Breathe." He inhaled and exhaled raggedly. "Good. Again."

In and out.

Isla smiled softly. "You're okay. It's over." She wasn't sure that was true, but he seemed relaxed enough, and their bond had come back into clearer focus. Still not where it had been before she'd lost her wolf, but it was where it had been hours ago. Isla chanced leaning forward, brushing her nose against his. "You're okay."

They separated on the wet forest floor, knee-to-knee, mud squishing beneath them as they faced each other. Kai hung his head, his curls nothing but gentle waves capped by water droplets. "What am I?" His voice broke. He was a man who had been hit by life again and again and now stood on the edge of breaking.

What am I—not *what's wrong with me*. They were clearly beyond that. They'd figured out he had additional abilities, but he was not a typical wolf. Not even close. Even just saying he had magic felt wholly insufficient.

"I don't know," Isla answered truthfully, bracing, always ready to catch him if he fell apart.

"If I hurt you—"

"You. Won't." She took his chin firmly in her grip, and he looked at her with eyes clouded in desperation. In exhaustion. "*You won't.* If we're going with this 'being here for a reason and being together for a reason' thing, I am me because I am yours. I'm made to take you, all of you, as you are, whether you're entirely wolf or not at all. My heart is yours. My soul is yours. And you are mine." She leaned in closer, growling slightly, "So I don't want to hear this hurting me nonsense ever again."

The tactic, blessedly, had worked. The corner of Kai's lips ticked up at her demand, at the fire she ensured shone in her eyes.

Still, his body slumped, entirely drained. "If I'm some kind of... monster—"

"Monsters are made," Isla fought, dropping her hand. "That is my belief, and you are not one. You're powerful, clearly. Different. That doesn't make you a monster."

"I killed—"

"I've killed." She cut him off. "By sword, by claw, by mind-breaking power, killing is killing. It's what we do to protect the people we love. It's a sacrifice of ourselves that we must make."

She had a feeling he already knew that, but she felt like he needed to hear it.

"What am I supposed to do?" Kai asked as the forest gradually came back to life around them. Wildlife warbling, cooing. "I don't know how to stop this. I don't know how to train this. I don't know what *this* is. There are no answers. No other alphas. No ancestry. No traceable history."

She swallowed. This may make things worse, but...

"I'd bet Cassius knows," she said, and Kai blinked. "If it somehow made you a bigger problem for him, knowing what you are, then that could be why he didn't elaborate with Adrien. He couldn't risk you finding out."

Kai scoffed. "That's not as comforting as I thought it would be."

Not even a little.

He added, "And not only him, but the witch knows, too. You said she needs me because I can break something, and the whole point of the challenge was to see what I was capable of, if something was true about me, if I'd stop holding back. And I did. I gave in."

"Completely?"

Her question earned furrowed brows, but before Isla could elaborate, a scream tore through the air.

~

"There's a body in the river!"

Isla's legs were like lead, her lungs burning by the time she and Kai finally reached the crowded riverbank amongst the city's rubble. The moment she heard the words, her heart stumbled. Sobs and gasps fell from the mouths of everyone around them, and something about all of this struck her as too familiar.

But there was no Wall here. No bak. No trainees.

"Ameera!"

Isla hadn't realized Kai was behind her again, and she hadn't noticed Ameera amidst the milling crowd. She remained rooted while Kai bound up to his friend, now wearing clothes he'd found somewhere.

The general turned, and the blanched look on her face made Isla's breath catch.

Oh, no. Isla spun, frantically searching for every other member of their family—Adrien, Sebastian, and her father. Rhydian, Jonah, and Davina.

Nowhere.

"Who is it?" Kai had his hands on Ameera's shoulders, trying to get her out of her trance-like state. "Meera, who is it?"

Ameera blinked, bewildered. "E—Eli."

The name clanged through Isla with all the power of the storm they'd just witnessed.

"Someone," Ameera gulped. "Someone murdered Eli."

Murdered.

"Isla!"

Isla hadn't known she was moving, running, *sprinting* down the river-bank to where a burlap canvas covered the body until Kai called after her. But she didn't stop. Couldn't, wouldn't stop, even as the guards looked ready to intervene, not realizing who she was.

But they stepped back, either recognition sparking or at Kai's instruction, because she knew he was behind her. Her next movements blurred together. Nearly slipping on the muddy ledge into the water, pausing at the edge of the corpse, the way she bent and pulled at the burlap, and all air vanished from the world.

Eyes closed and skin sallow, his chest and innards exposed as though he'd been clawed to high hell, lay Eli.

Isla stumbled back into a solid force, a body, her hand going to her mouth. It was only the unconscious remembrance that she was a queen that allowed her to hold down her bile.

"You don't need to see this," Kai whispered, his words caressing the shell of her ear. He tried to turn her into his chest, but she was stone.

She did need to see this. He'd told her that he wasn't safe, that he was in danger because of the Hierarchy and Cassius, and those claws that had sliced through him were not from a bak. The lines were too thin, too numerous. No—these slash marks were from another wolf.

"I'm dead in the water anyway."

How horribly fucking ironic.

A coldness like Isla had never known slid over her bones, became her breath, became her blood, became everything she was. Darkness clouded her vision. Her fingers twitched at her sides, ready to draw claws, and her gums ached as canines threatened to punch through. But there was no shift, just that cold, that dark, as she felt something within her rising. Pulling up, *up.*

"Isla."

Whoever did this, she'd kill them. Make it last. Make it *hurt*.

"Isla!"

Kai was in front of her now, his hands gone from her shoulders, now on her face, his eyes, those dark storm clouds bearing into hers. She noticed the tears that had escaped were now streaming down her cheeks. "Who did this?" Her voice was so broken.

Kai's thumbs stroked her skin, whisking the wetness away. "We'll find out, I promise, and they'll pay for it."

It wasn't enough.

Her mother. Lukas. Callan. Sandrine. Dante. Eli...

Isla turned away from the river and looked up at the bank, finding their family united. On one end of the shore stood Ameera, Rhydian, Jonah, and Davina, and on the other, her father, Adrien, and Sebastian.

Her stare fixed on her father, and she hated that it narrowed. Hated that it drifted over his clothes, his hands, searching for blood.

Let it go, General.

Isla was moving, trudging up the mud of the river's edges, the muscles of her legs bleating in protest, but all thought had eddied away. "Where were you?" she snapped at her father.

Malakai jerked back, clearly ambushed by the question, by her demeanor. "What?"

"Where were you?" Isla pressed, her hands balling into fists at her sides. "I haven't seen you all night."

Malakai blinked.

"Isla." She whipped around to her brother, whose brows buckled, assessing her disposition. "He was with us."

There was enough hesitance and question in his words that she pressed, "All night?"

Sebastian didn't respond, and that was answer enough. Even Adrien was stonily silent, his features paling. She knew that look. He knew something. All it took was a flare of her nostrils and a pointed squint for him to understand her question. He shook his head.

Not with them all night, then.

She needed to hear it from her father's lips. Malakai's eyes had drifted behind her to Kai.

"Did you talk to Eli tonight?" Isla asked, regaining his attention.

Malakai's throat bobbed as he absorbed the attention on him, the eavesdropping crowd around them. He let out a heavy breath. "Yes, I did."

That shouldn't have relieved her, but if he wouldn't hide that fact, it was a good sign... in her eyes. But it seemed he understood precisely what she was alluding to, and hurt, genuine, deep, gutting hurt, lashed across his face. She placed that final brick on the wall between them. Now, all she was missing was the mortar to set it.

Kai stepped forward and braced his hand on Isla's shoulder. "I think it would be best if you left tomorrow, Beta."

Malakai's nostrils flared. "I agree. Cassius will want to know about this."

That fucking name.

"By morning," Isla clipped before she could stop herself. Malakai looked down at her, eyes blinking in bewilderment.

She could take it back. She could change her mind and apologize. But when she closed her eyes, she saw Eli's face and everyone else they'd lost in too short a time. She wanted to scream about her mother, that Cassius, his alpha, his best fucking friend, had sent her off to hell and abandoned her, but she could only bring herself to repeat, "You should be gone by morning."

Sebastian didn't seem to know what to do with himself, his stare darting between his sister and his father.

Malakai's nod was rigid. "If you wish... Your Majesty."

Two words shouldn't have wrecked her so thoroughly.

Kai's hand had dropped to her back, drawing hidden, soothing circles as she trembled, telling her to hold it together just a little longer, and then she could break all she needed to.

Malakai turned away from her towards Adrien and Sebastian, and she bit her tongue to prevent a sound from slipping from her lips.

"You boys will come with me," the Beta said. Whether it was a question or a statement, Isla wasn't sure.

She glanced at her brother through blurring eyes. Sebastian's lips pursed as he let his gaze drift over them both again.

"If people are getting killed," he finally said, "I think I should stay. For Isla." His eyes slid to Kai for approval, and the alpha nodded—another strike in her father's book.

Next, the attention turned to Adrien, still in his pale state of shock. His mouth opened and closed. How much choice did the Prince of Io have? Isla knew the words that were coming before he spoke them.

"I should go home."

By the time Isla and Kai arrived back at the Pack Hall, there were only a few hours left until sunrise, but they were covered in too much mud, rain, and death to collapse into bed. The pack had gone into another lockdown, guards posted on every corner, searching for a killer—something becoming all too commonplace.

It could've been a rogue who slipped in, a spy, or someone tied to the Hierarchy, an unfortunate confrontation on Eli's part...

Either way, he was dead.

"You go first," Kai said, starting the shower's flow of water.

In a daze, Isla watched the patter of droplets cascading over the white ceramic floor like the rain hours ago.

When the steam began clouding before her face, Kai tested the temperature with his hand. "It should be good," he said gently and turned to walk out, but Isla grabbed his arm.

"You, too." She cleared her throat, hating how wrecked her voice sounded. "Unless you want to be alone."

She would've understood. So much had happened tonight, and most of the time, he needed that chance to process before he came to her.

But Kai stepped forward, his lips soft against her forehead. "I would never turn down a shower with you." Though the words could've been wanton, there was nothing impish in them or any of their next movements.

Everything—from how they removed each other's clothes to how they stepped into the water and began washing each other off—was gentle, intimate, caring, and grounding.

Isla took in a deep breath of lavender as Kai worked his fingers through her hair, washing the night off her body with every considerate caress of her skin. Her heart went into battle because here she was with the man she loved more than anything, and the world was crumbling around them.

A sob clawed up her throat, spilling from her lips as she dropped her head. Kai wasted no time spinning her around, pulling her into his bare chest. His wounds from the bak had healed now, but she felt the raised scars beneath her cheek. Scars he'd bear forever.

How much more death could she take? How much more would she *have* to take if they were going to war?

It felt as if someone had scooped a hand into her chest and ripped out her heart.

"I left him." The words cracked out of her as she wrapped her arms around Kai's torso, feeling the water cascading down the muscles of his back. "He told me he was in danger, and I left him."

"It's not your fault. You couldn't have known." Kai stroked her hair. "If anything, *he knew*. If the Hierarchy wanted him dead..."

He trailed off, knowing the sensitivity of blaming the Hierarchy, of blaming Cassius. The divide between her and her father was now clear. Rather than waiting until morning to leave, Malakai had been gone within a few hours, and Adrien with him. To get far, far away from her and this place.

She should've told him about her fucking mother.

Another sob wrenched loose, and Kai held her tighter. "There's only so much you could've done, Isla. You're not meant to save everyone."

"I haven't saved anyone," she rasped.

"I will be at your side while we figure this out and try to salvage as much as we can in the process. If there are rogues and spies, we'll keep them out. If there's war and rebellion, then we'll firm up where we stand and draw the line. If Deimos is at risk, we'll defend it. And if I'm... *something*," he swallowed. "Tomorrow, I'm going to Olyvia to get some wolfsbane."

Isla nearly jumped out of his hold. "What?"

Olyvia was the alpha estate's appointed healer. She'd been the one keeping an eye on Isla's recovery, one of the few who knew the truth of her shifting.

Kai let out a breath. "Somehow, this made me lose control of my wolf. My ability to mind link is how I'm able to get into people's heads. If I can keep that tempered with bane, maybe I can keep this under control." His jaw tightened. "I was moments away from using it on your father to get the truth. If I hadn't been so drained, I might've, and I could've killed him."

Despite the heat of the shower, of his body, Isla shivered.

"But if you take wolfsbane," she began, "you won't have your wolf. You won't be able to shift."

"I feel like I'm more of a danger with my wolf than a liability without it right now."

Isla found her fingers dancing over his shoulder blades, feeling the etching of his tattoos. "If you think it's best."

Kai nodded. "I do. At least until I can figure out how to control it. I can't have another day like today."

"Today was a disaster all around." Isla stepped back and grabbed the shampoo. She poured some into her palm while Kai bent slightly, and she returned the favor, lathering it into his hair. "Even with my nightmare this morning and you jumping out of bed, we were doomed from the start. And then I heard that woman again during the storm."

Kai wrenched up from her moving hands, her nonchalance, blinking just before he got soap in his eye. "You what?"

Isla waved him off, gesturing for him to get under the stream. After he rinsed out the shampoo, she explained, "In my dream, there was music, and in the craziness of the storm, there was *more music* and her voice. And I... felt her touching me. Felt her in my head."

"Touching you?" Kai asked, flabbergasted, while shaking out his hair. "In your *head*?"

Isla flinched away from the flying droplets. "That is what I said, yes."

He groaned and rubbed his hands over his face. "Are we narcissistic assholes to think that we're something... more?" Kai dropped his hands, and Isla's gaze snapped back to his face. "Or at this point, is it more than clear that we're fucking weird?"

"I think the universe has made its point."

"Wonderful. Glad that's settled, then."

Isla had never been so grateful to have his jaded sense of humor back.

Kai stepped forward, getting close enough that the peaks of her nipples grazed his chest as he placed a hand beneath her chin to tip her head up. He kissed her once. "Happy Coronation Day, Luna."

Isla's lip curled. "What an auspicious start to my rule."

"One for the history books," Kai mused, giving her one last peck on her lips. "Come on. We have a long few days ahead, and I'm ready for you to hog the bed."

CHAPTER 29

KAI

Kai didn't think he'd gotten an hour of sleep, nor had Isla. It hadn't been because of nightmares, though. There wasn't any opportunity for that. Instead, the moment both of their heads hit their pillows, their minds ran away from them.

There was just too much to discuss, and Rhydian was right: they were stubborn workaholic bastards.

They had spoken of the upcoming conflicts, the other packs, these growing rebellions, and all Eli had said. Then came contemplating who'd killed him and what Callan's bloody shirt meant. Whoever had him, dead or alive, had been taunting the general.

"It could be the witch," Isla had whispered from where she'd been sitting cross-legged on their bed, unable to lie down anymore. "Even if she doesn't have... certain people... doing her dirty work for her anymore, we know she has control over some rogues."

That would've meant the rogues had found a way to slip out of their territory and walk through the pack *again* without being noticed. But if she already had them with her in the Wilds...

Not understanding the full scope of the tunnel system between Deimos and Phobos was going to be a problem, especially if the witch was hiding behind the Wall. Kai had ordered searches for tunnel *openings* and had them sealed up or guarded, but he hadn't sent anyone on excursions deep within to create a new map. It was too dangerous, especially as there weren't many trained to handle the bak or the effect of the dark magic of the Wilds.

"We're caught in the middle of two battles," Isla said. "She hates Cassius, Cassius hates us, and we're trying to fend them both off."

What a mess. "We need a better understanding of her motives," Kai said. "If she has Raana, even if she helped us once, we don't know her, and she's a witch. She's a *fae*." An idea struck him. One that may have been mad—or just agitating. "I think it's time to pay Ezekiel a visit."

"Ezekiel?" Isla jumped back. "But he hasn't been talking."

Kai wouldn't look at her as he answered, "If it came down to it, he wouldn't need to."

Isla's brows lifted in shock and understanding.

Kai didn't want to do it, and he felt disgusted for even thinking it. But the pack and his family were in danger, so if he had to debase himself to protect them, he'd do it. Though going through Ezekiel's mind would be his *last* resort, reserved as a threat more than anything. Hopefully, having the wolfsbane in his system would help his control... if the power would work at all with it.

"It would help if you were there," Kai said.

Isla snorted. "You think I'd actually let you go without me?"

No, not really.

Once the exhaustion became too much to battle, Isla nuzzled beside him, tucked beneath his arm, her head atop his chest, and very much on his side of the bed. He didn't mind at all. It wasn't long before she cried. Not violent gasping sobs, but those silent, despondent tears as she drifted somewhere cold and dark inside herself.

He hated that all he could do was hold her.

Kai didn't manage to see Olyvia in the Healer's Sanctuary until midday, even though he was wrenched from bed an hour after the crack of dawn to meet with Marin, who'd been pacing the floor when he made it to his office. He'd left Isla since she'd finally been getting some rest. At least the secretary had brought tea, easing the blow as she greeted him with three words: *this is bad.*

From where he now sat on the ecru-colored examination cot, Kai reached for one of the wolfsbane elixir vials perched on Olyvia's rolling worktable. Four remained, tucked neatly in the velvety material of a compact wooden box—one each for the next few days. His lip curled as he shook the slurry, watching its dark, sludgy form fold over itself.

"It will taste better than it looks," Olyvia said, finishing cleaning out her granite mortar and pestle. "Not by much, but I added some peppermint leaves."

Kai brought the vial back down to the table. "Thanks."

Olyvia turned off the faucet, the drain gurgling as it flushed the remnants of the mixture away. She wiped her hands on her pale blue apron, shaking an ebony strand loose from her braid out of her face.

A couple of years older than him, she'd been the protege of the former head healer when Kai was growing up. She ascended above her mentor only last year when the elderly mender stepped down. He, Ameera, Rhydian, and Jonah had gotten to know Olyvia well in their youth, their appointments with the former head healer frequent due to the ruthlessness of the Academy—as well as when Rhydian and Jonah's parents had died long ago, and they moved in with his family here in the hall. Though his father had never approved of the arrangement, having balked at housing the sons of a criminal from a farming village, Zahra had been a great friend of their mother's and strong-armed him into it. They'd lived here until they graduated from the Academy at eighteen.

"The bane won't kill you," Olyvia said, tightening the lid on her jar of wolfsbane flowers. "It might not work at all, not entirely hampering your shifting, but it should still quiet these surges of power. We just don't know." When Kai met her emerald eyes, wary and amused by her uncertainties, she elaborated, "Alphas typically don't dose themselves with bane *voluntarily*."

"Fair enough." Kai leaned back on the cot. He likely should've been somewhere else, but it was quiet here, and he knew Marin had Isla. He gazed out at the rolling hillside, at the way the sunlight caressed the swaying grasses. No storms yet, and he couldn't sense any rain. Maybe the goddesses had decided to grant them a reprieve.

He turned back, saying as Olyvia crossed the room to him, "I appreciate your discretion."

A gentle smile slid across her lips that hadn't changed in the near decade he'd known her. "Of course, Alpha." She pointed to the box of elixirs. "Take this for a few days and come back to me. I'll assess, and we can adjust the dosage from there if need be." She closed the rest of the distance between them, her eyes trailing over his face. With her jaw set and brow pinched, she touched two fingers to his forehead, drawing them across and down to his temple, following a path of energy. When she'd drawn the trail to his neck, she paused, laughing. "I see Luna Isla has gotten her fangs back."

Luna Isla. He'd never get sick of hearing that.

Kai chuckled as the healer kept moving lower until she reached his heart. "That she did."

She lay her palm flat atop his chest and closed her eyes. Kai hoped they'd truly *been* shut so she couldn't see the slight grimace cross his face, remembering when Raana had done this to find Isla beneath the arena. Maybe it had been the same technique.

"Anything else return?" she asked, the corner of her eye twitching as if she sensed something. It was like a gift she had—to perceive their wolves' energies—which was likely what made her such a skilled healer.

"Her claws," he said. "And her eyes and lumerosi are glowing again." Olyvia hummed, and Kai's voice rang in admiration. "She's resilient."

She needed to be with all the shit going on around them that she didn't deserve.

A lift of Olyvia's lips. "A wonderful quality for a luna."

"Indeed."

Olyvia slowly dropped her hand and took a healthy step back. With her hand smoothing out her braid, she eyed him skeptically. Before he could question, she asked, "Can you call on your wolf for me?"

Kai did. From one breath to the next, he brought his wolf forward, just enough that his eyes and lumerosi burned, canines and claws threatening but contained.

She placed her hand on his chest again. "Do you feel abnormal?"

"I became alpha less than a year ago, and I'm newly mated. Nothing feels normal." Olyvia breathed a laugh, continuing whatever assessment this was. Kai braced himself before finally inquiring, "Would you be able to tell if it was magic?"

Olyvia's hand seized, her uptilted eyes wide as she scanned his face, seeing his sincerity, his uncertainty.

Maybe he had been too trusting. Maybe he should've kept that in. Died with it, perhaps. Others may have assumed he had some gifts after the way the challenge had ended, but being *gifted* and having *magic* were different beasts.

Olyvia's features softened, and she stepped back again, half-sitting on the worktable. "I don't know much about magic. How does it feel to Isla? Mate bonds are powerful. Sometimes, they tell us more about ourselves and our wolves than we could ever glean in our lifetime."

Kai pursed his lips, running his hand over his jaw. "When it gets bad, when I lose control, she can't feel me through the bond. Yesterday, she thought I was dying."

"And you were shifted?"

"Completely wolf."

She fiddled with her braid again, a nervous habit she'd never gotten rid of. "What do *you* remember?"

Kai lowered his gaze, feeling his insides twist, and a dark cloud cast over his thoughts. A part of him didn't want to recall any of it. "After I shifted, it became hazy, but I remember feeling myself losing control, and I got this horrible headache like my head was splitting, and my senses were heightened. There was too much of the world to take in. It was overwhelming."

Olyvia tapped on the table, thinking. "And that's unusual?"

"Compared to how I was before. Typical now."

"How you were before as a common wolf or as an alpha?"

"Alpha."

The healer narrowed her eyes like she'd struck something. "Did it start becoming unusual after you were mated?"

Kai thought back. He'd admit to always feeling something *off* about himself. There was a piece he hadn't quite understood that hid for most of his life, but it wasn't since the challenge—from the moment he met Isla—that something inside him had changed. That piece became exposed and began to flourish.

"Maybe even a little before it. When we met." Kai rested his elbows on his knees, brows drawn. "But she... she makes it stop or, at least, calms it. She makes it bearable. I don't know why—but I try to think of her when it gets to be too much." It was Isla who'd freed him from the fog last night... after he had nearly hurt her.

Olyvia smiled softly, a twinkle briefly coming to her eye. "Well, you are a part of each other, and because of that, she has a connection to you, your wolf, and your power that no one else in the world does or ever will. You use her to temper it, but she may be the key to understanding it, too. Rather than trying to lull it, has she ever embraced it, tried to feel and figure out what it is?"

For all they'd done intimately, Isla had never *dug into* his power. Though...

"The coronation ceremony is probably the closest she's ever gotten to that part of me."

"I heard it was quite the spectacle," Olyvia mused.

"It was." Kai gnawed on the inside of his lip, trying to remember how he'd felt when the fire erupted. A rush like no other; it was dizzying, intoxicating, and world-shattering like he'd been broken and reforged. And then there was only her and him at the beginning and end of all things. But there was a moment last night when she'd kissed him, when he felt himself unravel for her, and something inside him had pushed her away, not wanting her close.

He sighed. "Any ideas about what this is?"

Olyvia echoed his heavy breath with one through her nose. "None that would have any merit. I'll do some research and speak with my friend who's a priestess—discreetly, of course. She'll know more about mating bonds than I do, in a spiritual sense, at least." She ran her finger along the top of the wooden box. "I feel for most, it's just about romance and sex. Then, for alphas and lunas, you get into talk about power, but there's so much more to it when you think of it in a divine way. Why the goddesses gave us *mates* in the first place, it must mean more. Otherwise, why is it becoming so rare? Because they want us unhappy, or we're misguided? Are deities truly that petty?" Her eyes had grown distant as she spoke, her stare resting on the statues of the three goddesses by the window. Milky cheeks reddened as she seemed to snap back to herself. "I apologize. I'm rambling."

Kai offered a smile. "Don't worry about it. It's interesting to think about. I'll admit I was on team 'mates are for romance and sex' until this started happening. Now, I want to know what the deities' intent is with all of this." He rose to his feet. "Whatever you find out, if Isla or I aren't available, which I imagine will be common for the next few days, you can talk to Jonah... just don't mention the bane or the power."

He'd have to tell him eventually—all of them eventually—but not yet.

"Jonah," Olyvia breathed a laugh. "I haven't seen him in years. Even you and Rhydian haven't been around until recently. And, um, Ameera." Another fidget with that braid, and the red tinting her cheeks deepened. "How is she after Beta Ezekiel... or I guess, just Ezekiel... you—well, obviously, you know."

Kai raised a brow as she rubbed at her cheek as if trying to wipe the color away. This was the most flustered she'd been all morning.

"She's doing as well as she can, but Ameera won't ask for help, and I try not to push her." Something struck Kai then, remembering how often Ameera had found herself at the sanctuary as they'd grown. Sometimes, they'd thought she'd been dramatic with all the mending she needed— the boys may have been rough with her in sparring, but she was just as tough. "You two were close, weren't you?"

A smile, a frown, and another tighter smile crossed Olyvia's face before she waved a hand. "Yeah, but it's been a while. We haven't really spoken since she became a warrior."

"Warrior general now," Kai said, pride infusing his voice. Ameera might kill him for it, not being the biggest fan of *people*, but he offered, "You should reach out to her."

Olyvia had since risen and moved to begin cleaning a spot on the table that was already tidy. "I'm sure she's busy. I've heard she's been shadowing your council."

Goddess, word spreads fast around here.

Continuing to tout his friend, Kai said, "I want her as my beta."

Olyvia halted and turned, her wide eyes blinking. "What an honor."

Kai shrugged. "She deserves it."

Something flashed in the healer's eyes before they guttered, and without the bane in his system yet, Kai could sense pride melded with something like remorse.

"She does."

CHAPTER 30

ISLA

After wanting to throw her into a Deimos safehouse while she and Kai tried to avoid their mating bond, it was ironic that Ezekiel had been dealt that very fate.

Isla observed the brambles where the former beta's prison lay, the cottage marked by the faint scent of smoke on the wind as it billowed through the treetops from its stout stone chimney. It was one of five houses that Kai's family had spread through the region, a quaint space accompanied by a gurgling stream peppered with colored leaves fallen in the season's shift as mossy boulders slumbered beside it.

When they reached the precipice of the narrow dirt path leading to the doorway, Kai muttered, "A fucking vacation house."

His punishment should've been worse. Much worse. If anyone else had done what he had, then they would've been rotting in the dungeons beneath the hall.

"You did it for Ameera," Isla said, mapping the path of the moonlight over his shoulder blades, the night's darkness pressing on them both.

She didn't bring up his father, whose memory was more than likely also a motive. They may have fought, but the connection between him and Kyran's ghost remained.

As she and Kai drew closer, a set of guards emerged from the brush beside the front door, bowing deeply. They acknowledged them before silently retreating to the woods, still on patrol but allowing them privacy with Ezekiel.

The worn porch steps creaked beneath their feet, undoubtedly signaling to Ezekiel that they were approaching. Isla hated that her heart began to beat faster, hated that her dagger weighed heavier at her side. There was no battle here. Just a talk. *They* had the upper hand. And this would be the first time she addressed the beta as his queen.

Seeming to master himself as if he, too, had plummeted into reeling thoughts, Kai pushed the door open.

Goddess, this place is a hot spring.

Sweat percolated on Isla's brow as she followed Kai inside, able to take in the cottage's living area and small kitchen with one sweep of her eyes. Kai could likely cross the space in a few strong strides. A fire roared in the stone hearth while the earthy, gamey aroma of stew blended with the scent of burning wood as the pot steamed on the stovetop. No wonder it was so hot... and the soup smelled delicious.

"Alpha."

Isla's focus snapped to the high-backed armchair by the fireplace. Ezekiel rose, a smile like that of a fox, not a wolf, sliding across his lips as he tucked the book he'd been reading beneath his arm. He bowed deeply to Kai before shifting his attention to her.

Isla schooled her expression.

She hadn't seen the beta since before the challenge.

He appeared much more haggard than he had then, his salt-and-pepper beard lengthy and slightly unkempt, his sleek dark hair, much like Ameera's, nearing his shoulders. His eyes were tired, worn, and... seeking. Incredulous.

"And the Luna of Deimos, at last." Isla's eyes flared wide as he cleared his seating area, placing his book on the coffee table. "My queen."

He dropped to his knees, bowing his head.

Isla's eyes slid to Kai, whose features were a mix of discomfort, confusion, and the slightest bit of smugness.

But Isla still felt the condescending undercurrent of Ezekiel's gesture, and whatever glory was supposed to wash over her felt like grime.

"*Get up,*" she demanded, bracing her feet apart and folding her arms. "Don't embarrass yourself more than you already have."

Ezekiel lifted his head slowly and surveyed her, then turned to watch Kai.

"Your luna gave you an order," Kai said, no room in his tone for question or protest.

One foot at a time, Ezekiel stood. "I'll admit, I'm surprised by your visit. From what the smug bastard Sol has said, I figured it wouldn't be long until you cast me out as a rogue. But then you allowed my wife to visit, though we didn't have much... privacy from the guards."

"Are you complaining?" Kai deadpanned.

"No. I am grateful for your graciousness. I just wish it could've been my whole family."

"We extended the invitation to Ameera." Something wicked rose within Isla then, venom coating her tongue. She wasn't sure what exactly had set her off, but the poison felt good after everything they'd been dealt these past few months. "She has the freedom to come and see you. Any time. *All the time.* She just doesn't want to."

Her biting words clearly roused Ezekiel, whose eyes became slits.

"And yet, here you are," he seethed, and Isla felt Kai bristle at the tone. She stuck out a hand to hold her mate back, allowing Ezekiel to spew his vitriol. "I heard the Imperial Beta was here for the coronation. *Your father,* who sent your mate into a battle for his life. *Your father,* who aids the Imperial Alpha, who likely knows of the attacks—"

A blade whizzed just by Ezekiel's shoulder, wedging perfectly into the wooden mantle above the fireplace. It would've plunged into his heart if Isla had chosen to center her aim.

"You don't get to talk about my family. Not like that," she growled before steeling herself. "But Cassius's plans are what we're here for."

Ezekiel's chest rose and fell heavily.

"Sit," Kai told him. Isla hadn't even noticed he'd moved, now spinning Ezekiel's armchair away from the flames. The former beta wisely obeyed, lowering with his features pinched, eyes darting between them. Not cowering, though. This was prey that would put up a fight.

Goddess forbid this would be simple.

Kai went back to where he had been standing. "No more tricks, no more lies, no more games. People are dying because we don't know how to move, where to move."

"Everyone is hiding shit from us," Isla continued, waltzing to the hearth to retrieve her blade. She wrenched the metal from the wood and, for a moment, embraced the heat. Let the burn chase away her deep-set cold. "And that ends now." She turned away, leaning against the back of Ezekiel's chair, balancing her dagger on a point. "So, you're going to tell us *everything* you've been hiding. Everything you know."

"And if you miss anything, I'll know."

Kai's words seemed to affect Ezekiel the most, his throat bobbing as a crack fissured his cavalier armor. He'd been at the alpha challenge, and he understood enough to grasp his meaning.

Suddenly, his lips curled in perverse delight. "Look at you—both of you. Everything your father could've dreamed of. Powerful. Feared." His head twisted to Isla, still standing just out of his direct sight. "I never told you this, but despite everything, I think Kyran would've liked you."

Isla watched Kai's features twist at the words, torment flashing in his eyes.

"Do you know about the rebel units in Mimas, Tethys, and Iapetus?" Isla began.

It was a simple question, and the surprise that sparked on Ezekiel's face told her he hadn't expected them to be privy to this.

He drilled his face into neutrality. "Who told you?"

"Warrior General Eli," Isla said, her stomach pitting as his sunken features flashed into her mind.

No more tears. They would fix this.

Ezekiel scoffed. "Did he still think you'd be on Io's side?"

"No. He was hoping I'd be against them."

"Well, that's unexpected." He chuckled bitterly. "I should've given him more credit. Where is he now?"

"Dead," Kai broke his observational silence. "Murdered during the Equinox."

Ezekiel blinked. "By who?"

"We don't know," Kai said. "It could've been your witch or an order from Cassius."

At the mention of the Imperial Alpha, Ezekiel's eyes slid to Isla, who took her place at Kai's side. She fought to keep her features impassive. "Tell us everything you know about the rebellions."

Ezekiel took a long breath before settling further in his seat. "The peace amongst the packs has been treading a remarkably thin line since

Kyran and I began our tenures, and even before that. While Imperial Alpha Eoin was in power, he conspired to have Alpha Locke's line rule in Charon. Though we're a landlocked kingdom, the Imperials have had their eyes on Mavec for decades. Absorbing it into any one of our surrounding territories that Cassius has his claws in would give him exactly what he wants. Truly centralized power and better control of the kingdoms. He'd likely hand off Io's current land to his son and rule over all from new territory." Ezekiel paused, but one look at Kai and the threat of his power had him continuing, "He's allowed Charon to gradually tear itself apart so he can build it back up into what he needs it to be. Oberon, Callisto, Ganymede, Rhea—they're all on his side. Before I'd been put in here, I'd heard he proposed a marriage of the Imperial Heir to one of Baldor's daughters."

Isla started. Adrien hadn't mentioned that at all. Her mind reeled with all their previous talks. With memories of the influx of Charon's pack members who'd risked their lives to seek refuge within their borders.

"Alpha Verena and Alpha Deacon know about Cassius's witches. Verena knew your father had a plan, but she hadn't known exactly what it was. There are rebel groups in their territories, and it's safe to say they're not doing much to discourage them. If war is imminent, I'd imagine they'll be calling on them soon."

Isla's heart thundered in her ears. "Are there rebels here?"

"I'm sure they exist, but I have not found them."

Kai paced a few steps in the room, casually glancing down at his feet as he tucked his hands in his pockets, a picture of effortless regality. "If my father wasn't afraid of war, why did he stop working with the witch?"

Isla caught the slightest twinge of muscle in Kai's cheek.

Ezekiel might've, too, if the spark in his eye was any indicator. "He only told me it was to protect the family... to protect you." He presented it as if it were the greatest secret he'd ever kept.

Kai dropped his easy disposition, his body locking up. "Me? Protect me from what? Who?"

Ezekiel smiled like a canary who had just gotten a second chance at life. "I don't know. He said he'd tell me when he was sure, but"—he shook his head—"she killed him a week later."

Whatever Kai had been feeling, despite it no longer being visible on his face, Isla could sense it through the bond's fragments and mist. Something violent, twisted, and agonizing churned inside him.

Had Kyran known that Kai was... different?

She fought the urge to reach out to Kai physically, knowing he didn't want Ezekiel to see the effect of his words.

Kai cocked his head. "You never thought to mention that?"

"I told you that I was going to explain everything to you after the Hunt, but then your fated mate being the Imperial Beta's daughter complicated things. It all became a balance. But now, it's clear where our luna stands."

Isla twirled her blade in her hand. Goddess, his addressing her by that title shouldn't have made her skin crawl.

"How many times," Kai's voice had taken on a darkness that made Isla pause, and she swore red began to edge his irises, "did you meet with the witch after my father passed? When she nearly killed Isla, she said you were 'coming around' to her plans."

Ezekiel's disposition wobbled, his lips becoming a thin line.

Isla felt Kai's aura spill into the room like ink in water. Ezekiel's hand snapped to his head. Were Kai's abilities still so potent with the bane in his system?

"Twice," Ezekiel breathed. "Twice." He flinched.

"Is she responsible for the rogue attack during the banquet for Delta Atesh?"

More hesitation. A further push of Kai's power. Isla tried to gauge when to jump in and pull him back.

"Yes."

"Did you know about it? Did you help?"

She could've sworn the fire in the hearth sputtered, and Kai's essence became overwhelming, the bond pulling taut.

"I did not think it would be like that. She mentioned a few rogues slipping in to find something she'd lost. She promised no death. I swear."

Kai's eyes flared red, and Isla stepped closer. "And you trusted her? She'd just killed my family. Your fucking best friend. My brother, who was like a son to you." All lethally clipped words, sharp as blades, but a part of him was slipping a leash. "You kept meeting with her. You got our people killed and lied about it."

A small fleck of crimson dripped from Ezekiel's nose. Kai noticed.

He didn't back down.

Isla stepped in front of him, putting her hands on his forearms. "Not worth it."

She might as well have struck him across the face. "Not worth it?"

"That was supposed to come out better." She stroked his arm in apology.

Ezekiel, in Isla's granted reprieve, slumped in his seat. "She was our best chance." He coughed. "She was our best chance against Io."

"Well, now you have to take her out of the equation because she's after us, too," she said. He didn't need to know that she didn't want them dead. A tired question spilled from Isla's lips before she could stop herself. "Is there any way for this to end peacefully?"

Ezekiel shook his head. "Our alpha killed a man without touching him. We all saw it. We all lied to ourselves, saying the rogue had done it to himself, but we felt him. Fear makes us not question. Hope tells us it doesn't matter. Kai is stronger than Cassius is. And if he isn't, then he will be soon. And *that* cannot stand. It won't stand. So, in my opinion... no. I don't think there's any chance for peace while you exist."

CHAPTER 31

KAI

"I'm sorry for what I said."

Kai glanced over at Isla from where he'd been observing the lake's surface, the wind catching the wisps loosened from where she'd braided back her hair. The crescent pommel of the sword strapped to her back glinted in the moonlight. "What do you mean?"

She closed the distance between them, a map of Deimos in her hands. Across it, lines were scribbled, mimicking the ones Callan had drawn. "When I said it wasn't 'worth it,' I didn't mean..." She paused. "I didn't mean Ezekiel shouldn't pay. I know locking him up isn't enough of a punishment for all he's done—"

Kai stopped her with a crooked finger beneath her chin. "If you didn't stop me, I could've killed him, and we don't need that right now." Maybe it should've frightened him that there was very little tethering him *not* to do it. As it had before, even dulled to a whisper by the bane, the power called to him to kill. Ezekiel had a feeble mind, so easy to shatter and pick apart.

Moving him out of the safehouse and into dank, cold, ancient dungeons beneath the hall would do for now.

Isla pursed her lips, haunted azure eyes glittering with the stars. "Are you okay?"

I don't think there's any chance for peace while you exist.

He only told me it was to protect the family... to protect you.

It was his fault. All of it. His father and Jaden's death, his mother's heartache, and every horrible occurrence that followed. His. Fault.

Guilt settled like tar on his heart as he took in Isla's beautiful face, her despondent eyes—the face of a woman who would not know rest as long as she stood by his side.

I am me because I am yours. I'm made to take you, all of you, as you are.

Even if he was a fucking curse?

Kai forced a soft smile. "I will be." Saying anything else would be too heinous a lie.

Isla's grin was just as gentle as she pushed to her toes and pressed her mouth to his.

You are mine.

He was grateful that whatever void festered inside him didn't push her away. When they broke apart, he rested his forehead against hers.

"We're going to be okay," she whispered between them. A reassurance, a question, a plea. And hearing it from her lips, knowing the mental hell she'd been going through since Eli had been killed, meant everything.

He tilted his head down to kiss her nose. "We're going to be okay."

Isla took a step back, her hands going to the straps of her pack. After speaking with Ezekiel, they'd prepared for a small night of exploration in the tunnels.

"This was the lake you washed off in after the bak?"

Kai hummed in affirmation, remembering how he'd felt plunging into the water, no longer on the brink of death. "We should be close. Not long after that hill's decline, the slope feeds into a forest, and it's hidden by the brush."

"Let's keep moving, then." Isla took the lead, plowing ahead.

He may have given her a few extra steps while appreciating the view.

Unlike on the Equinox, the passage did not beckon him this time. All was quiet. Internally, at least. Around them, the forest felt alive, charged.

The scent of the tunnel hit him first. Acrid and vile. A clear echo of the abhorrent scent of the Wilds with its dark and twisted magic. Given how far away they were from the Wall, from Phobos, the odor was concerning.

At the cave's mouth, Kai peered into the blackness, barely lit by crystals in the walls, as if the Goddess and her light had been chased away from here. The stone floor, to his surprise, was splattered with dried blood.

His blood.

"Goddess above." Isla crouched. "There's so much."

Apparently, he'd been more injured than he'd thought.

Isla's wide eyes drifted further inward, tracing his bloodied path. "How did you even make it back home?"

Kai blinked. "I... recovered?"

Isla stood with a hand on her hip, and Kai could hear the ratcheting up of her heartbeat, the quickening of her breath. He couldn't deny struggling with confined spaces, but from what Isla had told him, for her, they were a nightmare. Why would she have proposed coming here at all?

He placed a gentle hand on her back. "We don't have to do this tonight, Isla."

She glanced up at him, hesitance flickering in her eyes before that warrior's steel settled over it. "No. If war is coming, coming soon, then we should understand all paths that leave us vulnerable—or that we can use. Getting the markers is important to map it all."

She took a sidestep from him before reaching back and drawing her sword, the metal sighing as it was released from the sheath. Kai couldn't fight the smile tugging at his lips.

Isla inclined her head at him. "What?"

Kai shrugged. "I shouldn't find you so attractive holding a weapon."

Lamp in hand, Kai led the way, taking them the first few yards beyond the cave's mouth. The air hollowed in his ears with each step, and there was the faintest sound of rushing water. His hand ran along the cool cave wall, keeping his eye out for any of those small wooden orbs etched with the swirls and symbols of his ancestors.

"How far in had you gone?" Isla's question was punctuated by the click of a dropped pebble, the glitter-painted rock laid to keep track of their path. She hadn't dropped them often, though, given his blood had already mapped their path. Given the volume, he had no idea how he was able to walk out of here and home alive.

"In another few yards, there's a split. You'll know which direction I took by my blood."

A few more feet, and they came upon the divide, and indeed, more blood, the most they'd seen because his wounds were freshest here. And the smell—Goddess, the stench made his eyes water.

Even Isla had brought her sleeve up to her nose. "Something tells me the bak weren't moved."

They came to a halt a few feet from the closest dead beast, the two others further away. Three throats torn to shreds by Kai's wolf. Swarms of insects and some tiny rat-like creatures now fed off the carcasses.

"Goddess," Isla groaned, her eyes flicking up and focusing on something. "There's a marker over here." She'd have to get close to the beast to wrench it from the cave wall.

"I'll do it." Kai extended a hand for the small chisel. To his surprise, she didn't argue.

While he drove the blade into the rock around the marker's edge, Isla examined the bak's corpse. "How did you kill this one?"

Kai glanced down from the stone wall, noticing her tipping the creature's chin with the blade of her sword. "What do you mean?"

"The throat is still intact. The others aren't." She gestured to the clear pools of blood beneath the other two and trained her eyes elsewhere along the body. "And I don't see any other injuries." Though the creature appeared very much dead, accompanied by a blank, vacant red stare, Isla lifted her sword high. She was about to bring it down, cleaving the beast's body, when she screamed and fell back on her ass.

Her shout still echoed as Kai abandoned his work on the marker, his wolf attempting to rise to the surface against the bane. "What is it?"

But Isla didn't speak; she just sat on the rock floor, sword at her side as she panted, wide-eyed. It took him a few darting glances to realize what she was staring at.

A minute, beady set of red eyes peeked from the large crevice between the bak's neck and shoulder. Then red eyes became a tiny head, half-drooped ears, and a small, wet snout. It had ashen-gray hair-covered skin and paws, without any skin-tearing, gutting claws. And when the creature *yawned,* those were not throat-tearing teeth.

Kai's whisper reverberated off the tunnel's walls. "You're fucking kidding me."

"It's a baby," Isla gushed, more confused, fascinated, and excited than he would've liked her to be.

The first two emotions, he agreed on. He'd never seen a bak pup before. Hell, he didn't know they... reproduced, but then again, they'd never explored much of the Wilds. And the bak had to come from somewhere with the Hunt going on for as long as it had.

Suddenly, one of the rats, no longer satisfied with its dead meal, dove for the bak pup. Its teeth nipped at the baby, a yelp and cry slipping its maw.

"Hey!"

Before Kai could stop Isla, she was lunging forward, scooping the pup in her arms, and impaling the rat with her sword.

The other rodents took a break from their feasting to turn on her, but one flash of her violet eyes, her wolf rising, sent them squeaking and scurrying away. "Yeah, you better run." She flicked their dead companion off her blade's tip.

Kai noticed the pup gazing up at her, its tiny red eyes drinking her in. A wolf, a predator. A queen. He was shocked when it didn't squirm or try to flee from her arms.

No, the little beast settled.

It took up the entire cradle of her arm, a decent size but nowhere near the size of an adult bak.

For a delirious moment, he could admit it was cute. Endearing, even, as it tucked into her for protection.

Then reality set in.

Kai asked, "What are you doing?"

Isla tucked the pup closer as she turned to him. She met his eyes, then followed his stare to the bak in her arms. They darted back to him, then to the bak again. She smiled weakly. "I don't really know." From its perch in her hold, the pup shivered as it stared at the dead bak below. Isla frowned. "I think one of these is its mother."

Kai observed the gruesome scene. It had been a melee of teeth, claws, and death. He hadn't noticed a mother protecting her pup. Though if they'd been calm in this makeshift den of theirs and they perceived him as a threat...

Of course, they'd fight.

He was surprised by the nausea that roiled his gut.

But these were *bak* in *his* territory. He had to get a grip.

"It's horribly trusting," he said.

"I didn't know bak had pups."

"Neither did I."

His mate glanced down at the small beast in her arms, then ran a finger over the back of its head, behind its ears. It seemed to lean into her touch, and she let out a small, incredulous sound. "We left all the food outside the cave mouth?"

"Yes, why?"

"It's so thin," Isla said, still petting. "And its heartbeat is weak. It probably hasn't eaten in days."

As it nudged into the cup of her hand, and she let out a small laugh—one of the most joyous sounds he'd heard from her in days—Kai sighed. "Isla." He fought to keep off a smile that mirrored her own as she met his eyes. "What are you thinking?"

The grin that slid across her mouth, though innocent, was far from it. "I want to feed it."

"Just feed it," Kai affirmed.

"Yes."

His mate, a lover and giver of the benefit of the doubt to all... including little monsters.

"Isla."

"Kai," she mocked his tone. "I just want to get it some food, and then we'll bring it back to the Wilds."

"We haven't fully traced a safe path directly to the Wilds yet."

"Well, now we have more incentive to."

As if it could sense his opposition, the pup turned to Kai. He narrowed his eyes, and the creature flinched, curling into Isla.

She gave Kai a deadpan look, caressing the creature between the ears. "Don't let the brooding fool you," she whispered to it. "He's a softie. He won't hurt you." Kai kept his features unwavering, and Isla sighed. "I just want to get it some food, and then we'll keep going. Maybe we'll find the direct path tonight."

"We're in Ifera."

It wasn't possible to reach the Wilds from here unless they intended to be out all night and felt like risking getting lost in this unknown maze forever.

Isla shrugged. "Maybe we'll get lucky."

When she began heading back the way they'd come, following her pebbles and his river of dried blood, Kai waited a few moments. Not to watch her walk away this time, but to glance back at the three dead bak.

At that one with the uncut throat and the maw of the tunnel beyond. Quiet. So quiet.

What had called him here?

Kai shook his head, knowing he wouldn't find the answer in this barrenness. With three more hard knocks to the marker, it popped off into his hand, and he followed her.

CHAPTER 32

RAANA

Raana could not get the image of the dead man out of her head.

Eli. His name had been Eli, and she only knew it because he'd tried getting through to Nerissa's soldier when the general caught them trying to flee through the storm.

Before the soldier had clawed him to bits.

After finding her way back from the stained-glass window to the throne room to collect the ash mixed with Kai and Isla's blood, Raana had been so exhausted that she could only manage to get them both out of the hall through the shadows before they had to navigate the rest of the territory on foot.

Then, the storm had raged, and it had become their saving grace. For some reason, with it, Raana had felt a new surge of power and was able to pull magic from somewhere deeper inside herself. But before they could flee, a man had been searching for Isla through the torrential downpour, and either her name or the man's voice had stalled the soldier.

That's when Raana learned his name was Callan and that he knew Eli. Well enough that Eli had nearly fallen to his knees in disbelief upon seeing him. Well enough that he'd wrapped Callan in a hug.

Enough that Raana saw Callan's mask falter until Nerissa's spell, a spell she'd reinforced herself, lashed pain through him, and he shoved his claws into his friend's gut.

Amidst the howling winds, Eli had been too stunned to defend himself. Callan's blows had the ferocity and skill of an apex predator striving for death, rendering him too weak to fight back, though a single shot of adrenaline had given him enough strength to send him and Callan tumbling down the riverbank.

But it wasn't enough.

Unable to contain her sobs, Raana had tried desperately to save him, heal him, as his blurring eyes blinked at Callan standing behind her. A man turned beast, whom she thought might deliver one final death blow, a clean slice along his neck, but he remained frozen, breathing hard and twitching as if still battling pain. Still battling Nerissa's magic.

It was when the storm had ceased that Raana had come to terms with Eli being dead, that she noticed Callan had taken her knife—Nerissa's knife—and was clutching it tightly in his shaking fingers. For a few thunderous heartbeats, she wasn't sure if he intended to use it on her or himself.

But like the drop of a lock on a cage, a familiar haze plummeted over his face again, and he let the knife fall into the mud. She didn't have a chance to save it from sinking to the bottom of the river.

And then, there had been Adrien.

There was a feeling first, a sense of blissful relief and a warmth she wanted to wrap herself in. Before the cold, brutal reality settled like the sediment beneath her feet.

And more so than the dead body that she saw every time she closed her eyes, she couldn't forget the look on Adrien's face. Hurt, disgust, confusion—and maybe a touch of something sweeter she'd been too shocked to grasp fully.

Upon their return to the Wilds, she and Callan were greeted by a motley army of Nerissa's other soldiers and bak. Despite her protests and screaming, the vial of ash and blood had been wrenched from her hand, and the two of them were violently separated. After all they'd endured on their journey, Raana had been too drained to fight back.

For a couple of days now, she'd tried to trace Callan through the halls, trying to recall how his aura may have felt, but with all the iron and magic here, it was hopeless. Though she'd carried on until blood gushed from her nose, her ears only knew ringing, and her head pounded so badly it brought her to her knees.

And for days, she hadn't been able to find Nerissa.

Until now.

"Where are you keeping him?" Raana asked by way of greeting when she entered what she could only assume had been a greenhouse before the dark magic took hold. Its arching glass was spotted with spidery vines of rot and decay, any chance of seeing beyond ruined by its cloudiness.

Her shadows were a whirlwind behind her as she approached, where Nerissa plucked decomposing plants from their perches, collecting leaves and bushels in a small wicker basket.

"You need to be more specific, child," she trilled, examining a fragment of the crumbling foliage.

Her nonchalance stoked an ire inside her. "*Callan*," Raana snapped. "His name is Callan. Where do you keep him?"

"The one who murdered his friend?"

Raana jerked back, the shadows catching at her sides as if they'd thought she'd truly fall. "How do you know that? I haven't seen you for days." She hadn't had the chance to tell her anything.

"He told me."

The *lilt* in her voice.

Raana's features twitched, and the shadows were a delightful bite at her fingertips. With her manacle already abandoned, she contemplated removing her lesser glamor to give Nerissa the full force of what she truly was. "Where. Is. He?"

Nerissa took stock of what was in her basket before stepping aside. Her inky hair had been braided back, her emerald robe vivid against the murky landscape—but her face did not have the same brightness, Raana realized. Her features seemed paler, worn, and the scar Isla had given her seemed more brutal. She seemed... weaker, like she was slipping.

"And why do you need to know?" she asked. "Are you going to have a chat? Use him to fill the void your prince left behind?"

"That's disgusting," Raana spat, her skin crawling at the implication.

Nerissa had moved to the middle of the glass, humming some tune Raana didn't know. It was so easy for her—all this death and suffering.

Raana shook her head, pointing. "You talk about wanting revenge on the Imperial Alpha, but how is *this*," she gestured around, shadows clearing the foliage as she stalked towards her, "any better than what he's doing to our sisters, whom you're supposedly avenging? All this effort. All this power, and you're using it to play games. Using everyone else to do your dirty work. You're a coward."

"Says the girl too afraid to embrace her own power." The elder witch's voice had darkened. "And do not patronize me, calling them *our* sisters. I doubt they were your sisters when you opened your legs for the prince. Now, while you still lust after—"

Nerissa's basket clattered to the floor, gasping as its cursed contents spilled, as Raana's shadows whipped out and pinned her to the wall. The entire decrepit greenhouse rattled, and Raana could've sworn the ghosts of this place, something greater and far more wicked, had peered in to behold her.

Like serpents, her darkness slithered along Nerissa's body, enveloping her in their violent iciness before coiling around her neck. Raana's bones, her breath, and blood had become nothing but ice, and she laughed, a horrible sound wrenching from some dark and hollow unknown part of her as she sensed Nerissa's conduits burning, her chants in the First Language, though whispered, loud in her fae ears.

Hopeless.

What had Nerissa done to weaken herself this much?

The smell of magic filled the room as Nerissa's nose started bleeding, her soft words of attempted control fading when she realized—

"Your magic doesn't work on me," Raana snarled, feeling the phantom of Eli dying beneath her hands.

Nerissa's features shifted from panic to some twisted pride as she smiled maniacally. "Then do it."

Raana's nostrils flared, and she called on her shadows to squeeze tighter and *tighter*.

Nerissa's eyes widened as she sputtered a cough, her feet lifting off the ground, kicking against the glass. Raana's lesser glamor had fallen away; she could feel it. Her fingertips burned with a power that rivaled the stars, her blood singing as it had as she stood before Deimos's stained-glass window. It had only been a slight fissure, but Raana could've sworn that darkness leaked from the space—a shadow greeting her.

"When you were there," Nerissa choked, blood from her still-bleeding nose dribbling over her lips, tracing her scar, "what did you see? What did you hear? Another—" A weak cough. "Another realm, perhaps?"

The shock was enough for Raana to lessen her hold.

Nerissa smiled, crimson staining her teeth. "Did you feel the world cleaving open during the storm?"

Answers. Nerissa had answers, so many answers, and Raana could only get them if she were alive.

Slowly, she lowered Nerissa to the leaf-littered floor but held firm. "How?"

"During the Equinox, the veil is thinnest, and you are a child born of two worlds. Your blood, your essence, defies the barrier between them, between all. *That* is what makes you so powerful. That is why all will fear you, why the High Witch will hunt you to the ends of this world and the next to ensure your demise." Nerissa scoffed. "Such an inflation of her own importance. She is a worm compared to you and what you could be."

Unfortunately, the useless attempts at flattery and bravado did nothing to stir her. Raana only wanted to understand. "I've been alive for plenty of Equinoxes. I've never felt or seen anything like that before."

"That begs the question, doesn't it? What's different now?"

A little looser. Raana's mind reeled through the options. "Does it have anything to do with the moon?"

"I can't be certain."

Raana bore her eyes into Nerissa's, seeking the line between truth and lie, lie and truth. "What do you need Kai and Isla's blood for?" A flicker of hesitation passed over her gaze. She retightened the shadow's hold slightly. "I got it for you. I proved my loyalty. Now, tell me what it's for."

"There are pieces of themselves that they do not yet know." She spat blood on the leaves beside them. "That they are yet to understand. Their blood will allow me to show them."

Raana narrowed her eyes. "Why can't you just tell them?"

"Because even if I did, they would not listen to me, and even *I* do not know the entire truth. Their past holds the answers, and blood is the key."

CHAPTER 33

ISLA

There were a few entrances into *The Bookshoppe*: the back door, the front, and then the set of storm doors down into Jonah's basement apartment. Though all would be locked this early, Isla knew where Jonah hid the spare keys in the nook of a tree behind the building. They'd basically become *her* set, after endless nights spent with him poring over books, though she always left them here.

Isla was elbow-deep in the hidey nook, her satchel banging against the bark as her fingers just grazed the cold metal of the keys, when she heard the back door of the shop fly open. Shrieking voices came next, a shouting match that dropped into harsh whispers once exposed to the open air.

Isla knew both men.

Abandoning the keys, instinctively knowing it would be best not to be seen, she took a few more steps into the wood and pressed her back to the largest of the nearby trunks.

Jonah and Sol continued their squabble, but the grit of their voices was hard to decipher at this distance without her wolf's hearing and with the obnoxious bird warbling its morning melody over her head. She glowered up at it, and it seemed to leer back, then flew away as soon as Jonah's back door slammed closed.

She heard the crunch of gravel beneath shoes as Sol passed by, and she risked a peek around the bark to catch a flash of his face, to find his features pulled into a scowl. Judging by his trajectory, he was heading towards the hall.

She frowned. What the hell had that been about?

Isla's mind began to spin conclusions—recalling Kai's story about all of them, including Jonah, being trained for the guard by Sol until he had quit to run the shop—but then she stopped herself.

Not my business.

Not wanting to make her eavesdropping known, Isla waited about ten minutes before circling back to the door. Though she knew Jonah was awake now, she still went to the nook for the key as normal.

She was through one of the three outside-facing locks when the other two clicked, and Jonah pulled open the front door.

Isla jerked back, forcing her face into an expression of pleasant surprise. "Well, you're up early."

Jonah's brow ticked up, his shirt hanging from his hand. Apparently, she'd disturbed him while changing. "I wasn't expecting you this morning."

Isla swung her satchel around, opening it to reveal three new markers, partially exposed within their cloth wrap. "I came bearing gifts."

Jonah laughed through his nose and leaned against the doorframe, musing, "More work for me? How nice." She knew he enjoyed this, despite his sarcasm. "I miss the pastries."

"Next time, I promise. I heard the place I usually go to makes the best apple tart in the whole city."

Jonah nodded, then dropped his head for a closer look. "When did you get these?"

"Last night. We found another tunnel in Ifera." Isla pulled her map from the bag, pointing to the tunnel's location in Deimos's northern region and the small stars she'd etched as the marker's locations.

Jonah's mouth pulled tight. "Bak?"

"Yes," Isla breathed, folding the map back up while Jonah looked on for her to elaborate.

Her mind flashed to beady red eyes atop a short, gray muzzle, to partially drooping ears flopped sideways as the bak pup tilted its head innocently this morning. *Innocent.* Goddess, she never thought she'd describe a bak as innocent. But then again, all of this was mad.

She'd brought the creature home last night, much to Kai's behest. But he would've died if they'd left him out there alone. Isla needed to address her bleeding heart.

"They had already been taken care of... mostly," she explained.

"Mostly?"

Isla closed the bag and sweetened her voice. "Mind if I come in?"

Jonah sighed. "Every time you have that look on your face, I get nervous."

"Many do."

He stepped to the side, opening a path for her. "You're always welcome, *Luna*."

Isla thanked him grandly and cleared the doorway.

Despite wanting to keep his business *his business*, Isla couldn't stop her wandering eye. But there was no answer as to why he and Sol were fighting in the lines of shelves carved into the walls and support columns, the various testaments to innovation hanging from the ceiling, or beyond the mezzanine to more books and reading nooks.

"I haven't seen you or Kai in days," Jonah said, drawing Isla's attention as he slid on his shirt and started on the buttons, covering up the tattoos he shared with Kai, Rhydian, and Ameera. Symbols of their bond, of the losses they'd suffered. "Not since the Equinox."

Isla's features fell, and she turned away, moving to play with a model car on the cashier counter. Suddenly, she felt a headache coming on. "We've been busy. He's in meetings all morning today." She'd join him for one with the council later.

"I'm sure." Jonah's tone wasn't sarcastic or mocking. "Kai seemed... *off* that night. More so than you just tiring him out. Has he not been feeling well?"

Isla was grateful she'd been turned away from him. "It was a long day." Schooling her features, she spun and caught the doubtful furrowing of his brows. Without Kai there to decide how much to share with his friend, Isla quickly diverted. "He said he told you about the dagger." Jonah nodded, though his look of skepticism didn't waver much. She gripped her bag strap tightly. "Any theories?"

"One, for now." He lifted his hand, gesturing to where the stairs down to his apartment lay. "Care to step into my office?"

Jonah's apartment could have been described as a cave or the hoard of a book-loving dragon. Her eyes trailed over the space as she slipped off her shoes, leaving them by the stairs and feeling the cement floor cool beneath her feet. Her eyes adjusted to the light of a lamp perched on a small table by Jonah's bed, the faint glow illuminating the open, marked-up book on his mattress.

The study in the corner had been an organized flurry of tomes, papers, and machine odds and ends. It was there, spread out over a worn wooden desk, that sketches, maps, books, rubies, and little balls of wood inscribed with ancient symbols lay. In the center of the mass sat the dagger and the broken diadem. All the random shit they'd gathered during the mess these past months had been.

She couldn't deny the draw she felt towards it all, now a little stronger than before. Jonah hadn't followed her towards the pile, moving to the kitchenette instead.

Isla perched her satchel on the chair before adding the three new markers to the rest they'd gathered, already searching for a pattern between the symbols. As expected, these newer ones had the swirling emblem that indicated the path connected to Deimos. She grimaced as battle strategies began forming in her mind.

As if they'd physically been tugging for her attention, Isla snapped her head around to the dagger, diadem, and the artwork of the woman. Her moon-white hair and violet eyes made Isla's heart stutter. She waited for that tapping, for her voice to slip into her mind, into her thoughts. But... nothing.

What? Nothing to say now?

"So, what's your theory?" Isla called across the room, nearly moaning at the pleasant, nutty aroma fluttering around her.

Jonah pulled out two mugs and began pouring the coffee. "She may be a priestess."

"A priestess?" Isla spread her hands over the table and gazed down at the artwork, tracing over the crown she wore, which wasn't a perfect match to the item they possessed, like the dagger was.

"It's a ceremonial blade." Jonah carried over two cups, and Isla took one with a cheery thanks. "And the crown in the painting may just be an extravagant version of the adornments priestesses wear today. She could've been from Ares. I feel like there was much more value put on the deities and those who had a connection to them back in the day."

"Way back," Isla mused. She had to be at least a thousand years old since that was when the split occurred and Ares ceased to exist.

She sipped from her brew, mulling over the words. Though she understood his logic, a priestess didn't feel right.

"Do you still feel drawn to them?" Jonah asked, cutting into her attention.

The liquid burned going down her throat as she forced a swallow. "A bit more now than before." Taking a breath, she ran her fingers over the blade's hilt. A dull, broken pulse shot through her hand, and she yanked her arm back.

That was new.

"Are you okay?" Jonah leaned closer.

Isla nodded, placing her mug down as she moved for the blade again. She weathered the feeling this time, gripping the weapon tightly. Lifting it towards her face, her eyes glided over the silver-toned metal freckled with the tiniest bits of gold, the ivory pommel, and its dark crystal accents. The same look as the blade she'd cut her hand with for the coronation, but the feeling...

"It feels broken."

"What?"

Isla shook her head, confusion knitting her brow as she swiped the knife through the air. She pointed the tip towards the three fragments of the crown. "In a way, it feels broken."

Jonah's assessing gaze traveled over her and their wares. He reached across the wood to snatch his leather-bound, well-loved notebook from the corner of the desk, the rich brown cover scuffed. He sifted through page after page of notes and translations before he found a blank sheet at the end. "It's in one piece, and it looks intact."

"I'm just telling you what I feel." Isla's eyes slid to the artwork of the unnamed woman. "I'm still dreaming of her, and it's always the same. There's a storm, there's war, she calls me Warrior Heart, and there's that music." The haunting melody and the violin that nagged at her. Had she heard it anywhere before? "She always talks about 'trying harder' and 'stopping him' and it's 'only been us.' And then she presses a blade, *this blade*," Isla shivered as she stared at the weapon in her hand, swearing it hummed its own melody now, "against my throat, my heart, and says, 'If you fail, then they all fall.'"

Even repeating it, it didn't make much sense.

"Who's they?"

Isla scoffed. "Who's falling? What's failing? She isn't into specifics. Never has been." She pulled out a chair at the table and slumped into it, placing the dagger on the slab and plucking up a piece of the diadem. "I don't know what to make of it. Any of it. Is she... me in a past life or something? It sounds ridiculous, but anything could be possible at this point, and I will take any answer just to knock this problem off our list."

"Well, do you believe in reincarnation?"

"Not really."

In her mind, they were all crafted uniquely by the Goddess; then Fate decided who their mates were and wove them together before ripping them apart. What was left behind? The smallest fragment of their other half within them, so their souls could find each other again through life. She was no one but herself—she felt and fully believed that.

She eyed Aneurin's journal a few feet away, gently placing the diadem back onto the table. "But history repeating itself, I might believe in that. Kai has his own theory that Deimos may be heading towards the same fate that Phobos was dealt and that we—we're supposed to stop it."

Jonah's features paled. "I figured everything was connected, but I was hoping it wouldn't be in that way."

Isla hummed in agreement. "It's all been so strange with the Wilds lately, and everything sounds so eerily similar to what you said Aneurin went through against the Imperial Alpha back then."

"I wish Kai would catch whoever killed his family so we could get answers from them. Though I'm sure everyone will want their head on a spike immediately."

Isla's stomach hollowed, and the rich brew suddenly tasted like ash. The image that flashed through her mind made bile crawl up her throat. Others learning the truth, her mother in chains and hauled before a bloodthirsty crowd as an alpha killer.

Her features strained to remain impassive while Jonah continued, "I mean, the killer gave us all of this: the journal, diadem, dagger, and markers, and they have communicated with us through these symbols.

They could probably answer all of this. They're clearly lingering around Deimos. Maybe you and Kai should talk about putting more resources into tracking them down?"

Isla's hands dropped to her lap, her fingernails gouging so deeply into her palms she felt the wetness of her blood. "I don't think they'll be much help."

It was such an illogical claim that Jonah's brows drew together, and he observed her with concern. "Why not?"

"Have you ever heard of something called the dark moon?"

Jonah took a large gulp from his mug, finally opting to sit. His analyzing eyes seemed to bore holes into her. "Never in my life."

This would be a pretty good distraction, then.

Isla breathed, relaxing her hands as she began to explain everything Adrien had told them about the moon and its effects. Jonah's hand moved so fast as he wrote that she was surprised smoke hadn't flown off the page. She kept Cassius wanting Kai dead vague enough that she didn't need to mention Kai's power or anything regarding Raana.

When she'd finished, Jonah remained silent. For five seconds, ten, twenty—

"You know how my face sometimes makes you nervous?" Isla traced anxious circles along the table's surface. "You being quiet makes me nervous."

Jonah still didn't speak, though; he only took a seat and flipped through Aneurin's journal, riddled with folded pieces of paper containing the shopkeeper's own notes.

"What's bothering you?" Isla asked.

"All of it."

Isla didn't have it in her to laugh. "What's bothering you *most*?"

"That something like this exists and that the Imperial Alpha is the only one who knows about it."

"Well, now we do."

"But we're likely missing the part that can actually be weaponized."

Isla pursed her lips. "Most likely."

Jonah kept flipping, grumbling that he needed a better tabbing system. "Do you know how rare auroras are in Deimos?"

Isla lifted her brows. "Extremely?"

"It's never happened before. At least, not in any of the written records

I've combed through these past few days—here." Finally, he reached what he'd been looking for and cursed in relief. His finger pressed down on the page riddled with ink. "My translation isn't great, but Aneurin talks about seeing *skylights* with Saoirse and calling it a 'Goddess's beckon.' I wondered if it was the same."

Isla had heard and seen in the papers that some had called the aurora a blessing—a sign that her and Kai's reign was about to be something special and Goddess-blessed.

"Who's Saoirse?" She hadn't realized she'd reached towards the dagger again until she felt the dull buzz of it along her fingers.

"Aneurin's mate. The last Luna of Phobos."

Isla slowly pulled her hand back. "Does he talk about her anywhere else?"

"Not really," Jonah said. "You would think he would—I think they were fated, too—but he mainly writes about rising to power. A lot of political meanderings, scheming, and nonsense. Then some of his own personal accounts."

Isla wrapped her chilling hands around her mug's warm surface. "What kind of personal accounts?"

"Nothing interesting. How he'd been feeling day to day. A lot about headaches he'd been having, but didn't want to tell anyone about it, so they wouldn't see him as faltering."

Isla nearly jumped from her seat. "What kind of headaches?"

"Bad ones?" Jonah offered, heeding her eagerness. "I could translate something like pressure. There could be more about them in his other journals. I'm sure there are many more. We barely scratched the surface of any war here, just some scheming."

Isla gnawed on her lip. "Where do you think those are?"

"My best guess would be the Wilds if anything. The Pack Hall, if it's still standing after the decimation."

Isla found her eyes tracing the swirls of creamy foam through the darkness eddying within her mug. Her mind reeled back to last night. "Would Alpha Kyran have kept journals like this?"

Would he have written about Kai, about why he wanted to protect him specifically?

Jonah cocked his head. "I could imagine. Kai hasn't seen them?"

She highly doubted Kai had gone through his father's things. "He hasn't mentioned them."

"Oh, the secrets those must hold." Jonah leaned back in his seat, gnawing on his pen, mulling something over. "For diaries like this, I think it's customary for them to be locked away where only other alphas can get to them. I doubt betas are told, and I wonder about lunas. Alpha Kyran may have only given the location to Jaden."

"That's... tragic." It was the only word Isla could find to describe any of this. "So, Kai would never know where to find them?"

Jonah frowned. "He wasn't Alpha Kyran's heir."

Isla huffed. "Someone *must* know. They can't just be lost forever." The corner of Jonah's lips ticked up slightly. "Don't look so giddy about it."

A full smirk graced the shopkeeper's mouth as he put his hands behind his head. "Another mystery to solve," he mused. "Hopefully, this one doesn't try to kill us."

~

Isla would've been content never to think again.

By the time she left *The Bookshoppe*, her mind was spinning, so filled with thoughts that she was surprised they didn't spill out of her ears as she ascended the hills back to the Pack Hall.

She'd made it nearly halfway home when the coughing started.

Her hand went to her chest, clawing at it as if she could free her lungs.

She hadn't realized it was happening before it was too late. Her body turned cold, her fingers trembled, and the overwhelm wrapped so tightly around her throat that she sputtered. Panic hit her like a blow to the head.

Isla ducked into the nearby woods and found refuge against a tree, sinking to the leaf-littered floor. She dragged her knees up to her chest as she breathed, breathed, *breathed.*

The forest around her was so tranquil, the wildlife at peace and trilling their melodies. Covering her mouth, she leaned her head back against the bark, catching glimpses of the sky through the trees' canopies.

This felt different than any other time she'd panicked or cried these past few days. She couldn't pinpoint what had set her off.

It was too much. All of this was far too much. And it didn't feel like there was any way out of it. No end. Never any sense of peace.

An abyss opened wide beneath her, threatening to drag her down and swallow her whole. That monster watched and waited, smarter than she was.

"Stop. You're fine. Get a hold of yourself." Her words fell on deaf ears, and her attempt at a smile failed.

A warrior. A queen... a joke. A liar.

She felt wetness at the corner of her eye and swiped it away, her shoulders shaking as she brought her forehead to her knees and sobbed through her teeth. A weight pressed down, harder and harder, preparing to crush her beneath it.

If you fail, they all fall.

She'd already failed in so many ways, failed so many people.

So much death.

Isla's thoughts eddied to an unrelenting cold, blanketing her bones and chilling her breath. She embraced it, sank into it, letting it carry her away.

Something beneath her skin writhed, clawing at her insides, through her chest, and up her throat. Her wolf?

Isla cried out, her back arching as a flash of pain shook her to her foundations. And then everything was dark and raw and frigid and... powerful.

She slumped, feeling like something had been ripped from her, and through her blurred, blinking eyes, she could've sworn that shadows of the forest shifted around her.

Glowing violet eyes stared at her through the dark.

The birds ceased their singing. The leaves around her had scattered.

Isla gulped down air, her teeth chattering and body shaking so violently she may have been vibrating.

Whatever had stirred settled now, but Isla still felt charged... yet, somehow, exhausted.

She scanned the forest again. There was nothing there.

The world swayed.

A possibility reared in her head, but she shut it down; she wouldn't accept it.

She dug the heels of her palms into her eyes, shaking her head, a tired whimper slipping from her lips. Nothing. It had to be nothing.

She couldn't handle much else.

CHAPTER 34

RAANA

Raana whipped her head southward as her shadows bit along her skin, buzzing with an energy she'd never felt from them before. She'd been in the final ascent of the mountain, just about to reach her cottage door, when she felt the pull. Not what she'd felt with Adrien on the night of the Equinox, but something... different.

Strange.

She spun back, focusing on her task: get her grimoire and get out.

It had been her own personal mission, her own small escape.

After she'd snapped in the greenhouse, something had shifted in her and Nerissa's relationship—if it could even be called that.

Nerissa had wanted her to embrace her true self, to get a taste for the breadth of her power. Perhaps, it was time for Raana to do just that. To brace herself to fight. And for that, she wanted all the weapons in her arsenal.

Her greatest?

Her mother's grimoire. Her family's secrets.

Sneaking away hadn't been difficult with Nerissa somewhere Raana couldn't trace her, busy working on the spell with Kai and Isla's blood.

Jumping between the shadows, it had only taken half a day's travel and rest to make it to her mountain home. When she'd walked these passes with Adrien only a few weeks ago, she'd been so weak, so slow.

Back then, he kept telling her to remove her iron ring and embrace her fae body, but she refused. Now, with only the lesser enchantment in place, she could see he had been right. Not only had it been easier to move through the darkness, but her body had been stronger, faster, and her senses were keener. Now she could avoid the paths that swarmed with Io's guards.

Her cottage appeared just as ghostly as Phobos's Pack Hall. A shell of itself, a remnant of a life once lived—her prison and her sanctuary. She hadn't been back since she'd learned of Helene's betrayal.

The potted flowers near the front door had died without her care. She sifted around their dried periwinkle buds and cracked stems until she found her rusty house key. It rasped as it slid into the keyhole and clicked as it turned.

A swirl of dust kicked up in the soft spill of moonlight that trailed in behind her after she shoved the door open. The cottage had never been a grand space, but it felt even smaller now after spending so long in the crumbling palace. From where she stood in the entry hall, she could see everything—the living room, dining area, washroom, and her bedroom.

Her heart clenched, morose homesickness wrapping around her throat.

This silence—she liked this silence. This bittersweet nothing.

Perhaps a few hours by the fire with a good book wouldn't hurt. Maybe, for once, she could forget. She could escape this world into the black-and-white pages, in this cage that felt like home.

The fire in the hearth roared to life after she struck it, its heat washing over her. Raana embraced it, her fingers playing in the light and shadows it cast, though she hated that being here tugged at a memory.

Adrien.

"Spirits," she grumbled, hanging her head.

Get over this. Get over him.

She swore she could feel him behind her, watching as he had been the last time they'd been here together. All his handsomeness, bravado, and aggravating—

Wait.

With her eyes wide and shadows swirling around her, Raana gently rose to her feet. Her hand slowly reached for the steel fire poker perched against the hearth's stone outlay.

Not possible.

But still, she moved on instinct, shadow to shadow, her body colliding with something hard, firm, and warm. She got her footing, one of her hands finding a shoulder while the other positioned the sharp end of the poker against the soft, delicate skin of a throat.

Raana's chest heaved as she stared into the golden-green eyes that had been the subject of every dream and nightmare. "Adrien?"

His gentle smile obliterated her while the firelight danced divinely across his face. "You're getting better with that," the prince said, tipping his head to the poker, his raven locks shifting.

This had to be a dream. She hadn't traveled here at all. She was back in the hall, corrupted by dark magic. Sleeping.

"Are you real?" She hadn't meant to whisper the question aloud.

But then she watched, wide-eyed, as Adrien's hand rose to feel along his own chest. "I feel real."

He certainly did.

The muscles of his arm tensed and relaxed beneath her touch in a way she'd come to know well, and her shadows didn't seem to protest his presence. In fact, they began weaving around their legs, drawing them together. The back of her eyes stung, and her heart galloped. "What are you—what are you doing here? How are you here?"

"Waiting for you. And I walked. Unlike some people, I don't have shadows to carry me across the world."

Smartass.

Raana's laugh was edged with a sob, and she squeezed his shoulder again.

Real.

She dipped into her magic, using it to get a sense of that aura of summer storms and living embers.

Real.

Him. This was *him.*

Waiting for her.

Still, she didn't drop the poker. "How—how did you know I'd come here?"

Adrien didn't flinch at the weapon still pressed to his throat. He nodded to the side. "You left me a friend."

Raana watched as a writhing sliver of darkness crept over his shoulder. Hers. But not from this cottage, not the ones that gravitated towards her. It dripped with her essence. This was one of her own making. Her brows twitched towards each other, her jaw slackening.

It slid over his shoulder to her hand, down her arm, and up her neck to her ear, where she felt it like a kiss against her skin. His kiss—that had been burned into her memory, burned into every intimate part of her body.

And then, she heard his voice—an unheard question. *Tell me you're okay. Please.*

Her features falling, Raana met Adrien's eyes, his tight smile as if, somehow, he'd known what it said to her. "I've been going out of my mind trying to figure out what happened to you."

The poker faltered, and Raana let it fall to her side. She tried to wrap her mind around it. All of this. "It told you where I was going?"

Had the shadow always been connected to her, connecting *them*?

"I get a feeling—I *got* a feeling, and I trusted my gut. It led me to you. Always does," he said. "I figured you were coming here and knew where you hid the key. So, I waited."

Raana could barely swallow as her eyes slid over his face. Darkness smudged beneath his eyes, and there was something more sunken and sadder about his features. She wanted to kiss away the bitterness, wrap herself up in him and use him, let him use her, and forget the world existed—their horrible coping mechanism.

But the past, all she'd done, slammed down between them, separating them like a great wave. She stepped back, moving from where they'd ended up by the dining table, and headed for the potion's cabinet to retrieve her grimoire.

Staying wasn't an option anymore.

"You shouldn't be here," she said, then cursed. No, that wasn't the right thing to say. There were too many apologies she owed. Raana paused at the kitchen counter and turned. She squared her shoulders and looked him dead in the eyes. "I'm sorry."

It didn't make her feel much better; it hadn't mended everything perfectly as she imagined.

Adrien had remained in his place, and for a moment, she feared again that he'd been an illusion. "For?"

Raana let out a breath. "Everything."

Silence.

Adrien's footsteps were heavy as he approached, punctuating every hard beat of her heart. He halted a few feet away. "Did you kill that man I saw you with at the river?"

His gaze was pleading, and though she understood why he'd think it, the hurt cleaved her chest. "You think I could?"

"No, I don't." Another step, and he leaned against the countertop, looming over her. So close again. *Spirits*, his mouth was perfect. "Which is why I'm confused."

Raana mastered herself and that traitorous organ in her chest. There was no reason to hide the truth from him. She looked away, searching for a knife to cut her hand, an offer of blood to open the cabinet. "It wasn't me. It was another of Nerissa's soldiers."

"Nerissa?"

"That's the witch's name." Raana tensed, realizing she'd never actually told Adrien where she'd gone. "She's the witch who—"

His features darkened. "I know."

"Oh." When the counter yielded nothing, she moved to the altar, their tribute to the Mother and Spirits. "The soldier's name was Callan."

More silence. One beat. Two.

"Oh, Goddess."

Raana turned to find Adrien had braced himself on the countertop. "You know him?"

"I—I grew up with him," Adrien breathed. "He's a warrior, and he dated Isla for a while."

"He knew Isla?" Raana's whispered question had been more for herself. It seemed Nerissa had taken so many wolves of Io into her clutches.

Adrien nodded, a grimace sliding across his face, his voice hollow. "I just had to talk to his family, Sandrine's family, and apologize for bringing her into the Wilds."

Raana's chest cracked, her mouth falling open. "I... I'm so sorry."

But was she?

She'd done this. She'd cost that woman her life. She'd chosen him— and she'd choose him again.

How had his father reacted? Adrien was alive, still standing, at least? Save for the tired look on his face, he appeared unscathed, though shadows danced in his eyes, a haunting of memories he hadn't wanted to share. She couldn't help but notice he took a step back from her, and her heart cleaved further.

"Why were you both in Deimos?" he asked softly, suspiciously. "What were you doing?"

Shame clawed its way up her throat. "I needed to do something—for her." His face blanched, and he took another step back. Heat flared her cheeks, and she wished the shadows would gather and whisk her away. "She would've done it with or without me, and if I hadn't done it, people could've died."

"People *did* die." Anger laced his words, and Raana flinched. The lines of his face softened only slightly. "So, Callan works for her now? Like her rogues?"

"He has no control over what he's doing. I've tried breaking the spell, but it just hurts him. That's why he snapped when Eli—" Adrien flinched. "When Eli called him by his name. It's unbearable to watch him try to break the enchantment. I can't imagine the experience... I tried to save Eli, but he was too far gone. That's when you showed up."

A muscle feathered in Adrien's jaw. "Where's Callan now?"

"Somewhere in the hall."

Adrien raised a brow. "In Phobos?"

Raana nodded.

"It's still standing?" he asked, clearly baffled.

"Barely," she said. "It's falling apart, and the dark magic makes the hallways move. So much of it is warded against the fae and crafted with iron that my magic is almost useless. I've been searching for him and anyone else she has enslaved, but I can't find them anywhere."

Adrien paced a few steps away, absorbing it all, shaking his head, and cursing under his breath. Raana tracked down her knife behind some crystals and pressed it to the fleshy part of her hand as he asked, "Do you know what she's planning?"

She cut too deeply. "Not really."

Lie, her mind screamed. *Lie. Don't tell him the entire truth.*

There was a chance he wouldn't forgive her if he learned who her task had targeted, but... she couldn't bring herself to spew the untruth.

Her palm itched as her immortal healing kicked in, the wound knitting together. "Nerissa says she doesn't want to hurt them. She's adamant about it. She even swore it to me by her blood." Raana braced herself and turned, using her magic to open the cabinet, feeling the pull and drain of her energy. Blood magic. There was always a cost. The spell Nerissa was doing would require her own sacrifice, too. "But she needed Kai and Isla's blood for a spell, and I had to get some of it from the coronation ceremony."

She wished there had been silence.

Wished she hadn't heard him roar. "She what?"

Raana had pulled the grimoire from the cabinet and shut it just as Adrien cornered her. The wood shook as her back collided with it, and his arms boxed her in. The gold in his eyes blazed, his temper fuming. "Why does she need their blood?"

Raana didn't find herself cowering from his fire—she matched it. "I don't know."

He bared his teeth. "Don't lie to me."

She exposed hers right back, tucking her grimoire close to her chest. "I. Don't. Know. Not fully." The air between them heated. "She said the blood will help her show them the past—their past—give them answers and help them understand themselves."

"Understand themselves how?"

"Maybe you should ask her yourself," she snipped, moving to slide away from him.

With his forearms flat on the cabinet's wood, he corralled her in entirely. His broad body lined up with hers, leaving her nowhere to go. The scent of him was intoxicating. The heat, the closeness.

She huffed. "You know I can just shadow around you, right?"

Adrien pressed closer. "Then, do it."

No.

She wouldn't admit it was because she enjoyed this... as frustrating as he was.

Her heart thundered, and her breath caught when his fingers dipped into her curls, pushing them back to reveal what was hidden beneath them. He ran his finger over the arch of her ear. "So, I get the real you—or part of you." She hadn't been able to glamour away the ears, only her sharpened teeth and glowing fingertips. "The enchantment's not as strong?"

"I lost my ring." She flashed her bracelet. "I've had to make do."

Adrien hummed and leaned closer, his breath a hot wash over the pointed shell. The question he whispered was not what she'd expected. "Why haven't you killed her?"

The interrogation felt unfair given their closeness. Raana couldn't think much beyond him to say anything but the truth. "I don't have anyone. Everyone in my life has died or abandoned me. So, I take what I can get, even allies who are just people with similar enemies."

Adrien fell back, a plethora of emotions moving over his face as he scanned hers. "You want my father dead?" A mutual desire between her and the elder witch... and many others, she was sure.

Raana inclined her head, her lips inching closer to his. "Do you?"

For a moment, there was only their mingling breath, the places their bodies barely brushed, and this cabinet whose contents wouldn't survive if he took her against it.

Adrien's throat bobbed, and then he straightened. Raana found herself gasping for air as he paced a few steps away.

He ran his hands through his hair in the way he always did when he was frustrated. In the way she wanted to right now. Her eyes flicked down to where he strained against his pants. She bit her lip.

"Is she expecting you back?"

Raana snapped her eyes up to meet his, seeking a dark and mischievous glint there, finding enough of a glimmer to set her blood and mind racing.

Sex with him would solve a lot of problems. Mainly short-term ones, and then create long-term problems. But life was short... unless she was immortal.

"She doesn't know I left," she said wantonly.

"That's good." Adrien matched her low tone. "Because I need you."

Raana's heart was about to burst through her ribcage. She stepped closer, leaving her grimoire on the counter and leaning against it. "For what?"

Adrien grinned, and it was every bit as reckless, damning, and charming as he was. "We're breaking into the prison."

CHAPTER 35

KAI

Kai was grateful for the bane flowing through his system because the battling personalities in the council chamber might have sent him spiraling, weaseling into minds, and ripping away words for some peace and silence to think. The news of Eli's death had ripped through the continent with a ferocity that would've impressed Kai if it hadn't caused him such a migraine. Since they'd discovered his body, the story had made it to the leader of every kingdom and had even littered the newspapers in some packs.

A warrior was dead in Deimos. *Murdered*. And not just any warrior—a *general* here to protect them from the rogues when "they couldn't protect themselves." Eli was a hero to some, a martyr.

In reality, he was an unlucky bastard, and Kai appreciated whatever the general had been hoping to do in going against Cassius to find Callan, despite any ill will he'd had towards either of them in the past. He'd ensured his body, cooling beneath the hall, had been cleaned and prepared with respect for his beta father's impending retrieval.

But Eli wasn't the only elite fighter who'd been dealt a poor fate on Deimos's grounds. Another was still missing. And that news, the greatest source of this headache, had been held back until now. He should've suspected, with Cassius's conniving ass being involved, that there was a cover-up happening, or at least that the Alpha was biding his time to hit with a hard blow of the second warrior's fate.

It was all so perfectly calculated, so fucking infuriatingly, perfectly calculated, that Kai almost had to admire how much of a prick the Alpha was. He had half a mind to storm the Imperial Hall and rip through his mind to learn the truth of it all, but if Cassius did know *everything*, then he'd be prepared. Kai would just end up with a blade in his chest while his family watched.

He glanced from where he sat on the council room's dais to Isla, seated behind a crescent-shaped desk as she watched Sol, their Head of Laws, and Afalin, their Head of Pack Relations, discussing their scouts. Though she looked stunning, every bit the queen in the room with her subtle adornment and navy dress that draped over her body perfectly, her stare was vacant, lost.

She was fighting so hard to keep herself together, but each day since they'd pulled Eli from the water had taken its toll. He could see it, feel it. She barely spoke, ate, or slept. And she was always... cold. *Physically* cold, particularly when her wolf rose to the surface. That was something to address another day with Olyvia.

Isla put on a brave face in front of others, in front of him, but he knew her. He'd seen and loved that fire in her eyes too much not to notice it guttering, and it terrified him. She'd told him in fragments about the girl she'd been before. How deep into darkness she'd fallen. He'd be damned if he let her become another in his long line of ghosts.

Shifting his attention to his right, he looked at Ameera. Though she hadn't formally been announced as the beta yet and technically still hadn't accepted, Kai had asked her to take that seat today. In his council room, he made the rules. Anyone who opposed may find themselves under the same scrutiny and dealt the same fate as the four council members Kai had stripped of their positions after the challenge, those who seemed too loyal to his father's ways and were replaced with others of his choosing.

"Our scouts did not return," Reuben, the High Commander of the Guard, said. "With all that's occurring now, sending in more would be inadvisable. We've caught two more of Locke's spies in rogue lands. Neither talked, despite our best efforts, before they were discarded."

"What do you do with the bodies?" Nia, his new Head of Coin, asked.

"Burning them makes it easier to pin on rogues," Reuben answered.

"Why don't you just bring them in? Give them a *proper interrogation* here."

"Because that worked *so* well with the rogues," Afalin mused.

They hadn't gleaned much at all from the rogues, but now that Kai knew of the witch, he wondered how much she and her abilities with memories and enchantments came into play with how little information they possessed.

"Rogues are a different breed," Reuben said. "They have no one to answer to. They just want chaos and destruction. It's a hive mentality."

Sol brought them back to the topic at hand. "Bringing Locke's spies into our territory and holding them is against the Code. We may already have breached that with Charon, but their pack members voluntarily entered our borders. It's different to infiltrate rogue territory and pull them out. If we're caught, the consequences on a continental stage are dire."

"Continental stage?" Reuben scoffed. "What good is it anymore to play by the rules? War is imminent within the continent. I imagine we should be bracing for more direct blows from the Imperials and their allies soon. Charon *is* our doorstep." Kai noticed Isla swallow out of the corner of his eye. "Especially if they've captured our scouts." Reuben suddenly turned to Kai. "I imagine that's why Alpha Verena has asked for an immediate audience with you, Alpha. Tomorrow, at the latest."

"So demanding," Afalin drawled with a condescending undercurrent to his tone. "Who does she think she is?"

"An alpha," Kai bit out. "Just as much as I am."

Though he had paused at the demand of the order from one of his father's longest friends. He wondered how much his father had told Verena about him, his errant son who had little respect for Kyran's rules and wishes.

"Well, today is nearly over, and Beta Sampson will be arriving from Iapetus tomorrow afternoon. We can't put them in the same room," Afalin argued before lowering his voice, seeming to know the name he brought up next was sensitive. "Remember what Ezekiel said about their recent confrontation at the Feast? Verena left Callisto. She didn't even stay to watch the hunters be sent off."

"Why would she?" Sol countered. "She hasn't had a trainee approved in years. I'm surprised she attended at all."

Kai hadn't noticed any confrontation, but then again, he'd been a bit preoccupied that night.

Afalin's agitation became more than apparent in the knocking of his fist on the council's bench. "So, what do we tell Alpha Verena? We can't afford to lose allies, particularly ones that could easily block our access to the Southern Waters."

Kai already had his solution. After allowing them enough time to debate, he spoke. "I will remain here to handle Beta Sampson. Luna Isla will go to Mimas with Ameera and speak with Alpha Verena."

The room went silent, looks of disbelief flashing across many faces before they righted themselves. Though most directed their eyes to Isla, who he felt tense through their bond hazed by the bane, Kai kept his pointed stare fixed on each of them. A cold and brutal calm washed over him. "Comments?"

No one offered any, but the unspoken words choked the room. Kai turned slightly to his mate, watching her fists clench and unclench over the skirt of her dress.

"*Come on.*" He pulled at the pieces of the bond, hoping the words came through, if not audibly, then through a coaxing phantom touch. "*You've never been one to back down from a fight, beautiful.*"

As if she heard it, or maybe it had just been her own courage, Isla straightened. "All of you have permission to speak freely." She met each council member's eyes, too, an ember flickering in hers that warmed him.

They remained quiet, though some exchanged wary stares.

It was Afalin who broke the silence. "I..."

He trailed off when Kai leaned back in his seat, hands folding over his stomach. He was a predator, a protector, stalking around Isla's feet. He could've sworn he felt his mate pull at him, telling him to stop being an overbearing bastard. It almost made him smile. He took that feeling, that tether, and tried his best to embrace it before it faded.

"I mean no disrespect to you, Luna," Afalin continued. "But your coronation was very recent. You're new to the position. New to Deimos. And Ameera"—he gestured warily to the general at Kai's other side—"is not the beta, as it currently stands. I don't know if answering an alpha's invitation without Alpha Kai is the best course of action. And your—"

He snapped his mouth shut, and Kai had a feeling he knew where he was heading next. The elephant in the room: Isla's lineage. Verena's dislike for the Imperial Alpha and his pack was not a well-kept secret.

Kai glanced at Isla, who did not look at him in question or for comfort. That warrior's stare was fixed on her opponent.

Suddenly, Isla sat even taller, tilting her head slightly, her hair shifting over a shoulder, the gold rippling in the pillars of sunlight spilling through the windows. "I may be new to this, Delta." Her voice was smooth, low, and lethal—and Goddess, did it turn Kai on. "But I have observed court my entire life. If where I come from has taught me anything, if becoming a warrior has taught me anything, it's brutal discipline, etiquette, and how to navigate overwhelming personalities—and Marin has also trained me into the ground. Believe me, when I set foot on her territory, I will know Mimas and Verena, her consort, heir, staff, people, and their strengths and weaknesses upside down and backwards." She let those words linger for a few heartbeats as she settled back, a demure yet confident smile on her face. "Any other questions?"

None.

Wisely, no one spoke, and Kai needed a cold bucket of water. Her words seemed to have worked for some, as cautious looks and tense shoulders eased. But not everyone. Not Afalin.

"Council adjourned, then." Kai leaned forward, resting his elbows on the bench. "As a reminder, though it should go without question, whatever was said in this room remains in confidence. Any breach will result in a penalty of the highest accord. Clear?"

A resounding, *yes, Alpha,* echoed through the chamber.

"Dismissed."

Each member of the council rose and bowed to him, then to Isla. That warrior's mask remained on her face as each exited the room, though gradually, it began to crack, piece by piece, and each fallen fragment tore a part of him with it.

First, the slump of her shoulders, then a downturn of her lips, a small, tired breath slipping the rosy softness. Then that fire sputtered to cinders, still hot but fading.

Shit.

When Sol, the final remaining delta, had left, Ameera rose to her feet, earning both of their attention. "I'll let you know of my decision after this trip."

Kai nodded, fighting his urge to ask what answer she was leaning towards. "Very well."

Ameera began descending the dais to leave Kai and Isla alone, as if sensing they needed to talk, but paused. She spun on a heel, and the shades of emotion in her eyes were nearly impossible to decipher.

"If you visit my father again, don't mention me becoming beta to him," were her only words before leaving the room, closing the grand double doors of the chamber behind her.

Isla's eyes had been fixed on where she'd disappeared. A few silent breaths passed before she said, "She wants to see him, but she's afraid she'll say something that she'll regret and ruin everything between them."

Kai studied her. "How do you know?"

"Because I do."

He pursed his lips. Not sure if it would be best to bring up her own father now or try to distract her from it. "You handled that beautifully, by the way. I thought Afalin was about to soil himself."

The small distraction seemed to work, the corner of her lips ticking up slightly. "He wasn't entirely wrong, though. I *am* very new."

"And you weren't wrong either. You've done everything you could to prepare yourself."

Isla leaned back, gazing up at the council room's ceiling. A scowl slipped across her features as she observed what was painted there. Just as they had in the throne room, the three goddesses loomed over the council chamber.

"Always watching," Isla mused, darkly.

Kai cast his eyes over the three women who seemed to hold their lives in their hands. "Yes, they are."

CHAPTER 36

ISLA

Isla awoke to a nudge against her face and a kiss of sunlight across her brow. Slowly, she cracked open her eyes, lifting her cheek from Kai's chest. She'd been using him as a mattress after they'd spent the night in a heap of blankets before their fireplace.

Last night, in preparation for their first time apart since they'd been mated, downing wine had led to soft kisses and caresses, which then became the stripping of clothes, then finally, her legs wrapped around Kai as he blew the world away.

Isla's vision cleared to find the bak pup as she typically did these past mornings, stubbed tail wagging, red eyes innocently gazing at her as if she were its entire world.

"Good morning," she whispered.

A glance up beyond Kai's still-slumbering features revealed the little sleep space she'd crafted him by the glass doors to their veranda. Isla had grabbed every blanket she could find, and the bak had tunneled a hole into them like a den.

He sniffed before padding forward on his notably clawless paws and shoved his head in the confined space beneath the brawny arm that had been looped around Isla's back. He pushed Kai's arm up until her mate roused just enough for him to get beneath it. As he snuggled in, Kai's eyes fluttered open. Confusion painted his face, then a mildly

294

concerned smile when he took in Isla's beaming grin. "Good morning, beautiful."

The gravelly baritone of his voice in the morning never failed to send a shiver down her spine.

"Morning, handsome," she cooed too sweetly for him not to frown.

He began to mouth something like *what did you do* when he finally clocked the leathery hide of something beneath his arm. He lifted it, and the bak yipped in protest. "Every morning that I wake up, I cannot believe this is real."

Isla ran a hand over the bak's head to get it to settle. He sidled closer to Kai's side. She laughed, laying her own head back on his chest. "He *is* cuddly, isn't he?" she said to the bak.

"Goddess, this is madness," Kai murmured, relaxing his head back to stare at the ceiling.

Isla felt his fingers stroke down her naked spine.

"Perhaps. He also seems to enjoy your heat. Maybe he can take my place in the bed while I'm gone."

Kai lifted his head, meeting her eyes, unamused. "Funny. And I don't need the reminder."

"I'm leaving in a few hours," Isla said, and Kai dramatically shushed her. She chuckled. "You made it twenty-five years without me. You can survive a few days." She pretended the words didn't feel like a blow to her chest.

"I don't remember what life was like before you, and I don't want to."

"Oh, you can do better than that."

Kai's chuckle reverberated through her body, and Isla sucked in a breath when he flipped them over, pressing her back into the floor and settling between her legs. His elbows bracketed either side of her head as he pressed his weight down onto her, her body igniting in response.

The bak stared at them, his head cocked to the side.

"Can you give us a minute?" Kai asked, and somehow understanding, the creature got to its paws and padded back to its burrow. Kai watched him the whole way, bewilderment twisting his features before he hung his head and just... laughed. It was something genuine that warmed her heart. "What the hell, Isla?"

Isla beamed, running her fingers through his curls, pushing them back from his face. "At this point, we should name him."

"This is sounding more and more permanent," Kai said, trying to sound stern, but those dimples bracketed his smile. Isla brushed her thumbs over them. "You do realize that he's going to grow into a ferocious monster three times our size. A monster we've killed many of."

That fact felt like a weight on her chest. "Well, right now, he's a baby without a mother, and if he didn't have us, he would die."

"He's a baby monster."

"Maybe not." Isla shrugged as she adjusted beneath him, her skin gliding along his. "Monsters are made."

That seemed to strike a chord with Kai. Though still, he argued, "Instinct is instinct. He could hurt someone." But then his features fell as a wave of thoughts and emotions passed over his face. "We'll talk about it when you get back." He kissed her once, chastely on the mouth, and when he pulled back, he said, "You're ready." Not a question.

Isla's stomach clenched. "Verena will not have great things to say about Io or my father. I just can't lose it. I need to detach myself, make them nothing to me." When they meant everything. "Do you think she'll speak plainly with me about the rebels? About what she wants?"

"I hope so. But I want you to be safe."

Isla tsked. "When have I not been?" Kai raised a brow, and her beam widened. Wrapping her arms around his neck and her legs around his waist, she pulled him closer. "I'll be safe, I promise. Ameera will be with me."

He brushed his nose against hers. "Okay." His kiss was soft and simple, but his following movements weren't so pure. He moved to her jaw, her neck, between her breasts. Then to one, then the other.

Isla breathed a moan, arching into his mouth. "What are you doing?" she asked, even if it was obvious.

He blazed a trail down her stomach, peppered kisses on her hips, gripped her thighs, and kissed her skin before settling her legs over his shoulders. He smirked up at her. "A little parting gift."

Even his wash of breath over her center had her bucking.

And then Kai leaned forward, sweeping his tongue over her once with that featherlight softness that drove her absolutely mad.

Isla let out a blissful sigh, fingers burying in his hair, undulating hips steadied by a firm hand on her coiling lower belly. She kept her eyes locked on his.

He kept things slow and soft, devouring her delicately yet holding her tight until her nerves were raw, until her skin tingled, until just one more perfect stroke would topple her over the precipice he'd gradually taken her to.

But he'd prevented that somehow, allowing the pressure to build, build, and build, her breaths becoming shallower as her muscles strained and her back arched. Her nails dug into his scalp, her thighs squeezing, but his mouth—biting, licking, and kissing—was as relentless as his name slipping off her lips.

Let go, beautiful. She swore she heard the words—felt them—through their recovering bond.

And let go she did.

Isla had one thing she wanted to do before she left for Mimas: find Sebastian. Though she was trying not to let it cloud her thoughts, the last time she'd seen their father still weighed heavily on her heart, and if anyone understood him like she did, it was her brother.

Sebastian hadn't been in his guest suite or anywhere else in the House, and it took asking the staff to learn he'd gone for a run in the nearby forest.

So, Isla had made her way to the woodland, perched herself on a moss-covered boulder, tall enough that her feet couldn't reach the ground, while she waited for her brother to return.

The crunch of leaves and twigs beneath heavy feet and labored breaths hit her first. Not long after, Sebastian crested the hillside, his body dampened with sweat and his golden hair half-pulled back to keep out of his face.

He skidded to a halt, his eyes wide and his hands going to his hips as he caught his breath. "Pudge?" A warm, sly smile broke across his face. "What are you doing here, Your Majesty?"

Her title shouldn't have grated her so thoroughly. She resisted the urge to ask him to drop the formalities and swung her feet several times, knocking her heels against the rock's surface. "Looking for you."

Sebastian's smile faltered. "Well, that can't be good." He wiped his brow once with his equally damp forearm before going for his shirt, which he'd removed and tucked partly into the waistband of his loose running pants. "Are you here to tell me to be on my best behavior while you're gone?"

Isla held in her laugh, leaning back and pressing her hands into the soft moss behind her. "Maybe I should be."

"Don't worry. I'll be a model citizen."

"Sure you will."

All he gave in return was a grin as he slung his shirt around his neck.

Isla, though less devilish, found herself returning it. She wouldn't tell him outright if only to prevent stroking his ego, but she was grateful he'd asked to stay. A war of guilt and relief waged inside her, touched with fear.

Maybe she should've put her foot down and told him he couldn't remain here, to keep him safe. She couldn't imagine him being dishonorably cast out as a rogue, unable to join any other pack.

"Why did you want to stay?" she asked. "You know the consequences of being out of the pack longer than you're supposed to be."

If the worst ever came to be, she'd likely make him stay here in Deimos, taking the brunt of the consequences and fighting anyone who tried to take him away.

Sebastian's features scrunched as if that were the dumbest question anyone had ever asked. "Because you're my little sister. A big, new house, a fancy title, a crown, and a mate who could probably kick my ass—those things don't change that. They haven't really changed you." He gripped both ends of his slung shirt and paced a few steps closer. "You're still terrible at asking for help and want to do everything on your own. You never want anyone looking out for you because you don't want to be a burden. You're stubborn to a fault..."

Isla narrowed her eyes yet fought to keep a smile from creeping on her face. "Please, go on."

Sebastian snickered. "I'm afraid we'd be out here all night, and you have a boat to catch."

Isla lifted her eyes, seeking the sun's position. She didn't have much time left. "Are you afraid you upset Dad?" she asked. Not the subject she should be focused on.

"Afraid? No. I definitely upset him. Or, at least, disappointed him and made his life hellish with Cassius." His features edged into a scowl before softening again. "But he'll understand that I'm here for our family. At the end of the day, after all the politics and bullshit, that's what matters."

Something deeper lay within the words, something raw, but Isla was too distracted to pick it apart.

Family.

Tell him. All of it. Right now. Don't be selfish.

Isla opened her mouth, closed it, and opened it again. "Do you want to take a walk?"

Sebastian laughed. "I just ran twelve miles worth of hills, but sure."

Isla slid down from her rocky perch, her legs shockingly unsteady. She crossed her arms over her chest, leading them down an easy path so she wouldn't have to brace as many inclines.

"Do you think I was out of line on the Equinox? Accusing Dad of— what I did." She wrung her hands together and took a few moments to survey the brush. "I just... need someone to be honest with me. Kai would, I'm sure, but he's also horribly biased in my favor."

Sebastian rubbed his neck. "Well, maybe you were harsh."

"Great." A pit formed in Isla's stomach. She snatched a twig off the ground to at least have something to do with her hands.

Sebastian ran a hand through the tree they passed by, ripping down a russet-orange leaf and pulling it apart at its stemmy veins. "What made you think he could? I mean, Dad and Eli weren't getting along, but I don't think he'd murder him. Let alone claw him to bits like that."

She hadn't really taken that part into account that night—the brutality of the killing. Eli had been eviscerated.

She wondered exactly how much her brother knew already, but she didn't hesitate to confide, "Eli mentioned trying to talk to Dad about Cassius covering some things up that Eli wanted no part of, and Dad shut him down. Told him he needed to drop it before he got hurt."

She paused, allowing the words to sink in, and where Isla had expected shock, Sebastian's features didn't waver. For a moment, deep down, some fractured part of her feared he had been some kind of double agent, but then his face pinched into a scowl.

He said nothing, so she asked, "Do you know anything?"

Sebastian tossed the skeletal remains of his leaf on the ground. "Most of what I've been told lately was only related to Deimos, Kyran, and how little we trusted them. Basically, everything I told you that night in your apartment. I haven't been told much of anything since the Hunt."

Of course not. Cassius likely suspected Isla and Kai were mates by then.

"But Dad did mention rogues and rebellions to Adrien and me before Eli showed up. He also said the continent wouldn't like seeing us play favorites for being at your coronation. Even though you're my Goddess-damn sister, you may as well be Adrien's, and you're his daughter. Cassius wants to prevent everything from collapsing."

Isla growled under her breath. "Cassius's definition of 'collapse' is everything no longer working in his favor."

When Sebastian didn't immediately respond, Isla feared she'd stepped too far. But he began, just as they reached the gurgling creek's edge, "I know he's technically my Alpha—well, until he banishes me—and I know he's Adrien's dad, but I hate that guy."

"I don't think I've ever agreed with you more."

"Dad's his Beta and has been his best friend for twice as long as we've been alive. He's loyal to him to a fault, and I can't blame him. I'd follow Adrien to war." His face curled at the last word. Not the best choice. "Sometimes, I think about whether he'd choose him or us."

Isla snapped her head towards him. "You do?"

"Sometimes," he repeated and didn't elaborate. Instead, he kicked a rock into the water and asked, "Do you know where Callan is?"

Isla's heart sank, and she looked away, trailing the water's flow and watching tadpoles mill about in the murk. "I have a suspicion, and I hope I'm wrong." She trailed off, and Sebastian eyed her expectantly. She kicked her own rock, her heart thundering. "I need... I need you to listen to me before you start freaking out, okay? Please. Listen to everything I say, and don't do anything rash."

Sebastian's brows drew inwards. "Anything that starts like this can't be good."

It's not.

Isla steeled herself. "I think Callan was taken by a witch."

Sebastian's expression didn't falter much to her surprise. "The one you've been hunting?"

"Yes." She felt her lungs squeeze, and she coughed. *Not again.* "She escaped a prison in Io where Cassius is holding witches, hoping to use them, I assume, against us."

Sebastian jerked back. "He what? How do you know that?"

"Kai." *Or Ezekiel.*

Sebastian blinked. "Does Adrien know?"

Isla rubbed a hand along her arm to warm herself. "He, uh, confirmed it."

Hurt and confusion crossed her brother's face. "Why didn't he tell me?"

"I don't know, but there's more. When the witch first escaped, Cassius needed to catch her before anyone found out. So, he..." *Goddess, spit it out.* "That was where he sent Mom and her team years ago. Their trip to the southern territories was to track her down for Cassius, and the witch ended up killing or capturing them all."

A weight simultaneously lifted and pulverized her chest.

Sebastian's eyes had gone so wide that Isla could find flecks of brown in the pine green as if he'd truly been crafted for the forest. "And how do you know that?"

"The witch told me, more or less, when she took me. Mom was captured."

Isla swore she could see Sebastian's heart pounding through his bare chest, beating straight through his rib cage. He paced a few steps back from her, his eyes glossing.

"Seb—" Isla started, but he cut her off.

"She's alive, isn't she?" A broken and hopeful smile slid across his face. "She's alive."

Isla went rigid. There was understanding in his voice.

But still, he said, "Say it," like he needed her to confirm the impossible. To make it real.

Isla swallowed a sob, her eyes stinging as she nodded. For a moment, she couldn't get the words out. "She's alive."

And just like that, the ghost that stood between them vanished.

A single tear slid down his cheek, and he didn't wipe it away until it reached the stubble of his jaw. His body shook as he laughed and cried in disbelief. She couldn't think of the last time she'd seen him like this... if ever.

Isla wiped the tears from her eyes, remembering her mother in that cave when they were finally, *truly* face-to-face again. How broken she had been, how much she'd gone through.

"Fucking hell." He paced a few steps away, rubbing the bridge of his nose. "I knew it."

The words struck her like a lash. "You knew?"

"I figured," he corrected, closing the distance between them again. "That's another reason why I stayed: to track her. I felt her in Abalys that night. I didn't know what to do. I thought I was going crazy and wanted to make sure before I talked to you or Dad... *Dad*." Sebastian took a few steps towards the hall. "We have to tell him."

Isla's stomach pitted when his face lit up at that.

"Wait, slow down. You have to let me finish."

"Finish once we get Mom." He ran a hand over his hair, shaking his head at himself. "Goddess, I'm not even asking the most important question. Where is she? Are you hiding her somewhere? How—how long have you known? Where did you find her?"

"Let me finish," was all Isla could say, and the softness of her tone spawned another frown on her brother's face. Nausea bubbled in her stomach. "She's been through a lot, Seb. The witch held her for years, torturing her."

Sebastian blanched, his fists clenching at his sides. She could've sworn she felt his wolf rising to the surface.

Isla couldn't pause. "She made her into—" *Monsters are made.* "She went through hell, and now, she's not the same. She did something really, really bad." That felt like downplaying it. Isla swallowed, bracing for another truth. "*She* killed the Alpha and Heir of Deimos."

Sebastian's body locked up, his eyes wide. His mouth opened to speak, but nothing came out.

Isla continued, "The witch uses her like a weapon, like she used the rogues. She basically stripped her sense of self and used her to kill Kai's family. She almost killed Kai."

"You're lying." Not an accusation but a plea.

"I wish I was," Isla said. "I haven't seen or heard from her since the night of the challenge."

"You saw her?" Sebastian's voice broke.

Isla nodded, her lower lip trembling. "She saved me, *has* saved me, more times than I ever realized. She saved you, too, that night." Apolla's face flashed through her mind again, and she winced.

Isla's expression and fracturing of words seemed enough for Sebastian to gather just how bad she'd looked. The fact that he'd felt their mother's touch that night she'd rescued him visibly rocked him. His features curled in anger. "Where is she now?"

"I don't know. She's skilled at remaining hidden... and I'm not sure she wants to be found." She didn't want to believe that.

Sebastian went quiet as he pondered the words, breaking them down. "Does Kai know it was her?"

She caught the unease on his face. "Yes."

"And how does he feel about all of it?" Careful, cautious words.

"I won't lie and say he's fine, or that he's forgiven her. But he understands she isn't the enemy. Honestly, we don't talk about it much," Isla said.

"How could you not?"

A defensiveness slipped into her voice. "Because everyone processes things differently, and that's how he is." She let out a long breath, Jonah's previously proclaimed desires ringing in her head. "I want to find her, I want to bring her home, but I don't think it's the best idea right now."

Sebastian reeled back like she'd punched him in the face. "Not the best idea?"

"Do you understand what she did? What could happen if it becomes known?" she gritted out. "She'd be arrested. Imprisoned at best or execute—" She couldn't finish the sentence. "Everyone here wants the killer's head on a spike. There's only so much I can do to protect her."

"That's where you'd draw your line?" Sebastian bit out.

The accusation in his tone made her blood boil, then ice over. "There's no line. There's no simple answer. This isn't easy. It's not just about me. It's not just us. Our family. Kai. She murdered a *king*. This involves all of Deimos, our allies, who want some form of justice. And once they're through with her, where do you think their attention goes next?" She paused, giving him a chance to answer. His falling features were enough of a response to show his understanding. They'd target her next, then him, their father. "I won't turn my back on my family. I can't, which means it would all lead to more suffering, more mess."

Sebastian blew out a hard breath, shaking his head. "So, what are we supposed to do?" He threw out his arms. "Pretend she's still dead? Like she doesn't matter, like she doesn't exist?"

"No," Isla snapped and then groaned. "Well, yes. She's better hidden. Safer."

"And you're sure she's safe?"

Isla's shoulders slumped. "No."

Sebastian let out an astonished breath. "What the hell are we supposed to tell Dad?"

"Nothing." Isla swallowed, guilt threatening to suffocate her. "If he knew the truth, he'd probably go after Cassius, and we know how that would end."

The warning worked two-fold. Sebastian couldn't try anything rash, either.

He shook his head, his features twisting in agony. It was too much. "This is fucked, Isla." His voice guttered.

"I know," she breathed. "I know."

A muscle feathered in Sebastian's jaw as a tense silence settled between them. Isla fought against the cold crystallizing her veins, against the stirring beneath her skin.

Not now. Not real. Not happening.

"How long have you known she was alive?"

She snapped her eyes up, watching the wind ruffle Sebastian's hair. And in a flash, he looked as he did the day they'd learned of their mother's fate. Though now, rather than agony and distress, his eyes gleamed with disappointment. "A few weeks."

"A few weeks," he repeated, his voice broken. His lips pursed, and he looked off as if he'd been recounting all the times he'd been with her, all the times he'd suspected their mother was alive, and thought himself crazy, sparing her his theories so he wouldn't reopen her old wounds while he suffered alone.

Isla stepped forward, her arm outstretched. "Seb—"

He retreated. "I need to think." He fell another step, backing down the hill. "Have, uh… have a good time in Mimas."

Isla didn't stop him, only watching as he disappeared into the brush.

~

When Isla looked into the murky river waters, she swore they still eddied with Eli's blood. She let the gentle rocking of it take her as she stood at the far edge of the dock while the crew readied the boat for their trip.

She didn't flinch when she heard the heavy footsteps on the wooden boards, only letting out a small breath when Kai came up behind her and wrapped his arms around her waist.

"Don't leave me," he whispered, with the perfect hint of drama, as he dropped his head to place a kiss on her neck. Isla wished it had been enough to crack the well of emotion in her chest. Better to fall apart and let it all out now with him than break down anywhere else.

Kai snapped his head up, examining the side of her face. "What happened?" When she didn't answer right away, his finger hooked beneath her chin and turned her gently.

She swallowed hard, her sky-blue eyes tumbling through the storms of his, seeking answers.

How much did he hate her mother for what she'd done? How much was he masking it for her sake?

"I talked to Sebastian, and now he knows everything." Her gaze lowered to the dock, tracing the rotted lines in the dark wood. "I should never have kept it from him. I had no right."

Kai fully turned her so he could take her in his arms. A simple, loving embrace to any outside eye while everyone was surely, secretly watching.

She should've done better to keep up appearances. Who knew how the gossips would spin her looking so downtrodden.

"No, it wasn't," Kai said softly. "You did what you thought you needed to do to protect him."

Isla wrapped her arms around him, sinking into his warmth and wishing they could stay like this forever. "All I did was put off the inevitable and found a way to hurt him more."

She felt Kai comb his fingers through her hair. "Where is he now?"

"I don't know." Worry clenched her heart like a fist. "I asked some of the staff to keep tabs on him, but I don't know where he went."

"I'll find him."

She pulled back to meet Kai's eyes again. "Thank you."

Kai took her face in his hands, crooning in a slightly mocking tone, "Anything for my beautiful mate."

Isla rolled her eyes, a smile tugging at her lips as a lightness spilled into her chest. And then, he closed the distance between them.

She sighed into the kiss, relishing the feeling of his mouth on hers, the way the world melted, and nothing else mattered in his embrace.

One of Kai's hands had gone to her waist, while the other angled her head, taking a little more of her lips as he traced his tongue along them. That *damn* tongue. Heat flooded her cheeks and pooled in her lower belly.

She could feel him smiling.

"Unfair," she whispered into the kiss, and then there was the sound of a cracking flashbulb nearby.

They broke apart, heads turning to where a reporter, not so smoothly, tried to hide behind a stack of barrels after snapping their photo.

With his narrowed focus remaining on the man, Kai asked her, "What do you think the headline will be?"

Isla groused, "Alpha is the world's biggest tease."

Kai chuffed a laugh and turned back to her. "This morning wasn't enough for you?"

"No." Her simple answer seemed to amuse him further, but then something dawned on her. Her eyes darted to either side of him. "Where's the pup?"

"At home."

Her eyes snapped to his. "By himself?"

"He was sleeping last I saw him."

Isla gaped. "But he's going to be terrified when he wakes up!"

The concern that edged her voice had surprised her as much as it seemed to surprise Kai. She couldn't explain how the little creature had captured her heart. Maybe it was his innocence. A monster not yet forged.

Hope. Most likely horribly misplaced hope.

Kai took her in frankly and lowered his voice. "Well, I can't bring a baby bak with me through the hall."

Isla sighed, gnawing on her lip in thought. "We're going to have to figure something out. Someone to watch him when we're not around."

"Oh, that'll be an easy sell," Kai mused. "Please watch our baby monster. We apologize if he decides to eat you."

Isla deadpanned, "We'll. Figure. Something. Out."

Kai's eyes slid over her face again, a smile tugging at his mouth. "If you're like this now, I can't imagine how you'll be with our pups."

The statement made Isla's stomach toss and flutter, but she snipped back, "If this is a test run, I'm afraid how you'll be." A lie. She couldn't wait to see him as a father and knew he'd be an amazing one. "Probably letting them run amok."

Kai poked at her side. "We'll just have to get there, won't we?"

Get there... when everything stopped being so shitty.

"One day." Isla smiled tightly.

Kai flicked her nose. "One day."

In the distance, she could hear the crew yelling that the ship was set to go, followed by the vessel's horn, which sent all the perched birds into flight. "I need to go."

"Technically, you go when you want to go," Kai said. "You are the queen."

"Okay, I *should* go. Any last words of advice?"

"Just be you."

"You can't do better than that?"

He huffed, muttering something about her being hard to please. "If you meet a guy named Jax, don't believe anything he says."

Isla furrowed her brows in amusement. "Why?"

"Because he tends to embellish stories of our youth."

"Ah." Isla grinned and reached up to pinch his cheek. "Tales from the rebellious little prince days."

Kai hummed in agreement before leaning down to kiss her, the embrace not lasting nearly long enough.

He pulled back just enough to rest his forehead against hers, murmuring, "I love you."

Isla brushed her mouth against his one last time, burning its perfect shape into her mind. "I love you. Stay out of trouble while I'm gone and expect me back if I feel anything wrong."

Kai laughed and echoed her mock threat. "Let's see if we can make it a few days without anything freakish happening."

Isla held back her scowl, feeling phantom ice fill her veins again.

Later. She'd tell him, worry him, later. They just needed to get through the following few days.

She stole one more kiss before they finally broke apart, then Isla headed to the boat and her first true test as queen. Kai watched her from the dock until they sailed from sight.

CHAPTER 37

ISLA

From her position at the bow, Isla gazed down the gradually broadening river, the wide expanse of the bluest water yawning back to the sea on the horizon. She would admit that she loved the sea as much as thunderstorms. The waters off Io's shores were one of her favorite places to relax. On the edges of cliffs, on warm sands, listening to the waves and gulls, having the smell of salt tickle her nose, and feeling the coolness of the water on her skin against Io's brutal heat.

Isla inclined her head, breathing in so deeply she hoped to catch a whiff of anything she could tie to those memories, but all she found was river and burning fuel from the vessel's engine.

How comforting.

Sighing, she glanced down at her mating ring, the gemstone glistening in the fading sunlight. She could survive being away from Kai. It would only be for a few days, and she was her own person. She'd made it a month without him—granted, they hadn't been mated then.

A shadow cast over her as someone approached and settled at her side. Ameera splayed her folded arms on the boat's rail, a breeze sweeping back her hair as she surveyed the distant southern waters.

"Are you okay?" She spoke with a jarring gentleness.

Isla must've looked morose if even the general was attempting to offer some warmth.

There was no need to be dishonest... and maybe her truth could inspire another. "I will be," Isla said, echoing Kai's words from last night. "What about you?"

Ameera laughed through her nose, understanding the tactic. She met Isla's seeking eyes with a sidelong look of her own. "I will be."

It was more of an answer than Isla had expected.

The two warriors fell into silence, the air filling with the sounds of the milling crew behind them and the slosh of water against the side of the vessel. Isla realized that Ameera hadn't asked about how their conversation with Ezekiel they had some nights ago. As the potential beta, what they'd learned was something she likely should've been privy to, but Isla understood her now more than she ever had. When Ameera was ready, maybe they could work together to find a way out of their family ordeals.

As they began sailing further inland, a sandstone wall rose above the shoreline, growing taller along the coast. Beyond it, Isla glimpsed the red thatched rooftops of buildings, but nothing more. There were occasional breaks at the wall's base, each crevice sprouting a dock spotted with fishermen yanking in their hauls from the day. Some threw their hands up blindly to wave, others noted who they were—the royal entourage—and bowed their heads.

Isla waved back, a gentle smile on her face. Ameera hadn't bothered.

Isla slowly lowered her hand. "You've been to Mimas?"

Ameera turned, leaning her back against the rail and surveying the boat's deck. "A few times. A couple with Kai, a couple without. They're lenient with us going in and out of the pack. If I had to describe it, it's everything I imagine Io *isn't*." Isla furrowed her brows, and Ameera elaborated, "Much more free-spirited, laid back."

"Io isn't just rigid, narcissistic assholes with sticks up their asses," Isla countered. "You've met me, my brother, and Adrien."

"My point exactly," Ameera snickered, and Isla bumped her with a hip. The general cracked a smile, one that reached the rich brown of her eyes. "I *mean*, I see how desperate the three of you are to break free from there, which leads me to believe you aren't the norm."

Isla's lips turned downwards. "Considering how we grew up, and the people we grew up around, I don't think we are the norm, no." She cast her eyes out, seeking the ocean again, her fingers winding circles over the wood of the rail. "But the rest of the city, of the pack, away from all everyone typically knows us as, is just... people, living their lives like anyone else in any other kingdom."

She hung her head. *People who will get caught in the crossfire.*

Ameera said nothing.

Silence blanketed them again, but it wasn't much help against the chill of the wind that swept by. Ameera wrapped her arms around herself, offering, "Another difference is it's much colder down here."

"Well, Kai's not here to warm the bed. Will you spoon me if I catch a chill tonight?"

Ameera's genuine laugh, light and melodic, made Isla's smile stretch wider. "If you ask nicely."

As the buildings neared and the sandstone wall stretched higher, Maeve appeared from where she'd been below deck. She fiddled with the pendant around her neck—a simplified rendering of the deities in metalwork shapes, representing the Goddess, Fate, and Eternity—as she asked Isla if she wanted some help freshening up.

A wry glance down at her disheveled attire was all Isla needed to know.

She opted out of wearing a dress, instead keeping to a cloud-gray tunic tucked into high-waisted pants. She probably should've appeared queenlier, but this was easier to move in, if need be.

When she finally breached the sunlit surface again, the vessel had slowed to a stop just before the towering northern gates of Mimas's Pack Hall.

The darkened wrought iron stood in sharp contrast to the sandstone pillars it was set into. Top-set flags, the colors of pale seafoam and overcast skies, billowed in a breeze kissed with salt, while wildflowers bordered the gravel pathway from the dock to a sprawling courtyard. In the distance, Isla could see the spires and turrets, red-tiled roofs, and identical pale stones of the palatial structure.

She wasn't sure why, but she hadn't expected Mimas to be so pretty.

Ameera appeared at her side again, bracing herself as the vessel hit the dock's edge.

"There are a lot of guards," the general noted under her breath as the bridge was lowered for them to disembark. "There has never been this much of a presence at this gate. There's no need to guard so heavily from the water, especially the river that's only shared with Tethys and us." Ameera tracked her eyes across the surrounding land, and Isla followed them to the trees swaying in the gentle wind. "I can sense more in the forest, too. A lot of them—and shifted."

Isla held back her frown at the fact that she couldn't detect much. Even if she could never fully shift again, she'd at least like her wolf senses back. Digging inside herself, she sought her wolf. It brushed against her stronger than it had in a while, but what nudged alongside it made her frown deepen.

Not now.

She snapped back to focus and prayed Ameera hadn't sensed anything. "This is odd for a pack that should view us as an ally."

Ameera met her eyes.

Isla's heart clenched. "Is it because of me?"

Ameera didn't disagree. "Kai is new to being alpha, and I'm new to being... this... and his father, my father, and Verena were close. I'm sure she knows more about us than we care for. It's probably a precaution. She just needs to know our packs continue to be on good terms."

Isla loosened a breath and wished her, hopefully, future beta's words had been more comforting.

A large company suddenly appeared from just out of sight beyond the wall's stone.

That, Isla could sense.

Alpha Verena didn't need the adornment atop her beautiful twist of curls for Isla to know who she was. Her aura was undeniable. Unquestionable.

Isla knocked back her shoulders, Marin's words echoing in her mind. *Approach all you do as a warrior—assess, strategize, execute—but hold yourself like a queen.*

Alpha Verena was the only current reigning female alpha on the continent, and one of the only five in history since the law had been passed allowing daughters to inherit the titles of the alphas who preceded them. She was the eldest of seven children, five of them male. She'd nearly been killed twice by her own radical groups, who'd wanted one of her brothers to take the throne instead. So, she was strong-willed, to say the least.

At her side stood her consort, Theon, formerly her guard who protected her from said radicals, and was himself, formerly from *Deimos*. Verena had not been his fated. In fact, his fated had rejected him entirely, opting to marry a wealthy merchant in Rhea, choosing a life of luxury over what a soulmate bond offered. Alpha Rainer, Kai's grandfather, as Kyran had not come into power yet, had allowed Theon to defect from Deimos to escape the heartbreak, as Mimas and Deimos had good relations. Somewhere along the way, the rejected male had captured the then-alpha heir's heart.

Isla had been racking her brain for the eldest of their four children's names when her eyes snagged on two faces amidst Verena's party. Unlike most of the others, they didn't seem to be guards. One she recognized immediately, and the other, who seemed keenly interested in Isla, given his smirk and stare, she hadn't known at all.

As they descended to the dock, Ameera snorted. "Well, this will be interesting."

Isla's eyes slid back to see what, exactly, would be interesting, and took in the familiar woman with ink-dark hair and blue eyes that shone like sapphires. Amalie.

Kai's Goddess-damn ex.

Isla vaguely remembered her being related to the Alpha of Mimas, but no one had mentioned that she'd be here.

She shook her head, clearing away the distraction. Why did she care if Kai's ex was here?

The man beside Amalie elbowed her the moment Isla's attention had shifted her way, a devious smirk playing on his mouth before Amalie laid her own jab in his ribs.

"Luna Isla." Verena's voice was like velvet, smooth and assured as their groups came to a head, each taking their turns bowing to the other. Isla felt the commanding tone like a shot down her spine.

Strategize. Execute. Strategize. Execute.

"Alpha Verena." Isla expertly matched her poise. Though Verena was an intimidating presence, Isla wouldn't let herself become small.

"Welcome to my home." The alpha gestured to the beauty around them, and as if in answer, a gull cawed as it speared for the ocean in the distance. "I appreciate your answering my invitation."

The political refinement of this woman was so diplomatic, even in the cadence of her voice. It was somehow soothing, but Isla had been gripped by every word.

Isla smiled gently. "Of course. I appreciate you extending it."

Verena's brows raised slightly, just able to look down at Isla, her height similar to Ameera's. It seemed she'd been making her own assessments. "I also want to congratulate you on your mating. Such a shame Alpha Kai couldn't join us."

"A shame, yes." Isla noted the way Amalie shuffled at the mention of Kai. "But Kai sends his best wishes."

"Busy times, I understand," Verena answered, though somehow, it felt more like a question than a statement.

Goddess, what a monotonous dance this was. No wonder Adrien and Kai had hated attending court growing up.

Verena went on to introduce Isla to her mate and sons—she didn't have any daughters—making the pointed observation that Isla was around the same age as her children.

Then Verena stepped back, gesturing behind her. "And this is my niece and nephew, Amalie and Jax." She beckoned them both forward, and they obeyed.

So, this was the infamous Jax.

Of all the family members Verena had between her siblings and their children, *these two* had been the ones she'd chosen to greet them. And given the look on Amalie's face, she hadn't wanted anything to do with it. So, if she'd shown up because her aunt *made her*, there was a point here. Some test, maybe, in Verena's eyes.

Making a point of Isla's young age and bringing forward her mate's former lover? Perhaps she wished to assess Isla's poise and self-control.

Her eyes flicked to Jax, his devilish grin prevailing. So, what was his purpose, then?

Seemingly through with Isla's introductions, Verena drew her attention to the warrior general at her side. "It's wonderful to see you again, Ameera." Her voice lowered, the slight dipping of her head making the pearls of her crown glimmer with the dusting of silver highlights along her olive cheeks. "I'm sorry to hear about your father—and Kyran, Jaden.

And General Eli and his missing warrior as well." Now, she looked between them. "I'm not sure how close all of you within the program are."

She'd certainly done her own research.

Ameera had schooled her features, bowing her head. "Thank you, Alpha."

Isla offered her own gratitude, fighting the narrowing of her eyes. She could only weather so much of this obvious pressure before her instinct had her wanting to snap back.

"We," Verena gestured to her close family, the sleeve of her pale green robe billowing, "must be going, but I'll see you both in the morning for breakfast, and the others will see you at the party tomorrow evening."

Isla tried not to appear too surprised. "A party?"

"In honor of your visit, *Luna of Deimos*," Verena crooned. "I'm assuming we're your first trip away from your own soil?"

Isla forced a sweet smile. A party meant mingling with people she hadn't been briefed on. When Marin found out, she'd have a heart attack. "You would be correct."

Verena barely seemed phased by the confirmation; she'd already been certain.

"In our absence, Jax will escort you through the hall." Her nephew stepped forward confidently, and Isla calculated every swaggering movement of his. "He will answer any questions you may have about the pack. If anything dire comes up, though, please reach out to me."

Though her cheeks already hurt, Isla wouldn't let her smile falter. "Very well."

She nearly groaned in relief when she could finally relax. At least, relax her face.

She, along with Ameera, Jax, and Amalie, lingered in the opening of the courtyard as the rest of the groups disbanded. The guard and staff Isla had brought with her from Deimos hauled off their things in small horse-drawn carriages, which, she had to admit, were remarkably charming. She hadn't seen many of those as motor vehicles became more widespread.

When the gardens had been filled with only them and the surrounding wildlife, Jax suddenly bowed deeply to her, his reddish hair burnished orange in the fading sunlight. "*Luna.*" When he rose, he leaned towards Amalie, speaking out of the side of his mouth. "You left out that she was gorgeous when you described her, Cousin."

Isla was suddenly particularly curious to hear how *exactly* Kai's ex had painted her to the family, her aunt included.

She chanced a look at the alpha's niece and caught her eyes drifting from the ring on Isla's finger to the mark on her neck. Her nostrils flared before her gaze collided with Isla's. Her eyes flashed with surprise, and Isla didn't back down. She wondered if she remembered her from the banquet.

"Kai is," Jax lifted a hand, correcting himself as he gained Isla's attention again, "apologies—*the Alpha of Deimos* is a very lucky man."

Isla didn't bother putting any type of regality behind her expression. "You're too kind."

Jax seemed to enjoy the drop in her façade. "I'm afraid to ask if he mentioned me at all."

"Only a little," she said. "Nothing too bad, don't worry."

"How boring you must think me, then," Jax drawled before exhaling. "Kai became the most of us all—the sons that didn't matter. With no birthrights, we got to have all the fun since no one gave a shit about us." He gestured widely as he looked between her and Ameera. "But now look at him, with two beautiful, powerful warriors at his right and left hand. He's doing something right. Fate is most certainly on his side."

Isla would counter that Fate most certainly hated them.

Jax glanced behind her to Ameera, whom he'd somehow known had been Kai's choice for beta. News really did spread. "Hello again, Meemee."

Ameera folded her arms, smiling despite the narrowing of her eyes. "I never gave you permission to call me that."

Jax returned the grin. "Has someone finally captured that stone heart of yours?"

Isla tried not to look too intrigued.

Ameera smiled venomously sweet and flipped him off, before saying, "As much as I enjoy standing here for your pageantry, we're tired and would like to go to our rooms."

"Of course." Jax bowed again, then turned fully to Isla. "Though I was hoping that I could show the luna the *true beauty* of what our pack has to offer later tonight. It's not the mystic, mysterious beauty of Mavec or the lavish, glittering gold of the Imperial City, but we have our own wonders."

"Oh, Goddess," Ameera grumbled as if she knew exactly what he was talking about—and also knew that the way he'd said it made Isla's ears perk up.

Isla smirked and matched the smoothness of his voice. "I'm listening."

CHAPTER 38

KAI

When Kai entered *The Bookshoppe* at closing time with the pup wrapped in a blanket, hidden beneath his arm, he hadn't expected Rhydian and Davina to be there. Initially, he had planned to slowly introduce everyone to their new *addition*, starting with Jonah, but that had quickly gone out the window. *Very* quickly, in fact, since the moment the pup heard new voices, he squirmed in Kai's hold enough to peek his head out, all but one of his floppy ears on show.

What had started as joyous greetings from his family rapidly fell to wide-eyed, flabbergasted looks and frozen stares.

"You've got to be fucking kidding me." Jonah seemed to understand exactly what Kai held, despite never having glimpsed a bak in person.

A baffled Rhydian sat up in the chair he'd been lounging in across the study table from Davina, whose own eyes were wide with intrigue, confusion, fear, and that same touch of endearment he'd found in Isla's. "Is that what I think it is?"

Kai pulled the blanket back further and adjusted his hold so the pup was fully in view. "Depends on what you're thinking."

Rhydian's gaze remained fixed on the red eyes, the wet, twitching nose, and the sallow gray skin. "A bak?"

"A *baby* bak," Kai corrected, as if it made it any better.

Jonah braced himself against a book-laden column, his appearance conflicted. Kai knew exactly why. A bak was rare to see, but one that wasn't actively trying to kill you, even more so. "Why did you bring it here? Why do you have it?"

Kai felt like he shouldn't have found their befuddlement so amusing. Maybe it was because he'd already gone through it himself.

"Because Isla didn't want me leaving him home alone." He absent-mindedly scratched the pup beside one of his ears, which he seemed to appreciate. "Apparently, he gets scared."

Though he'd said it mockingly, Kai didn't bother mentioning Isla had been entirely right. When he got home, the pup had been whining and whimpering in his crate in their bedroom. He'd also destroyed the blankets they'd left him. Kai was shocked when he practically leaped into his arms when he opened the crate's door, and again when he jumped from Kai's grip and sniffed about their rooms, clearly noticing Isla's absence.

Davina's jade doe-like eyes were fixed on the baby as she asked, "Why do you have it?"

"It's kind of a long story."

And they had time, so Kai enlightened them. He had nowhere else to be. No one to go home to but Sebastian, who he hoped was at the House so he could honor his promise to Isla. Otherwise, it was going to be a long night trying to track him down to make sure he didn't do anything rash.

Kai began his tale further back than the night they'd gone searching the tunnels. Instead, he spoke of Isla's coronation morning when he'd initially found the bak in the passageways and fought and killed what had likely been the pup's mother. He refrained from mentioning the flare-ups of his power, if only because the guilt for what he'd nearly done to Rhydian reared its head and made him so sick he needed to sit down in a nearby armchair.

His brother hadn't seemed to notice or realize what happened that night, and none of them had ever really commented on what he'd done to Brax, but Kai wondered how horrible it made him not to warn them about all he could do, what he felt. How dangerous he truly was when he could slip and break any one of them if he lost control.

But he had the bane now, and it seemed to be working. Granted, it had only been a couple of days, but he'd taken the victory.

By the time he'd disclosed his and Isla's voyage into the tunnels that night, the pup had located one of his mate's sweaters behind the shelves. Any attempt to wrench it away had been futile while he dragged it everywhere he went, wrapping himself in it as if he'd already come to know and miss her scent. Kai tried to pinpoint when exactly the creature had become so obsessed with her, but there had been so many small kindnesses from her that night and beyond.

Kai couldn't deny the soft place it warmed in his heart. He, most certainly, would become a fool when he saw her with their own children.

One day.

Once he'd finished explaining, his eyes settled on the pup and Davina, who'd slid to the floor to play with him. He rolled onto his back and exposed his smooth gray belly.

"He is a cutie," Davina cooed, rubbing the pup's stomach while he let out a tiny, satisfied sound. She giggled.

"Don't even think about asking for one." Rhydian's voice held a hint of caution as he remained firmly in his seat, his typical bravado cracking from the memory. Kai knew the guard had seen a bak once before, the one Isla—or her mother, technically—had killed in the house within the wasteland. That one had been dead but also an adult, likely ten times the size of the pup—what they had to look forward to in the future. Dead or not, the shot of fear when one glimpsed the legendary monsters never went away.

He asked Kai, "How are you sure this thing isn't going to try to eat you?"

They weren't.

"His teeth are barely sharp enough to cut through meat. Isla had to chop up and tear every morsel we've fed him into bits." He'd had to do the same just before they got here. Maybe he should've brought more food with him. He had no clue how big his appetite was.

"Mother of the decade," Jonah commented from where he'd been shielded behind the stacks, having gone to get things from his apartment. "Hasn't she killed like twenty of these things?"

Six, Kai was pretty sure.

He twisted his head as his brother resurfaced in the main lobby, a haul in his arms. He had some of the things he and Isla had discussed earlier that morning, and most importantly, alcohol.

"She has a strong maternal instinct." Kai watched as Jonah placed each item on the study table where Rhydian sat: the diadem, the dagger, Aneurin's journal, and that woman's picture. Despite the bane, he felt that void within him twitch, bite, then recoil.

Strange.

Only Jonah seemed to notice the way his features pinched and relaxed, but he didn't comment.

Rhydian mused, "Clearly."

It took Kai a bit to realize they were still speaking of Isla. He watched Rhydian cast a keener eye over the pup and noted how his shoulders eased at the melody of Davina's laugh. It filled the belly of the room as the bak lapped at her hand with his pinkish-gray tongue.

Kai could've sworn a smile tugged at Rhydian's mouth. "How long are she and Meera gone?" he asked.

Kai frowned. "Two days." He couldn't keep the grumble out of his voice.

"Two days, and after only five hours, you've shown up here with a baby monster," Jonah said, lining up a few glasses. "I fear what you'll have for us tomorrow."

"In my defense, I was with her when we got him."

Davina tied her hair back when the pup became too intrigued, playing with the long, brassy strands. "What's his name again?"

Kai accepted the liquor Jonah had poured for him. "We haven't given him one yet."

Rhydian reached out to his twin for his own glass. "A name sounds permanent."

"That's what I said." Kai took a drink, savoring the burn in his throat, grateful for it. It was going to be a long night. It had been over a month since he'd been in their bed without Isla, and he wasn't sure how well he'd handle the empty space beside him. "We're taking suggestions."

Davina rubbed the pup between the ears. "I'll see what speaks to me. I doubt you want to call him *adorable little button*." She gushed the last words, bringing her face closer to his. "Because that is exactly what you are, isn't it?"

Kai snorted. "I'll keep that one in mind, but yeah. Maybe keep trying."

Davina gave him a deadpan look before going back to playing with the baby.

When Kai pulled out a seat at the study table, he realized Jonah had been watching him.

He lowered himself into the chair. "Isla never got to tell me what you two talked about the other morning."

"Well, she never mentioned him." Jonah nodded towards the pup in Davina's lap and then to the spread of wares on the table. "We discussed all of this. Same old, same old. Though she says she feels like the dagger's broken."

Kai observed the finely worked blade, his brows knitting as that essence seemed to tuck tighter within him. "How?"

"She just said it feels broken," Jonah repeated exasperatedly. "And then she told me about the dreams she's still having. My theory right now is she's a priestess."

No, that felt wrong.

Kai's eyes dropped to the artwork of the white-haired woman. For a heartbeat, Kai swore the answer to who she was lingered right on the cusp of his mind.

Before he could say anything, Jonah asked, "Do you know where your father's journals are? His personal accounts."

Kai snapped his eyes up to meet his, feeling like he had punched a hole into his chest and squeezed his heart. Jonah shifted his focus back to his mapping, seeming to know Kai hated the vulnerability slashing across his own face.

He wished his voice hadn't sounded so damn vacant. "No, I don't."

He should've known, though, shouldn't he? So had been the tradition for the newly anointed alpha to study the wisdom of their predecessor. Kai should've started keeping his own records.

"You didn't come across anything in the old archives when you were down there?" he asked Jonah. The catacomb-like cavern beneath the hall held some of their oldest books.

His brother shook his head.

"Why do you want them?"

"Isla asked me if I'd seen them."

And just like that, Kai had seen how that wonderful mind of his mate's worked. Maybe they could find out why his father had wanted to protect him.

He had an inkling of where he could begin searching, and his stomach turned. "I'll see if I can track anything down."

∽

Kai told himself he wasn't a coward because he was doing what he'd promised. Thankfully, Sebastian hadn't ventured far. He was under the pergola in the backyard, so Kai not only didn't have to scale the city to find him or have to leave the pup alone for too long, but he also had an excuse to put off riffling through his father's study.

Sebastian's back had been to the door, only one of the several hanging lanterns lit to illuminate him, and nothing much beyond in the darkness of night. Hunched forward, his elbows rested on his knees while the handle of a bottle of Kai's good whiskey dangled from one of his hands. Kai had already gone through a decent amount, but the Io-born wolf had clearly done much more damage.

Kai eased the back door open and stepped outside. Sebastian hadn't turned or even flinched. The pup, tucked comfortably under his arm, sniffed at the air before huffing. Kai wrinkled his nose in turn. Even he could smell the booze from this distance.

Rough night.

Kai eased the pup to the ground, knowing he wouldn't venture far, and crossed the patio to swipe the bottle from Sebastian's hands just as he leaned forward to fill another glass to the brim.

"What the hell?" Sebastian whipped around, and Kai immediately noticed the purple smudges under his widening eyes. His voice sounded gravelly, but the words weren't slurred. He either had a remarkably high tolerance, or he'd stretched this all day.

"You should've sensed me coming," Kai told him. "I wasn't trying to be quiet." Sebastian was inebriated enough that he failed to hide his emotions—shock, fear, and wariness. Kai gestured to the seat beside him. "Care if I sit?"

He didn't wait for an answer as he pulled out the chair and fell into it, catching the pup sniffing around some of the furniture, his tail wagging. He'd likely caught Isla's scent again.

Not bothering to reach for a glass, Kai brought the bottle to his lips and took a long drink.

When he brought it down to his side, Sebastian lunged for it, but Kai tore it back. "You smell like a tavern. You've had enough."

Sebastian growled under his breath but didn't protest. He just turned away, rubbing at his face and covering his eyes. "Did Isla tell you to come talk to me?"

"No." Sebastian peeked out to shoot a doubtful glance his way. "She told me to keep an eye on you. Somehow, I missed you inhaling my liquor cabinet."

Sebastian snickered, and that was it before silence fell. Kai didn't mind it.

He shifted his gaze up to the moon, the Goddess, tracing its edges. He wondered if Isla would be doing the same.

"I'm sorry."

Kai turned. Sebastian hadn't lifted his head. "For drinking my good liquor? I can buy more."

"No," Sebastian said. He sighed a heavy breath. "*I'm sorry.*"

Kai understood with a spear to his chest. Lips thinning, he took another large gulp. "You didn't do it," he rasped through the burn. And there was that slight slam against his ribcage.

Murderer.

Sebastian lowered his hands and leaned back in the wicker chair. His golden hair gilded by the lantern as he tipped his head back to also trace the moon. He sniffed. "Still, I never said it, and I'm sorry. I can't imagine it. If it had been Isla and my dad."

Murderer, murderer, murderer.

Kai cleared his throat and took one last gulp of whiskey before setting the bottle as far away from himself as possible.

Sebastian's scream made him jump back to his seat. "What the fuck is that?"

Kai averted his eyes to the base of Sebastian's chair in time to see the bak pup scurrying away to hide behind Kai's legs. A deadly monster, easily frightened.

Chuckling, Kai leaned down to scoop the baby up. "Your sister adopted a new pet."

Sebastian remained agape. "Is that a bak?"

"Yes, it is."

"I... I have so many questions."

"I'm in for a long night, so ask away."

And so, Kai went through everything he already had earlier at the shop.

Sebastian asked his questions and finished with, "Goddess, she must have you wrapped around her finger."

"Oh, entirely." Kai gave the bak a slight bounce. "But I'll admit, he's growing on me."

Sebastian nodded his brows and dared to reach forward. The bak recoiled initially, but with Kai's mutter of encouragement, he inched towards Sebastian's touch. "I've done a lot of wild shit in my life, but this might take it."

"This is definitely up there for me," Kai responded.

Sebastian's fingers slid beneath the pup's chin. "None of this feels real," he confessed. "Like it's a nightmare and a dream at the same time."

"That's how I feel pretty much every day."

Sebastian's eyes met his at the gentle frankness, the apology and sorrow still lingering. "Be honest with me."

"Okay."

Both leaned back in their seats, a beat of silence settling between them.

Sebastian swallowed. "What would you do if you saw her?"

Murderer, murderer, murderer.

Kai sniffed and could see how every second he hadn't answered tightened the muscles in Sebastian's body.

"Honestly?" Kai affirmed, and Sebastian nodded. "I've thought about killing the person responsible more times than I'll ever admit to Isla. It's what kept me breathing sometimes. And even though I know it wasn't her will, *she* is the one who took their lives. Who watched their last breaths." Sebastian's nostrils flared, but Kai continued, "But I love your sister more than anything in the world, and I would never, *ever* do anything that would hurt her. So, I have to put it behind me, and I will. For her. The witch is the true killer."

Even saying the words, he felt his power grating along his bones.

Murderer.

"Isla is just as upset as you are and is trying her best to get through it. I... I can only be so much for her, especially with this. With your family," Kai said. "She needs you now more than ever."

Sebastian glanced at him once, then up at the stars. "I need her, too."

CHAPTER 39

ISLA

When darkness became their cover, Isla and Ameera fled their rooms in the hall. With the hood of her cloak over her head as instructed, if only to avoid watchful, curious eyes, Isla allowed the general to lead the way. Apparently, this had been quite common for her when she and Kai visited.

The island is a party that never stops, Jax had offered, and Ameera had confirmed once she and Isla reached their rooms. Just off the coast in the Southern Waters, the small island was the prime location for day and nighttime enjoyment.

Isla took some time to admire the scenery as they wove through meandering garden paths to reach a gnarled oak tree twined with pale twinkling lights that had apparently been their meeting spot of choice these past years. In its distance, below its curling branches, she spotted Jax leaning against the bark, finishing off what looked like an apple.

Isla stopped short when she caught someone sitting on the bench behind him.

As she and Ameera closed in, it was Ameera who asked, "So you decided to join us?"

Amalie, still stunning despite her sour look, with her hair pulled back from her face and a swipe of glitter along her charcoal-lined lids that brought out the blue in her eyes and dress, gave her a narrowed smile. "Didn't have much of a choice."

Her eyes made impressively quick work of surveying Isla's attire, another combination of a tunic and pants, before slipping to her mating mark, her ring.

Isla recalled what little she knew about Amalie and Kai's relationship: on again and off again, a beautiful couple appearance-wise that the pack and its gossips adored, but behind closed doors, their compatibility was only physical. If they weren't all over each other, they were fighting about something. At least, that's what Belle had told her months ago when she began training with the guard.

Isla blanched.

Either out of sympathy or her own selfishness, wanting to evade the awkwardness that had sprouted between them, Isla craned her neck to observe the tree and its glow. "This is beautiful." She cast her eye to the other trees of the forest, which hadn't been lit and didn't have seating as this one did. "Why is it the only one like this?"

Jax slapped his hand against the bark and threw the apple's core deep into the woods. "My great, great, great grandfather's—or he might be an uncle, technically—luna, for some reason, loved this tree and used it as her place to reflect. So, when she died—tragically, of course, as it always goes—he made this in her honor. Apparently, when he was withering away, he spent his last days right here, talking to her and waiting to be with her again. I don't think he was that old when he died. They were fated mates, and she was his world. A broken heart killed him."

A somberness cleaved her chest. "That's..." She couldn't find the right word, and her eyes dropped to her ring.

"Love is a devastatingly powerful thing," he said. "For all it blooms, it destroys with even greater force."

Isla's eyes flicked back up in time to realize he'd also been observing her ring.

"You know, that may be the most poignant thing to ever come out of your mouth, Jax," Ameera commented from behind her.

Jax bowed his head. "I try."

Then his cousin rose from the bench, wiping something from her dress. "If only you hadn't bastardized the monument by making it a meeting spot for your debauchery."

"*The island* does not always equal debauchery, Cousin," he said over his shoulder before turning back to Isla. "Though the most lecherous nights have been the most fun. I'll let your mate tell you some of those stories."

Isla quirked a brow. "He may have mentioned you tend to embellish."

Jax's jaw fell unhinged. "Nonsense, that prick. Is he still trying to be on his best behavior around you? Even after he put that mark on your neck?"

"He's a gentleman when he has to be." Isla laughed.

Jax cocked his head. "And other times?"

"Wouldn't you like to know."

"Can we go, *please*?" Amalie snipped. By the time they all looked at her, she was already heading for the lantern-lined cobblestone path behind her.

"Why is your aunt making her do this?" Isla finally asked when she was decently out of earshot. Jax seemed surprised she'd drawn the conclusion. "It's not hard to tell she doesn't want to be here."

"The day I understand my aunt's motivations is the day the world ends. I simply obey," he said.

Isla scoured his face for truth, which he seemed to be telling.

The alpha's nephew gave her a smirk before sweeping his hands in a grand gesture to the rock path cast over by a yellowish glow. "Well, to the sea we go, Your Majesty. We don't want to miss the ferry."

"Lead the way."

They headed down the path one by three. Isla was intrigued by Jax's stories as he explained more of the Pack Hall's expanse and the royal city of Ciryn that was home to those buildings she'd spotted glimpses of behind the sandstone walls. As they drew closer to the coastline, before they walked along its edge, Isla sucked in a breath. In the distance, the island's lights glimmered like stars, not with the ethereal glow of Mavec's crystals, but in a way that was a bit more ostentatious.

She hadn't realized she was beaming until Jax commented, "You and Kai really are a pair."

"What do you mean?" she asked.

"You both look at everything like it's a challenge. Something to be conquered." He pointed to the island. "You're about to have the time of your life over there, and nothing's going to stop you."

Isla laughed, tipping her head back as a salty nighttime wind kissed her face. Having the time of her life didn't sound bad, though she wished Kai had been here with her. "I've missed the ocean."

"Have you ever been to the south of the continent?" Jax asked.

"Before Deimos, I'd never really left the north. It was one of the reasons I wanted to be a warrior, other than protecting people," Isla said. "I wanted to travel the continent."

Jax snickered. "So small-minded."

"Excuse me?"

"Why only desire traveling the continent when there's a whole world out there?" He nodded towards the water. "You know, they say if you squint hard enough, you may be able to see a siren's tail kick above the water."

"Really?" Isla focused, widened eyes narrowing and seeking anything over the rippling blanket of dark.

Jax nodded and, as if he could hear her next question, said, "Technically, they're not allowed this close to the continent, but by the time someone gets in the water to fight them off, they're long gone. The sea makes its own laws after that until you reach their isles." His lips thinned. "So much out there, and yet we're here, wolves amongst ourselves."

Wolves, some witches, and a part fae... apparently.

Isla caught the longing in his voice, the spark in his eye. "Is there anywhere you want to see?"

"The fae ruins of Naerel," he answered immediately. "Their architecture was extraordinary. I mean, the entire city was crafted by magic. No mortal builders could ever compare. And now, it just sits there. Not many go to appreciate it, given the fae were so..."

"Heinous?" Ameera finished for him. She was silent for the most part, but the general was always listening.

Isla's skin itched, the hair on the back of her neck standing. *Not now.* "Were they really all like that?"

Jax shrugged. "I mean, I'm not a thousand years old, so I wouldn't know. I've never met one, but an entire people couldn't be evil. I read some even stood by mortals during the War of Realms and offered their lives along with the others who sacrificed themselves to seal the veil and keep them out forever."

Isla vaguely remembered that part from her history lessons. Wolves, witches, sirens, crawlers, humans, and fae, it had taken everyone to end the war—even the deities.

Jax's final word echoed in her head. *Forever.*

She swallowed, glancing at the ocean again and then up at the sky as if she could see the veil shimmering there. "Do you think the fae would ever be able to return?"

"Of course."

Isla snapped her head his way, her eyes briefly snagging on the ferry boat they closed in on, the line of revelers fifty-deep.

Jax clarified, "History always repeats itself. We never learn. We'd just better hope it's not our lifetime. They're immortal; they can wait forever."

Isla's stomach pitted.

"What could we even learn from the war to prevent it?" Ameera asked, fiddling with her necklace—the pendant on a gold chain, like she always wore.

Jax's following words clanged through her. "Never trust a fae."

～

The air of the island had been electric.

Lights shimmered everywhere that Isla turned as infectious, upbeat, foot-stomping, hip-swaying music flooded her ears, her veins.

Jax had let out a triumphant howl the moment he stepped from the docking sands to the boardwalk. Some of the passersby echoed him, and it wasn't long until the sound traveled distances far beyond what she could detect.

A party that never stops.

Isla had never seen anything like it. It was the perfect escape from their worries. Even Ameera was beaming as she took it in, and she swore Amalie's sour look had lifted, too. She felt like a child on Solstice.

"Welcome to the best night of your life, Your..." Jax trailed off, his eyes questioning.

Isla smiled. "You can call me by name; I won't tell anyone."

He grinned back. "Very well, *Isla*." He began leading them through the masses. "Can you communicate through your mating bond from this distance?"

Isla raised a brow, carefully dodging bodies. "Uh, this far away, it's more tugs and feelings, but if Kai felt anything strong enough, I'd know."

Jax considered. "And it's the same for you?"

Isla nodded slowly.

"Well, tug at the bastard and tell him he's an asshole for missing a good time." She laughed, fully intent on doing so, when Jax continued, "What's your drink of choice?"

Isla shrugged. "Anything but whiskey, honestly. I'm not picky."

The four of them headed to the closest bar, a shack styled with the vibrancy of someplace tropical, its drinks served with what appeared to be miniature palm fronds.

Isla squeezed herself onto one of the mahogany stools that had just been freed while Jax shifted to get the bartender's attention to order drinks. Her eyes greedily gulped down all that lay around her, partly as a warrior's assessment. People surrounding her ate and drank, flirted, and played cards or dice. The smoke flitting by her nose from a man's pipe smelled sweet, addictive even, enough so that she'd elected not to inhale too deeply.

As Isla noticed couples walking hand in hand—some engaged even *more* closely—she decided to reach inside herself, find a thread, and give it a small, loving tug. She tilted her head to observe the moon, the Goddess watching above. Hopefully, he and the pup were okay.

When Isla turned to rest her back against the bar, she found Ameera a few yards away, catching a server and likely placing an order for food. Amalie had vanished entirely. Isla didn't blame her.

"Excuse me?"

Isla's gaze shifted as a petite woman with cropped ebony hair sidled up beside her. Her heart jumped into her throat. Did she know who she was?

She was around Davina's size, so Isla had several inches on the woman and extensive levels of training. Though looks could be deceiving. The blade she kept hidden under her jacket bit at her side.

Isla gave the woman a polite smile. No one else seemed to pay them any mind. Jax and Ameera hadn't noticed either. "Yes?"

From a stack in her hands that she'd kept tucked so close that Isla nearly missed them, she handed Isla a flyer. "If you don't have plans for later in the night, I think you might enjoy the show."

Isla peered down, examining its bold-colored surface, an epic splash of red hues. She held it back to view the clearer image of a man's face partially shielded by his tipped hat. Printed in white across its surface was a calling card: "*Silver the Magnificent*."

Isla furrowed her brows. "A magic show?"

Funny. Magic was entertainment as long as it wasn't real.

"I'd say so. There's certainly magic in Silver's words. The show is inspiring. I think you'll leave with a fresh perspective."

Isla's gaze dropped back to the paper. "Uh, thank you. I'll see if we have time to..." When she looked back up, she was gone.

"Who was that?"

Isla whipped around to Jax, who held two palm-frond-decorated drinks. The scent of coconut wafted up to her, though she wasn't sure how they'd settle in this nervous pit forming in her stomach.

Isla flashed him the front of the flyer. "Some woman just gave me this for the magic show tonight."

"Magic show?" Jax leaned over. Isla watched the slight widening of his eyes, though it vanished quickly. "Oh, that?" He left her glass on the bar behind her. When she turned to reach for it, she felt the paper being smoothly eased from her grip, realizing it too late. "You don't need that."

Isla's eyes narrowed to slits. "Why not?"

Fear flashed over Jax's face as if he'd just remembered who she was. He'd torn it away from a queen. "The show's not that great, trust me. There are many more entertaining things to do, and we'll probably be gone anyway."

"It's only in a couple of hours."

"We have the breakfast early in the morning." He crumbled the pamphlet in his hands before gesturing out to the crowd. "Come on. There's much more of the island to see."

For now, Isla decided she'd give in.

She'd already formulated a plan.

"Let's wait for Ameera," she said, gentler, allowing Jax to let his guard down. While he moved back a few steps to throw the pamphlet away, Isla shrugged off her jacket and hung it beneath the bar.

She could've sworn she heard Kai's voice in her head, his laugh tiptoeing down her spine. *You can never let anything go, can you?*

No, she couldn't.

Eventually, Ameera showed up with their food, a dish of chicken skewers slathered in a dark, sweet sticky sauce that smelled as divine as they tasted, and they set off.

Isla allowed them to drift a good distance away with a fair amount of weaving before she let out an aggravated huff. "Ugh, Goddess, I left my jacket by the bar."

Jax swore, running his eyes over her body as if it would appear. "Don't worry, I'll get it."

Isla put her hands up. "No, it's fine. I've got it." She ducked away before he could follow.

Her jacket had thankfully still been beneath the bar when she approached. She excused herself as she slid a hand past the man who'd taken her seat and retrieved it, before going to the trash.

It had only been about ten minutes, and it seemed just as filled as it had been, but the crumpled flyer was gone. She'd watched him throw it in there, right?

"Looking for something?"

Isla whipped around, shocked to find Amalie, her arms folded with the leaflet ball in her hand. Had she been watching them from wherever she'd disappeared earlier?

Isla flashed her a befuddled look. "You dug in the trash?"

Amalie tossed the paper at her. Isla caught it smoothly. "If you want to go, I'll take you," she said.

Suddenly, going didn't seem like a good idea at all.

Isla unfurled the paper, reading over the creased surface. What could be so bad about this? "Why?"

Amalie's smile didn't reach her eyes. "We brought you here for a good time, didn't we?" She took a step closer to Isla, lowering her voice, "But you'll have to leave your guard dogs behind."

〜

A couple of hours later, Isla had left her "guard dogs," but not far behind. Ameera, though hesitant, had been willing enough to go along with her plan.

Isla subtly kept a hand on her blade as she followed Amalie to the western end of the island, away from some of the main attractions and writhing crowds. The alpha's niece had thrown the hood of her cloak over her head, clearly wanting to remain hidden. Isla, wanting to follow suit, had quickly purchased a straw hat from the nearest vendor. Not the most fashionable, but it would do. She'd braided her hair and tucked it into the back of her jacket.

Her heart thundered in the growing silence as they approached a row of white-and-midnight-blue striped tents for shows and performers. They didn't go inside any of them, but went around. There had been one more set further behind them that all appeared blood-red in the darkness of the night.

A burly man stood at the tent flaps, his sharp eyes scanning flyers and allowing people inside.

Shit. Were those supposed to be a ticket?

"I don't have the flyer," Isla muttered to Amalie as they closed in on the tent's entrance.

Her sapphire eyes narrowed, but then Amalie sighed. "It's fine. I'll take care of it."

Isla clenched and released her fists.

When they reached the entrance, the man's expectant eyes had fallen on Isla first. She appeared like nothing but a disturbance, it seemed. He glanced at her hands and saw nothing, his features tightening.

"She's with me."

He shifted his gaze to Amalie, who'd dropped her hood, his face barely softening as he nodded and stepped back.

So, they knew her here.

Isla sucked in a breath before she dove beneath the tent flaps into uncharted waters.

For a magic show, everything seemed a bit... morose.

Rows of seating had been set up, all facing a long but narrow stage fitted with one singular microphone and some speakers.

Amalie nodded towards the back at some empty seats, slightly separated from the rest of the crowd.

Swallowing and fighting an innate urge to flee, Isla followed, eyes trailing over the people they passed on the way. Some of them, she noticed, wore similar dark uniforms, and for every person who seemed excited about a *magic show*, there had been someone else who was like stone. Her stomach turned.

They sat just as grating feedback ripped from speakers. The uniformed attendees began a rhythmic stomping—an introduction, a greeting.

What the hell was this?

Howls from people, not wolves, rang through the tent, and Isla snapped her attention forward as a man—unnaturally handsome, tall, and broad-shouldered—powered onto the stage. He wore a dark uniform, just as the others, though his had been pinned with the gleaming symbol of a moon and sword. Not quite the warrior insignia, something just a little more brutal.

Silver.

"Brothers and sisters," he began, his voice authoritative and robust yet charming somehow. The crowd quieted. "Thank you for being here today. Thank you for your support while we stand to make history. While we stand to bring down a regime that has stood for far too long."

Oh, Goddess. *Oh, Goddess.*

"Pay attention, Luna of Deimos," Amalie whispered, the title dripping with silent venom as a lethal smile crossed her lips.

Luna of Deimos... Daughter of Io.

Isla's body went cold, her spine became steel, and her fingers itched for her blade. To protect herself.

She didn't need to ask Verena about the rebellions. Amalie had brought her right to one of their secret gatherings.

CHAPTER 40

KAI

It had been nearly six months since his father passed, and Kai hadn't done anything with his old study on the second floor of the House.

To this day, he'd only opened the door three times.

When his mother still stayed in a wing here, he knew she'd sit in the space sometimes, either because he'd caught it ajar or could hear her crying, whispering as she talked to his father's ghost.

He'd felt like a coward then, not going to comfort her, and he felt like one now, standing in front of the oak door, hesitating.

He had to get over this. It was a fucking office. It wasn't as if his father's spirit was going to come out and berate him for being there.

As if he, too, wanted Kai to *get on with it,* the pup squirmed in his arms, lunging forward. Kai held him tighter. "Okay, relax."

He stopped wiggling, and Kai could've sworn his red eyes narrowed.

He eyed the door again, giving it one last long, slow drag before taking the biting cold handle in his hand. "Fuck it."

The door opened with a squeak so glaringly loud in his ears, and the light spilled from the hallway, mixing with the moonlight in the room. He'd only ever made it in a few steps each time before he left, and even now, six months later, the scent of smoke from his father's pipe smacked him in the face. It still sat there on his desk, abandoned. Kyran had likely been in here just before bed that night.

Kai closed the door behind him as if caging himself in. He'd get through this. It was just a room.

There was a blanket lying on the small couch—one of his mother's favorites—likely left from all the times she'd sat or slept in here. *Why did you leave me?* He'd heard her sob once, and it still haunted him.

The scent of smoke choked him.

Kai suddenly became very aware of the heartbeat beneath his palm, the warmth pressed to his chest. The pup didn't squirm, only nuzzling closer. He flexed the fingers of his other hand, wishing again for his mate, wishing he'd had her floral, rain-kissed scent to chase away some of this smokiness.

He drew closer to the desk and didn't bother turning on the lamp because then he'd clearly see the unfinished paperwork that remained there, his father's handwriting scribbles somehow legible.

Plopping on the couch, something sharp poked at his leg, and he let the pup down with a warning not to piss on the floor. He reached beneath the blanket to pull out a framed photo. He recognized the grainy, discolored image as being taken by his mother's old camera. Of course, it would be here.

It hadn't been his entire family. Only his dad and his two sons, with his mother behind the lens, posed on the deck of the family's riverboat. Jaden had his lumerosi across his chest, which meant he had to be at least fourteen when he'd fully mastered his shift and been granted them, meaning Kai had to be around eleven. Up on his father's shoulders, while Jaden stood in front, the wind pushed through his hair that had been curlier then, as he threw his arms out, beaming without restraint. He almost wondered if the kid was him at all.

He was trying to protect you.

Ezekiel had to be lying, or perhaps Kai just needed him to be.

He rested his elbows on his knees and leaned forward, leaving the frame to the side and putting his face in his hands.

Suddenly, everything in the room pressed down on him: the darkness, the quiet, the barest truths that he never truly let himself feel.

They were dead. They weren't ever coming back. He'd never see them again, never find them, no matter if he turned the world upside down and inside out. They were nowhere.

And that suffocated him with every word he hadn't said and any remark he wished more than anything to take back. It suffocated him with the realization that he wanted to hear his father's advice. About being an alpha, a mate, a father... even if he may have disregarded it anyway.

He wanted Jaden's, too. Wanted to keep growing up with him, start each of their families as they'd always talked about, and figure out who would be the cooler uncle. He wanted him to tease Kai mercilessly for being so stupidly in love, but then come to understand why, like he always did.

A dampness crept into the corner of his eyes, and he swiped it away, never giving it a chance to slip. He leaned back in the chair again.

There was no room for tears, no room for breaking.

The sound of scraping and shuffling, of soft growls and grunts, carried to his ears. Kai craned his neck to see the pup's tail wagging and butt wiggling as he pulled something from beneath his father's desk.

"Hey! Stop that," Kai called across the room, but the pup didn't cease. Whatever it was, it had to be heavy, or the little beast's strength hadn't quite kicked in yet.

Kai groaned, pushing to his feet. "Little one." His gritted voice echoed in the room, and he sounded more like his father than he ever had in his life. He reached down, scooping the pup up in an arm and bringing his face close to his. His red eyes blinked naively at him. Kai couldn't be swayed. "What did I say?"

The pup lunged forward in response, lapping Kai's nose. His breath was horrendous.

That was truly bak.

Kai grumbled, wiping away the wetness. "You and Isla will be the death of me—*fuck.*"

Reeling forward, Kai grabbed what he could to support himself, his father's bookshelf holding his weight. His chest felt like it had been cleaved open, his entire body numb and cold with panic.

Not. His.

Isla. The bond.

Kai had felt terror like this, pure, genuine fear, from her enough times to know that something was wrong.

And he had nowhere near enough time to get to her.

CHAPTER 41

ISLA

Isla's skin itched, her head throbbed, and her throat burned, but she forced herself to remain in her seat. She forced herself to listen while speeches and anecdotes were given of small triumphs against the Imperial Pack and its allies, confirming what she'd learned from Eli about the brewing southern rebellions.

From the "warriors" trained from birth to serve as spies in Ganymede to rebels using the rogue territory to slip through poorly guarded borders in Rhea and setting up a secret stronghold, the packs had been a patchwork of silent warfare occurring right under their noses during these times of *peace* for years.

It was when Silver spoke of Charon and Locke, of Cassius, her father, Imperial Luna Marlane, and Adrien that she knew she needed to leave—not only that tent but the island entirely. Someone stronger might have endured it, but she was unprepared and had no one to turn to as they unleashed their vitriol. She could only watch Amalie's nerve-skewering smile as she felt the desire for her family's blood dripping from every emphatic spoken word.

Had Amalie always been a part of this?

The alpha's niece said nothing as Isla slowly rose from her seat after the most recent orator's conclusion. She kept low as she snuck through the wooden seating. Thankfully, her movements were drowned out by the chittering crowd. In the short intermission, spectators spoke amongst themselves, some clearly roused by the cause, invigorated by the possibilities of shredding the hierarchy apart. Others had been understandably wary, aware that pretty words and speeches only masked the catastrophe that this could be, the destruction it could lead to, and the lives lost.

Isla had just reached the sandy ground when she caught Silver returning to the stage again. Someone had been tailing him onto the platform, but stopped just short of the wide spotlight. Her heart leaped into her throat when she recognized the petite build and black-cropped hair. It was the woman who'd handed her the flyer.

"As you may or may not have heard," Silver boomed over the crowd, his tone smooth and assured, while Isla dipped back to shield herself in the structure's shadow. "A few days ago, our brothers and sisters in Deimos crowned their new luna. Alpha Kai, a victim of a tragedy that could've been prevented had the Imperial legions done their duty and kept sorceresses from breaching our lands, found his fated mate." From some, whoops and whistles went through the air, but others released low grumbles.

Isla's entire body went numb.

"His fated is a warrior born of Io." Those noises of approval slipped into sharp breaths. Clearly, they hadn't known. "The Imperial Beta's daughter."

More gasps and now chatter had begun, frantic words of confusion and begrudging words cursing the Goddess.

"But I've learned she is one for our cause."

The chatter ceased.

Isla scrunched her brows. What was he talking about?

"It has been relayed with confidence from our most trusted allies that before the luna accepted her role at the alpha's side, they devised a plan, and she bravely returned to the Imperial Pack, risking her life to gather intel. From her, we learned of an arsenal of witches that Imperial Alpha Cassius is harboring in Valkeric, their mountain prison, preparing to unleash them upon us all."

Cries of shock and fear erupted, and Isla had to resist her own.

None of that had been true. At least, not the part of her involvement or why she'd gone home, but she bit down on her tongue and her urge to jump out and refute him.

Because she was smarter. She understood.

She was a chess piece on a much bigger board—a symbol.

She couldn't control the misinformation they spread, the propaganda, and couldn't change who and what they wanted her to be. These people would believe what they heard today. Everything.

It was better for her if they believed it. The fact about the witches had been true, anyway.

"With her knowledge of Io, her strength, and Alpha Kai by her side, whose power is unlike anyone we have ever seen—the ability to *kill* without touching an opponent—" More gasps and urgent chatter. "We are stronger than we ever have been, and now—now is when we rally. Now is when we prepare to strike. The luna is here," Isla nearly choked, "in Mimas, visiting our alpha, our pack, preparing for our fight. She arrived at the Pack Hall just this afternoon."

Isla's heart stopped entirely when Silver's eyes, the color of his name, flitted in her direction. Brief enough not to draw attention, but with enough of a flash that—

He knew she was here.

She was leaving.

Now.

After a glimpse of Amalie, who wasn't looking her way but still donned that serpentine smile, Isla turned on her heel.

She kept her steps casual as she exited the tent, feeling the entry guard watching her closely. But once she rounded a dune, shielded from sight, Isla sprinted. She sprinted until her feet ached, until her lungs burned, until that ridiculous hat was lost in the wind.

She didn't run for the central part of the island. She couldn't handle people right now, couldn't handle that chaos. Her mask needed to be reforged, and the only way that could happen was if she broke and gathered herself again.

The southern beach had been deserted and was a thin stretch of sand compared to what she'd glimpsed of the northern end closer to the ferry entrance. Isla was grateful for the barrenness as panic pressed on her chest with cold, clawed hands. Squeezing, shredding.

With her chest heaving, Isla looked down at her own splayed fingers, prickles forming over her chilling skin, her insides writhing, twisting.

"Please don't." Darkness pressed in and gathered.

This couldn't be real.

"Isla?"

Isla snapped her head up to find Ameera approaching.

Isla went ramrod-straight, quashing whatever brewed inside her, throwing fire at it to burn it away.

Not now. Not now.

She'd forgotten Ameera lingered nearby.

One hand over her heart, she tried to master her breathing while the other waved Ameera off. "I'm fine!"

The biggest lie in the world.

Ameera broke into a sprint towards her, moonlight gleaming off her hair and sand kicking up in her wake. With that warrior general's keen analysis, she inspected her. "What the hell happened in there?"

Isla clenched and released her fists, choking out a breath. "It wasn't a magic show. It was a meeting for the rebellion. Amalie is—" Isla shook her head. "The things they want to do, I—I..."

Ameera's features hardened, and she pointed to the ground. "Sit."

Isla paced a few steps, her body wired. "I can't."

"Sit," Ameera commanded again. "*Breathe.*"

Isla stared at her for a few moments, trying to choke down an inhale before she lowered herself to the grit. The texture of the beach was a welcome, soothing sensation as she dug her fingers into it.

Ameera eyed her, ensuring she was settled before turning away. With her head down, she scoured the beach for something. Isla couldn't muster up enough energy to ask what. Eventually, she scooped up a decent-sized shell and filled it with ocean water.

Trudging back to Isla, she held it out. "This is the best I can do."

"You shouldn't drink salt water." Isla blinked.

Ameera flashed her a deadpan look. "Close your eyes."

Isla didn't know why she obeyed so quickly. She flinched when the cool water splashed over her face, then sighed into its salty scent. With sandy hands, she balled up her shirt and wiped her eyes. "That feels nice."

Ameera left again to get more, but Isla scrambled to her feet. She followed her to the shore's edge and kicked off her shoes, rolling up the legs of her pants. Her breaths moved like the wind and the waves as she dug her toes into the cool, wet sand, letting the water lap across her feet.

Breathe.

Her eyes traced the strip of moonlight on the water before she let her eyes slide closed.

Breathe.

"Are you okay?"

Isla wouldn't look at her as she nodded, shame coiling in her gut. Goddess, she was falling apart.

"Barely." She hung her head. "I don't know if you've realized this about me, but I hate not being in control. I—I can't handle it. Being pushed and pulled by someone else, not having a say in my own future... I don't trust myself to handle whatever it is."

She peered at Ameera, who only eyed her with consideration, no judgment. Just a listening ear, thank the Goddess. She needed it.

Isla cleared her throat. "When I broke down last year, I was lost. I felt like I had no purpose, and now I have too many. I went from wanting someone to just see me to wishing I could hide because now everyone is looking at me, and I don't know what I'm doing. I'm cracking. It's too much. It's too fast."

Silence fell between them with nothing but the sloshing and a gull's soft caw.

"Do you wish you fought harder?"

The words were a bludgeon to Isla's skull. She turned her head. "What?"

The general pursed her lips. "Do you wish you fought the bond harder?"

Isla shook away the nagging in the back of her mind. "No. Kai is my choice, and even if this is what it costs to have him, I'd choose him again and again. I'll get stronger. I'll get better. We both will, and we'll have each other when we do it. But the road to being okay is hard."

"Isn't that the truth?" Ameera scoffed, her eyes going distant as she thought. Her features softened in the wake of the gentle wind as if it had blown away her mask. Her hand went to the chain around her neck. "Did I ever tell you why I became a warrior?"

Isla shook her head, eager to understand the inner workings of the general's mind.

She didn't notice the creature slithering through the waves and onto the sand—not until it snapped around her leg and dragged her into the water.

CHAPTER 42

ISLA

Stars shone in Isla's vision as the back of her head slammed into the sand, a momentary blackness blanketing her thoughts until the icy ocean water bit into her shoulders, weighing down her clothes.

"Isla!"

Ameera.

Isla's ears hollowed around the sound of tearing cloth, then an imposing wolf appeared as she blinked. Blinked. A wave crested. Crashed. Her breath sharpened as her head went under, the saltwater burning her throat and nose, choking her.

You need to move.

Ameera's lumerosi burned bright as she dove into the sea, trying to sever what felt like a tentacle's grip around her calf. It tightened its hold, squeezing so much that Isla thought her limb would be ripped off entirely.

Move!

She felt a tug at the core from that darker part of her while the voice in her head bellowed.

Distant, so distant, but there. As if, somehow, Kai had crossed the breadth of land and water and drove his power into every void between them.

Move!

It was her own voice this time. A chant. A war song.

Isla twisted, gritting through the pain in her leg as she dug her fingers into the sand.

Move!

A steady roll of thunder shook the skies as she hauled herself up the shore, arms straining as she pulled and kicked out at whatever held her.

Ameera's wolf yipped, and Isla cried out at the release of pressure, her face slamming forward into the sand.

Move!

Isla clambered to her feet, wrenching her dagger free from where it had been strapped to her leg.

Ameera.

Her wolf's front leg leaked crimson, and Isla met her halfway as she limped over. She strained to hold her wolf up, to walk.

Ameera shifted back, grunting and clutching her shredded arm. "Shit, the salt stings."

Isla's eyes dragged over the injury as the flesh slowly mended, then at Ameera's clothes in tatters across the beach. She shrugged off her jacket. "Here. Keep the wound covered." She helped her slip it on. "Run or kill it?"

They were both warriors. If whatever this was posed a threat to others, they needed to take care of it.

Ameera never had the chance to answer.

The creature that slinked from the water was unlike any Isla had ever seen.

Two sharp points emerged first—murky green ears that speared the air like lances. Pitch-dark eyes absorbed the night above a slitted nose and thin mouth, pulled back to reveal razor-sharp teeth that still had a chunk of Ameera's flesh embedded in them. Humanoid, the creature trudged onto the sand, its long, slick body the same muddy green as the tentacles stretching from its back and trailing over the sand like the train of a gown.

"I should've brought my sword," Isla muttered, the cold slithering along her body.

"I'm not healing fast enough," Ameera panted. "It could be venom. We need the high ground. There's a forest over there for some cover, and we'll get it away from the water."

Isla felt the bond tug inside her as the thunder rolled again. "Okay."

Her body tensed when the creature's eyes fell on her. "Isss it you whom I ssseek, mortal?"

She held in her gasp.

Was *this* a siren? She'd always imagined them prettier and with… tails. Not these lengths of leg with taloned, webbed feet.

"The sssea and ssshadows sssay it's so."

Every instinct in Isla fired to run. If this was a siren, they didn't stand a chance if it got them into the water. She and Ameera stepped back, knowing that if they turned now, the tendrils at its back would be long enough to reach them.

"Who are you looking for exactly?" Isla asked, readying her blade in her grip. She had one shot at this—only one to distract it.

And then she'd need another weapon.

The creature tilted its head. "The bridge, the cursssed one, the anssswer, the key." The way it said the words had almost been melodic. "Which are you, golden one?"

Isla sent up a prayer and hurled the dagger. "None."

She and Ameera didn't linger to see if she hit her mark.

The creature shrieked, and Isla's legs bleated in protest as they pushed her against the sands, moving faster and *faster*. They needed to get to the forest, to higher ground. She needed a weapon, her dagger back. Or…

Shit, shit, *shit*.

She had one more weapon in her arsenal. One she hadn't attempted to use. One she knew there was no coming back from. But they'd die if it got to them, dragged down into the watery depths.

Isla dug deep, hurling herself towards her wolf. She embraced the cold, the power that waited, and darkness met her. She punched through it, pulled from it, falling to her hands and knees as her foundations trembled.

"Isla!"

One of the tendrils snapped at her leg, tried to wrap around it, but recoiled.

And then the world shifted, for she had not.

Isla might have screamed—she wasn't sure—but the pressure inside her exploded as darkness and cold bled from her.

With her arms nearly buckling, she turned and faced upright, choking when she met the glowing eyes—violet eyes—of the creature she'd glimpsed in the woods back in Deimos. A wolf crafted of shadows, of the deepest darkness between stars.

Her wolf.

Given a new form, new life.

Because somehow, when she'd healed her, when she'd brought her back from near-death, Raana must've given her magic.

That had been the unending cold, the dark veil blocking her from shifting completely. Her wolf had become... this.

She had no time to dwell on it. The impossibility, the catastrophe if this was forever.

"Go," Isla commanded through gritted teeth, willing her wolf forward, dredging up every scrap of energy she had to let it take charge.

Ameera appeared behind her, bringing herself to her feet. And then they watched the creature of the sea square itself, its claws out, ready to tear through bone and flesh—only that wasn't what it faced.

Her wolf moved faster than Isla could blink.

Moved as she would have if she'd been shifted, only it had no weak spots. At least, none that the creature could connect with.

Where it swiped with taloned hands, the wolf became as elusive as air, its body only smoke. But when the wolf struck, it became hard as stone, sharp as a blade, powered by the ferocity of a luna. Her ebony canines sank deep into the creature's neck, and it barely had time to shriek before its head was ripped from its body.

Pearlescent blood sprayed as its corpse dropped to the ground, its serpentine head caught in the jaws of her wolf, the creature's black eyes wide and vacant.

Isla met her wolf's gaze, willing it to drop the head as the world swayed. She obeyed, and they watched it thud and roll across the sand.

Nausea overtook her, but not from the gore.

"Come back," she rasped, as her wolf became nothing but mist that blew over her. Isla's breath caught as she felt the creature settle right where it always had, ready to be called on again.

Ameera struggled to hold her upright as Isla's legs gave way. "What the hell was that?"

Then everything went dark.

CHAPTER 43

ADRIEN

"Well, you definitely made getting in easier than I'd originally planned. Last time I snuck over here, I had to scale that whole cliffside by myself," Adrien whispered, raising the burgundy fabric of a guard uniform from a folded pile and comparing it to his body. Deeming it too small, he tossed it to Raana, whose eyes had been taking in the dimly lit space. She still hadn't drifted far from the now-closed tunnel door.

She caught the shirt just before it could hit her in the face and narrowed her eyes. "It couldn't have been that bad."

Of course, not for her.

Her power allowed them to just appear on the rock face, whisking them through the shadows and into the tunnel. His previous attempt at sneaking into the High Ground involved lying flat on his stomach on the rust-colored cliffs, his scent masked and his sweat dripping as he elbowed himself through the plumes of stone dust.

"Let's see you climb then, Scornn," he teased.

Raana shrugged and allowed darkness to dance along her fingertips. "I'll never need to." She held up the fabric. "I also don't need this. Isn't the point that I use my shadows to blend us in and move us around? You'll observe your father's meeting, and I get to find the other witches, then you find your friend."

Adrien wouldn't exactly consider Lukas of Tethys a friend, but he had been an unwitting victim.

Plus, Adrien couldn't shake the nagging feeling that there had been a reason his father had been keeping the former Hunter prisoner, other than to cover his ass when it came to there being a witch on the continent.

So much treason to accomplish in one night. But he was done with being a bystander to his father's games.

"Well, in case that doesn't work, the uniforms will help." He reached for the back of his shirt and pulled the garment over his head. The humid air of the laundry room kissed his skin, and he caught Raana staring. She hadn't bothered averting her eyes like she'd done many times before.

No, now her gaze dipped down every contour of his chest and abs, her eyes darkening.

Goddess, spare him.

He'd scented it back at her cottage, too, when he'd pinned her beneath him against the cabinet. She wanted him, and he'd be damned if he didn't want her. Even if he still debated the level of trust he had.

His mind drifted, images percolating of what they could've done back at the cottage. How he could remap all those places that left her screaming his name...

"Focus, Scornn," he said, meaning it more for himself. Her eyes snapped up to meet his.

And there was that blush as if she hadn't realized she'd been ogling him.

It fell away to a flat look before she turned away. Adrien mirrored the action, giving her privacy to change.

Only a few moments passed before he heard footsteps approaching. Too close—they didn't have enough time to hide.

Small, icy hands suddenly gripped his arms, and darkness enveloped him.

When his vision cleared, they were back in the escape tunnel again, just behind the door they'd shut.

Because, of course, shadows.

Shielding Raana's body against the wall, his arms bracketing either side of her, he faintly heard a female's melodic humming. The laundry room door opened. A laundress?

He knew the general staff they employed at the prison typically couldn't shift, so her senses wouldn't have been so keen. And Raana, bless her mind, had also swept their clothes up with them when they'd hidden.

So, they just needed to wait this out.

Adrien glanced down at the witch, his animal eyes able to see her faintly through the darkness. Even if he couldn't see, he felt her.

He also scented.

She hadn't managed to get her uniform on yet. He also hadn't fastened the buttons on the tunic. So, the peaks of her bare breasts were pressed against his own naked chest.

Adrien made to step away but found himself bumping into cool, writhing ebony. The shadows were still swirling around them. Gentle kisses peppered over his back and neck, and one mimicked Raana's pounding heartbeat.

It felt like they'd remained there for eternity, staring at each other, sharing breaths in the dark. And they stayed forever still, even when the humming faded away. Even when the laundry room door opened and closed again.

They should've moved.

They should've fought the tension, the allure, the constant drags towards each other.

Adrien felt it looming, then. Every conflict between them. Every impossibility that had been so easy to forget when they were together. Raana had been ready to leave Morai not long ago, and now she was working with the witch who wanted his father dead. Who probably wanted him dead, too.

They had no future.

And yet.

He. Couldn't. Move.

Raana's hand was a cool touch to his scorching chest as she eased him back. For a moment, he swore guilt flashed over her face. "We should go."

Adrien swallowed, savoring the feeling of her. "Is that what you want?"

Raana's eyes dropped to where their bodies skimmed, where their hearts beat in time. "I can't have what I want, Prince."

Before he could respond, his face nearly struck cold stone, Raana having fallen back into the darkness.

~

"Eli is dead. Beta Sampson is grieving. And he was like a son to Alpha Ivander. Alpha Kai of Deimos should be held responsible. We know he's planning something."

Hidden amidst the shadowed steel rafters, just out of sight, Adrien peered into the cavernous meeting room. The shock of Alpha Locke of Charon's presence was enough to distract him from whatever had occurred between him and Raana earlier. She'd gone on her excursion, tracking down the witches.

"You know I cannot force anyone's hand, Locke," Cassius said, scratching at something Adrien couldn't see on the table of sleek black stone they sat on one side of—who would take the other? "The continent cannot descend into chaos for the sake of selfish vendettas."

Not for the sake of selfish vendettas? What else had approving Kai's challenge been? All of this had been about eliminating a threat only *he* seemed privy to.

Locke clenched and unclenched his fists, trying to rein in his composure. "We can vote—"

"It must be unanimous, and Verena and Deacon would never vote against him. They were friends of Kyran's, and even under Kai, Mimas, Deimos, and Tethys remain close." Despite his own even disposition, disgust dripped from his father's voice. "And if he were forced to step down by vote, it would not be a quiet endeavor."

Adrien had nearly forgotten about that part of the Code—a vote to allow all alphas to decide if power needed to be shifted away from a bloodline without the need for a challenge.

His own bloodline could've been forced to step down at any time, but his father treated allies well. They'd never vote against him.

Locke pushed, "We're also losing Southern Iapetus. Ivander is struggling to maintain control, and his land is divided. Eli's death—"

"Means nothing."

Adrien flinched at the harshness of Cassius's voice and tucked in closer at the tiny creak of the beams. Luckily, neither man glanced up.

"It only sows distrust," his father said. "Alpha Kai did not commit the murder. We cannot use that for grounds."

"How do we know? He was in rogue territory. You know he left that message."

"Above *your* bounty hunter. Go to Deimos and accuse him, then. I'd love to see how it plays out."

"I would not go down as easily as a rogue," Locke snapped, and at a glower from his father, a warning, he retreated. "I refuse to bend in fear to a child."

Cassius drummed his fingers on the table, checking his pocket watch. Whoever was supposed to meet them was late. "It's not fear; it's acknowledgment of the unknown. And calling him a child is ignorant. He has a weakness. Everything, everyone does."

"What about Imperial Beta Malakai's daughter?" The malice on his face, the cruelty, was undeniable. His eyes flashed like a myriad of wicked ideas had just sprung to his mind for how to use Isla against Kai.

Adrien imagined himself springing from the shadows and running his claws along Locke's throat.

Even Cassius didn't seem to appreciate it. "What about her?"

The lower alpha schooled his face, seeming to tuck some of his ideas away. "Does she not have any shred of loyalty to her homeland? To her family?"

"Alpha Kai is her fated mate. That holds precedence, by law and Code."

Locke's jaw set, his eyes narrowing as he chuckled bitterly with a shake of his head. "It's unbelievable, actually."

Cassius raised a brow and turned his head with predatory slowness. "What exactly?"

"They were at the feast, they were in the Hunt together, and some saw them speaking in the fields before it. Alpha Kai saved her Goddess-damn life. If they were mates, they knew it, and then she returned here, did she not? The Alpha of Deimos's fated mate was right under your nose, likely spying for him, and then you permitted her warrior assignment to his kingdom. How could—"

Locke cut off as Cassius's claws dug into his throat.

Crimson eyes flaring, the Imperial Alpha rose to his feet, his aura of power a near shockwave through the room. Locke cowered beneath him as blood dripped down his neck, soaking his white shirt.

Locke trembled but didn't fight, knowing Cassius held his life in his hands. One move and he'd cleave open his throat entirely. "I apologize," he rasped. "I—I'm sorry, Imperial Alpha. I didn't mean—"

"Do you take me for a fool?" Cassius snarled.

Locke went to shake his head and regretted it. A whimper slipped from his mouth. "No."

Cassius's claws seemed to bury deeper. "Nothing I do, nothing I allow in my kingdom, on *my continent*, is without intention." The low, lethal words pierced the air. "Do you doubt me, Alpha?"

"N—no."

"My father put your miserable bloodline in power, pulling them from nothing. Don't think I won't undo it just as easily."

Locke attempted to nod as a knock came at the chamber's doors. The inferior alpha's eyes darted to it, then back at Cassius, who didn't release his hold. Adrien's grip on the rafters tightened as his leash on his tempered heartbeat loosened, but there was enough chaos in the room to disguise it.

Slowly, Cassius removed his claws, the sound of wet flesh echoing up to where Adrien lay. He used Locke's shirt to clean off his blood-smeared hands and didn't dilute his power—or sit.

"Come in," Cassius called out, and the door swung open.

Two Imperial Guards stepped into the room, their features like stone as they bowed to his father. "Imperial Alpha."

Adrien caught the bodies behind them, two women clad in black robes, their faces shadowed by their hoods, familiar crystal pendants hanging from their necks. He knew that within their folded sleeves, there were several hidden weapons. He also knew the woman who stepped forward—regal, deadly, and beautiful beyond reason—before she was introduced.

"I present Her Highest, Ellena Hale, Matron of All Witches."

Adrien's breath stalled.

Why would his father meet with the matron? The world's leaders typically convened only once, and that summit always occurred in the spring.

Fear tightened his chest, thinking of Raana roaming these halls.

Just as dangerous to her as his father was her people's queen. A collector of sorts, she'd told him, especially of potential threats, of rivals in power. He wondered if she had sensed the other witches first, if her kind had a keener sense for her, too. Had he known the matron was a part of his father's meeting today, he would've never asked her to come with him.

Below, Cassius inclined his head, acknowledging the authority Ellena carried. "Matron Hale. I appreciate you meeting me on such short notice."

Beside him, Locke shifted, clearly unsettled, but he didn't interrupt. Blood still stained his collar, his earlier bravado muted under the weight of the matron's presence.

Ellena's lips curved faintly. Not a smile, but a small threat. "I would have preferred not to come at all," she said calmly. "But we are clearly out of time, and you are unbelievably unprepared."

Adrien's heart stuttered when the doors opened again.

More witches entered—four this time—moving in perfect, silent coordination. Between them, half-carried, half-dragged, was a slight, limp figure.

Iron shackles bound her wrists, etched with runes that made Adrien's skin crawl even from this distance. Her head lolled against one witch's shoulder, dark curls veiling her face but exposing the arch of her ear. A thin line of blood trailed from her nose, dripping onto the stone floor in slow, sickening drops.

The world narrowed to a single, unbearable point.

Raana.

Adrien's control shattered, his wolf erupting to the surface.

His heartbeat roared as he launched from the rafters, shifting midair, bones cracking and reforming as fur and muscle tore through skin. The impact shook the chamber when he hit the stone floor, claws scoring deep grooves as he landed between Raana and her captors, his father and Locke.

A line would be drawn with the move he made next.

"Adrien." His father's voice boomed behind him, and he could feel the Alpha's stare digging into his back.

Adrien didn't turn.

"What is the meaning of this, Cassius?" Ellena asked, her voice heavy with warning. Adrien could feel the power radiating from her. Knew she possessed the spells able to take him down.

But he didn't care. Not as Raana's blood pooled before him.

Bracing himself with a small prayer to the Goddess, the traitor prince launched forward. Making his choice. Fighting for what was his.

CHAPTER 44

ISLA

Isla was in the Wilds. She recognized the feel of the rotting earth beneath her feet, the ghastly odor, and the lingering essence of dark, destructive magic seeping from every pore. But again, she knew she was dreaming.

She wasn't only dreaming; she was in a memory.

Donning not her warrior's uniform but her crimson ballgown from the night of the feast when she first met Kai, she lifted her leg over a decaying log as she pushed through the brush. Thorns scratched her arms and face, snagging on her dress as she fought through them.

A tug came—a pulse from deep inside her.

When she felt the thick forest would never end, she stumbled into a clearing, and there, in the distance, she watched herself with Kai.

They'd been shifted, and he loomed over her, a bak dead on the ground behind him—the one he'd killed to save her life. They moved around each other like a dance, doing all they could not to touch when the desire to do so had been so rooted within them.

"You were always meant to return to our greatest failure."

Isla sucked in a breath, whipping around to seek the woman with violet eyes.

But there was nothing, just the endless horror of the cursed woodland.

When she turned back, she and Kai had vanished, but the bak still lay there.

"Where are you?" Isla called, her voice hollow in this place that was not a place.

"*Everywhere*," the woman said, a resounding echo in Isla's mind. *"I always have been."*

Isla's nostrils flared. *That's not an answer.*

"Are you me?"

Silence greeted her, and she stepped forward. Her feet were bare, sinking deep into the muddied earth, the beautiful dress she'd remember forever torn in the thorns.

"We are the same." The words came from beside her.

Isla turned.

Nothing.

"Cursed with the same burden."

She felt an icy breath against her cheek, gasped, and turned, only to catch a flash of white hair before she was pushed.

The world shifted, and Isla tilted, faltered, then fell to her hands and knees somewhere new—somewhere she never had been. But it tugged, *tugged.*

A palace of crumbled stone towered before her, a phantom peering from the shadows. Its seeing eye opened wide—a window left vacant in the wake of shattered stained glass.

Tug, *tug.*

Her heart pounded in her throat.

She fought to her feet. "What is our burden?"

Steeling herself, Isla pressed forward, but no matter how many steps she took, she never got any closer to what she suspected to be Phobos's Pack Hall. It was a haunting shell of its former beauty, an alarming echo of a dwelling she now called home. The full moon shone behind it, accentuating the shadows.

"Come to me, and I will show you." Isla didn't turn at the breath on her neck that shot shivers up her spine.

She didn't need to ask where to go. She knew.

The Pack Hall reached out to her with clawed hands, calling her as she had always felt the Wilds did. It wailed for another bid at her blood, one she could never resist answering. One that may have been destined.

"Why can't you just say it? End these games and tell me."

Though she couldn't see her, she felt the violet-eyed woman bristle. *"Because it is not enough to speak it. I already tried, and ignorance cost us everything. You must see, Warrior Heart. You both must."*

Both?

Before Isla could ask the question, the woman trilled, *"Two souls bound by secrets and blood. They've all been watching. Waiting."*

Isla furrowed her brows, spinning. "Who?"

Wind blasted by her.

Isla threw up an arm.

It meant nothing when the gale had been strong enough to bring her to her knees. A violent crack of thunder sent her hands to her ears, the ground shuddering beneath her. Then the rain, icy, skin-tearing droplets, began as lightning cleaved the world.

Another memory—but Isla didn't have Kai to shield her from the storm this time. Not again, when that familiar solemn aria played, slithering around her mind and body, coiling and crushing her.

She did know them. Knew this woman, knew this melody, but...

Isla cried out when the dagger sank straight through her chest, piercing her heart. She lifted her head, the metallic taste of blood in her mouth, to find the violet-eyed woman stoic. Behind her, the moon had vanished.

"Come now, Warrior Heart. You're running out of time."

PART IV
A QUEEN'S DARKNESS

CHAPTER 45

KAI

Kai knew when he felt Isla dying the night of the alpha challenge, something within him broke. Not just a fracturing of their bond, but something in *him*. It was a shattered piece that mended every day he looked at her—every day he heard her, touched her, or felt her against him—but he didn't think he'd ever be as he once was.

So, when he'd felt the bond straining, felt her struggling, fading away, *then change*, he'd be damned if he didn't try to get to her.

There weren't many other thoughts in his head as instinct drove him out of Deimos. He'd left a note for Sol, left the pup with Sebastian, and dredged up every scrap of power he had, pushing past the eddying bane in his blood, and shifted. He'd been nothing but a blur of red-laced shadow through the night, through the city, and along the river's edge.

It was when he reached Mimas's borders that he felt himself faltering. Not long after, he was stopped by Mimas's guard, a mere hour from dawn.

They'd tried saying they needed to speak with Verena before they let him in, but Kai wouldn't hear it. It was possible he truly looked like he'd kill someone, or maybe he'd let that deeper, darker power of his flare, as they agreed to let him pass and brought him transportation. And clothes.

Now, here he stood before Ameera in the doorway of her guest suite in the Pack Hall because he knew Isla hadn't been in hers. He'd felt it.

Kai's lifelong friend blinked wide eyes at him before giving a disapproving shake of her head. "You crazy bastard. What are you doing here? Don't you have a meeting with the Beta of Iapetus?"

He did, but Kai didn't need a lecture. Not now. "Where's Isla?"

Again, he must've been a sight as Ameera dropped her fight. She side-stepped, her lips in a thin line. "In bed. She's still sleeping."

A small beat of relief.

Kai entered the sitting room, scanning for any threats. His nose twitched at the faint scent of rot and ocean water. "What happened last night?"

He wasn't keen on how Ameera's features paled or when she breathed, "Oh, Goddess, you felt it."

Kai clenched his jaw. "What happened?"

She narrowed her eyes at his biting tone. "A lot. I'll let her tell you when she wakes up. It's better if she explains it." As if she could see the words he was about to speak, she added, "Let her rest. She's probably fine, just tired."

Kai swallowed, his throat dry from the run and worry. He caught Ameera rubbing her left arm, and his features softened. "Are *you* okay?"

For a second, she hesitated, and he was impressed with the ease with which she relaxed her posture—that would have convinced anyone else but him.

"I'm fine." She snickered, returning to where she had been seated, reading a book, when he'd knocked. "Goddess, you mated men are no better than fussing mother hens. You could've just called to check on her."

She was probably right, but Kai couldn't ignore the crater in his chest. He closed the distance to the bedroom. "I can't lose her," was all he said before he quietly slipped inside.

Kai had been dozing in the armchair beside the mattress for an hour before he felt an oddly charged breeze sweep across his face. The curtains rustled behind him, though the window was closed.

Isla began to stir.

"No," a cracked whisper fell from her lips as she twisted in the wide bed. "*No.*"

More wind eddied, the temperature in the room dropping as Kai shot to his feet, his wolf edging to the surface as the air hollowed. His eyes jumped between each corner, where darkness seemed to gather. Isla thrashed, murmuring. Kai lunged for the bed, for her, and—

Goddess, she was freezing.

He gripped her shoulders. "Isla!"

Her heartbeat was erratic, her body trembling, her breath staccato. It had to be another nightmare.

The bond flickered.

Kai's eyes flared as he dragged her to him, sitting her up in his lap and leaning her against his chest. Her shivering had been violent enough that he needed to steady himself.

"Isla." He didn't yell but whispered her name, allowing the warmth of his breath to cascade over her face. "I need you to wake up."

She didn't.

Her heartbeat faltered, and her hand moved up to claw at her chest. Trying to rip something out, to rip something free.

Kai placed his hand over hers, not letting himself panic when he felt something burn beneath his arm wrapped around her shoulders. Her lumerosi glowed, seared, while the rest of her was frigid. She must've been fighting something, something he couldn't see. "Isla, *wake up.*"

She didn't.

Shit. Kai tugged at the bond, tugged at her, trying to pull her back. "*Isla.*"

For a blink, he swore shadows moved along her body, and something felt very, *very* wrong.

He didn't want to do this; he didn't want to risk it. Guilt settled as he plunged into himself, spooling a thread of power and casting it across their bridge—right to the edge of her mind.

Break in. Get her out—a fleeting thought of his own.

But another came as he toed the cliff, and a small door creaked open. *Break in—and destroy her,* his power said.

"*You're running out of time.*"

Kai recoiled and snapped back into himself at the new voice. *Her voice.* That woman.

Isla's eyes flew open, amethyst-illuminated, and coughs spluttered from her lips as her gaze darted around the room. She gripped him so tightly she could've torn his flesh away, her chest heaving with each shuddering, sobbed breath.

Kai bore against the pain and held her tighter to him. "You're okay. It was a nightmare. I'm here. You're safe."

Isla's panting slowed, her eyes fluttering up to meet his. "Kai," she rasped, her shaking touch reaching for his face. Her fingers were cold as they brushed over his lips, his cheek.

"We couldn't even make it a few hours," he forced through a soft chuckle.

She exhaled something between a sob and a sigh before hugging him tighter to her, eventually ending up with her knees beneath her and her legs wrapped around him until there was no space left. Their chests lined up as their hearts beat together. There was nothing lustful about it; she just... needed him.

And she could have him, all of him.

Kai buried his face into her neck as she had done his, taking in her scent and running his fingers through her hair, avoiding snagging them in the salt-laced waves. "You're okay."

He felt her shake her head in disagreement.

He held back his frown. "What?"

"I have magic."

The words had been so quiet he thought he'd misheard her. "Come again?"

Isla pulled back from him slowly, her stare colliding with his, her eyes bloodshot, gleaming, and desperate. "I think Raana somehow gave me magic when she healed me."

Kai's features twisted. His mind flashed to the shadows he'd clocked just moments before along her skin. "How?"

Isla opened her mouth, then closed it. "I don't know how she did it, but when I try to shift, I don't, but my wolf still comes out. It's just... it's made of shadow."

Kai blinked, trying to make sense of the bizarre picture. "You're shadow?"

"No. I remain *me*, but my wolf manifests as shadows. I can see her, talk to her, control her—but I also feel like I can't. Magic is the only way I can explain it. I always thought it was possible that she'd inadvertently done something to me, but I never... I never thought this..." Panic washed over her face.

He tried wiping it away with the stroke of his thumb across her cheek. "When did you figure this out?"

She peered at him cautiously. "We were attacked last night."

There it was.

Rage slithered alongside his confusion. "Who and by what?"

"Ameera and I were on the beach. I don't know what it was, but it emerged from the water and tried to drag me in. Ameera managed to get it to let go, and with few other options left to fight it, I took a risk and called on my wolf. It paid off."

That explained Ameera's arm.

Isla's face flickered with horror and pride. "I've never felt anything like it. It was me attacking, but different. I felt powerful in a whole new way." Her shoulders slumped. "But I'm exhausted, and all of me feels broken and wrong." Her throat bobbed. "If this is going to happen every time I shift, we're in trouble."

Kai let out an even sigh, keeping his agreement at bay. "You're alive, and you're safe. That's what's important."

She nodded but then went rigid. Her eyes scanned over his face with stunned clarity. "Wait, what are you doing here? Don't you have a meeting today? Where's the pup?"

Kai snorted. "And Ameera called me a fussy mother hen. The pup's fine. He's with your brother."

"With *Sebastian*?"

"You do only have one brother," Kai said before explaining his previous night of familial introductions, then explaining how he'd felt her, how he'd run there.

A somber smile slid across Isla's mouth as she ran her hands over his chest. "You didn't—"

"You know I had to." His hands settled on her hips as her legs encircled his waist. "It may make me a shitty alpha, but my greatest duty is to you. If you call, I'll answer. Every time."

His heart stumbled when she brought her mouth to his.

Her lips were chapped, but the kiss was smooth. It deepened slightly, from one breath to the next, but Isla pulled back just as Kai felt something dark twisting in him, recognizing her.

She spooled her fingers in his hair, twisting the curls at his nape. "There's, uh, something else."

A shot of pleasure coursed down his spine at the tug of her hands, but the words and the way she'd said them dampened his mood. "And what would that be?"

She flashed him a wary, beaming grin. "We need to go into the Wilds. Today."

CHAPTER 46

ISLA

Isla wasn't sure which Kai had taken in better stride—her plan to go to the Wilds, the severed head of the ocean creature Isla had killed that Ameera had kept, or her news of the rebel meeting Amalie had taken her to.

"You were gone for half a day. *Half a day*," he blurted from the sitting room couch, staring at the vacant black eyes of the creature within the large box Ameera had stolen to stow it off the island. It peppered the air with the scent of the ocean and death. "All this in a few hours."

"We're nothing but impressive, aren't we?" Isla crooned, the sheepish grin only ever leaving her face when she scowled at the sea creature's head. While she'd been unconscious, Ameera had dragged its body back to the ocean, letting it be carried away. She'd felt it better to keep the head separate—not knowing if it had some capacity to reform—and to be able to show Alpha Verena what was terrorizing their shores. Thankfully, due to their wild nights and desire to hide from pack gossip, Jax had a more discreet route off the island and back to the Pack Hall.

Ameera, apparently, didn't have to spin too wild a story, showing Jax the head and saying Isla had gotten too tired after fighting tooth and nail to save his pack from being eaten alive by the monster. Maybe an embellishment, but it worked well enough.

"Impressive is one way to put it," Kai grumbled, dragging a hand through his curls.

Isla responded by kissing his cheek.

Ameera's blanched expression as she sat opposite them was a mix of perplexity and disturbance. Isla had caught her and Kai up on everything. Each tidbit of information they lacked—Kai on the happenings here in Mimas, and Ameera the rest. About her magic, her dreams, the moon, their thoughts and theories on Deimos's fate. And yet, still, she said, "Explain again why you think you need to go into the Wilds *tonight*."

Isla huffed, slumping back in the seat. Her limbs still felt off-kilter and wobbly, her head foggy from magic use. And yet, even if it drained her... she wanted to call on her wolf again. Wanted to see her, feel her, and be complete again in whatever way she could.

"It sounds bizarre, I know. But it's not like everything else hasn't been," Isla said. "I think the pack's in trouble, just like Phobos was. This could be the final piece we're missing. This woman can show us."

Ameera inclined her head. "You don't even know who she is, and you trust her?"

"Yes." Isla didn't hesitate. "Not only because we don't have many other options, but because... because I feel it. This is genuine. She's done all she could to get to me."

"But you think that witch is in the Wilds, right?" Ameera asked. "With that..." She furrowed her brows with her next nonsensical words. "With that fae, who's also a witch that gave you magic?"

"Yes."

Kai, who'd gone silent for Isla to take the floor, added, "She doesn't want us dead. They're working together, the witch and this woman, to get to us, I think. At least, both want us for something. We just have to stop avoiding them and find out what it is."

Ameera shook her head. "This is insane."

Neither Kai nor Isla denied it.

Kai said, his voice deep and authoritative, "Let's see what Verena truly wanted from the invitation, and then we'll skip the party and—Goddess, I can't believe I'm saying this. We'll go tonight."

Isla could feel the unspoken response that choked the room, so she added, "We are facing danger, enemies, and death everywhere we turn.

At least with the Wilds, we know the only thing we can do is survive." She rested a hand on Kai's thigh, a comfort for her or him, she wasn't sure. "And if they need us to stay alive, it would be foolish for her to draw me in there just to kill me."

Ameera seemed to absorb her words with lethal focus. "You're not going just the two of you—we're not even going as just the three of us. We're stronger as a pack."

Kai stiffened beneath Isla's touch. "No. No one else. I don't even want to risk you in there. You could get—"

"*Stop*," Ameera snapped, making Isla jump as the general bared her teeth. Even Kai looked taken aback. "Just stop. No more, '*no one else is getting hurt.*' No more doing things on your own."

She rose to her feet and squared herself before him. Kai straightened, too, but he didn't stand. Isla saw it then, the two forces that they were.

"If you want me to be your beta, let me have your back. Let Rhydian, Jonah, and Davina. Let anyone else who fucking wants to," Ameera seethed, her words holding the weight of months, of years. "You are our alpha, and more importantly, you are our friend. Our family. If I die protecting you, so be it. I know what I'm getting into, and it's my choice."

Isla's hand remained on Kai's leg. She swore she could hear his heartbeat, could feel the guilt that contracted and released with each pulse. Her own shame coiled in her belly. She and her mate were two sides of the same coin.

Kai's eyes burned into Ameera's as if reading her thoughts and emotions, but Isla didn't feel that power rising from him.

Eventually, he sighed. "Okay."

Ameera nodded, not showing any mirth or sign of triumph at his reconciliation. "I'll see if I can get to a phone. Then I'll call Jonah and get him to relay the message."

Kai's jaw tensed as he clenched and released his fists. Isla could see the thoughts, the fear pelting him. "Tell him to bring only those we trust, and that we need his maps and food. We'll convene at the house in the wasteland. The three of us will go there right from here... I need Sol, too. Get him to come so I can talk to him. He'll be in charge while we're gone. Depending on how far the Pack Hall is from our entry point, it could be days."

It was the Hunt all over again.

Ameera nodded, a warrior and a general to her king, before turning to leave the room.

When she'd shut the door behind her, leaving Isla and Kai alone, Isla rose to carefully close the box with the creature's head and stow it in the corner of the room.

Back at Kai's side, she slid in close and kissed him once on his neck, on the mark she'd left there. His eyes were haunted, likely clouded by visions of a grim future, a horrendous fate beyond the Wall.

When she leaned her head on his shoulder, he slid his arm around her waist, tugging her close and resting his head on hers. Then he sighed—a tired, defeated, and determined sound. "This needs to be over."

Though she'd been thrilled to see him, Isla couldn't help but wonder if Kai's sudden presence would undermine her in Alpha Verena's eyes. The meeting with her to find out the true intentions of her invitation didn't take place in her office; instead, the alpha, Isla, Kai, and Ameera traveled through a winding tunnel system until they reached the dungeons and catacombs beneath the hall.

Isla may have clung to Kai a bit tighter than she would've liked, but found some joy at the thought of being able to rub it in Adrien's face that she beat him to discovering this pack's secret tunnels.

Unlike Deimos, there were no crystals to light their path as their steps echoed across the stone. Instead, torches cast menacing shadows around them, and Isla blinked every so often when she found herself instinctively seeking her wolf within them, even though she felt it tucked away safely inside her.

She timed her pace with the thudding of the creature's head against the side of its box that Ameera held.

They'd shown Verena and Theon in the alpha's office, and upon seeing it, they'd paled and said they needed to show them something. So, Theon had taken over any other obligations for the morning, while Verena had rushed them down here.

When they came to a halt before a solid iron door—which Isla knew from the way her wolf, now laced with fae magic, recoiled—Verena placed her hand atop it. "On the night of the Equinox, this was caught in

Ciryn. It slaughtered several of my citizens, destroyed their homes, and killed my guards before it could be subdued."

Fear struck Isla's heart, and it only faded to confusion when they all stepped inside and beheld what lay upon a metal worktable, illuminated by more torchlight. A creature just like the one that attacked them last night. This one was similarly missing its head, now perched on a separate table.

It had also been carved open.

Every organ, its oddly shaped heart and lungs, eyes, tongue, and every other part that Isla had trouble identifying, had been stored in different glass jars perched on various rusted iron shelves. Even its blood —a pearly goo that seemed to shimmer in the fire's glow—had been collected.

"There were two of them?" Ameera asked, dropping the creature's boxed head onto one of the few unoccupied spaces, disgust crossing her face.

"Clearly." Verena, despite her typically settled appearance, seemed wracked with distress. "And now I fear more may have slipped through."

Isla tried to calm her racing heart. "Slipped through what?"

Kai, his eyes haunted and distant, knew the answer with stunning quickness. "The veil." His gaze trailed over the vats of tissue and blood before he met Verena's eyes. "This is fae, isn't it?"

"That's our theory, yes," she said, terror trickling into her voice as it beat through Isla's chest. "Other than being unlike anything I or any of our Elders have ever seen, it was only harmed by iron, though it was the beheading that killed it. One of my advisors believes that the aurora on the night of the Equinox was a consequence of a tear between worlds."

Isla's mind reeled back to that night, recalling how it felt as if the world had broken, had cleaved open.

"The aurora happened here, too?" Ameera asked, eyes wide at the monsters on the table. Verena nodded. "And the storms?"

Verena glided languidly around the table, pulling out a pad of notes with scribbles, diagrams, and drawings of the creature to study herself. "She believes those are connected as well. If the veil is being tampered with, or the fae, or anyone, have been trying to break through it, then the storms could be manifestations of that chaos."

Isla's head spun as she stared at the murky green, desecrated corpse, the creature's words replaying in her mind.

Is it you whom I seek, mortal?

The bridge, the cursed one, the answer, the key. Which are you, golden one?

Isla shook her head, glancing at Kai, who'd gone silent, tumbling away into his own thoughts.

She asked Verena, watching her study the monster intently, "You didn't invite us here to speak of rebellions or war, did you? You wanted to talk about this."

"Yes, yes, and yes," Verena answered, earning stares of perplexity from them all. She flipped a page of the notes. "There have been wars of many kinds in our history. It's an inevitable sickness. Wars amongst wolves, wars between continents... wars between realms." Isla felt her heart stutter as she lifted her gaze to the immortal body draped across the table. "I fear that in our strife, our rebellions, and our battles, we may be blinding ourselves to an even greater threat, and our division will be our downfall."

As her words sunk in for them all, the only sound was the low hiss of torch fire.

Verena slipped a hand into the pocket of her coat, withdrawing a folded piece of correspondence. Isla raised her brows at the parchment, thick and marked with a familiar Imperial seal.

"This came this morning," the alpha said quietly, unfolding it. "From Imperial Alpha Cassius."

Isla's stomach tightened.

Verena scanned it once more before lifting it to show them. "He's calling for a summit in Io—all alphas, lunas, and betas. The subject is pressing matters—regarding an external threat. I'm sure yours is waiting for you when you return home."

External?

Isla's eyes slid to Kai, who stood rigid beside her, jaw set, his gaze fixed not on the letter but on the dissected creature sprawled before them. She knew he was thinking as she was, that the summit was less about unity and more about him—about Deimos, about the power he carried, about what Cassius already knew.

Io... she'd be returning to *Io*.

Though she couldn't dawdle much on the thought—on any fear

regarding seeing her father or excitement about seeing Adrien—because she was too focused on Kai, still deep in thought.

He finally broke his focus to ask, "When?"

"Five days." Verena refolded the parchment and tucked it away. "I won't pretend Cassius doesn't plan three moves ahead, or that he's not cautious of what may be occurring here in the south. I will go prepared. If he has anything peculiar in mind, I intend to see it coming." She leveled her stare with Kai's, unspoken words lurking in her gaze. "If you strike, we stand by you."

Isla's brows lifted. *If we strike?*

Kai's features remained set as he nodded, his next words dark and chillingly sincere. "If Cassius tries anything, I'll kill him where he stands."

CHAPTER 47

KAI

Kai hated this. He knew Ameera had been right, knew he couldn't bear every burden on his own, and knew he had to allow his friends to make their own choices, but as he took in his family, scattered around a house ravaged by rot and destroyed by a monster, all he felt was dread.

They'd left Mimas by noon with an excuse about an urgent issue back in Deimos, but Kai knew Verena had been agitated by their early departure.

That was two members of the pack leadership he'd pissed off today. According to Sol, who'd just left to return to Deimos, Beta Sampson hadn't appreciated Kai not being there to speak with him when he'd come to retrieve Eli's body. Kai's extended condolences through his delta would only go so far. But that was a fire he would worry about another day.

Finishing off the last of the chicken Jonah had made and wiping the sleep out of his eyes from the nap Isla had forced him to take when they'd beaten everyone else here, he watched his mate, now reunited with the pup slumbering happily in her lap. At the same time, Jonah attempted to piece together a logical route into the Wilds from the markers they'd gathered.

Unable to shift and having not trained with the guard in years, Jonah wouldn't be going with them. Neither would Davina. They, along with the pup, would linger here. Their small pack consisted of Kai, Isla, Ameera, Sebastian, Rhydian, and Magnus. Not *entirely* clued into what was happening, the guard could finally live out his warrior dreams and see what the Hunt was made of. Magnus had one job: kill bak and have their back. And tell no one about the pup.

Isla had leveled that threat with glowing violet eyes and a dagger while the pup wagged his tail in her arms.

Magnus and Rhydian were the only two who hadn't gone through the Warrior Rite, and Kai couldn't deny that it had only bolstered his own unease. Especially when he saw the way Davina clung to Rhydian and how she'd been shaking. He knew what it felt like to lose a mate, and he hadn't even *lost* her. But any soft request or mention to Rhydian that it was okay for him to stay behind had been met with vehement opposition.

By him, by everyone.

No one else will get hurt, Kai could at least affirm it in his own head.

Kai leaned back against the broken frame of the threadbare chair, destroyed by the bak who'd chased Isla through this house when they'd first discovered it. The bane had entirely left his system now, and given where they were heading, he wasn't going to risk hindering himself at all.

He could feel it now, the Wilds' twisted call. His ancestor's past... and maybe his pack's future if they didn't figure this out.

He shook away the idea, his power, almost angry at being suppressed, writhing with his fear, pulsing with the thought that had nagged him since they'd spoken with Verena.

The storms. The manifestations of chaos.

He could sense one brewing with the roiling within him now, as if his body had always known what had been happening, and he'd just never drawn the connection. How far did these senses of his go?

"This path will likely be your best bet," Jonah said through an exasperated breath, his finger gliding along the map. "But it's risky. You need to be sure that this first marker you found is meant to be the opening into the Wilds."

The first marker. The one that Isla's mother had left for her and Lukas as a hint. A clue.

Isla nodded, stroking the back of the pup's ears. "I'm eighty percent sure."

"I've been up against worse odds," Sebastian said from where he'd been with Ameera and Magnus, discussing strategies to handle the bak with some overexaggerated hand motions.

Jonah placed his finger somewhere on the map. "Once you're above ground, potentially *here,* then you get to the Pack Hall, which is, to my estimation, *here,* closer to the western coastline. It'll likely be a one or two-day trip, depending on if you..." Jonah hesitated, and Kai knew he was about to say *shift.*

"Isla will be on my back," he said, and her eyes flashed to him. They'd already discussed it between themselves—and she'd made the quip about being "great at riding him."

Around them, everyone seemed surprised. It was unheard of for an alpha to allow anyone to use them like that. But this was Isla.

"I don't know if we've decided this yet," Sebastian began, adjusting the fabric of the guard uniform they'd given him, "but that witch is there, right? Who gets to kill her?"

Ameera, in her warrior's garb, folded her arms. "Well, she killed Kai's family."

Kai's hands clenched and released from fists.

Sebastian's jaw ticked. "But she took my..." He snapped his mouth closed and ran his tongue over his bottom lip. His eyes flickered to his sibling across the room. "Sister. And me, too."

A truth, though it was more of a reason for Kai to be the one to rip the bitch's heart out.

Unspoken words passed between the three of them who knew the entire truth, and they came to an unspoken agreement. The person who got revenge would be the one who landed the killing blow. No one cared as long as she was dead.

"And what about everyone else we come across?" Rhydian asked. "She has the other witch." Raana. "And then the rogues, and probably Callan, too. What do we do about them?"

Silence fell.

One beat. Two.

"Win the battle," Kai said, and everyone's eyes were on him, looking to him for orders, for guidance.

You are no—

He cut off the destructive thought and swallowed, his eyes meeting Isla's, who gave a soft smile.

They were going to be okay.

Kai leaned forward, his elbows resting on his knees. "If it's down to you or them, you're the one walking out. We try to save who we can—*if* they can be saved." He broke down the plan again. "We go in, we make it to the Pack Hall, we find our answers—"

However they were supposed to do that.

"We kill the bitch—"

Or *that.*

"And then we all come home, alive and safe." His stare slipped to Davina's, who'd been nodding, crying. Then everyone else. Everyone who'd been trying to get him to let them in for far too long. "No one else is dying on me."

A smile slid across Ameera's mouth at his nearly choked words. "Yes, Alpha."

An echo of the agreement followed, a lightness settling between them before they entered an eternal darkness.

Sebastian jumped to his feet, shaking out his shoulders. "Let's get this over with." Kai knew he was energized by the opportunity to slay the witch. "To hell we go."

To hell, indeed.

CHAPTER 48

ISLA

Isla had never imagined she'd have to enter the Wilds again. And yet, here she was, with her family at her back, and her mate's hand occasionally brushing hers. Finally able to touch him. So different from the way things had once been. Everything was so, so different.

She was no longer a Warrior of Io.

They'd been traveling for almost a day, sensing that night approached beyond the dense canopy. Isla remembered well the disdain of not knowing the minute, the hour, or the day here—the Wilds' endless gray. Thankfully, the map of the tunnels—the path her mother had given them through the markers—had been right. She'd consider it a blessing from the Goddess if it hadn't felt like something much worse was coming.

It took everything to maintain her steel will and composure. Panic was an ever-present knot in her throat, and every now and then, magic would tingle along her skin. She still didn't know how to wrap her mind around it.

She had magic.

And it wasn't the magic of witches; Raana's shadows were immortal in nature. This power, and how they'd wielded it, had been part of the reason fae were viewed as heinous and cruel. So horrible that many had sacrificed their lives to lock them out forever.

Isla glanced down at her hand, narrowing her eyes as if to will darkness to her fingertips, but nothing came. The shadows must've only been within her wolf.

At her side, Kai suddenly flinched. She twisted to look at him as he rolled his shoulders. The two of them led their unit as Sebastian and Ameera took the rear, while Rhydian and Magnus, their *honorary warriors*, stayed protected in the middle. Kai had promised them that if they both made it out alive, he'd tattoo a warrior's crescent on them himself.

"Are you okay?" she asked, feeling the gentle brush of his aura against her as he cast his senses out, clearly needing an outlet. He, like the other wolves, had been alternating between his shifted and human form to conserve energy, while Isla alternated between getting on and off his wolf's back, keeping her shadow wolf in her back pocket for now.

Kai took a breath, and her eyes dragged over the scars beneath his guard's uniform. "It feels different here."

"Different?" she echoed. "Like worse?"

"Like *different*." He cast his eyes around them, checking the forest. "Or maybe it's just me."

"Your senses," Isla suggested before lowering her voice. "You didn't take the bane, so—"

"So, this thing is mad at me for trying to suppress it."

Isla felt a chill and nodded in consideration. "You, uh, speak like it's something else entirely." And she remembered the night of the Equinox, when he'd transformed into something else right in front of her.

"It feels that way." Kai's throat bobbed, darkness and uncertainty passing over his face as though he was becoming uncomfortable in his own skin again. "There's so much to feel out here. I don't know. I'm just on edge."

She was, too, but it didn't hurt to attempt to be a grounding force. She took his hand in hers and tugged him down into a kiss.

"Goddess above, can you two give it a break up there?"

Isla whipped around to where Sebastian had called from his position. She flipped him off.

"Were you even in the Hunt?" Ameera chastised him. "Keep your voice down."

"They've killed a million bak between them," Rhydian drawled back at her brother. "If they want to make out in the cursed woods, let them. Everyone has their thing."

Isla scoffed, unable to deny appreciating the tactic, bringing some light in so much darkness.

"It's unsettlingly quiet," Magnus commented through a cough, still getting used to the Wilds' atmosphere, the suffocating magic. Isla would admit she'd been impressed by him so far; his years of training had prepared him well. She could imagine his frustration, being denied year after year when he'd deserved to enter the Hunt and become a warrior.

"The Hunt took me nearly a week, I think. The whole purpose is to *hunt* the bak; they usually keep to themselves," Isla said, pulling out the map. *At least, they used to.* "It's only been a day, and we're making good time. We should reach the hall soon."

"Or now," Kai said, and everyone followed his eyes to where he'd been gazing beyond.

He must've sensed it first because it took a few more paces before Isla finally saw it. The cracked spires, the shattered window, and the rubble. The corpse of Phobos's Pack Hall. Isla's blood iced, and she felt her wolf try to rise.

The hall, the crown, and the heart of this territory seemed to pulse with the deepest, darkest magic. Perhaps that was why so few hunters had ever glimpsed it, having been so repulsed by its energy.

It was exactly as Isla had dreamed it.

Kai's steps stuttered, and Isla braced him. Before she could ask what was wrong, the hall's great double doors creaked open.

They all halted.

Shifted.

All but Isla, who drew her sword and called her wolf forward enough that her eyes and lumerosi glowed. Raana's magic—*her* magic—ghosted across her fingertips.

But she had no control over it and had to leash it, saving it for use only as a last resort. She couldn't risk becoming as depleted as she had been on the beach this deep into the Wilds.

Keeping her wolf composed became a feat, though, when a familiar figure crested the staircase of the Pack Hall. Even at this distance, Isla knew the witch. Her anger boiled, and her wolf's howls for blood nearly sent her charging forward.

They needed to be smart about this. The witch knew this territory better than any of them.

Isla took quick stock of what lay around them. Where was her army of rogues and monsters? Where was Raana? Where was Callan?

"The Alpha and Luna of Deimos," the witch trilled in that sickeningly melodic tone. She appeared more haggard than when Isla had last seen her. Sallow skin, brittle hair, and sunken cheeks, as if the life had been sucked from her. The scar Isla had left was an angry pink over her features. "I meet you together, at last."

Isla felt a presence at her left. Sebastian stepped forward, his wolf towering over her, a snarl across his maw, and murder flaring in his eyes.

"Wait," she commanded her brother through gritted teeth, but she felt like she'd already lost him. Their mother had been tortured and forced to work for this witch against her will for a decade. Had been forced to commit the highest treason—the reason she may never be able to come home to them.

Ice cascaded over Isla's body, but she willed herself to calm. *Not now.*

"Is that your brother?" the witch called across the palace courtyard. "How fun it would be to have a matching set. It's been so long now, but I do remember your mother rambling about wanting to see you two again."

Sebastian exploded.

Isla had no time to lunge for him as he darted across the clearing, fury powering his swift strides. Fury blinded him as a bak appeared.

In one powerful swing of a claw-tipped paw, Sebastian went flying backwards.

He landed a few yards away, his wolf letting out a whimper.

Not a death blow.

Not a death blow.

Isla hadn't realized she'd been running for him, that they all had. Hadn't realized she'd lost her hold on her magic. Shadow rippled from her body, threatening to take form. When they'd all surrounded her brother, shielding their pack member, her darkness swept across their feet.

No one would die. They were all making it out of here alive.

Attack. Defend.

They froze as the witch's battalion, at last, emerged. Three rogues. Seven monsters.

No, eight, nine...

Isla swallowed hard as several more bak poured from the trees and lined up before the hall like soldiers.

How was she this powerful?

"Very interesting," the witch cooed, and genuine shock seemed to ripple across her face as she took in Isla. "I see Raana is as careless with her power as she is with her own body. Did you know that there are covens who have settled in the fae ruins of Naerel, hoping the land will gift them power as the immortals once could? As they once did. It's all a trick, though. Even a trickle of fae magic is too much for a mortal body to contain. A seed that blooms into an uncontainable wildflower, destroying you from the inside."

Isla bit down on her shock, her fear. She couldn't care right now.

But beside her, Kai bristled. Isla sensed the bond tug, release, and fade, and she turned her head to find he'd moved a step ahead of them. He leveled his crimson stare across their opposition.

Death incarnate.

She couldn't let that power sweep him away.

She tugged him back.

Stay with me. Stay focused.

"I didn't come to listen to you talk." Isla firmed her grip on her sword. "You've already subjected me to enough of that. Where is she? You're working with her, right?"

"Yes," she said. "As it turns out, everything about you is true. I suppose I should be thanking you, Luna of Deimos."

Isla scowled. "Thanking me for what?"

She readied herself as the witch took out a small blade and pressed it to her palm. She cut deep, crimson pooling and pouring onto the cracked Pack Hall stones.

The earth trembled as a rush of wind swept through the forest, kicking up the foliage and sending Isla stumbling into Kai.

Then came the mist, a blend of light and dark, swirling around them, burning her skin. The scent of magic flooded her nose. Magic that fused with her blood, her essence.

A howl of pain rang out from behind her along with the sound of tearing flesh, but Isla had no time to see who'd been attacked.

Nothing could've prepared her for the plummet.

CHAPTER 49

ISLA

Isla was falling. Falling and falling and falling. At least, it felt that way until she snapped back into her senses.

She righted herself, blinking her eyes against the soft glow of a lantern on a vanity she'd never seen before. Her body felt... unfamiliar. Her hips were narrow, as was her waist, and her arms and legs felt weaker than they should.

"Saoirse!"

Isla spun.

No, no... she didn't spin. But she saw it happening through another's eyes, felt it through their bones and blood.

Saoirse.

Saoirse glanced back at the mirror, checking over her appearance. Her night-dark hair gobbled up the light, and chestnut eyes with a rim of gold reminded Isla of the sun.

Saoirse.

Not the white-haired, violet-eyed woman.

But, Saoirse, the Luna of Phobos.

"Warrior Heart."

"What the hell?" Isla whispered into the chasm of darkness from which she watched life unfold through Saoirse's eyes. Her ire flared. "Where are you?"

"Play the part," the violet-eyed woman crooned. *"Make it to me, and you will see."*

Isla couldn't be here, couldn't do this now. Her family was in trouble. That howl rang and rang and rang in her head. One of them was hurt. One of them could be dead.

"Where's Kai?" Her voice echoed. "You said this involved both of us."

"You will find him. As we always have."

So, he was also caught in this spell. Relief and dread crashed through her. Their family was facing the witch and her army without them.

Sebastian, Ameera, Rhydian, Magnus...

"I can't do this now!" Isla shouted through the darkness, desperation scratching her voice. "I need to get back, and then I'll listen to whatever you—"

"Play your part, and they will be fine. If you do not learn, if you do not see and understand, *then they will all fall to ruin."*

Isla didn't know how much she could believe her, but she didn't have much of a choice. She'd have to follow along or try to find a way to break out. The latter could waste too much time.

Something was pulling her arm. No, not *her* arm—Saoirse's arm. And not something, someone.

The person doing so had their face turned away; their entire figure seemed to shimmer... blur.

Saoirse sighed, running her hands over the many skirts of her gown. "I don't know, Eva."

"Oh, come now," Eva drawled, turning and pushing back her tawny locks that had fallen from her intricate coronet. Still, an aura seemed to shine around her. "We've been waiting for this day."

"You have," Saoirse corrected. "You dragged me here."

Eva heaved a breath. "Every she-wolf of age dreams of being invited to this ball. The whole purpose is to find your mate, and we both know *you* need one." She sidled closer as she forced Saoirse into step, and the two of them exited the cramped powder room.

Plucking thoughts as they flew by, Isla tried to gather what she could about where they were and who Saoirse was as a person. There had been nothing notable about her bloodline, and, though she was putting on a jaded façade, Isla could feel the eagerness powering her blood. But she hadn't been able to shake her nerves, sneaking off to this room hidden away on one of the upper floors of the Pack Hall after sweet-talking a guard to let her by to escape the madness below.

And madness it was.

Isla couldn't help but marvel along with Saoirse as she took in the grandeur of Phobos's Pack Hall in all its glory. Not yet a victim of dark magic, the halls were littered with finely dressed pack members, their gowns and suits more embellished than anything Isla had ever seen anyone wear. Five hundred years might do that, she supposed.

A symphony of joyous, resplendent music rang out from the ballroom they approached as they descended a broad stone staircase, pine winter garland twined around the rock.

"You know…" Eva leaned close to her ear, and Isla could practically feel the energy rippling off her. It emanated from no one else. "I also heard that Alpha Heir Aneurin is seeking *his mate*."

Isla could feel something within Saoirse tremble, as if a part of her had already known where her future lay.

You will find him. As we always have.

"He's courting someone, isn't he?" Saoirse asked, trying to sound indifferent.

"Only until he finds his fated." Eva waved her off before craning her neck to see over the masses once they'd reached the bottom of the stairs. "I don't want to fall to the end of the line to meet him. He may get bored and leave before he gets to us."

Saoirse scoffed. "Well, that already makes him sound like quite a charmer."

Eva poked her side as they spilled into the mingling ballroom crowd, and from within, Isla was awestruck by the beauty of the stained-glass window. She couldn't help but wonder why Deimos's window was so high up and away from everyone else. The aura that this window cast over the ball's guests, a rippling sea of night, was nothing short of magical.

"Keep that scowling look on your face, my dear," Eva said. "I'm sure you'll dazzle him."

CHAPTER 50

KAI

Kai had no idea what the fuck was happening.

One moment, he'd been running for Isla, and the next... he was here.

Phobos, in the past.

Honestly, there wasn't much that could shock him anymore, but he needed to find a way out, to find Isla and their family. He'd heard the howl before this magic took him, but dredging up his power and slamming it against its confines had yielded nothing. Roaring into the void for that woman to explain this had been met with silence.

But there had been a flicker of their bond, and Kai knew, deep within himself, that Isla was here. Isla was safe, and he just needed to find her.

He'd figured out that he was Aneurin fairly quickly. And with that same otherworldly sense that he'd felt the thunderstorms, Kai knew the strange power he possessed also lay dormant beneath Aneurin's skin.

Did he understand why he was seeing everything through Aneurin's eyes? Not really.

But had he figured that the best way to find Isla would be to find Aneurin's fated mate, Saoirse? Yes.

Too bad he had no control over this damn body.

At an aggravatingly leisurely pace, Aneurin strode through the Pack

Hall's corridors, high and curved like the ones in Deimos, with his best friend, whom Kai had learned was named Viktor, at his side.

"If you don't find her tonight, just *choose* someone," Viktor said. "It's becoming more common. You can't go this long without a mate. You're the prince."

Aneurin bristled and ran a hand over his dark hair. Kai caught the feeling that Aneurin didn't even like Viktor much, but he'd been the son of his father's beta, so he felt he had to be his friend. He supposed it didn't work out for everyone.

"Fate is on my side tonight," Aneurin said, the seal ring—not quite the orientation of wolves and moon Kai had in Deimos, but similar— glinting on his finger. "I'm going to meet her. I can feel it."

He certainly could. There had been a tugging at his gut as he stopped at the top of the grand staircase and stared into the packed crowd, a nagging at the back of his mind.

Saoirse—*Isla*—was here.

When they approached the ballroom's double doors, trumpeters blared their instruments, and the revelers who'd been mingling and dancing came to an abrupt halt.

"May I present," a voice proclaimed from the dais set at the head of the ballroom, "His Royal Highness, Alpha Heir Aneurin of Phobos."

The crowd cheered and clapped as Aneurin ascended the stairs to his small throne, where one after another, his guests would greet him, most of them unmated women.

He cast his eyes along those who already lined the dais, heeding that gut-deep feeling to see if his wolf would react. But no. Nothing.

But she was here. Somewhere, calling to his blood, bones, and breath.

Kai had felt it, too. Felt it now and felt it then when he'd first seen Isla across the room at the feast.

All of this seemed so typical. Why was it crucial for them to see this to understand themselves?

"I'm going to take a walk around first," Aneurin told someone who seemed to be his equivalent of Marin, and didn't wait for his answer—or for Viktor to catch up—as he descended the dais stairs.

The women around him became a flurry of abashed giggles and sultry stares. He smiled at each of them and bowed his head, but—

Not her, not her, not her.

Until—

He, or maybe it was Kai, had seen a luminescence first. An aura of gold surrounded a dark-haired girl he did not know, which eventually flashed to the one he did—the one he loved.

Neither Kai nor Aneurin could have moved fast enough. There had been the strangest sensation of *pulling* before he saw Isla emerge from Saoirse, and then he finally felt like he was standing—though airy—on his own two feet.

"Oh, thank the Goddess," Isla muttered, wrapping her arms around him, embracing him. Though even this felt light, and she didn't have her scent. Like they were only illusions of themselves.

She pulled back to examine his face, her eyes dropping over him. "You're in your clothes."

He glanced down at his attire, then at hers, neither of them in this day's fashion, before scanning the rest of the crowd. No one seemed to notice them. No, they were looking at Saoirse and Aneurin, the will of Fate before their eyes. The air hummed between them. And as if he were still tethered to the other alpha, Kai felt the dormant power within Aneurin crack from its shell.

"How do we get out of here?" Kai asked Isla as the ballroom floor cleared, leaving Aneurin and Saoirse in the center of it. The future alpha had taken his mate's hand, preparing to dance. They'd both started at the touch, the first brush of skin against skin, but that had been it. They surely had better self-control than he and Isla had.

As if she were afraid they'd get separated again, Isla held Kai close. "She said the only way we get out is once we understand, once we *see*, and everyone will be fine if we play our parts, so, I guess—*Goddess*."

"What?" Kai whipped his attention around as Isla craned her neck, seeking something while the orchestra had begun a new aria. This one started with a simple, hauntingly beautiful violin.

"This is it," Isla breathed. "This is the music I keep hearing—the one from my nightmares and my dreams, it's always been this."

"The song from their first dance?" First meeting, first dance, first touch.

Isla furrowed her brows. "Yes, but—"

"But what?"

"This doesn't feel like *why* I remember it."

"What do you—"

Before Kai could finish the question, they plummeted again.

CHAPTER 51

ISLA

Isla had a vague sense of having lived an entire life. A sense of a love that was not perfect, but one that had been... enough.

She watched, still separated from Saoirse, who had become the Luna of Phobos, while the dark-haired queen stared out the window at a light rainstorm, a hand resting on her swollen belly.

"Hello, darling," Aneurin purred, stepping into her bedroom, separate from his own.

But this Aneurin did not hold Kai.

Isla checked the bond. It was distant—a spark. But there... still there. Perhaps he was in a different hollow of the past.

Isla steeled against her panic, forcing herself to remain, learn, listen, and see why all of this was so important.

"You're back." Saoirse smiled, but there was a tiredness in her eyes. Even Aneurin seemed to have aged, his hair graying at the sides and on his beard.

"I am," he said, leaning down to place a kiss on her neck, sliding a hand over hers on her stomach. Isla fought back against the uneasiness of intruding on an intimate moment.

"I feel like I've barely seen you," Saoirse breathed, her voice vacant as Aneurin kissed her again. Gentle, but not tender.

"There's much to be done, dear." Aneurin's voice had an underlying darkness as he stepped back from her, heading for her side table to pour himself a glass of water from the crystal pitcher. He pinched between his brows.

"Are you still having those headaches?" she asked.

Aneurin took a long drink. "Nothing to worry about."

Saoirse's features fell, and she hesitated before saying, "I heard something today... Is it true? Are we really going to war with Io?"

Isla's heart stopped, and something lethal flashed in Aneurin's eyes. She could've sworn she felt the room tighten, the aura shift. "If I have my way, yes."

She knew the same dread that sluiced through her ran through Saoirse, too. "There has to be another way—a better way. I don't want to bring our child into a world of bloodshed and death. Can't you come to an agreement?"

Aneurin's nostrils flared, his voice gravelly. "The Imperial Alpha will never relinquish his power, you know that. And as long as we are under his thumb, we will not thrive. *None of us* will. None of us but *them*." He rose to his feet.

"Wait," Saoirse called out, and there had been years of these abrupt ends to conversations and quick goodbyes. "You just got back. Won't you spend the night with me?"

Aneurin pursed his lips, hesitating, scanning his mate, then her bed. "I need to leave for Iapetus before dawn. If I spend the night with you, dear, I won't be doing much sleeping."

The innuendo didn't do much to rouse Saoirse's lips. She looked away from him. "Why bother coming back at all? Weren't you just in Tethys?"

Aneurin sighed, closing the distance between them. "I came to see my mate and child. Our future alpha." He leaned down, placing a hand on her belly and kissing her again. "I am doing this for us, my love. *All of us*. For our future. It will be brighter than any ever was."

"I can't imagine how bright it could be shrouded in so much darkness."

Aneurin said nothing, only kissing her once more and leaving.

Isla gritted her teeth, her nails digging into her forearms as she watched Saoirse cry.

In the emptiness of this bedroom, it all rushed by her. Their love had not been perfect—and it had *barely* been enough. Aneurin valued power above all, even her.

She glanced around the room, seeking out Kai, feeling the hours pass by like wind against her cheeks as Saoirse rested.

Until a knock came at the door.

The luna hadn't been asleep. She'd just been staring out into the dark void before her, so she shot up at the sound. A shadow lingered below the door before disappearing.

Carefully, Saoirse padded to the entrance, calling out for an answer that never came, and opened her bedroom door to find a box at her feet. Atop it, three symbols had been carved, and Isla recognized them as the emblems of the Goddess, Fate, and Eternity.

With furrowed brows, Saoirse slowly walked with the box to the chair Aneurin had sat in, sneering at his discarded water glass as she sat. Lighting her lantern, she carefully pried the case open, and Isla gazed over her shoulder to look inside. She swore she felt the white-haired woman over her shoulder, pushing her to *see*.

Isla's heart started as she looked upon a diadem and dagger—*the* diadem and dagger. She could feel them call to Saoirse the way they called to her.

Though here, in this time, they were entirely intact.

CHAPTER 52

KAI

Kai was home.

Well, *not truly*. But he was in Deimos. The world seemed darker now in this part of the past. That void within grew greater, a chasm primed to swallow him whole. He wasn't sure how much time had passed, but he knew that time certainly had.

Deimos appeared different, ancient, as he peered down from his overlook, sneaking away from Aneurin, who'd been meeting Alpha Orin, who looked very different to Kai, though he was his many greats great-grandfather. Kai probably should've taken a closer look at the documents on the desk in his study.

"Do you know how horribly a war with Io would go? No one will win," Orin said.

Kai let out a hard breath, not bothering with the door to step back inside the room, his magic-laced form able to easily slide through walls.

"I've already gotten Iapetus and Rhea on our side," Aneurin said from where he sat in the seat across from him. Something about him had become... darker, more unhinged. "We cannot cower. *This* is the time."

"*This is the time*," Orin mocked, making Aneurin's power flare. He wasn't sure if Orin had felt it, too, but it knocked the breath from Kai's lungs, making his own beat in response.

One and the same.

"How do you figure *now* is the time, Aneurin?" Orin asked, folding his wrinkled hands.

"Because," Aneurin gritted. "The goddesses have blessed me with a weapon like no other in the world."

The weapon Jonah had told them Aneurin spoke about—the one he'd used to convince other packs to join his cause.

Orin scratched his beard, clearly not taking this as seriously as Aneurin intended. "And that is?"

The Alpha of Phobos ground his teeth before a lethal calm settled over his face. "It's better understood by demonstration, I believe."

"Very well, and how—"

Kai's breath caught with Orin's, feeling his own power writhe as Aneurin's lashed out. It speared straight for the walls of Orin's mind, tearing through and leashing it as if it were as easy as breathing. In the distance, Kai swore thunder rumbled.

Orin blinked, his eyes wide and bloodshot as he choked and spluttered while Aneurin's mental claws held tight. No matter how much Orin, *another alpha,* fought and thrashed, he couldn't get free.

Kai felt sick over what he sensed.

It was an intoxication with such undiluted, undisputed power to shape the world as he wished.

Maintaining his hold, his eyes a glow of bleeding crimson and shadow, Aneurin had risen, going to the window and peering out. "You won't breathe until I wish it. You will think nothing but what I allow. Every memory you have, every feeling you've ever felt is mine." He ran his hand over the stained glass, and Kai blinked when he thought it had gleamed. "I can see, feel, taste, and hear the world like no other. It's *mine.* All of it is mine." He slid his hands into his pockets. "And you know what the most interesting part is?" He chuffed a laugh. "I can't be killed."

Kai couldn't feel his body while his own mind whirred, while those last words bludgeoned him over and over.

He should've been dead after fighting the bak in the tunnel.

"The Beta of Iapetus stabbed me right in the heart." Aneurin tapped his chest. "It was supposed to be a nice dinner, too—a celebration. I'd gotten them to agree to my plans, but you can't trust anyone, I suppose. I bled, and that was it. I healed. I made him use the same knife to slit his own throat."

Made him.

Kai was going to be sick.

Aneurin squinted, seeing something beyond the glass, and Kai felt, despite the power, whatever this was frightened him—*reached* for him.

Aneurin jerked back, and Kai felt the power straining as if something else were trying to pull his strings.

The Alpha of Phobos spun, facing Orin on the brink of asphyxiation. He released him and casually sat back in his seat as the Alpha of Deimos slumped in his chair, his face beet red as he clawed at his chest for air.

"It's a shame the gift didn't pass to us both, cousin. We could've returned our bloodline to its former glory. A powerful Ares once again. I don't understand why our forefathers split it."

He sniffed the air, scrunching his nose.

Orin had pissed himself.

He let out a deep sigh as he slid a piece of parchment across his desk with a quill. "Now, you're going to write a letter for me, and then we're going to make a public address."

CHAPTER 53

ISLA

Saoirse was dreaming, meaning Isla was dreaming with her. Saoirse's slumber was filled with death, blood, and a war-torn landscape that wasn't a far cry from what will soon be Phobos's reality.

Phobos's northern city was in shambles, a consequence of a long-fought battle, an attack by Io and their allies of the north. But that didn't matter to Aneurin—her alpha, her mate—because his armies had conquered and destroyed parts of Oberon, Callisto, and Ganymede. They were in such ruin that no one thought they would recover. All on his march to Io's doorstep.

She hadn't seen him in nearly six months now, neither had their son, and the man she glimpsed had become a shell of what he once was. As if the possession of a power as great as his had feasted on him from the inside.

He was unstoppable, *unbreakable*. The world had gone dark as chaos reigned. No one could touch him. Even his allies—his own soldiers—were frightened by the breadth of what he was, so much so that they considered assassination. A fool's game, when he'd simply tear through their minds the moment the thought arose.

But he was doing all of this for them. He wasn't trying to take more than he thought they were owed. He was trying to help protect his family, their family, from the person he perceived as a monster.

He still loved her, in that cold way of his. He was still her mate.

"Saoirse."

Isla was stunned to hear that familiar voice say anything other than *"Warrior Heart."*

"No!" Saoirse shouted, suddenly right beside Isla, though she didn't acknowledge her as the dark winds ripped around them. "I won't do it. I won't."

Won't do what? Isla thought, lifting her hand to shield her eyes, even though it meant nothing here.

"He's my mate!" Saoirse screamed, sobbing. "It can't be me."

Finally, the woman appeared, her focus set on the broken luna who was ready to go to her knees.

"That is why it can only be you," the violet-eyed woman said. "Only *you* share his power. Only *you* can get through his defenses. Everyone else has tried and failed, and he will destroy *everything* unless he is stopped."

Isla suddenly found it hard to breathe as something sparked in her. A conclusion so horrendous it nearly made her vomit.

That couldn't have been what this was.

"Even if he showed repentance and remorse, the power would not allow him to do it himself. *They* would not allow it. It can only be you," the woman said.

Isla stumbled back, looking between the two women, clarity ringing like a bell.

But, no.

No, no, no.

The woman added, "Find comfort in the fact that you are not the first with this fate, and you will not be the last."

Isla couldn't breathe. She needed to find Kai. She needed to get out of there.

"Stay, Warrior Heart." Now the distant voice called to her. *"See and understand."*

"Tell me who you are," Isla gritted, her voice wobbling as her eyes stung. As she felt Fate lingering in this place that was not a place, in every beat of her warrior's heart. In the thread she'd drawn from her soul to another—a direct line through his defenses.

Finally, the woman said, *"I was the first of us."*

"The Luna of Ares," Isla breathed, feeling like a piece of a puzzle had fallen into place.

"*Andromeda,*" she clarified.

Ares, Phobos, Deimos.

Three lunas, three queens cursed to...

To...

Isla needed to find Kai. Needed to get him out. Get him away from all of this. *Now.*

She closed her eyes and dug for the bond, but met resistance. A cold, dark shell of the man Isla loved more than anything.

"Let me go to him!" Isla shouted over the winds that had grown stronger. "This isn't us. That isn't him."

Kai wasn't Aneurin. He wasn't a monster. And he wouldn't become this, even if their power was the same.

"Let us out!" Isla reached to her side for a blade that wasn't there. "I understand! I see!"

"*No, you don't.*"

"There has to be another way," Saoirse cried, and Isla snapped her attention back to her. "If it's a curse, why can't we break it?"

"There is not enough time to seek that answer," Andromeda said. "Even going into my own past, where it began, I cannot figure out how the power was bestowed and how to eradicate it." She closed the distance between them, her features cold, deadly. "You have already taken *too long.* The world is on the brink of collapse, and he's grown too strong. If they get hold of him, it's *over.* The crown and dagger are your answers. *You* are the answer, the only one who can wield them— Goddess-blessed, Goddess-chosen, soul-bound. You end it, Saoirse. Now."

CHAPTER 54

KAI

Kai needed to get the hell out of here and find Isla. *Immediately.*

From the corner of the empty ballroom, he watched Aneurin peering through the stained-glass window as plumes of smoke from pyres of the fallen rose from his city to fill the storm-clouded sky.

He'd felt disgusted watching him tear through the continent, destroying everything he passed and losing the lives of so many wolves. But he was a man with all the power in the world, and nothing had come close to stopping him.

A *gift*—one that Kai felt in his own soul.

This power, this Goddess-damn curse.

Would he end up just like Aneurin? Corrupted by this... thing, the entire world falling to chaos by his own hand. The power clawed at him from within now, called him to use it, *embrace it.*

This was what he had to see. Perhaps to understand what he stood to become. He needed to tell Isla, but how could he explain that he was a monster? That it might already be too late, and they would need to find a way to stop him.

"I am me because I am yours. I'm meant to take you, all of you, as what you are."

Goddess above.

"Darling." Aneurin turned with the word, sensing Saoirse with the power he'd cast across the entire palace before she'd even crossed the threshold of the ballroom.

Kai straightened from where he'd been leaning against one of the ballroom's many pillars as Saoirse, beautiful in an amethyst gown, swept into the room, carrying a music box. Kai had seen Aneurin gift it to her and knew it played the aria from their first dance. Saoirse wore a diadem —one that looked an awful lot like *the* diadem.

"You look stunning," Aneurin said, and Kai didn't pay attention to what came next because that's when he saw her.

"Isla!"

He ran to where she kneeled on the floor, barely able to catch her breath, her face splotchy and tear-stained.

"What happened?" he asked, and she peered up at him like she was seeing a ghost. He held her face in his hands and swiped her tears away, but they just kept falling. "Breathe," he told her as she'd once told him. "It's okay. We'll find a way ou—"

"No, it's not," she cracked, her body trembling. "It's not okay." She turned and sucked in a breath, her eyes widening. "No, no, no."

Kai turned, seeing that Saoirse had opened the music box and the aria was playing. She wrapped her arms around Aneurin, but though the image of them was loving, the air was tense.

Something was wrong.

"Warrior Heart."

Now, Kai heard it. That woman's voice, and when he looked beyond Saoirse and Aneurin, he saw her there. Something about her struck him as familiar.

"Let us out," Isla whispered, grabbing onto Kai's shirt and holding him tighter as Saoirse's hand dropped behind her, back into the folds of her skirts. "Please. I see it. I understand."

"See what?" Kai asked, his eyes not knowing where to land.

He hadn't been prepared for Saoirse's cry or her mighty lunge as she plunged a blade towards Aneurin's heart.

Hadn't been prepared as he glimpsed the dagger clutched in her trembling hand, stopped not by Aneurin grabbing her wrist but by his power as it took hold of his mate's mind.

The world around them pulsed, the ground beneath them shook, and the stained-glass window cracked. Radiating and jagged, the fractures spread, a network of gleaming vines, rivulets of shimmering blood.

Aneurin looked between the blade and his mate—the woman the goddesses had blessed him with. "What is this? Saoirse?"

Isla held Kai tighter, and he wrapped his arms around her, fighting back against the void inside him that attempted to push her away.

"I have to do it," Saoirse sobbed through gritted teeth, fighting against his hold and her own will. The violin continued its serenade. "I'm the only one who can."

"What?" Kai breathed and felt Isla shudder.

He met her gaze again. The look in her eyes as tears fell, as she mapped and memorized every plane of his face, shattered him.

Thunder and lightning rattled the skies, making the Pack Hall tremble so violently that Kai had to brace himself.

The diadem glimmered atop her head as Saoirse regained her strength. "You won't stop. *It won't stop.*" Her limbs shook as Aneurin's body locked up as if she had pulled at a leash, pulled at their bond, her link to his power. She seemed to hold him in place as the diadem glowed brighter, and as the dagger burned. Kai could've sworn some runes pulsed on the blade, on the hilt.

Aneurin's eyes were murderous, crimson and shadow, and his hands shook. He'd kill her; Kai felt it within his own power. And Saoirse seemed to see it now, see the monster he was and would be forever.

With tears streaming down her face, she firmed her hold on the dagger and steeled herself. "You will destroy everything unless I... I... I'm sorry."

With one more cry that rattled the realms, the Luna of Phobos plunged the dagger into her mate's heart.

Everything stopped.

The world went quiet.

Still.

Saoirse and Aneurin dropped to their knees, the blade driven in to the hilt. The aria came to an end.

Aneurin swayed then slumped onto Saoirse's shoulder as she sobbed. She laid him down on the marble floor and then folded over him, his blood coating her as she cried over his chest, repeating that she was sorry and that she loved him.

Isla was trembling, holding onto Kai like he'd vanish, and shaking her head. "I won't do it," she whispered to him, to Fate. "I won't."

As if in answer, thunder crashed, and lightning streaked so brightly it cleaved the room. The world quaked. He felt it *break*.

Aneurin's blood began flowing from red to black, darkness leaking from him like ink in water. His power, Kai's power, spread through the palace floor like vines—veins of rot and destruction.

Kai held Isla, shielded her, when the world exploded. When the floors quaked, the glass shattered, and the hall itself collapsed.

He held her when he lifted his head and beheld his fate, her fate, the reason they'd been bound together, why they'd found each other on that terrace.

Kai still held her when he peered outside, quiet once again.

Quiet because nothing lay beyond but the Wilds.

EPILOGUE

CASSIUS

"What do you mean, he can't be killed?"

Cassius sat back in his seat, swirling the glass of liquor in his hand. "Exactly as I say it. Alpha Kai cannot be killed. At least, not in a way that we know." He didn't avert his eyes from the Imperial City's landscape to Malakai, finally returned from Charon, as he took a long drink. He could feel his Beta's eyes on him, urging him to explain. "Back during the War of Realms, in the height of the battles with the immortals, Alpha Kai's ancestors turned on us. The Alpha of Ares made a bargain with the fae or a demon; those who wrote it did not know, but no one had been aware of it until the war concluded, and the alpha was poised to make himself a god. He met his end, eventually. No one knows how, and the continent entered an age of relative peace until his power rose again, five hundred years later, with Alpha Aneurin of Phobos."

He paused and finally turned to examine his lifelong friend's expression. Malakai's features had paled. He'd never been privy to any of this; tales such as these had been in diaries kept in the catacombs far below the Imperial City. The secrets of all Imperial Alphas past were meant for Cassius's eyes alone... until he was to pass them along to Adrien.

Or, at least, he would have, had his son not been such a disappointment.

His eyes narrowed on the Valkeric Mountains in the distance, where Adrien remained shackled with his harlot.

Both he and Raana should've heeded his earlier kindness. Should've obeyed and done as he'd wanted them to do. It was by his grace that both still lived after Adrien attempted to free her. Ellena wanted to use their bones as a necklace, regardless of the treaty between witches and wolves.

But... they were both too valuable, as the end of the world as they knew it loomed.

"Aneurin ruled during the decimation," Malakai said, drawing back Cassius's attention.

"Yes," he said. "That's what's believed to have killed him."

"So, Kai can be killed by a witch." His friend's voice wavered, understandably. Even with all the Alpha of Deimos stood to take from them, it didn't change that he was his daughter's mate.

So, Cassius would have to give him a better reason to oppose the alpha. A greater desire of his heart. His *greatest desire,* a long-forgotten dream, an impossibility.

He checked his watch. A reason that should arrive any minute now.

Cassius took another long sip. "A witch didn't cause the decimation."

Malakai jerked back. "That's what's been told."

"That is better believed than a villain who can't be slain. My ancestor, during Aneurin's reign, spent most of his time hiding from him beneath this city. *Hiding.* He was a coward. At least with the tale that the decimation had been a witch, potentially orchestrated by his hand, it strikes fear. Better to be viewed as ruthless than weak."

Malakai let out a long breath, falling silent as he stared down at his hands, thinking. "They'll be here in a few days. I don't trust Locke, and I don't trust Kai wouldn't kill him if he felt the slightest bit threatened."

Fool.

"Then let him die by his own ignorance. There's nothing we can do. After that, you'll likely take up the helm in Charon until we select someone better."

And then they'd figure out how to destroy the Alpha of Deimos.

"Do you think Isla's in danger?" Desperation dripped from his voice. "Sebastian's there, too. They're all I have, Cas."

For now, Cassius thought, and perfectly timed, a knock came at his office door. "Isla is the only thing buying us time if what I suspect of the dark moon is correct." He leaned over and tapped his friend's knee. "But enough of this. I have a surprise for you, brother."

Malakai lifted his brows, his features uneasy. "Your surprises are typically hit-or-miss."

"I think you'll like this one," he said before rising to his feet, plastering on a smile. "Come in, Ravona!"

The door eased open, and Ravona, Winslow's assistant, entered, but she wasn't where Malakai's eyes fell. It was the woman behind her, freshly bathed and finely dressed, who had become the center of his world.

A ghost made flesh.

Malakai's hulking body trembled. "Apolla?"

Apolla's darkened blue eyes filled with tears as she fell to her knees. Her burnished gold hair fell around her as she dropped her face into her gnarled hands and sobbed.

Ten years. She'd been lost for ten years, and Cassius had brought her home again.

Malakai charged up to her and dropped to his knees to take her in his arms. Apolla flinched away.

One moment passed. Two.

They met each other's eyes, and then, with one last sob, she settled.

Cassius turned back to his city, giving them their moment as they embraced on his office floor. Mates reunited.

He gazed up at the moon, the Goddess watching over them, and smiled.

AUTHOR'S NOTE

Thank you so much for reading **A Queen's Shadow**! I hope you've enjoyed reading it as much as I've loved writing it.

This book, oh, man, this book took it out of me. In the best way, of course, but oh, man. I apologize for leaving on such a cliffhanger, but it was too much to resist. **A Kingdom's Curse** is about to be *wild*. The stage is set, true fates have been revealed, we're "running out of time", and we've seen small glimpses of the greater world beyond our continent. I. Am. So. Excited.

Words cannot describe how grateful I am to each and every one of you for coming along this journey with me. Weaving together this story and crafting these characters has been such a joy. Isla and Kai hold such a dear place in my heart—along with everyone else, of course—but Kaisla's love story, to me, is just something else. A love that could make or break everything. I cannot wait to share the rest of their journey with you. Keep an eye out for more news on AKC!

If you enjoyed the story, I would love if you'd consider leaving a review on Amazon or Goodreads. Reviews mean so, so much and are greatly appreciated.

To best keep up to date with series news, you can find me on social media or visit my website, www.melissakieranauthor.com, to sign up for my newsletter. I absolutely love connecting with you all, so please don't be afraid to say hello!

Until our next adventure, my friends!

- Melissa ♥

PRONUNCIATION GUIDE

Names

Isla: eye-lah
Kai: k-eye
Raana: rah-nah
Adrien: ay-dree-n
Ameera: ah-mee-rah
Davina: dah-vee-nah
Rhydian: rih-dee-n
Jonah: joh-nah
Sebastian: seh-bas-chihn
Cassius: ka-see-uhs
Marlane: mar-layn
Kyran: kee-rihn
Zahra: zah-rah
Jaden: jay-dehn
Malakai: mal-ah-ky
Apolla: ah-paw-lah
Locke: lawk
Maeve: may-ve

Amalie: ah-mah-lee
Jax: jacks
Verena: vah-ree-nah
Theon: thee-on
Saoirse: sor-shah
Aneurin: ahn-ur-en
Andromeda: an-droh-meh-dah
Orin: or-in

Locations

Morai: mohr-eye
Cataea: kah-tay-ah
Io: eye-oh
Deimos: dee-mohs
Phobos: foh-bohs
Ares: air-ees
Callisto: kah-lihs-toh
Charon: shah-rawn
Ganymede: gan-ee-meed
Iapetus: eye-ah-peh-tuhs
Oberon: oh-ber-on
Rhea: ray-ah
Mimas: mee-mahs
Tethys: teh-thihs
Ehime: eh-heem
Auren: aw-rehn
Elsun: el-suhn
Naerel: nay-rel
Mavec: mah-vehk
Abalys: a-bah-lihs
Ifera: eye-feh-rah
Surles: suhr-lehs

Other

Aeterna: ay-ter-nah
Destinare: des-tin-ar-ay
Bak: bahk
Lumerosi: loo-mer-oh-see

ACKNOWLEDGMENTS

As I write this, I realize it is for the third time, and I honestly cannot believe it. First, I have to thank you, the reader, for making this possible. A Warrior's Fate was essentially my first book ever, and Wolves of Morai is my first ever series, so to have your support on this journey means the absolute world to me. I cherish each one of your messages, emails, posts on Instagram and TikTok, and the general support you've given me and this series. I could not have imagined this book reaching the readers that it has, and it's all because of you. Thank you for making it possible for me to do this. I still feel like I'm in a dream.

Shelly, thank you so much for being my sounding board, my moral support, and keeping me sane during this process. I owe so much to you.

Kirsty, this book would not have existed without you. Thank you so much for putting up with me and my bizarre scheduling. Thank you for making everything sound so much better.

Fran, thank you so much for your talent and for creating such beautiful covers for this series.

Anna, thank you for being my beta reader, for your feedback, and for listening to my many plot tangents.

Kelsey and Rosie, thank you for helping me keep organized and sane.

My family, also still out of the loop about this series and my 'being an author', thank you for believing in me, even though you don't know exactly what's going on.

Until the next! ♥

ABOUT THE AUTHOR

Melissa Kieran is a Massachusetts native, who fell in love with storytelling and fantasy at a young age. Though, she began her author journey writing young adult romance when she was fifteen on serialized fiction sites, fantasy romance has taken her heart. *A Warrior's Fate* was her fantasy debut.

When she isn't writing or dreaming up new stories, you'll probably find her searching for some sunlight, doing something "sciencey" (she has her degree in biology), or binge-watching a show she's likely already seen twice...or five times. She loves connecting with her readers, so don't be afraid to say hello on social media!

facebook.com/melissakieran.author
instagram.com/melissakieran.author
tiktok.com/@melissakieran.author
goodreads.com/melissakieranauthor